GERALD SEYMOUR

A LINE IN THE SAND

A NOVEL

SIMON & SCHUSTER

NEW YORK LONDON TORONTO SYDNEY SINGAPORE

SIMON & SCHUSTER
Rockefeller Center
1230 Avenue of the Americas
New York, NY 10020

Originally published in Great Britain by Bantam Press, a division
of Transworld Publishers Ltd.

SIMON & SCHUSTER and colophon are registered trademarks
of Simon & Schuster, Inc.

Designed by Jeanette Olender
Manufactured in the United States of America

10 9 8 7 6 5 4 3 2 1

Library of Congress Cataloging-in-Publication Data
Gerald Seymour.
  A line in the sand / Gerald Seymour.
    p. cm.
  1. Intelligence service—Great Britain—Fiction.
  2. Retirees—England—Fiction. 3. Assassins—Iran—Fiction.
  I. Title.
PR6069.E734 L56 2000
  823'.914—dc21   00-020771
ISBN 0-684-85477-5

TO HARRIET

THE PERSIAN GULF

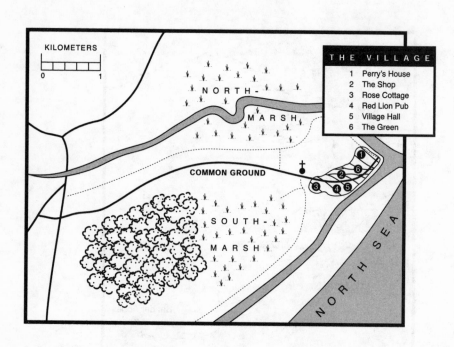

KILOMETERS
0   1

NORTH-

MARSH

COMMON GROUND

SOUTH-

MARSH

NORTH SEA

THE VILLAGE

1 Perry's House
2 The Shop
3 Rose Cottage
4 Red Lion Pub
5 Village Hall
6 The Green

PROLOGUE

He knew it was the last time he would be there.

He stepped through the double door of the administration building, held open for him, and the sinking afternoon sun blasted against his face. He blinked hard, momentarily blinded, and stopped disorientated in his tracks. He lowered the glasses from the crown of his head onto the bridge of his nose. They were all around him, crowded in the doorway, and they were his friends—more than just the people he did business with, true friends.

The car was waiting. The driver stood beside the rear door and smiled at him with respect. The technicians, engineers, and managers pressed close to him to shake his hand, hold his arms, and brush-kiss his cheeks. The friendships had been nurtured over many years. When he had left the office of the project manager, three or four minutes before, he had started a stuttering progress down a shadowed, cool corridor, stopping by each door to make his farewells. He had been wished a good journey, a safe return home, and he had been told how welcome he would be when he came back the next time.

He knew there would not be a next time.

The sun, full and gold turning to scarlet, hit his face and pierced the protection of his darkened glasses. He grinned and responded to the friendship and trust that was shown him. He had betrayed their trust. The project manager took his arm, led him towards the car, murmured appreciation that he had fallen in with the change of schedule, and squeezed his arm in implicit thanks for the present of a Toshiba laptop. On each visit, three times a year, he brought many presents with him to the complex, and they had a sliding scale of value dependent on the position in the complex of his friends. He brought with him computer equipment and gold or sterling silver ink pens, toilet soaps, and packs of toothpaste. He had come, as always, five days before, his bags weighted with the gifts that cemented the friendship and bound the trust. The vomit was in his throat, and he swallowed hard. As their friend, each time he came, he was invited to restaurants to eat battered prawns or shrimps, or whitefish, and he was invited to their homes. It had taken years of visits to build the friendship and the trust that were a sham.

The driver opened the door of the car. The project manager was flicking the buttons of a personal organizer, a secondary present from the previous visit, to confirm the date on which he would next return. He looked past the project manager at the straggling line by the double doors, all smiling and waving. He said it again, as he had said it many times in the last five days: it had been no problem for him to change his schedule and come a week earlier than originally planned. He wished them well. He did not know what would happen to them. It was the mark of their friendship, their trust, that they had left the cool, air-conditioned offices and design rooms to stand in the ferocity of the sunlight to see him on his way, and he had betrayed them. He could not look into their faces or into the eyes of the project manager.

Before he ducked down into the car, a last time, he raked the buildings, scarred by the sun and the salt carried from the sea by the winds, as if it were important that he should remember each final detail.

What Gavin Hughes saw . . . The complex was a series of wire-fenced compounds. Above the wire mesh fences around each compound were the silver- and rust-colored coils of razor wire. At the gates to each compound were sandbagged sentry points that were covered with decaying canvas to give shade from the sun. The watchtowers at the corners of the compounds were built on weathered wood stilts, and the dipping sunlight caught the barrels of the machine guns jutting above the parapets. Between the compounds were four antiaircraft defense positions, two with multiple-barrel Oerlikon guns and two housing a cluster of squat ground-to-air missiles. If it had not been for the friendship and the trust, Gavin Hughes, who was a salesman in engineering machinery, would never have gained access to the complex . . . He saw the entrance tunnel to the building with the buried concrete walls and bombproof ceiling, and that was Project 193. He saw the dun-painted building, into which he had never been admitted, that housed Project 1478. He saw the building where the hot-die forge was installed, where heated metal for the warhead cone was compressed and then cooled for turning and grinding and milling, the home of Project 972. The buildings were spread out across the bright sand, scattered inside the complex perimeter that stretched three kilometers in length and two kilometers in width, and contained the lathes, mixers, presses, and machine tools. He would be asked the day after, or the day after that at the latest, what he had seen, what was different from before.

He dropped down into the back of the car and the driver closed the door behind him. He wound down the window and reached out to shake the project manager's hand, but still could not look into his eyes. He freed his hand and waved at the crowd by the double doors as the car pulled away.

They drove past the three-storey dormitory block that was used by the Chinese. He had never met them; he had seen them from a distance; they worked on Project 193, where the lathes shaped the solid fuel charges . . . and past the tennis courts, which were floodlit in the cooler evenings and had been built for the Russians, to whom he had never spoken. He had passed them in corridors but his friends had never made the introductions; they worked on Project 1478, where the machines he had supplied mixed the coating capable of withstanding the temperature of 3,000 degrees generated in the core of the missile tube . . . and past the volleyball court scraped from the coarse sand and stone by the North Koreans and played on in the half-light of dawn.

The driver slowed as they approached the main gate of the complex. Gavin Hughes was sweating and he loosened his tie. He twisted and looked through the rear window, back at the small group still

standing by the main doors of the administration building, toy figures waving him on his way.

Two guards came forward. When he had first come to the complex
they had scowled and taken their time over studying his papers.
Now they grinned and saluted, their automatic rifles slung casually
on their shoulders. Three visits before he had brought one a Zippo
liquid-fuel lighter with a Harley-Davidson motif. On the last visit he
had brought the other a carton of Marlboro cigarettes.

This would be his final visit. He would never see these men again.
It had been made plain, at the last briefing. In a discreet second-floor
room of a Georgian house behind the line of gentlemen's clubs in Pall
Mall, the satellite photographs of the complex had been mounted on
a display board. The images of the roofs of the buildings were pinpoint sharp, and the entrances to the underground workshops, the
tennis courts, even the volleyball area, and the positions of the antiaircraft defenses.

This was Gavin Hughes's kingdom. He had access. He was a salesman for standard engineering machines and could tell them what
they needed to know when the images failed them. At the last briefing, the night before he had flown, over the tired sandwiches and the
stewed coffee, he had told them why his visit had been moved forward a week, what was happening at the complex on the days that
he should have visited if the original schedule had been maintained.
None of their satellites and high-optic lenses could provide them
with that kernel of detail. The meeting had been suspended. For two
hours he had been left in the room with only his controller, an un-
giving and aloof woman, younger than himself, for company. When
the meeting had resumed, the senior man requested he repeat the
ground covered earlier, why his visit had been put forward. In the
second session two new men had been present. An American, per-
spiring in a suit of brown herringbone tweed, had sat behind him
and to his right, and never spoken. A leather-faced Israeli, a Star of
David in gold hanging in the chest hair under an open-necked shirt,
had been equally silent.

Afterwards the controller had walked him back to his hotel, and
warned her agent to go carefully on this visit, take no risks. Her last
words, before they parted, reiterated what would be his fate and his
death if he created suspicion . . . as if Gavin Hughes did not know.

As the guards shouted their farewells, the barrier at the gate was lifted and the car powered away on the straight road through the dunes. It would be half an hour to the airport and then the feeder flight without formalities to the capital.

If . . . if he made it through the security check, another car, another driver, would be waiting the next morning for him when he came off the flight at Heathrow, to ferry him to another briefing. If they knew the depth of his betrayal and were waiting for him at the final security check, then they would hang Gavin Hughes, as his controller had told him, from the highest crane . . . He didn't know what would happen at this place in the next few hours or days, and hadn't an idea what his own future held.

1

The harrier contorted to clean the clammy mud from underneath its wing feathers. It worked hard at the clinging dirt as if its primitive, wild mind demanded cleanliness before the start of the day's long flight north. The dawn sunshine glossed the rusted gold of the feathers. The bird worked at them with its vicious curved, sharpened beak, pecked at the mud, spat, and coughed it down into the marsh water below the perch on a dead, stark tree. At first light it had hunted. It had dived on a brightly crested duck, the bone-stripped carcass of which was now wedged in a fork of the dead tree. The mud had speckled the underneath of the wings when it had fallen, stone fast, onto the unsuspecting prey.

Abruptly, without warning, it flapped with a slow wing beat away from the perch and abandoned its kill. It headed north, away from the hot, wet wintering grounds of west Africa.

It would fly all day, without rest, on an unerring course that retraced its first migratory route. As a killing bird, a predator, the harrier had no sense of threat or hazard.

They had been right over the tent camp, bucking in the strength of the gale, before they had seen it. They had searched all morning for it, forced lower by the lessening visibility from the whipped-up sand. The pilot of the lead helicopter had been sweating, and he was supposed to be the best, with many hours of desert flying experience, good enough in Desert Storm to have flown behind the lines into Iraq to supply the Special Forces. They had been down to a hundred feet, where the wind was most treacherous, and the wipers in front of him were clogged by grains of sand. Only a minute after he had rapped his gloved fist on the fuel gauge and muttered into their earphones that they had little time left, the Marine Corps major had spotted the camp, tapped the pilot's shoulder, and pointed down. The colonel of the National Guard had softly mouthed his thanks to his God.

Duane Seitz had heard the excited voices on his headset and thought this might be a good game for kids, reckoning himself too old for this sort of serious shit. They had put down beside the tents. The two following helicopters, which were also flown by Americans, were talked in and disgorged the local National Guardsmen. The rotors lifted away two of the camp's seven tents, but the pilots had refused, no argument accepted, to cut their engines. They wanted out and soonest.

As the thirty National Guardsmen corralled the camp, the rotors and the wind threw the fine grains in stinging clouds into their faces. The two tents had come to rest in bushes of low scrub thorn a hundred yards from the camp, but the bedding that had been with them, and the clothes, were still in loose flight, scudding over the sand. The pilots broke their huddle. They shouted into the ear of the Marine Corps major: the storm was not lifting, the gusting sand would infiltrate every aperture in the helicopters' engines, they should get the fuck out—not negotiable—now. It was already clear to them, to the Saudi colonel, to the men of the Saudi Arabian National Guard, and to Duane Seitz, that the raid had failed.

The man they sought had evaded them.

Seitz felt it keenest. He stood in the center of the camp, huddled against the wind and the blast of the rotors, the sand crusting on his face, and gazed around him. The information had been good. It had come from the interception of the signal of a digital mobile telephone. The antennae on the eastern coast had identified the position across the Gulf from which the call had been initiated, and the position in the Empty Quarter where it had been received. It should have led them to the man Duane Seitz hunted.

There was one prisoner. He was heavyset, jowled, and lay on his stomach with his arms bound behind him at the wrist and his ankles tied sharply. He wore the clothes of a Bedouin tribesman, but his physique and stomach were too gross for him to have been from this group of camel herdsmen. Seitz knew the face of the prisoner from the files, knew he came from Riyadh, was a courier for the man he tracked.

The tribesmen huddled on their haunches around a dead fire surrounded by scorched stones. The colonel yelled at them, kicked them, and they keeled away from him. Twice he whipped them with the barrel of his pistol, but none cried out even when they bled. They were small men with twig-thin bodies, impassive in the face of his anger. They could be shown the blade of a sword or the barrel of a gun but they never talked.

The camels were hobbled to pegs and kept their heads away from the force of the wind. Seitz thought the nameless, faceless man would have ridden on a camel into the blast of the driven sand. There would be no tracks and no chance of pursuit from the air. He knew only the man's reputation, which was why he sought him as if he were the Grail.

The patience of the lead pilot was exhausted. He was gesticulating to the colonel, pointing at his watch, at his helicopter, and back into the eye of the storm. The colonel gave his orders. The prisoner was dragged, helpless, towards a fuselage hatch. Above the scream of the wind, Duane Seitz heard behind him the crash of gunfire, then the camels screaming. Without their animals the Bedouin would either starve or die of thirst or exposure in the wilderness of the Empty Quarter. It was a shit country to which he was posted, with a shit little war, and he had failed to find his enemy.

Perhaps it was because one of the emaciated tribesmen ducked to avoid the blow of a rifle butt, but for a brief second the dead embers of the fire were no longer protected against the wind. Seitz saw black shreds of paper lifting in the gusts between the charred wood. He scrambled through the Bedouin and the National Guardsmen, fell to his knees, whipping out the little plastic bags that were always in his hip pocket.

Carefully, as he had been taught at the Academy at Quantico more than two decades ago, he slipped the scraps into the bags. As he squinted down, he fancied that there were still faint traces of Arabic characters on the fragments.

He was the last into the helicopter, holding his bags as if they were the relics of a saint. They lifted, and the camp in which he had placed such hope disappeared in the storm of driven sand.

"No."

"I appreciate that this is a difficult moment for you, but what I am telling you is based on information gathered within the last month."

"No."

"Of course, it's a difficult situation for you to absorb."

"No."

"Difficult, but inescapable. It's not a problem that can be ignored."

"No."

"They're serious people, Mr. Perry. You know it, we know it. Nothing has changed . . . For God's sake, you were in Iran as often as I'm in the supermarket. I cannot conceive that you are incredulous to what I'm saying. But this is not accountancy or commerce, where you would have the right to expect definitive statements. I can't give you detail. It is intelligence, the putting together of mosaic scraps of information, then analyzing the little that presents itself. I am not at liberty to divulge the detail that provided the analysis . . . You have been there, you know those people . . . If they find you, then they will seek to kill you."

Geoff Markham stood by the door watching Fenton doing the talking and recognizing already that Fenton had made a right maggot of it. The man, Perry, had his back to them and was gazing out the front window as the late-winter rain lashed the glass panes. As the senior operative, Fenton ought to have made a better fist of it. He should have sat Perry down, gone to the sideboard, routed for a whisky bottle, poured generously, and put the glass into Perry's hand. He should have communicated warmth and commitment and concern; instead, he had trampled with the finesse of a buffalo into Perry's home. Now it was fast going sour. And as it went sour, so Fenton's voice rose to a shrilling bark.

Geoff Markham stood by the door and remained silent. It was not his place to intervene when his superior fouled up. He could see Perry's hunched shoulders tighten with each new assault.

Perry's voice was low and muffled, and Markham had to strain to hear the words.

"You're not listening to me . . . No."

"I cannot see what other option you have."

"My option is to say what I have said . . . No."

"That isn't an option . . . Listen, you're in shock. You are also being willfully obstinate, refusing to face reality—"

"No. Not again. I won't run."

He heard the hiss of his superior's exasperation. He glanced down at his watch. Christ, they had not even been in the house for fifteen minutes. They had driven down from London, come unannounced, had parked the car on the far side of the green onto which the house faced. Fenton had smiled in satisfaction because there were lights on inside. They had seen the face at the window upstairs as they had opened the low wicket gate and gone up the path to the door. He had seen Perry's face and he had thought there was already a recognition of their business before they reached the door. They wore their London suits. Fenton had a martinet's mustache, painstakingly trimmed, a brown trilby, and a briefcase with the faded gold of the EIIR symbol.

There was no porch over the front door, and Perry would have recognized them for what they were, a senior and a junior from the Security Service, before they had even wiped their feet on the doormat. He made them wait and allowed the rain to spatter their backs before opening the door . . . Fenton was not often out of Thames House: he was a section head, consumed by the reading of reports and attendance at meetings. In Geoff Markham's opinion, Fenton had long ago lost touch with the great mass of people who surged back and forth each day along the Thames embankment under the high walls of the building on Millbank. To Fenton, they would have been a damn bloody nuisance, an impediment to the pure world of counterespionage . . . Markham wondered how he would have reacted if strangers had pitched up at his door, flashed their IDs, muscled into his home, started to talk of life and death.

Fenton snapped, "We have conduits of information, some more reliable than others. I have to tell you, the information we are acting upon is first class. The threat is a fact—"

"I won't run again."

Fenton's right fist slammed into the palm of his left hand. "We're not urging this course of action lightly. Look, you did it before—"

"No."

"You can do it a second time."

"No."

"I have the impression that you wish to delude yourself on the strength of the threat. Well, let us understand each other. I am not accustomed to leaving my desk for a day, journeying into this sort of backwater, for my own amusement—"

"I won't run again—final."

Fenton brayed, at the back of Perry's head, "There is evidence of a very considerable danger. Got me? Hard evidence, real danger . . ."

From where he stood at the door, Geoff Markham thought that Perry's silhouetted shoulders drooped slightly, as if he'd been cudgeled. Then they stiffened and straightened.

"I won't run again."

Fenton ground on relentlessly. "Look, it's a pretty straightforward process. Getting there is something we're expert at. You move on, you take a new identity . . . A cash sum to tide you over the incidental expenses. Just leave it to us. New national insurance, new NHS number, new Inland Revenue coding—"

"Not again. No."

"Bloody hell, Mr. Perry, do me the courtesy of hearing me out. They have your name, not the old one, they have Frank Perry—get that into your skull. If they have the name, then I have to examine the probability that they have the location . . ."

Perry turned from the window. There was a pallor now to his cheeks, and his jaw muscles seemed to flex, slacken, and flex again. There was weariness in his eyes. He didn't cower. He stood his full height. He gazed back at Fenton. Geoff Markham didn't know the details on Perry's file, had not been shown it, but if he deserved the threat, then there was something in his past that required raw toughness.

"It's your problem."

"Wrong, Mr. Perry. It's your problem because it's your life."

"Your problem and you deal with it."

"That's ridiculous."

The voice was a whisper: "Men like you, they came, they told me of the threat, they told me to quit, run. I listened, I quit, I ran. I'm not spending the rest of my life, every day that remains of my life, like a chicken in a coop wondering if the fox has found me. It is your responsibility, it's owed me. If the fox comes, shoot it. Understand me? Shoot it . . . What did *you* ever do for your country?"

Geoff Markham heard Fenton's snort, then the cut of the sarcasm. "Oh, we're there, are we? Playing the patriot's card. A man of letters once said that patriotism is the last refuge of scoundrels."

"I worked for my country. My head was on the block for it."

"While lining a damn deep pocket . . ."

"I am staying, this is my home."

It was a good room, Geoff Markham thought. There was decent furniture, a solid sideboard and a chest of dark wood, low tables. It suited the room, which was lived in. He could see it was a home. When he was not sleeping at Vicky's, he lived in an anonymous, sterile, one-bedroom apartment in west London. Here, a child's books were on the floor, an opened technical magazine, and a cotton bag from which peeped a woman's embroidery. Invitations to drinks and social functions stood on the mantelpiece above the fireplace. If it had been Markham's, he, too, would have tried to cling to it . . . But he had seen bodies, in Ireland, of men who had not covered their tracks, had made themselves available to their killers. He had seen their white, dead faces, the dried blood pools below their cheeks, and hair matted with brain tissue and bone fragments . . . They could whistle up the removals company; there were people who did discreet business for them. They could have him loaded within twenty-four hours, gone, lost.

Fenton jabbed his finger at Perry. "You won't get the sources from me, but I can tell you they have given this matter—your life, your death—a very considerable priority. Are you listening?"

"I am not leaving my home."

"They are starting on a journey. We don't know when they began it, could be a couple of weeks ago. For them, Mr. Perry, it is a long road, but you can be certain that at the end of it you are their target . . ."

. . .

The dhow had brought dried fish and cotton bales across the Gulf. The cargo for the return journey was boxes of dates, packaged video-cassette recorders and television sets from the Abu Dhabi ware-houses, cooking spices bought from Indian traders, and the man. The dhow's large sail was furled, and it was driven by a powerful en-gine. The man was the important cargo and the engine was at full throttle. He sat alone at the bow and stared down into the foaming water below. The previous night, each of the five crewmen had seen him come aboard in the darkness, slipping silently down the quay-side ladder. Only the boat's owner had spoken with him, then imme-diately given the order for the ropes to be cast off, the engine to be started. He had been left alone since the start of the journey. The call to his mobile telephone had come just after the crewmen had seen him lean forward and peer down to watch the dark shape of a shark, large enough to take a man, swimming under the bow wave before it dived.

None of the crew approached him except to offer him a plastic bottle of water and a bag of dried dates. Then the man had lifted his face. The scarred redness around his eyes, the upper part of his cheeks, and his forehead were raw. The crewmen, swabbing the deck, stowing ropes, taking turns at the wheel, understood: he had come through the stinging ferocity of a sandstorm. He had talked quietly into his telephone and none of them could hear his words in the several minutes the call had taken. It would be late afternoon be-fore he would see the raised outline of the city's buildings, the mosque minarets, and the angled, idle cranes of the port. They did not know his name, but they could recognize his importance be-cause they had sailed with their hold half empty, at night, to bring him home.

He wore the torn, dirtied clothes of a tribesman, he smelt of camels' filth, but the crewmen and the owner—simple, devout men who had sailed through the worst gale storms of the Gulf waters—would have said that they held this quiet man in fear.

Later, when they had a good view of the buildings, minarets, and cranes of Bandar Abbas, a fast speedboat of the *pasdaran* inter-cepted them, took him off, and ferried him towards the closed mili-tary section of the port used by the Revolutionary Guards. They felt then as if a chill winter shadow was no longer on their dhow, and they tried to forget his face, his eyes.

"The last time I did what I was told to do."

"For your own good. You were sensible, Mr. Perry."

"I had only two suitcases of clothes. I even cleared out the dirty washing from the bathroom basket and took that with me."

"Self-pity is always degrading."

"The men in bloody raincoats, they packed all my work papers, said I wouldn't need them again, said they'd lose them. Where did my work life go—into a landfill?"

"Dredging history rarely helps."

"I had six hours to pack. The men in raincoats were crawling all through my house. My wife—"

"As I understand, about to divorce you, and with a 'friend' to comfort her."

"There was my son. He's seventeen now. I haven't seen him since—I don't know what exams he's passed and failed, where he's going, what he's doing . . ."

"Always better, Mr. Perry, not to sink into sentimentality."

"I had damn good friends there, never said good-bye, not to any of them, just walked away . . ."

"I don't recall from the file that you were under duress."

"It was a good company I worked for, but I wasn't allowed to clear my desk. The raincoats did that."

Fenton sneered. "The directors of that company were lucky, from what I've read, not to face a Customs and Excise prosecution, as you were lucky."

"You bastard!"

"Obscenities, Mr. Perry, in my experience are seldom substitutes for common sense."

"I gave up everything!"

"Life, my friend, is not merely a photograph album to be pulled out each Christmas Day for the relations to gawp at. Little to be gained from wallowing in the past. Life is for living. Your choice— move on and live, or stay and write your own funeral service. That's the truth, Mr. Perry, and the truth should be faced."

The rain was heavier outside, beating a drumroll on the window-panes. The darkening cloud came out of the east, off the sea. Geoff Markham stayed by the door. He could have reached beside him to switch on the lights to break the gloom, but he did not.

Markham knew his superior's performance was a disaster. He doubted Fenton had the sensitivity to appreciate the castration of a life—Perry had run away from a wife who no longer loved him, a son, friends and neighbors, even his office, the banter and excite-ment of the sales section, everything that was past. Frank Perry was a damned ordinary name. If there had been six hours for him to quit his house, then the time allotted to choosing a new name would have been about three short minutes. Maybe the raincoats had sad-dled him with it.

Perry had turned back to the window, and Fenton paced as if he did not know what else to say . . . Markham wondered whether Perry had gone, a year or two later, to watch a school gate from the far side of the street, to see the boy come out from school, a leggy youth with his shirt hanging out, his tie loosened. Maybe the kid would have been alone, still traumatized from his father's disappearance. The raincoats would have told him that kids couldn't handle secrets, that they blabbed, that he endangered himself and the kid if he made contact . . . They would have tracked Frank Perry's former footsteps, his onetime life, until they were convinced that the trail was broken. Fenton wouldn't have understood.

"You have to face facts, and facts dictate that you move on."

"And my new home, new family, new life, new friends?"

"Start again."

"Dump my new home, put my new family through the hoop?"

"They'll cope. There's no alternative."

"And in a year, or three years, do it all again? And again after that, and again. Do it forever—peer over my shoulder, wetting myself, keeping the bags packed. Is that a life worth living?"

"It's what you've got, Mr. Perry." Fenton rubbed his fingernail against the brush of his mustache. Despite the gloom, Markham could see the flush on his superior's cheeks. He didn't think Fenton was an evil man or a bully, just insensitive . . . He'd do a memo—they liked memos back at Thames House—to Administration, on the need for counseling courses in sensitivity. They could set up a sensitivity subcommittee and they could call in outside consultants. There could be a paper—"Sensitivity (Dealing with Obstinate, Bloody-Minded, Pigheaded 'Ordinary' Members of the Public)." There could be two-day courses in sensitivity for all senior executive officers.

Fenton beat a path between the toys and the embroidery.

"I won't do it."

"You're a fool, Mr. Perry."

"It's your privilege to say so, but I'm not going to run, not again."

Fenton picked up his coat from the arm of a chair and shrugged himself into it, covered his neatly combed hair with his hat. Geoff Markham turned and quietly opened the living room door.

Fenton's voice was raised. "I hope it's what you want, but we're going into an area of unpredictability . . ."

It would be in the third week of its migration. The bird would have left its sub-Saharan wintering grounds around twenty days earlier, have stored weight, strength, and fat in the wetlands of Senegal or Mauretania. It would have rested that last night in the southern extreme of the Charente-Maritime, and hunted at dawn.

He sold insurance for a Paris-based company—annuities, fire and theft, household and motor, life and accident policies—in a quadrangle of territory between La Rochelle in the north, Rochefort in the south, Niort and Cognac in the east. The trade to be gained at a weekend, when clients were at home and not tired, was the most fruitful, but in March and October he never worked weekends. Instead, early in the morning, he left his home at Loulay with his liver white spaniel and drove a dozen kilometers into the winter-flooded marshland of the Charente-Maritime. In the boot of his car was his most prized possession: an Armi Bettinsoli over-and-under shotgun. Every Saturday and Sunday morning, in the early spring and the late autumn, he parked his car and carried the shotgun, wrapped in sacking, a kilometer away. His sport, as practiced by his father and grandfather, was now opposed by the city bastards who claimed to protect the birds. It was necessary to be covert, to move after each shot, because the bastards looked for men enjoying legal sport, to interfere. In the remaining months, he shot pheasants, partridges, rabbits, and foxes, but the sport he craved was in March, when the birds migrated north, and October, when they returned south to escape the winter.

That Sunday morning in late March, he saw the bird first as a speck and swung his binoculars up from his chest to make the distant identification. He had already fired and moved twice that morning. The dog had retrieved a swallow crushed by the weight of shot and a spotted redshank, which had been alive. He had twisted its neck.

The swallows flew in tight, fast groups and were easy to down. The spotted redshanks came in clusters and were not too difficult to shoot. But the bird coming now, from the south, low over the reed beds, was a true target for a marksman. He knew the markings of the harrier, could recognize them with his binoculars at half a kilometer's distance. It was a worthy target: those birds always flew singly, low, at near to fifty kilometers per hour, a ground speed of 140 meters in ten seconds. A marsh harrier would pay for his weekend's cartridges: his friend Pierre, the amateur taxidermist, always paid well for a raptor, and top price for a marsh harrier. He crouched, his breath coming in short spurts. The bird had such good sight, but he was low down and hidden by the marsh fronds.

He rose and aimed. The bird was straight ahead and would pass directly over him. He could see the ginger-capped crown of the bird and the ruff at its neck. It would be a juvenile, but it had fed well in the African winter. He fired. For a moment the bird dipped, bucked, then fell. The dog bounded forward, splashing into the marsh water. He fired the second barrel and shouted, urging the dog forward into the wall of reeds. He was still reloading when the bird came past him, within five meters. Its flight was level to his head, and then it was past. It had a labored, fractured flight; the wings beat unevenly. His hands shook and a cartridge dropped from his fingers into the water. He howled in frustration. When the gun was loaded and the dog was back beside him, he swung. The bird was beyond range but he heard its scream. He watched it for a long time with his eye, then with the binoculars. It went north, for La Rochelle. If it had the strength, it would pass by the estuary at Nantes and the river at

Rennes, then reach the Channel coast. He thought his pellets had hit the muscle, ligament, or tendons in the wing, but not the bone: bone fracture would have brought it down. From the look of it, the bird would not survive a crossing of the Channel to an English landfall.

They were crowded in the hallway, pressed close together against hanging coats. The family's boots were scattered on the tiled floor. There were tennis rackets in the corner, a bright plastic beach bucket and spade, a chaos of stones from the shore. It was the same comforting clutter that Geoff Markham knew from his own parents' home.

Perry reached past them and pulled the door open. There was an old bolt on it and a new lock. Geoff Markham shuddered—in Belfast the psychopaths had sledgehammered through doors to do their killing.

Fenton tried a last time. "Is it that you're frightened of telling her?"

"Who? What?"

"Frightened of telling your wife what you did. Is that the problem?"

"They never told me what I'd done. Said it was better I didn't know."

"She doesn't know about before?"

"She didn't need to know."

"Lived with the secret, did you? Festering, is it?"

"Get out."

"My advice, Mr. Perry, is to come clean with her, then fall into line."

"Tell them, back where you came from, no."

"So much better, Mr. Perry, if you'd had the guts to be honest with your wife. Isn't she just common-law?"

Fenton was on his way to the gate when his feet slipped on the wet brick of the path. He stumbled and cursed.

Geoff Markham was going after him when his sleeve was grabbed. The rain ran on Perry's face. He hissed, "This is mine. It's all I have. I'm not running again. Tell them that. This is my home, where I live with the woman I love. I am among friends—true, good friends. I won't spend the rest of my life hiding, a rat in a hole. This is where I stand, with my woman and my friends . . . Do you know what it's like to be alone and running? They don't stay with you, the raincoats, did you know that? With you for a week, ten days, then gone. A contact telephone number for a month, then discontinued. You are so bloody alone. Tell them, whoever sent you, that I'm sorry if it's not convenient but I won't run again."

Fenton was at the car, crouched behind it to protect himself from the rain. Markham reached it and opened the door for his superior.

He looked back. Perry's door was already shut.

2

Behind the cottage homes of brick and flint stone, where climber
roses trailed and the honeysuckle was not yet in leaf, the ornamental
trees in the gardens were shredded of color and the sea was slate
gray, with white flecks. Between the houses and through the trees, he
saw it stretching away, limitless. A solitary cargo ship nudged along
the horizon, maybe out of Felixstowe. The sea was like a great wall
against which the village sheltered, a barrier that had no end to its
width and to its depth.

"God, don't spare the horses."

It was the reason he'd been fetched out for the day. Fenton
wouldn't have wanted to drive or have to face the vagaries of train
timetables and a waiting taxi. Geoff Markham's function was to
drive, not to play a part in what should have been a reassuring and
businesslike making of arrangements for the removal van's arrival.
He had the wipers going but the back window was a disaster, as if a
filled bucket had been tipped on it. He reversed cautiously, couldn't
see a damn thing in his mirror, then swung the wheel hard. The car
surged forward. Fenton was writhing out of his dripping coat and
nudged Markham's arm so that he swerved. He veered towards a
woman in a plastic cape pushing her bicycle. Before he'd straightened up, the tires sluiced the puddle over her legs. There was a shout
of abuse.

Fenton grinned. "First sign of life we've seen . . ."

Markham should have stopped to apologize but kept going: he wanted away from the place. He knew nothing of the sea and it held no particular attraction for him. He thought it chill and threatening.

They went past a small shop with pottery and postcards in the window, from which faces peered. They would have heard the woman's protest. There was a tearoom beside the shop, shuttered for the winter. They swept past the village hall, a low-set building with an old Morris outside. Then there was a pub with an empty car park.

"Thank the Lord, the open road beckons. Could you live here, Geoff, in this dead end?"

They'd both seen it. The estate agent's For Sale sign was propped in an untrimmed hedge beside a crazily hanging gate with the faded name on it, Rose Cottage. Beyond was a small overgrown garden, then a darkened cottage with the curtains drawn, no lights showing. The rainwater cascaded from the blocked gutters, and tiles were missing from the roof. It would be "three bedrooms, bathroom, two reception, kitchen, in need of modernization." And it would also be, down here on the Suffolk coast, £90,000 before the builders went in. But all that was irrelevant to Markham. He was wondering how Perry was facing up to the devastation they'd left behind them.

". . . Sort of place, Geoff, where the major entertainment off-season would be screwing your sister or your daughter or your niece. Eh?"

Not since he had come back from Ireland and gone to work on the Mid East (Islamic) Desk had he heard his superior utter anything as crude. He was shocked, wouldn't have believed Fenton capable of such vulgarity. The bitter little confrontation with Perry had rattled him.

They went up a long, straight road, flanked first by terraced houses, then, as he accelerated, by larger houses oozing prosperity, set back in gardens with tarpaulin-covered yachts in the driveways. The church was on their right. Geoff Markham was good on churches, liked to walk around them, and this one, through his side window, looked to be worth a quarter of an hour, a fine tower solid as a fortress, a wide nave safe as a refuge. Beyond it was a stark façade of flint ruins, the clerestory windows open to the concrete gray of the clouds. He turned his head to see the ruins better. There was a chuckle beside him.

"About as dead as the rest of the wretched place."

Fenton, he knew, lived in Beaconsfield, not on his own salary but on family money; couldn't have managed Beaconsfield, the restaurants, the delicatessens, and the bijou clothes shops where his wife went, on a desk head's wage. Money was seldom far from Geoff Markham's thoughts, nagging like a dripping tap. Vicky and his future were about money. He was driving faster.

It was strange, but he hadn't seemed to register the village when they came into it, less than an hour before. It had not seemed a part of the present and the future. The village was history, to be left behind once the removal van had arrived. But no removal van was coming, and the village—its layout, entry and exit route, topography, community—was as important as any of those isolated white-walled farmhouses in south Armagh, Fermanagh, and east Tyrone.

Fenton was again massaging his mustache and showed no interest in what was around him. Through the trees was the shimmer of silver gray from stretching inland water. The road in front was straight and empty; he had no need to concentrate. Markham's mind was on the landscape, as it would have been if he had been driving in Ireland.

They reached the crossroads, and the main road for Ipswich, Colchester, and London. He paused for traffic with the right of way, and the smile brightened on Fenton's face. He checked the distance they had come since leaving the house.

"About bloody time. You never said—could you live there? Damn sure I couldn't."

It wasn't for Markham to pick a pointless argument with his superior. "I couldn't, but it's right for him."

"Come again?"

"He chose well, Perry did."

"Don't give me riddles."

Markham pulled out into the main road and slashed his way through the gears for speed.

"He wants to make a stand, he won't run . . . It's good ground for him. One road in and the same road out. The sea is behind and it can be monitored. Natural barriers of flooded marshland to the north and the south with no vehicle access. If you were in a city street or a town's suburban road, you couldn't get protection like that. He chose well, if he's really staying."

They would be back in London, on Millbank, in three hours. Then the bells would start clamoring and the calls would go out for the meeting.

He went, like a sleepwalker, around the ground floor of his house, and seemed not to recognize the possessions they had collected over four years. Frank Perry felt a stranger in his house. He had made himself three cups of instant coffee, sat with them, drunk them, then paced again.

Of course he knew the reality of the threat. Whatever had been done with the information he'd given in the briefings at the house behind Pall Mall, he would have made a lasting enemy of the authorities in Iran. He'd assumed that the information had been used to block sales of equipment and chemicals from the factories of the old Eastern bloc and from Western Europe, from the works of his old company in Newbury. There would have been expulsions of Iranian trade attachés, the loss of their precious foreign exchange resources, and the program would have been delayed. Of course the threat was real, and he'd known it.

However hard he had tried to put the past behind him, it had stayed with him. Sometimes it was a light zephyr wind on his face; sometimes it was a gale beating against his back. For four years, it had always been there. He had never been able, and God, he'd tried, to escape the past.

Through those years, Frank Perry had been waiting for them. He couldn't have put features to their faces, but he'd known they'd come in suits, with polished shoes, with a briefcase that wouldn't be opened, with knowledge that would be only partially shared. They'd be so recognizable and predictable. From the moment he'd seen them run from the car to his front door he'd known who they were and what they would tell him. He had rehearsed, more times than he could count, what he would say to them, and had finally said it.

He stopped pacing. He stared out of the window, across the green.

His fists were clenched. Everything he could see, the homes of his friends, the shop, the hall, and the pub at the end of the road, were as normal and unremarkable as they had been before the men from London had come. It was hard for Frank Perry to believe that anything had changed, but it had and he knew it.

His fingernails pressed hard into the palms of his hands. He would fight to hold everything that was precious to him.

Meryl Perry held the umbrella over the child's head and sheltered him all the way from the car, through the gate, up the path to the front door. The child shivered as they waited for the door to be opened. The Carstairses lived in a fine house on the main street, the only road through the village. They both worked and had good positions; she would only just have reached home, and he wouldn't be back for an hour. The child bolted through the open door.

"You're a saint, Meryl. Thanks ever so."

"Don't worry about it, Emma, wouldn't let him get soaked."

"You wouldn't, others might. Look, you're drenched. You're a sweetheart."

"I'm doing tomorrow, and you're doing the rest of the week, right?"

"Actually, Meryl, I was going to ask you—can you do all this week? It's a real bash at work, and Barry's in too early to take them. I'll make it up the week after."

"No problem, what friends are for."

"You're brilliant—don't know what I'd do without you."

The door closed on her. Her ankles were sodden, her stockings clammy. She liked Emma Carstairs, and Frank was Barry's best friend. They had good times together. The school run to Halesworth had been their first touch point. She hadn't had friends, not like Emma and Barry, before she had moved to the village. She hurried back to the car, the rain lashing her while she furled the umbrella. Off again, taking Donna home. She turned by the village hall, then went back past the church and up the lane to the council houses. She dropped Donna at her front gate.

"Thanks so much, Mrs. Perry."

"You'd have drowned at the bus stop."

"Vince didn't stop, nor that stuck-up Mary Wroughton."

"Leave off, Donna—probably they didn't see you."

"I'd have ruined my hair, you're really kind."

"And I'll see you next week, when Frank and I are out."

"Always enjoy baby-sitting at yours, Mrs. Perry. Thanks again."

The girl was out of the car and running for her front door. Her Stephen was scowling beside her, but he was eight and any child of that age objected to baby-sitters. She poked him, he put his tongue out at her, and they both laughed. He'd had behavioral problems in the city, but not since they had moved to the village; the best thing she could have done for Stephen was bring him here. She drove back into the village. There were no cars in front of Mrs. Fairbrother's, no guests checked in. Past the Martindales' pub, too early to be open. Vince's van was outside his terraced house; strange that he hadn't seen Donna at the bus stop. Dominic Evans—he was always nice to her—was running back into his shop with the ice cream sign, probably going to shut up early. He was always helpful, and Euan. She parked as close as possible to their front gate and Stephen scampered for the door. Peggy's bicycle was askew against the Wroughtons' garage door. Meryl was locking her car, umbrella perched over her head, as Peggy came down the Wroughtons' path.

"Meryl, hold on."

"Yes, Peggy."

"I've that typing for you—you said you would?"

"Of course I did."

"For the Red Cross and the Wildlife."

"No problem."

"Can't thank you enough, don't know what I did before you came. Oh, Meryl, you couldn't manage the Institute's minutes? Fanny's got an awful cold—I think there's a lot of it about."

"I'll do it."

"Thanks, Meryl."

"You should get on home, Peggy. You look like a hose has been turned on you."

"I tell you, Meryl, those people seeing Frank when you were out—they drove right through a puddle, could have avoided it. I used the F-word and all. Quite made my day, using the F-word."

Stephen had left the door open and the rain was driving onto the hall tiles. She took off her coat and shook it hard outside. She called, "Frank, we're home."

"I'm in the kitchen."

There was no light on downstairs. Stephen would have gone straight to his room, for his books and his toys. She went into the kitchen. He sat at the kitchen table, but it was too dark for her to see his face.

"You all right, love?"

"Fine."

"Had a busy day?"

"No."

"Visitors?"

"No, no visitors."

It was the first time in the four years she had known him that she could have proved he had lied. She said she would make a pot of tea, and switched on the light.

Kicking a cat would have been too easy, and beating his balding head against a wall would have been poor satisfaction. Seitz wondered if they knew in Audubon, Iowa, the good, solidly ignorant folk, as they scratched a living and paid taxes, where their money went. Did they know in California or South Carolina where it ended? In Texas? In Montana? If it were not for the tax money, Saddam Hussein might have been in Dhahran and the ayatollahs might have made it to Riyadh. And they treated him, the representative of those taxpayers, like a dog's turd, but he kept smiling. All day he had waited at the guarded headquarters of General Intelligence, and been shuffled between various air-conditioned offices. They offered him fruit juice and cake, polite talk, and he had achieved nothing.

The prisoner—for Seitz he was a number, 87/41—had most probably been below him all through that day, in the basement holding cells. It was the fifth time he had tried to win access to the prisoner, without success. The man would be in the cells, and maybe his mother would not recognize him. Maybe he was without fingernails. Maybe a fine cord had been knotted tightly round his penis while water was poured down his throat.

Seitz did not have the name of the man he hunted, nor the face. He had footprints. The prisoner might have told him the name, described the face.

His driver took him back to the embassy. He could demand time of the ambassador and shout a bit, and the ambassador would shrug and mouth sympathy. He could send another protest signal to the Hoover Building, and it would be filed along with the rest.

Later, he would be in his windowless office behind the bombproof door guarded by the young Marine, and he would stand in front of the big wall map of the region, with his herringbone jacket loose on his shoulders, and look at the footprints, at the bright-headed pins. It took two weeks, from the event, for Seitz to be able to put another pin in the map, to mark another footprint. From the pins hung little paper flags, carrying a date. For two and a half years he had followed the footprints, and they made a pattern for him.

There was a digital mobile telephone that made scrambled, voice-protected calls from and to an office in Tehran of the Ministry of Information and Security. The computers could not break through the scrambled conversations but they could locate and identify the position from which the call had originated or been answered. His pins, with their carefully dated flags, were scattered over the map surface of Iran and Saudi Arabia. It was two and a half years since the explosion at the National Guard barracks in Riyadh in which five of his countrymen had died; the pin was there and dated the day before it happened. Two years since the lorry bomb at the Khobar Tower air force base outside Dhahran had killed nineteen Americans, and that date pin was there, the day before the massacre. Each atrocity enabled him to track a man without a name and without a face.

It took two weeks for the computer to log the locations. There was a pin in the Empty Quarter, dated forty-three days back, and he had bypassed every bureaucratic instruction, ignored every standing order, worked the contact game, won the onetime favor, tasked the Marine Corps helicopters and the Saudi National Guardsmen, and still been too damned late. And there was a pin in international waters along the trade route between Abu Dhabi and the Iranian port of Bandar Abbas.

No name, no face, only footprints for Duane Seitz to follow as if he were a shambling, slow-going bloodhound.

Mary Ellen brought him the day's communications from the cipher section, and coffee. Sometimes she put whisky in it, which in this arrogant, ungrateful, corrupt country, was almost a beheading offense. She was blue chip, a college graduate from Long Island, and seemed to regard it as her life's work to look after a middle-aged man from a farming family in Audubon, Iowa. He was lucky to have her.

It took sixteen days from the time the antennae or the dishes sucked in the streams of digital information for the computers to locate the positioning of the receiver and transmit it to Duane Seitz. She passed him two pins and two dated flags. Mary Ellen was too short to reach that far up the wall map into northern Iran. He grunted and stretched. He drove home the pins where there were two tight clusters.

He drank the coffee.

She said, and he did not need her to tell him, "It's where he always goes. He calls from Alamut, then the next day from Qasvin, then silence, then the call again, then the killing. It's what he always does . . ."

"That paper we got, the burned paper, what did Quantico scratch out of that?"

She shrugged, as if the Hoover Building hadn't bothered to report back what the forensics at Quantico had learned.

"He's going for a killing, yes?"

"It's what the footprints say. He calls from Qasvin and the day before from Alamut, like it's his ritual. Then he moves and then he kills."

Hasan-i-Sabah had called for a volunteer to strike down a vizier. A young man without fear had stepped forward and Nizam al-Mulk was stabbed to death as he was carried in a litter to his wives' tent. Hasan-i-Sabah had inscribed, "The killing of this devil is the beginning of bliss."

The words had been written 906 years before, in the place where the man now sat. Every wall of the mountain fortress constructed by Hasan-i-Sabah was now broken. It was the eighth time he had climbed the mountain, taken the narrow path used only by the sheep, wild goats, and foraging wolves over the scree slope. The drop beneath him did not frighten him, but if he had slipped on any of those climbs he would have died. He was two thousand meters above sea level, perched on a small rock high over the valley. It was where he found strength.

Among the fallen stones of the fortress, it was difficult for him to imagine it as it had been. In the valley had been the Garden of Paradise. In the fortress had been the discipline of self-sacrifice and obedience. The young men who gazed down on the garden and learned their skills in the fortress were the Fida'is. Their trade was killing. They understood their duty and the personal sacrifice it required. They yearned for their reward, a place in the Garden of Paradise, where there were groves of sweet fruit trees, clear tumbling streams, and women of great beauty. He had slept in a tent by a small fire, and at dawn had packed up and started his climb on the path over the scree. Whether in sunshine or in the winter's mists, whether the snow had fallen and the path was treacherous, he made that pilgrimage to the destroyed fortress. He would reach it and sit for hours with the silence of the valley below him and consider the mission he had been given, the requirement for obedience and self-sacrifice, and the reward of a martyr's glory. When the sun lowered or the clouds darkened, he would make the call on the digital phone given him by the man who was like a father to him, like Hasan-i-Sabah had been to the Fida'is, and he would start the descent. He would reach the four-wheel-drive vehicle as darkness fell and drive back to the camp at Qasvin. From Qasvin he would start on his journey as, long ago, the Fida'is had started theirs.

"What's the matter with it?"

He put down his fork noisily.

"Isn't it good enough for you?"

He pushed away the plate. Now he looked down at the table mat.

"It's not much—it's what Stephen likes. A bit late to start complaining, you've had it before."

He'd cut through half a sausage and eaten it. He'd forked a few chips, and hardly any of the beans.

"What's the problem, Frank?"

Her boy had cleared his plate. He had a muted fear in his eyes, a child's loathing of adults' argument.

"All right, it's not much, but I had a long day. I did that typing . . .
Come on, Frank, what's it about?"

He shook his head, jerked it from side to side.

"Are you ill? Do you want an aspirin?"

Again he shook his head, more slowly.

"For God's sake, Frank, *what* is going on?"

There was the violent scrape of Stephen's chair as the boy fled the
kitchen, the clatter of his feet on the stairs. Then his bedroom door
slammed.

"You know what? He did really well in his English assessment,
better than he's done before. He was bubbling to tell you but he
didn't have the chance, did he? Come on, Frank, you're always so
good with him."

His head was sunk in his hands.

They hadn't spoken, not properly, since she had come home and
had recognized the lie. She had been in the kitchen, doing the typing
for Peggy before cooking supper, and he had been in the living room.

He still hadn't put a light on. He had turned his chair away from
the unlit fire and the television so that he could sit and stare out the
window. Dusk had come early and he hadn't drawn the curtains. He
gazed out onto the green and the streetlight on the far side. He had
not listened to the news bulletin as he usually did, or opened the paper she had brought him.

Meryl had never known him lie, and she felt a desperate anxiety.
When she had met Frank Perry, four years before, she had been a single mother without a name for her son's father, working in a small
company in east London, pushing paper, when he had come to advise
on the engineering required for the heating system in the old factory
floor. He'd made her laugh, and God, it had been a long time since
anyone else had. Next week, when Donna came to baby-sit, they were
going out to celebrate the fourth anniversary, April 3, since she and
Stephen had come to the village with their cases, all that they owned,
and moved into the house that she and Frank had found.

He didn't earn a great deal, but the checks that came in were sufficient to keep them in a lifestyle that was equally far from luxurious
and distant from frugal. He had a solid grasp of engineering and
seemed to come up with the ideas frequently enough that lifted

small businesses out of a problem hole. The work came by word of mouth from satisfied and grateful customers. He'd be called out around once a week, and then solved those problems at home. She was used to working around him in the house, bringing him cups of coffee and tea, leaving him sandwiches for lunch when she was out. His work brought them all the comfort she wanted; there was an absence of stress; she was free from anxiety. She didn't understand the engineering problems he was paid to solve, but her ignorance never seemed to offend him. Living here with him, she would have said, had given her and Stephen the best years of their lives.

She touched and tugged at her fair hair nervously. "Is it about me?"

"No."

She took Stephen's plate, stacked it under hers. "Is it about him? Has he said something—done something?"

"No."

"It's about you?"

"My problem," he said. His words were muffled through his hands.

"Aren't you going to tell me?"

"When I'm ready."

She was up from the table, carrying away the plates. "Of course, we're not husband and wife. We're only man and woman with a bastard child. Makes a difference, doesn't it?"

"Don't talk such rubbish, don't hurt yourself."

"Frank, look at me. Is it what we don't talk about? Is it that forbidden area, the past? Two men came, and you lied. Did they come out of the past?"

He pushed back his chair, took the plates from her, and put them in the sink. He held her close against him and his hands were gentle on her hair. He kissed her eyes as tears welled. "Just give me time, please . . . I have to have time." He gave her his handkerchief, then went upstairs to Stephen's room to ask about his English assessment.

She tipped the food from his plate into the bin, wiped the table, then went back to typing the Institute's minutes and the details of the Wildlife Field Day and the Red Cross bring-and-buy morning.

She heard him talking with her boy. Because two men had come from the past and he had lied, she thought, somewhere in the darkness outside the window there was danger.

The previous evening, four men and a woman from the Mujahiddin-e-Khalq had been brought in a closed lorry to the camp at Qasvin. Normally it was the corpses of executed criminals—rapists, drug dealers, and murderers—that were dumped at the Abyek camp, but because the four men and one woman were filth and apostates, they were alive. He had heard them singing in their cell in the night, low, chanting voices.

They had headed north from the training base in southern Iraq and crossed the frontier in the mountains between Saqqez and Mahabad, and been ambushed by the *pasdaran*. Most of the raiding party had fled, but five had been captured. After interrogation, trial, and sentence, they had been brought to the Abyek camp at Qasvin.

Normally the corpses were propped against bare wood chairs or low walls of sandbags, but once, when an air force officer had been found guilty of spying for the Great Satan, he had been offered as live target practice.

It was not a camp like a military compound but was constructed as a small town, on the outskirts of Qasvin. It was a miniature Babel, for the recruits spoke in many dialects, with a sprawl of concrete houses and shops, a market that sold vegetables, meat, and rice, and a mosque. For many years the Abyek camp had deceived the spy satellites of the Americans, but no longer. Now there was stricter security around the perimeter and greater caution on all methods of communication. Only the best, the most determined, of the Palestinians, Lebanese, Turks, Saudis, Algerians, and Egyptians were brought to the camp to finish their training.

Many came to watch, marshaled by their instructors into small groups of their own nationality. In front of them, in the sandscape that stretched to the perimeter wire and then the open country, were the low heaps of sandbags and the chairs. He wore a scarf across his face. Even the most dedicated and determined of the recruits might be captured, interrogated, might not have the resolve of those who had gone from the mountain at Alamut. He did not cock his Kalashnikov automatic rifle until the terrorists were brought out from their cell and were within hearing range of the metal scrape. They were not blindfolded.

They were led to the chairs and the sandbags. Their ankles were not tied. The air force officer who had spied for the Great Satan had tried to run, which had made for a better shot. It would be good if some of them ran. They were between thirty meters and a hundred meters from him. They were denounced by the commander of the camp, who read from a page of text. There was a silence and the sun caught their bared faces. He shot two with a short burst and saw them spill over, dead. He fired a long burst into another, a dozen rounds, and watched as the body kicked in spasm. He used many shots on the fourth man, but his mind was clear enough to reckon when he had one bullet left. She was farthest away, the last. She stared back at him. None of the men had given him the satisfaction of running, and neither did she. He shot her in the forehead, and she fell backwards. There was applause. He cleared his weapon, and walked away.

As the recruits blasted at the corpses—it hardened them to fire at real bodies—he made a call on his digital telephone. He was ready to begin his journey.

"I cannot fashion it out of nothing. I can only pass on what I've been given by the Americans, and I've done that. I've gone to the edge of my remit. If you can't shift him, that's your problem."

Penny Flowers had cycled over from Vauxhall Bridge Cross to Thames House; a rucksack and a mauve helmet sat beside her chair. It was the end of her day and she was tired, Geoff Markham thought. She wanted out and the ride home. She was older than him, and more senior. She didn't acknowledge his presence. He sat at the far end of the table and took the minutes of the meeting.

"May I just go over the ground once more. Stop me if I'm wrong. We have FBI material . . . on a raid into the Saudi deserts, following an intercepted but scrambled telephone link. They miss their target but retrieve sheets of burned paper, which are sent to their laboratories for examination."

Barnaby Cox was a high flier, and Geoff Markham had heard it said often enough that promotion had come too fast for his slender ability. He headed G Branch, with responsibility for the prevention of Islamic terrorism and subversive activity in the United Kingdom. His route to survival, as Markham had heard it, was a dogged pursuit of detail and a fierce avoidance of decision taking. The weight of responsibility had prematurely aged his features and grayed his hair.

"Which is what I told you yesterday afternoon, Barney. Their forensics came up with the name of Frank Perry, in capitals, roman characters, a date and time, and a wharf number in the port at Abu Dhabi, in Arabic. There was a secondary call the next day from a position located as mid-Gulf, between Abu Dhabi and Bandar Abbas. The Americans checked the name—Frank Perry—with their own computers, drew blank, tried us. We registered, it's what I told you yesterday."

It was not Harry Fenton's style to show deference to the younger man who had leapfrogged him on the advancement ladder. Fenton was back on tried and trusted home territory. He had private means and didn't care about the pension, but he had failed that day and there was an exaggerated edge to his voice. Geoff Markham doodled on his pad, waiting for something of value to note.

"Unless I'm given facts from which a threat-level assessment can be made, there's not really much point in me sitting here. Resources don't grow on trees. Frankly, it's pathetic that a man at risk cannot be persuaded to move to a safer berth." The superintendent from Special Branch spoke. He had come into the room and jerked off his jacket, ready for a fight. Geoff Markham knew the spat for influence between the Branch and the Services was already explosive. It amused him to watch.

"Fatal, the use of businessmen, never worth it," Cox mumbled.

"He's simply a silly little man without the wit to know when he's being offered common sense," Harry Fenton said. "But we, dammit, are obliged to react."

"I'll need some facts, if it's to come out of my budget," the superintendent shot back.

So, pass the load to Geoff Markham. The junior would write a report, and decisions could be suspended until it was circulated. Beside his doodles of Victorian gravestones, with a couple of church steeples, he wrote down Penny Flowers's extension number at Vauxhall Bridge Cross and the policeman's number at Scotland Yard. He left them, as a whisky bottle was lifted out of the cabinet, and went back to his cubbyhole between the partitions on the outer walls of the open-plan area used by G/4.

There was a photograph, blown up by the copier, above his desk. The Ayatollah Khomeini glowered down at him, fixed him with a cold, unwavering stare. It was good to have the picture. It helped him to understand: the image on the wall was better than anything he read or was told. It was a snapshot of suspicion and hostility. He rang Vicky to tell her he couldn't make dinner. She was giving him the treatment, and he put the phone down on her, didn't bother to continue a scrap with her. He opened the file on his desk and gazed at the three useless sheets of paper that dealt with an identity change five years previously. Nothing was in the file about a life and a name before that change. They'd gone down to the country at half cock, underprepared, the familiar story. He rang Vicky back, made his peace, and said at what time he would meet her.

He wrote on a sheet of paper the questions he would have to answer if he were to write a decent report. What was the history of Frank Perry? What had he done and when did he do it? What were the consequences of Frank Perry's actions? What should be the threat-level assessment? What was the source of the American information? What was the timetable for an attempt at a killing? The one thing he wouldn't write was that he'd rather liked Frank Perry.

The area was quiet, the partitioned sections either side of him empty. The face above him peered down. The eyes, long dead, preserved in the photograph were without mercy. He rang Registry, told them what he needed. Geoff Markham lived a good safe life, and he wondered how it would be if he were alone and threatened by the enmity of those eyes.

He walked along Main Street. The rain had eased, left only a trace in the gathering wind. There were few streetlights and no cars moving. He did not know what he would tell her or when. He could recall each day and each hour, five years back, of the first month after he had left the cul-de-sac house in Newbury with his two suitcases; two days with the minders in an empty officer's quarters in the garrison camp at Warminster; four days with the minders in a furnished house at the Clifton end of Bristol; five days with the minders in a hotel on hard times outside Norwich, after which they had left. Two more days, alone, in that hotel, then three weeks in a guest house in Bournemouth, then the start of the search for something permanent, and the absorption of the new identity, the move to a flat in southeast London. In those first days, he had felt a desperate sense of shamed loneliness, had yearned to call his wife and son, the partners at the office, the customers in his appointments diary. In those endless briefings on his new identity, for hour after hour, Penny Flowers had demanded he put the old life behind him. She had no small talk but emphasized coldly, and reiterated, that if he broke cover he would be found, and if he were found he would be killed. And then she'd gone with the minders, had cut him off, left him, and the night they had gone he, a grown man, had wept on his bed.

"Evening, Frank."

He spun, coiled, tense. He gazed at the shadow.

"Only me—seen a ghost? Sorry, did I startle you? It's Dominic."

"Afraid you did—obvious, was it?"

"Like I was going to shoot you. Just taking the dog out . . . I hear Peggy's lumbered Meryl with the typing for the Wildlife Field Day. It's very good of her. I was doing the group's accounts this evening— your donation was really generous, thanks. Prefer to say it myself than just send a little letter."

"Don't think about it."

"It's worth saying. It was a good day when you and Meryl came here—wish all the 'foreigners' slotted in as easily."

"We love it here."

"Can't beat friends, can you?"

"No, I don't think you can."

"Well, we've had our little piddle, time to be getting back, and sorry I startled you—Oh, did Meryl tell you about the field day, for the Wildlife, in May? And the RSPB lecture we've got coming up? Hope you can come to both. We're doing the marsh harriers on Southmarsh for the field day—anytime now they're back from

Africa. It's an incredible migration—fierce little brutes, killers, but beautiful with it. Better be getting back. Goodnight, Frank."

The footsteps shuffled away into the night. Dominic seemed to love the dog as much as he did Euan. Perry walked on and took the path beside the course of the old river, now silted and narrow, and across the north edge of Southmarsh. He climbed, slipping and sliding, over the huge barrier of stones the sea had thrown up, and went down onto the beach. His feet gouged in the sand, wet from the receding tide. From between the fast cloud that carried the last of the slashing rain, moonlight pierced the darkness around him. The silence was broken only by the hissing of the sea on the shingle. He scanned for a ship's lights, but there was nothing. He did not know what he would tell her of the past, nor what she should know of the future.

He walked in the darkness, grinding his feet into the fine pebbles and the emptied shells. He turned his back to the sea. The great black holes of Southmarsh and Northmarsh were around the clustered lights of the village. He felt a sense of safety, of belonging. It was his home. He moved on, retraced his steps, and came back into the village. Brisk footsteps were hurrying towards him, a bouncing torch beam lit the pavement, then soared and found his face.

"Hello, Frank, it's Basil. Choir practice drifted on, why I'm late out, and—same as you, I suppose—I felt like a prisoner in the vicarage with that dreadful rain today. Got to get out, get a bit of air before bed."

"Evening, Mr. Hackett."

"Please, Frank, not the formality, not among friends—even those, forgive me, whom I do not see on Sundays!"

"A deserved slap on the wrist."

"Not to worry—it's what people do that matters, not where they're seen to be. If all my worshipers were as involved in the welfare of the village as you and Meryl, I'd be a happier man . . . You look a bit drawn, had bad news?"

"Everything's fine."

"Before I forget, I hear Meryl's visiting Mrs. Hopkins. She's very kind, a great help to that lady, awful when arthritis cripples an active woman—and I've got you down for churchyard grass cutting this summer, on my rota."

"No problem."

"Well, bed beckons. Night, Frank."

"Good night."

He walked across the wet grass of the green towards the light above the front door and his home. He still did not know what he would tell her or when.

3

The atmosphere hung like gas, poisoned, in the house, and had for three days and three evenings. It clung to the rooms, eddied into each corner, was inescapable. They went their own ways, as if the atmosphere dictated that they should separate themselves from each other. The stench of the silence they carried with them was in the furniture, in their clothes, and had seeped into their minds.

He stood on the green, beyond his front gate, and gazed out over the rooftops towards the expanse of the gunmetal gray sea.

Stephen came down the stairs each morning, gulped half of his usual breakfast, and waited by the door for his mother to take him to school, or by the gate for the other half of the school run to collect him. He came home in the afternoons and bolted for his room, came down for supper, then fled upstairs again. The atmosphere between his mother and his stepfather had filtered into his room. Twice, from the bottom of the stairs, Perry had heard him weeping.

It was a bright morning, there would be rain later, and the wind brought a chill from the east.

Since he had pleaded for time, Meryl had not spoken of his problem. She was brisk with him, and busy. She called shrilly to him for his meals, dumped his food in front of him, made sharp, meaningless conversation while they ate. It was as if they competed to be the first to finish what she had cooked so that the charade of normality might be over more quickly. If he spread work papers on the table in the kitchen, then she was in the living room with her embroidery. If she had an excuse to be out, she took it, spent all of one of the three days helping with the nursery class and staying late at school to scrub the floor. He knew that she loved the house and the village, and that she feared that both were being pulled, by the poison, from her. They slept at night in the same bed, back to back, apart. The space between them was cold. She had looked into his face once, the only time that her eyes had flared in anger, when she'd pushed him aside and run up the stairs to her son's room, in answer to his weeping.

He watched the gulls flying lazily over the sea, and felt jealous that such matters did not trouble them.

His life, many times in those three days, played in Frank Perry's mind. He remembered his many friends at Shiraz, where the gases were mixed, before the project's move to Bandar Abbas, where the warheads were constructed, and more friends there. They had entertained him and kissed his cheeks when he gave them gifts, and were deceived. At the thought of his betrayal, he screamed silently across the winter-yellowed grass of the green, and the rooftops where the first smoke of the day crawled from the chimneys, and the open depth of the sea. It was not his fault: he hadn't been given a chance to do otherwise.

Emma Carstairs drove up, smiling and chirpy. She pushed the door open and belted her horn. Stephen ran past, without looking at him, and dived for the car as if to escape.

Frank heard Meryl's brisk shout behind him. The car drove away. There was a call for him. The Home Office in London. He went back into the house and heard her washing up the breakfast things. She hadn't asked him why the Home Office had rung. He picked up the telephone.

He felt like a Philby or a George Blake. Bettany, who had rotted in jail on an Official Secrets Act sentence, would have felt like this when he'd made his first communication with the Soviets. He took the phone card from his wallet. Geoff Markham had come out of Thames House, doubled back behind the building, scurried up

Horseferry Road for the first bank of telephones. The brewery answered, through to Marketing, a shout for Vicky. He felt he was breaking faith, and the furtiveness exhilarated him. He told her that the bank was giving him an interview for a place in investment brokerage; his application had been short-listed down to the last three. She squealed, she said he was brilliant. He gave her the details. She growled that she would bloody murder him if he blew it, and started on about her teaching him interview technique. She had wanted him out of what she called that creepy job and into proper work since they'd first shared a bed. He rang off. He wouldn't have dared make that call inside Thames House. He felt elation that he had been short-listed, and the same sense of shame as when he'd sent off the application to the bank with the necessarily limited personal background. It was what Vicky had told him to do—she had torn the job advertisement from the Situations Vacant.

He took the backstreets to the bridge, crossed over. The great building, the home of the Secret Intelligence Service, the green and cream and tinted-glass monstrosity, was enemy territory to most of his seniors at Thames House. When Cox or Fenton went across the river to Vauxhall Bridge Cross, they always said, after they'd legged it back, that they felt they ought to wash their hands. He asked for Ms. Flowers, and the security staff at Reception looked at him and his Security Service ID as if they were both worthless.

She took him into a bare interview room on the ground floor. She laid a file in front of her on the table and leaned her elbows over it, covered it with her bosom.

He talked. "We went down underprepared to see him, went with big holes in what we knew. We knew that his new name and identity were blown open—how and where is what we did not know. We told him his life was under threat, but we didn't know the extent of the threat . . . It was difficult to assess who was the blind and who the one-eyed. We're sending him the Blue Book. We need help and have to have answers to questions."

She snorted derisively. "Ask away. Whether I'll answer, that's a different matter. And you should know the importance we give to the Iranian weapons program. Attention, among the ill-informed, was directed towards Iraq, which is just comic cuts, cartoon-strip stuff.

Iran is the big player. Iraq has no global following, Iran is a focus point for billions of Muslims. Iran matters." She guarded the file with her elbows.

"Who was Frank Perry?"

"His name was Gavin Hughes. He was a pushy young salesman in an engineering manufacturing company at Newbury. He sold commercial mixing machines, mostly for export."

"What was the Iran link?"

"The Iranians wanted mixing machines for their program of WMD development. You know what that is, don't you? Weapons of mass destruction, microbiological, chemical, and nuclear."

"But the export to Iran of those machines is blocked by legislation, enforced by Customs and Excise. Isn't that right?"

"The machines are dual-purpose—you were informed of that, and the Customs interest. The same machine can be legally exported to mix chewing gum or toothpaste to industrial quantities, and illegally exported to mix explosives and the chemical precursors for nerve gases and biotoxins, which are the anthrax or suchlike end of the business. His company's machines, with falsified export declarations, were for the equipment of military factories."

"What was his importance?"

"He's a sharp salesman, as I said, everybody's good guy. People warm to him, people want to be his friend. The man who is liked and makes friends, he gets access. The access was disproportionate to the importance of the product he supplied. No need to go to Tehran to meet him, have him down to Shiraz or Bandar Abbas, sort the problem out there and save time. He's a popular man and not stupid. He doesn't push his luck, just keeps his ears and eyes open, and he oils the friendships with gifts. It gets so that he's hardly noticed when he's there. I'm not exaggerating—he was remarkable, one of the most valuable assets we've ever had."

"Who was the controller running him?"

"Ran him a bit myself at the end, when it was leading up to the sensitive time. We were into him about eighteen months before it finished. We'd picked up the illegality bit. He faced a Customs and Excise investigation and he'd have gone to prison. We had him well stitched, and he knew it. He was always very cooperative. You don't need to know who recruited him, did the heavy stuff, and pulled him on-side—they wouldn't give you the time of day."

"What happened 'at the end'? What finished it?"

"We and other agencies became aware of the pace of the development of chemical warheads. We needed to obstruct, or at least impede, that progress. Necessary action was taken."

"What was the action taken?"

"You should never try to run, Mr. Markham, before you've learned to walk. That's not your concern."

"Sorry, but it is my concern if I'm to be in a position where I can assess the contemporary threat level."

"If you've ever rammed a stick into a wasps' nest, then you make the wasps angry. They want to sting you. At which point you're advised to get the hell out. That'll have to be good enough for you."

"How would the Iranians have known that he was the source of information?"

"They're not idiots, certainly not in our eyes. At the same time they were clearing up the debris, he'd disappeared, left home and work. Yes, they could put that together. They would have been very angry."

"Has he been looked after?"

"What you already know—new life, no Customs and Excise feeling his collar, new identity. We treated him well and expensively."

"That's a minimum of five years ago. Would their anger have lasted?"

"With the action that was taken, yes. The anger might have matured, but it wouldn't have diminished."

"What are we supposed to do now?"

"God, why'd you ask me? Water under the bridge, as far as we're concerned. He's no earthly use to us or anyone now, just another engineer doing whatever engineers do."

"But if he was brilliant and remarkable, we owe him."

"Understood you've done that, offered help. I know his reaction too. He's made his bed. We don't acknowledge debt to civilians, businessmen. They work for us, we explain the risks, they stand on their own feet. Actually, we were surprisingly generous in this case. Nothing is owed."

"One last thing. What was the quality of the information on the re-
newed threat?"

"There's an American in Riyadh, from the FBI. He's their Iran
guru. He dug up Perry's name, a little consolation on a failed raid. If
you call him, don't have a pending appointment and don't expect
him to draw breath and let you get a word in. Get the message—
Perry or Hughes is a spent cartridge, he's of no importance. The
American in Riyadh is Seitz . . ."

The electric fan always distorted the television picture, and the
cranking air conditioner set in the wall did the damage to the sound.
Mary Ellen was responsible for catching the local-language news
program because Seitz found it hard to remember schedules. He
was at his desk, the fan blast riffling the papers in front of him. This
small section of the embassy building that he used with Mary Ellen
and the larger area in an adjacent corridor, the Agency's place, were
not served by the building's main air-coolant system. The pipes had
been cut off and sealed. A security review, two years back, had decided that the Bureau and the Agency should be protected from the
possible hazard of lethal gases being fed into the system, so they had
their own air conditioners, a nightmare of noise and unreliability
that needed the backup of electric fans.

The local-language news bulletin was usually a catalogue of the
king's palace meetings and the public appearances of the prime
princes. The picture was awful, the sound worse, and the content
negligible, so he let her monitor it. Even above the clatter of the air
conditioner and the whine of the fan, he heard her gasp. Seitz swung
in his chair.

The man's head was down, his voice a monosyllabic whisper. God-
dammit . . . The man was dressed in a white *thobe*, the long shirt-
dress, was round-shouldered as if the hope had gone from him.
Under the loosely draped *gutra*, the scarf covering his head, his eyes
had lost their light. Damn, shit, damn . . . The man mouthed a rehearsed confession. Seitz listened as he confessed to terrorism and
subversion of the kingdom. He was shrunken, as if dehydrated, from
when Seitz had last seen him, dragged in the sand towards the waiting helicopters. The bastards, the lying, deceiving, double-talking

bastards . . . He grabbed his herringbone jacket and ran, a fast wad-dling gait, for the door, the corridor, the grille gate where the Marine stood guard, the elevator, and the ambassador's floor.

He stood to his full squat height, and his body shook with anger as he hammered his complaint.

"It is just obstruction. I have been blocked at General Security six times and I have made two dozen, more, calls to General Security, the ministry, God knows who else. I have not only been denied the chance to talk to this man myself, I have not been permitted to read the interrogation dossier. They are supposed to be fucking allies—I know, sir, about their delicate sensibilities, and I know they are a proud and independent people, and please don't tell me to humor them, but I don't give a shit what happens in this country. The place is a cesspit, it is corrupt, devious, lying, complacent. Americans died in Dhahran and Riyadh. If this man is on TV and making a confes-sion, then he has been tried, convicted, condemned. Five Americans died in Riyadh, nineteen in Dhahran. Finding the killers of Ameri-cans is my job. This man, sir, was in contact with an organizer who I am paid to track and find. This man could give me the name and the face of that organizer, but I am blocked. When he has been, one-way ticket, to Chop-chop Square, I have lost the chance to get from this man that information. I was so goddamn close. So what the fuck are you going to say to our good sweet allies? I have been working more than two years for this one chance so I can hunt the bastard down. *What are you going to say?*"

The ambassador wrung his hands and said he would make tele-phone calls, which was what he always said. Seitz went back to his section. The fan blew the papers on his desk and Mary Ellen put a decent slug of "brown" in his coffee.

The coffee, laced with whisky, might just make him forget that he had no face and no name to work towards and that he did not know where the footprints led.

The wind whipped about her and could not move her. The sea swell bucked beneath her and did not shake her.

She was out of the Kharg Island terminal, the property of the Na-tional Iranian Tanker Corporation. Her call sign was EQUZ. Her length, bow to stern, was 332 meters; her beam, port to starboard, was 58 meters; her draft, the waterline to the lowest point of the hull, was 22.5 meters. She was loaded with 287,000 tonnes of Iranian crude. Her speed through the water, regardless of weather conditions, was a constant 21 knots. She had been at sea for thirteen days, routed from Kharg Island, past the port of Bandar Abbas, through the Strait of Hormuz, north up the Red Sea to the canal, away from Port Said and into the Mediterranean. After navigating the Strait of Gibraltar, her last reported position had her giving a wide berth to the sea lanes leading to Lisbon. She was two days' sailing from the western approaches of the English Channel. Her crew complement was always thirty-two Iranian and Pakistani nationals, and the master would give that number, in truth, to the immigration authorities at the Swedish refinery. She was a monster, carving her way forward, moving remorselessly towards her destination.

"Just read it, Mr. Perry, it's all in here. I can't say it's anything that pushes back the frontiers of science. It just states what's sensible."

When she walked out of the front door Meryl had been crying. She'd tried not to cry in the house, but she'd cried when she was on the step, and going down the path. Perry had seen her dab her eyes when she reached the car and then he'd closed the door. He was not ready to tell her. It would have been easier if she'd confronted him. He had been leaning against the hall wall, head in the coats, when the bell had rung. A card had been proffered, Home Office Central Unit, and a smiling, middle-aged man had been following him into the house.

"It's all in the pamphlet—what we call the Blue Book, because it's blue. Vary your route to and from your home, keep a constant watch for strangers whom you might suspect of showing a particular interest in the house. You haven't a garage, I see. Car parked on the street, that's a problem. Well, you look like a handyman, get an old car wing mirror, lash it to a bamboo pole, and check under the car each morning, under the main chassis and especially that naughty little hidden bit above the wheels, doesn't take a moment. Imagine anywhere under the car, or under the bonnet, where you could hide a pound bag of sugar, but it's not sugar, it's military explosive, and a pound of that stuff will destroy the car, with a mercury tilt switch. Always best to be careful and do the checks, doesn't take a minute."

They wandered through the house, as if the man were an estate agent and the place was going on the market—but it wasn't, he was staying. No quitting, no running. The furniture was eyed, and the ornaments and the pictures, and the fittings in the kitchen. He'd made them both a mug of tea, and his visitor had taken three biscuits from the jar, munched them happily, and left a trail of crumbs behind him.

"It's mostly about the car. You shouldn't think you're alone. I don't get many days in the office. So many Army officers who were in Northern Ireland, they all need updating. I've a lovely list of gentlemen I visit, and judges and civil servants. You shouldn't get in a flap—nothing's ever happened to any of my gentlemen. But what I tell all of them, watch the car . . . I'll be leaving brochures of the locks on offer, doors and windows, all fitted at our expense. You know, we spend five million pounds a year on this, and me and my colleagues, so don't get depressed and think you're the only one. They didn't tell me, never do, who you'd rubbed up the wrong way . . ."

They came down the stairs. The biscuits were finished and the mugs were empty. The man darted back into the living room. There was a grimace on his face, as if he had forgotten something and that was a personal failure.

"Oh, the curtains."

"What's wrong with them?"

"Dreadful of me not to have noticed. There are no net curtains. There should be—your wife can knock some up."

"She hates net curtains."

"Your job, Mr. Perry, not mine, to make her like them. I'm sure that when you've explained it—"

"Do you have net curtains at home?" He hadn't thought, and realized his stupidity as soon as the question was asked.

"No call for them. I'm not at threat, I've not trod on anyone's toes. Net curtains, you see, absorb flying glass from an IED, that's improvised explosive device—a bomb, to the layman."

He was grateful for the time and advice. He wished him a safe journey back to London.

"Final advice, be sensible, read the Blue Book, do what it says.

Don't think that from now on, what I always say to my gentlemen, life ends, you've got to live under the kitchen table. If there were a specific danger, say threat level two, they'd have moved you out of here, feet wouldn't have touched the ground—or, God forbid, there'd be armed police crawling all over your home . . . Good day, Mr. Perry, thanks for your hospitality. Let my office know what locks you want, and don't forget about the net curtains. I'll call again in about six months, if it's still appropriate. Good day . . . It's not that bad or you'd have the guns here—or you'd have been moved out . . ."

After he had read the pamphlet, he hid it among his work papers, where she never looked. Frank Perry still did not know what and when he would tell Meryl.

A jammy old number, the Branch men in London called it, a proper trolley ride for the geriatrics, and let them try it. He cursed. He was fifty-one years old, working out the time to retirement, and too damned old for this caper. He had a pride in his work and that was the cause of his annoyance. In his private moments, out of sight of family and colleagues, his chest would swell in the satisfaction of being a part of what they called the Branch; he followed in the footsteps of those elite Scotland Yard detectives who had been drafted in to form, more than a century before, the Special (Fenian) Branch, with the task of combating Irish nationalist attacks on the mainland. But in a hundred years, Special Branch recruitment had never kept up with the widening of the terror threat. His problem, that day, he was trying to do single-handedly the work that should have been given to a four-man detail.

It had been fine at the terraced house, where he'd picked up his target easily enough. The target had walked, and the detective sergeant had trailed him on foot into the center of Nottingham. Into a camping equipment shop. The detective sergeant had fingered wet-weather coats while the target had selected, then paid cash for, a sleeping bag, heavy-soled walking boots, wool boot socks, camouflage trousers and tunic that were ex–military stock. He might have been old, near to retirement, but the detective sergeant still registered his target's height and the size of the boots, which were at least two sizes too small for the target's feet.

All the university cities in the country had a pair of Branch men attached to the local police station. Used to be Irish work, not any longer. It was the Islamic thing that preoccupied the detective sergeant and his partner, Iranian students studying engineering, physics, chemistry, metallurgy, and the zealots who recruited among the campus kids. It was work for a dozen men in this city alone, not for two poor bastards. The Security Service provided the names and addresses, and bugger all else, leaving the detective sergeant to tramp the streets and type the bloody reports.

The target was careful and had twice ducked into shop doorways and let him come past. His shoes, new, hurt his feet, and he was bursting for a leak. The detective sergeant was trained in surveillance, but it was damn difficult to make the tail when it was down to one man. They had ended in a bookshop. He'd eyed the paperback thrillers while the target had been searching, very specific, on shelves across the shop.

He had not had this man before. There were usually so many targets that they came round on a rota every four weeks or so. It was only three months since the young fellow, wet behind the ears and up from London, had given the sparse detail of the Security Service interest in Yusuf Khan, Muslim convert, formerly Winston Summers. One of many, the tall, wide-shouldered Afro-Caribbean was under surveillance around one day in thirty, nine in the morning to seven in the evening. He did not know why this thirty-year-old cleaner at the university was on the list for sporadic surveillance . . . His was not to reason why, his but to do and bloody die—and bugger all glory for his pinched feet and aching bladder.

The target had taken a book, gone quickly to a vacant cash desk, and paid in notes and loose change before heading out into the street. The detective sergeant was good at his work and conscientious. He checked the shelves where the target had searched: UK Travel and Guides. The man was out on the street now. A woman was at the cash desk, with a child in tow, choosing a gift-token card. He'd lost half a minute before he'd used his shoulder, shown his warrant card, and demanded of the assistant what book her previous customer had purchased. The dumb girl had forgotten, had to check back in the point-of-sale computer.

He stood on the pavement outside the shop and cursed.

He could not see his target, and narrow arcades led off both sides of the main street.

He swore.

He quartered the arcades and the precinct, checked the bus stops and the precinct, but could not find the bobbing head he sought, or the bright-colored shopping bags. As his son would say, when his birthday came round, when the detective sergeant had to dig in his wallet to pay for the amplifier or the tuner, "Pay peanuts, Dad, and you get monkeys." They paid for one man to do a surveillance once every thirty days, and by eleven o'clock in the morning the monkey had lost its target.

He would find a place to leak, then walk back to the dismal street of little terraced houses to sit in his car, fashion the excuses, compose his report, and have not an idea why Yusuf Khan, formerly Winston Summers, had purchased boots, camouflage trousers and tunic too small for him, heavy wool socks, a sleeping bag, and a guidebook to the coastal area of north Suffolk. What the policeman knew of that area from a wet, cold, and miserable caravan holiday twenty-two years back was endless gray seas and marshes. But it would go in his report for want of something better.

"Were you followed?"

Yusuf Khan did not think so.

"Have you done anything to create suspicion?"

Yusuf Khan knew of nothing.

The intelligence officer was a man of sophistication and poise. He came from a childhood spent after the revolution in a villa of quality set in the foothills of the Albourz. The previous owner had fled in 1980 and his cleric father had been awarded the property, which looked down on to Tehran's smoggy sprawl. He was fluent in German, Italian, Arabic, and English, and could pass in casual London society for Palestinian, Lebanese, Saudi, or Egyptian. To the unaware he might be from the deep south of Italy, perhaps Calabrian or Sicilian. He had been three years in London and believed he understood the heartbeat of the British psyche . . . and that understanding had led him to recruit Yusuf Khan, formerly Winston Summers, Muslim convert. He was a religious man himself, prayed at the given hours when it was possible, and the obsession of the converts to the faith was something he found ridiculous but useful. He preyed on the converts, trawled for them in the mosques of the splinter communities who set themselves aside from the traditions of the Sunni and Shi'a teaching. He searched for them in the universities. The best he found, those who displayed a fervent adoration of the imam Khomeini, he recruited.

Yusuf Khan had been subject to police investigation in Bristol, following a knife attack on an Arab businessman who had kissed a white woman on the street outside a nightclub. Unemployed, embittered, and alienated, living in the east Midlands city of Nottingham, attending the mosque of Sheik Amir Muhammad, Yusuf Khan had been identified three years earlier for the intelligence officer. Twenty-three months before, with the trust already built in their relationship, the intelligence officer had told Yusuf Khan how he might best serve the memory of the imam. It had been a long evening of persuasion. The following day, Yusuf Khan had walked away from the faith, taken a job as a cleaner at the university. He monitored the attitudes, friendships, conversations of Iranian students in the engineering faculty. He found and befriended a girl who was now converted to the faith, and was useful. The trust grew.

The intelligence officer met his man in the car park of a restaurant by the river. There were too many high cameras in the streets of the city and at the entrances to the multistorey car parks. The engine ran, the interior heated, the windows misted. They were unseen and alone.

"You will not be missed from work?"

His friend, the girl, had telephoned the university and reported his head cold.

"You are certain that you have not created suspicion?"

Yusuf Khan was certain.

He was told that he should not go home again until after his part in the matter was finished, to where he should take a train, where he should hire a car, the grade of car, and where he should sleep before the given time. His list was checked, the clothing, the boots, the sleeping bag, the rucksack of khaki canvas he had bought the day before and collected from left luggage at the bus station. Everything was checked, the book, the maps, the photographs, and he was passed another tight-rolled bundle of banknotes. He was told of the affection for him of men in high places, far away, whose names he would never know, of their gratitude for what he did, and of how they spoke of him with love. The intelligence officer watched the swell of Yusuf Khan's pride and smelt the chili on the man's breath. He reached into the back of the car, unzipped a big sausage bag, and revealed the contents. He saw the bright excitement in Yusuf Khan's face. He showed him the launcher wrapped in a tablecloth, the shells, the automatic rifle with the folded stock, and the loaded magazines. He opened the canvas rucksack beside the bag, revealed the grenades. He held the man's hand, squeezed it to give him reassurance, and drove him to the railway station.

He said that, in the Farsi language, the imam was known as Batl Al-Mustadafin, and that was the Champion of the Disinherited, and therefore he was the champion of Yusuf Khan. He said that Yusuf Khan would deserve the love of all those who followed the word of the imam Khomeini. The intelligence officer did not tell him that the cornerstone of his work in London was "deniability."

When they reached the forecourt of the railway station, he told Yusuf Khan what the ayatollah Fazl-Allah Mahalati had said. He spoke with fervor. "A believer who sees Islam trampled underfoot and does nothing to stop it will end up in the seventh layer of hell. But he who takes up a gun, a dagger, a kitchen knife, or even a pebble with which to harm and kill the enemies of the faith has his place assured in heaven . . ."

He watched Khan into the station, carrying the rucksack and the sausage bag, which sagged under the weight of the weapons. On the way back to London he would call in at a small mosque in the town of Bedford, to a cultural association for which his embassy's support was well known, for a meeting that would help create the necessary factor of "deniability."

"Don't mind me saying it, Frank, you look bloody awful—had the tax man round? You look like I feel when he pushes his bloody nose in!"

Martindale belly-laughed without enthusiasm. He kept the pub in the village, the Red Lion, and had enough cash flow problems not to need the burden of his customers' difficulties.

"Say nothing, admit nothing. If you have to say anything, tell them the dog ate the receipts. Come on, Frank, don't bring your troubles in here. Trouble-free zone, this bar. Come on . . ."

Frank looked into the thin face with its dour smile. He had been nursing a pint for half an hour. The regular gang was in and there had been whispering before the landlord had come over with the cloth to wipe the spotless table. It had been good of Martindale to fetch him up to the bar.

Vince cuffed his shoulder. "Not right, not that you've got the tax man on your back, not you. What about a game of arrows, Frank? Tell you, each time you go for treble twenty you reckon that's the tax man's face. Last time they came sniffing round me, I told them to piss off. Oh, I can get down and do that chimney of yours next week, don't think I'd forgotten . . ."

Vince was the local jobbing builder, a one-man band. The previous November's big storm had shifted some of the roof tiles, and he'd gone up a ladder in the wind and rain with the surefoot grip of a mountain goat. If he'd waited for the storm to blow out, the rain would have been in the attic and dripped into their bedroom, and it would have been a hell of a big job. Vince talked too much, played at being a hard man but wasn't.

It embarrassed Frank that he'd brought his problems into the pub. If a guy was asked here how he was, he was supposed to say he was fine. If he was asked if he was well, he was supposed to say he was in good shape. Everyone there had problems, came in for a drink to forget them.

There was a short, awkward silence, then Gussie said, "Shall we throw together?"

"Why not, Gussie?"

"You've an education, do you know about Australia, Frank? I'm thinking of going there, next year. What a team, you and me—you take first throw. If it dries up a bit, a couple of weeks, I'll be down to dig your garden—you should be thinking of getting your vegetables in."

Gussie passed him the darts. He was a big, strapping, amiable youth. Thick as a railway sleeper, not the full shilling, but he kept his mother and the younger children on the pittance he earned as a laborer in the piggery. He propped up the bar most nights and talked to the older men as a breadwinning equal. He dug the vegetable garden in less than half the time it would have taken Frank, and charged too little. Nice boy, but he'd never get to Australia.

Paul took the empty glass from his hand. "No argument, my shout—be a pint, right? You've had one quiet one, time now for three noisy ones—right, Frank?"

"That's very kind of you, Paul, thanks."

"I'm thinking of coopting you on to the village hall committee, you being an engineer. Won't be any problem, they'll do what I tell them. Place'll fall down if we don't do something, and I'm the only one with the wit to realize it. I reckon we'd work well together, being friends. Of course, I'd take the main decisions. You up for it?"

"Be pleased to help."

Paul was not the chairman of the village hall committee, or of the parish council, but his way always won through because he was better briefed than any of the others. His life was the village, as had been his father's and grandfather's. Inquisitive but harmless. If his ego was massaged, he gave his friendship without condition, and Frank Perry, former salesman, could manipulate vanity with the best of them. He even quite liked the man.

He played darts with Vince, Gussie, and Paul through the evening. He didn't talk much, but let the conversation ripple round him and warm him.

"You heard, Paul, what's happened at Rose Cottage?"

"Heard it was under offer—do you know what they were asking?"

Gussie chipped in, "I was told it was over a hundred grand, and there's more to be spent."

"The last thing this place needs is more bloody foreigners—no offense, Frank."

"We only want people here who know our ways and respect them."

As the games were restarted, as the pints kept coming, Frank threw more accurately—it was his home, his friends were the publican, the jobbing builder, the piggery laborer, the big man of the village hall committee and the parish council . . . God, he needed friends because there was a blue-jacketed pamphlet hidden among his papers where Meryl wouldn't find it. He and Gussie lost both their games and it didn't matter to him.

He stepped out into the night.

They were going their own way, and behind him Martindale was switching off the bar lights. His friends shouted encouragement to him.

"Good luck, Frank."

"Keep smiling."

"Frank, I'll be in touch about the hall, look after yourself."

For a year he had been without friends. From the time the last of the minders had driven away, left him to his own devices, until the day he had come with Meryl and bought the house on the green with a view to the sea, twelve endless months, he had been without friends. He had lived in a one-bedroom flat in a new block a couple of streets away from the center of suburban Croydon. In all those months, trying to wear his new identity, he had never allowed himself more than half a dozen words on the stairs with any of the other tenants. They might have been good, kindly, warm people, but he hadn't felt the confidence to test them. Fear of a slip, of a single mistake, had isolated him. The first Christmas had hurt. No contact with his son, he hadn't sent a present; no cards hanging from ribbons; no visit to his father and mother in the Lake District for the New Year. Through that twenty-four hours he had sat alone in the flat and listened to the televisions, the laughter, the cheerfulness echoing up the stairwell, and he'd seen people arriving, arms loaded with wrapped presents. His company had been a bottle. When he ventured out to pubs as the evenings lengthened, he always took a chair and table farthest from the bar and the camaraderie. He had learned that he mattered to no one. He had sunk, the signs were clear enough to him, and it had taken a supreme effort to shake off the loneliness. He had started to read the trade magazines and look for small freelance work. The second company he'd visited had employed Meryl. He could remember, so clearly, that he had bounced away from the company's offices with a contract in his pocket and her smile in his mind.

He waved over his shoulder and their laughter, fun among friends, roared after him. He walked on and wondered where he would find an old wing mirror to lash to a bamboo pole.

"What makes you think, Mr. Markham, that you have any of the qualifications required for modern banking?"

"I'm used to high-pressure work. It matters when I make decisions that I've chosen the correct option. I can work on my own, and I can work with a team."

She sat wrong way round on the chair, leaned on the back of it, splayed her legs either side of the seat so that her skirt rode up.

"Balls, about 'high-pressure work,' but the right sort of balls. Hit 'team,' it's an emphasis word, they like that. Why, Mr. Markham, do you wish to walk away from the security—ha, ha—of safe civil-service employment? You could join us, you could be found unsuitable and out on your ear with your bridges burned. Why?"

"My present work, and you'll respect that I'm bound by confidentiality, has been challenging and responsible—but, the nature of the beast, it's limited. I'm capable of spending more time in the fast lane. I don't expect to be found unsuitable."

"Great, that's what they want, arrogance—and they want the rounded man. Mr. Markham, what are your hobbies, recreations? Shit!"

It was the telephone.

"So, they don't want to hear about Herefordshire churches . . . No?"

The telephone stayed ringing.

"Hill walking—give them long-distance hill walking, exploring the inner man. You can't move for bloody bankers on Snowdonia or Ben Nevis, for Christ's sake, and skiing."

He couldn't ignore, any longer, the ring of the telephone bell.

"I'll field it."

It was Fenton, opening with a caustic, savage quip about clock-watching. Had he gone on the stroke of five? He was to get back in, soonest. There was no apology for the time of night at which he was summoned back. He left Vicky. If he'd stayed longer she'd have killed him or lifted the skirt higher. He drove into central London, against the homeward traffic from the theaters and the restaurants. He parked on a double yellow as the Big Ben clock hammered out the midnight chimes.

Fenton showed him the single sheet of paper, a Special Branch detective sergeant's report of a routine surveillance. Markham knew Yusuf Khan: convert, zealot in the Hizb-ut-Tahrir, pupil of Sheik Amir Muhammad, cleaner at Nottingham University, knew him as well as he knew a hundred others from the files. The report was the familiar story of a fuckup. The target had been followed, lost, not found again. While he was followed, before he was lost, he'd been on a shopping jaunt. A cleaner, no skills, at the university took home not more than £125 a week after stoppages. Three weeks' wages gone in an outdoors shop, cash—and out of generosity because the boots wouldn't have fitted. And the book . . . There was a giant wall map in Fenton's room, floor to ceiling, which Montgomery would have appreciated or perhaps Wellington. Fenton used a snooker cue to do the business. Its end rapped the area covered by the guidebook, north Suffolk, then stabbed a line where land became sea, and rested there. The guidebook covered a "dead-end place," a "one-street hole." He held in his hand the routine report from Special Branch, and he felt the night cold.

"I'd ring her if I were you, Geoff, and postpone the nookie—and don't get to be a timekeeper." Fenton smirked. "Go to work, because I want it on my desk at lunchtime—the threat, what it is, where it's coming from."

He had said it himself: "He chose well, if he won't run." The cue end was beside the name of the village, which a man wouldn't leave, where a home was protected only by a door with a new lock and an old bolt.

The wind whipped about him and snatched at his coat. He was alone in the darkness. The sea cried beneath him and he sat on the deck far forward of the lights of the tanker's bridge. The night hours were precious to him, when he could escape from the claustrophobic confines of the cabin, which was like a prison cell during daylight because he had been told he must not attract the crew's attention. He stayed there until darkness came, and then he slipped out, glided silently along the hushed corridors of the accommodation block, and eased open the watertight door that led to the wide length of the deck space above the crude's tanks. In the night, in the darkness, with the great throbbing power beneath him, he felt the strength of his people and of his God.

Frank Perry had walked for nearly an hour past the green, down to the darkened boatyard with the stilted walkways over the river mud, then out on the raised path towards the Northmarsh.

He was at the place where the tidal river merged with the inland water mass and the slow-swaying reed beds. There was a crescent moon up and a shallow light on the beds. The silence was broken only when he disturbed a swan that clattered, screaming, away. He rehearsed what he would say, what he would tell her, and he peed the beer out of his bladder and into the still water at his feet. If they had had their way, Fenton and the younger man who had not spoken, then he, Meryl, and her boy would by now have been rootless flotsam. Maybe they would have been in a hotel, or an Army camp, or in an empty chalet complex that was available because the holiday-makers had not yet come. There would be nothing to hold on to but the handles of packed suitcases, forever. If he had moved her on, if they were now in an unknown bed, listening for danger in the night, alone, perhaps she would have stayed with him for three months, a year, but finally she would have gone . . . It was his home, and her home, and her son's home, and he prayed, mumbling, that she would understand . . . He would stay where he was safe, where she was, where his friends were, and her friends . . . He was drunk. He had accepted two more pints than was good for him. It was so long since he had been drunk, the Christmas before last, lights on the tree, Stephen in bed with his new toys around him. They'd shared a bottle of whisky, sprawled on the sofa, her head on his waist, and stayed there until the bottle was finished, then helped each other up the stairs, tittering. He had thought himself blessed.

But he could remember as clearly when he had thought himself cursed. It was the second night after the minders had checked him into an Army barracks, and at his insistence they had permitted him a single phone call. They'd huffed, complained, left him in no doubt that they were doing him a great favor, and would only drop the rule book that once. Perry had rung his father. Every moment of the call was seared sharply in his memory. "Hello, Dad, it's Gavin. Dad, please don't interrupt me and don't ask me questions. And don't try to trace this number because it's ex-directory and you'll only waste your time. I've had a difficulty overseas and I'm changing my identity. I don't exist anymore. I have a new name and am starting out on a new life. I've left home. They don't know where I am. I won't be able to make contact again. It's for the best. If I came to see you and Mum I'd be endangering you as much as myself. Don't, please, think badly of me. There were good times and we should all cling to them. I don't know what the future holds, but I won't ever forget your and Mum's love for me. Forgive me, Dad. I'm not Gavin anymore. He's gone. Look after yourself, Dad, and kiss Mum for me." He'd rung off.

The minders had been round him and they'd nodded coolly as he put down the phone, implying that he'd done well without bothering to say so. His father had never spoken, there had been only the silence in his ear. That silence on the line had been the moment when he'd known he was cursed . . .

He would not quit again. He listened to the retreating cry of the swan, watched its ghostliness over the reed beds and the quiet water, and turned for home.

His car was parked in front of the house. He paused beside it, then crouched and felt with his fingers into the hidden space above the front near side wheel for a bag of sugar.

"Got a flat one? Got a puncture?"

Jerry Wroughton stood in his door holding his cat, a spiteful little beast that killed songbirds. His neighbor always put it out last thing at night.

He lied. "Thought I had—false alarm."

The cat was dropped and ran to the cover of darkness. Wroughton asked, "Are you all right? You've not looked yourself the last few days, Frank."

"Haven't I?" He straightened and rubbed the dirt off his hands.

"What I wanted to say, and Mary, if there's anything wrong, and we can help, you've only to shout."

"Do I look that bad?"

"You said it, chief. Pretty grotty. Just yell, it's what neighbors are for."

"Thanks, Jerry, I'll remember that—you're very kind, both of you. I appreciate it."

He went inside, locked the door, and pushed the bolt over. He went to bed, alone, his back to hers, cold. He would tell her in the morning. It could wait until then.

4

They walked on the beach, their feet crunching on the smoothed stones of red agate, opaque quartz, and pink granite, and on the pebbles of cysterine, slate, and Torridonian rock, and on the broken scallop, whelk, and mussel shells. He did not speak until they were quite alone, away from a pair of winter shore anglers with their long rods resting on triangles of gawky legs, away from a woman and her toddler, who threw flat stones that bounced then sank into the first wave line, and away from the sight of their village behind the sea barrier of raised shifting rocks, away from the world. He had told her, at the house on the green, that he was ready to talk. She had made two curt telephone calls to cancel her commitments for the morning, and she had seen her boy, Stephen, charge for a sort of freedom into the Carstairs car. They walked together, but they were apart. Her hands were deep in the pockets of her coat, as if she intended to prevent him taking her fingers in his.

Perry didn't work his way round to it. There was no delicacy, no subtlety. It would have been kinder to her if he had come upon it slowly, but kindness wasn't in his script. He wanted the weight of deceit off his back.

"You tell a lie and each day it is harder to retract. The lie breeds a life of its own. You get so that the lie becomes the truth. You become comfortable with it, even though you dread the moment the lie will be found out. The lie is easy at the beginning, but it becomes, gradually, more and more, the hell that you carry." He paused, stared at the stones and shells under his feet, then pressed on. "Frank Perry is a fraud and doesn't exist. A woman gave me that name. She asked if it was all right for me, and I said that I didn't care. I had a new name, new numbers, a new life. It was to block out the past . . ."

He wanted to reach her, to close the gap between them. She was pale with shock, never looked at him. The waves beside them broke on the shingle pebbles, and were spent on the sand.

"Everything I am telling you now is the truth. My name is Gavin Hughes. Gavin Hughes, until this week, was dead and buried. He died so that Frank Perry could survive, was buried for my protection. Gavin Hughes was a chancer, everybody's friend, the good guy with good fun and good chat. Gavin Hughes had a wife, and perhaps she had seen through him and was growing out of love with him, and he had a son. Gavin Hughes had a job, selling, and responsibilities, and was envied. He was the good guy who won trust. Gavin Hughes falsified the sale dockets, betrayed all those who trusted him, went and sold mixing machines in Iran, and reported back to the intelligence people. Everything about Gavin Hughes was a lie . . ."

Above the bluster of the wind and the rumble of the spent wave surges on the pebble shore were the cries of the birds on the Southmarsh behind the sea's barrier. Gulls and curlews, whimbrels, sandpipers, and avocets wheeled and dived. She never lifted her head or helped him.

"The machines were for military use in Iran. It was illegal to export them for the manufacture of weapons and missiles. All the documentation was lies. I betrayed my company and my colleagues, and they didn't ask questions because the order book stayed full and the end-of-year bonuses kept coming. I had good friends in Iran, kind, ordinary, decent friends, and I broke their trust and gave them presents and sat their kids on my knee in their homes, and reported on everything I learned to the intelligence people. Something was planned. I don't know what because I wasn't on the need-to-know list—I was told that it was better for me that I did not know. There was a last visit to Iran and a last debrief back in London, and the links were cut, like a slice with an axe. Gavin Hughes died overnight.

I walked out of my home with two suitcases and was buried by the following morning. Whatever was planned, from the information I gave, made the death of Gavin Hughes a necessity. It was for my own protection."

At the top of the wall behind the beach, where the sea never reached, the straggling plants grew from the stones; glasswort, sea lavender, wormwood, and beet. As he had known the names of each of the integral parts of the mixers—the screws, nozzles, end-plate jackets, the cored blades, the air-purge seals—now he knew the names of the plants and the pebbles.

"What I told the intelligence people was used in an action against the Iranians. My life was considered in jeopardy. I ran, I quit. For a few days, not many, I was like a package that was moved around, a parcel in a sorting office, thrown between military bases, safe houses, empty hotels. I left behind my family, my job, my friends, everything I had known. And I started again, and I found you. With you, I made a new home, new family, new friends . . . I was so damned lonely before you came . . . I have never been back. I didn't tell you, but two months ago I went to see my father. They'd done that appeal, what they put on the radio when a parent is dying and has lost track of a child. Imagine what they thought in the hospital: an old man is sick and his middle-aged child has disappeared out of his life. I told you I had a business meeting. He didn't die, he wept when he saw me, he called me by my real name. I didn't tell him who I was and where. I came home to you and the lie was alive again. I thought the lie would last forever . . ."

He walked on, towards the far distant bright little shapes of beached boats hauled up high for the winter. It was a moment before he realized she was no longer abreast of him. He turned. She sat on the stones where they made a line against the wet sand that marked the extent of the tide's encroachment. He went back and sat close to her.

"Take a transcript—spit, pick your nose, urinate in the corner. Anything is permissible provided you've taken a transcript," Fenton had said.

Geoff Markham was slumped at his desk.

He had spent the night at his desk, and his head ached enough for him to have taken two paracetamols washed down with the corridor dispenser's coffee. His mouth was foul, his socks smelt, and he had broken his house rule: there wasn't a clean pair in his desk drawer. A runover with the electric shaver didn't help. He was raddled.

Fenton had been in at six, scrubbed fresh, following behind the cleaners with their sprays, Hoovers, mops, and buckets. Fenton would not have had more than four hours' sleep and it didn't show.

The hookup was complicated. They needed voice security and there were two choices. He could go to Vauxhall Bridge Cross and have the FBI agent attend the British Embassy in Riyadh's diplomatic quarter, walking distance from his own workplace, or he could take a cab over to Grosvenor Square, into their London embassy's FBI section, and have the hookup direct to the American's office in the Saudi Arabian capital. He chose to travel himself. He was exhausted. He would get more help from Grosvenor Square than Vauxhall Bridge Cross.

"A transcript is accountability—neither party can then wriggle off the hook," Fenton had said.

What hurt most, Geoff Markham had been asleep when his superior had opened his door. By his watch, he had been asleep for nine minutes, woken abruptly by a little hacked cough from the doorway. He had been up all night, playing linkage with the small network of night-duty officers in London, talking, pushing, trading favors with the Special Branch night duty officer and the woman at Foreign and Commonwealth and the man at Vauxhall Bridge Cross. The minute he had drifted off to sleep he had been discovered. It hurt.

"And where's the zealot, where's his guidebook? His known associates, where are they?" Fenton had asked, a rasped voice.

Through the night he had been searching for those answers. Alone in his small partitioned section, his eyes flicking only occasionally towards the pinned-up snapshot of Vicky, he had been with the sub-file on Yusuf Khan, and with the mother file of Operation Rainbow Gold. The mother file was the net result of the most expensive operation, in resources and manpower, with which Markham had been involved since his return from Ireland. Rainbow Gold was the setting up of a United Nations inquiry front, grandly named: the United

Nations Committee for the Eradication of the Harassment of Ethnic Minorities (Islamic). Rainbow Gold had started up New York and London offices for UNCHEM(I). Resources had been found for the rent of offices and for the printing of the UNCHEM(I) literature, and the wages of correspondence writers and the telephone answerers, manpower for the writers and researchers.

Those who knew of it in Thames House called Rainbow Gold a bottomless well in the budget of G Branch (Islamic), but out of the hearing of Barnaby Cox, who was the suckling parent of the operation. It was the only way to dig deep: Islamic society was damn near impossible to infiltrate. The religion, the culture, the hatred of the Muslim radicals in the United Kingdom could not be penetrated by the usual tried-and-tested procedures. Researchers, vetted and hired, carried the literature to the selected mosques of the UK, talked, listened, explained—it had taken three years of resources and manpower for Rainbow Gold to begin to win trust, and a desperate amount of G Branch (Islamic)'s budget. So slowly, water dripping on stone and eroding lichen, Rainbow Gold had opened a small door into the world of the radicals. They had tried with the Irish, with the Committee of Human Rights for the Irish in UK—CHRIUK—but they'd been too smart to buy it.

The name of Yusuf Khan, formerly Winston Summers, was a product of Rainbow Gold, and the name of Sheik Amir Muhammad, the spiritual teacher of Yusuf Khan, was from UNCHEM(I). Farida Yasmin (formerly Gladys Eva) Jones, associate of Yusuf Khan, had also been trawled in by UNCHEM(I). It had taken Markham all night, between the nagging phone calls to Special Branch and the other night-duty officers, to turn up the name of Farida Yasmin Jones. And when he had found it the waves of tiredness had caught him, and he'd slept.

Markham said, "SB have a base camp outside Yusuf Khan's place. Since they lost him there's not been sight or sound."

"Typical . . . Try and keep your eyes open, or do you want a bed moved in?" With the sarcasm was the twinkle in Fenton's eyes. "Associates?"

"Just one, a woman—I'm about to get SB to put surveillance on her."

"Their IOs?"

"The big boy was out of London most of yesterday—we picked him up at that study college at Bedford that gets its funding from Qom. The little guy was in the embassy all day. If I need you, where'll you be, Mr. Fenton?"

Markham's father had gone to work each day in a worn suit with the fear of redundancy haunting him. He had preached the need for financial security to the young Geoff. In his last year at Lancaster University, studying modern history, he had gone to the milk-round careers day. The crowds of students had been thickest round the stalls offering graduate opportunities with British Airways, the big accountancy firms, and Imperial Chemical Industries, but he'd avoided the crush and gone to the Civil Service display. He'd said to the earnest woman on duty there, blurted out a whisper, that he wanted to join the Security Service. It had seemed to offer a winning combination of a job for life coupled with clandestine excitement. The woman hadn't put him down, had merely filled in his details, and he'd dictated a hundred words to her for the application about his wish to contribute to the safety of his country.

He'd sat the Civil Service examination, done adequately, and been called to a shapeless interview in an anonymous London building. His parents had been told by the neighbors, murmured over the garden fence and in their street, that they'd been asked questions about young Geoff. No skeletons had been found in the positive vetting because there weren't any. He'd been accepted. He had done three years, as a probationer and dog's body, of excruciating boredom in front of computer screens, with occasional days for surveillance training and tracking East-bloc trade attachés across London; everyone said it would get better when the probation time was completed. Three years of similar frustration on the Russia Desk, but the Cold War was over and the team had the lethargy of yesterday's crisis; everyone said it would improve when he was transferred to Ireland. Three years in Belfast had turned up interesting and occasionally frightening work; everyone said he should wait for promotion. He'd come back from Ireland and been put on the Islamic Desk, and in London his salary chit seemed to go less far every month.

Islamic Desk was hardly the stuff of Defense of the Realm, and

ran a poor third to the obsession with Ireland and the East Euro-
pean culture. He'd met Vicky. Vicky and he were engaged, and she'd
found the advertisement in the newspaper and urged him to go for
it. He hadn't yet faced up to the big problem of when to tell his parents that he wanted to jack in the Security Service and go for a life in
the uncertain world of finance. They were so pathetically proud of
what he did because he never told them about mediocrity and paper
pushing. It would have been cruel to disillusion them, tell them that
nothing he did mattered or affected an individual's life. He could recognize the change in himself since he'd applied for the job. He was
sparkier and more daring, and quite prepared to ask the blunt questions that raised Fenton's eyebrow.

"If it's any business of yours, I'll be in my room arranging lunch
dates—I'll scalp you if there isn't a full transcript . . . Remember
what I said, young man, about us going into an area of unpredictability. It's looking like it might be a good deal worse than that."

The great leviathan shape of the tanker, monstrous in the thinning
mist, crossed at right angles ahead of the course of the ferry. It was
huge against the size of the closing car ferry. She glanced at it, saw it
merge again into the mist wall, then turned away. From the cross-
Channel ferry, Charmaine, disappointed by another romantic cul-
de-sac, pointed at the speck in the sky.

The bird flew low over the churning mass of the sea, only just beyond the white whip of the ferry's bow wave.

The unsuitable object of her imagined affection shrugged. "Just a
bloody bird—what's special about that fucking thing? Come on,
come on back down . . ."

"Piss off," she said, and turned to watch the bird.

Its wing beat should have been perfect in its symmetry. Charmaine watched it through a film of tears. Its right wing rose and fell
in a tired and flailing way, and the left wing flapped harder as if to
compensate. She was on a high deck, where she'd hoped the amour
would not find her, and the line of the bird's flight was beneath her.
She did not understand how the crippled bird had the strength to
make the great sea crossing.

It was down near the breaking crests and the spume of the bow wave. The bird dropped and the talons, startled and outstretched, would have splashed and skimmed the water. She heard its agony cry, and saw the frantic effort to climb again, to survive. She did not believe it could make the landfall. If it fell again, if the water covered its wings . . . She wept uncontrollably. The ferry sailed on, fast, and the bird, even when she screwed her eyes to see it, was lost in the bank wall of the mist.

"Stop."

The driver braked, then crawled forward again.

"Do it. Stop. Stop the car."

The eyes of the driver flickered uncertainly, as if an illegality was demanded of him. But he had worked nine years for Duane Seitz and knew better than to question. He stamped again on the brake pedal, then coasted the Jeep to the kerb. They were on Al-Imam Torki Ibn Abdulla Street.

"Don't look where I look, Mary Ellen. Take a point in the other direction, fix on it. Don't look."

Out of her window, she took a point as instructed: the telephone office at the far end of Al-Dhahirah Street. He kept his eyes on the square between the central mosque, the Palace of Justice, the big souvenir shop, and the mud-brick Masmak fortress. All the old embassy hands called it Chop-chop Square.

There was a good-sized crowd. Word would have spread fast. It was never announced first, but the sight of men bringing out plastic bags of sawdust was enough to gather a crowd. He had seen the man pitched out of the back of the closed van. He recognized the prisoner, and the colonel beside him. He doubted that his ambassador had made the promised telephone calls, or had bothered to pull rank. In the long distance he saw the drawn, frightened eyes of the prisoner, and the easy stride of the colonel as if he were going to a picnic lunch on the beach. It was the square where the crowds had gathered to see the beheading of the Princess Mishaal, and of some of those fanatics captured after they had invaded the Grand Mosque at Mecca. It was where they beheaded Yemeni thieves, Pakistani rapists, and Afghan drug dealers.

He lost sight of the prisoner behind the wall of heads and with him went the last chance to put a name and a face to the footprints. They would never understand in the Hoover Building, the assistant directors who flew to Saudi Arabia not more than twice a year, and the desk analysts who never left DC, why cooperation was denied him. He dictated reports, endlessly, that were typed up by Mary Ellen, cataloguing the Saudi deceit and vanity that denied him co-operation. On Mary Ellen's insistence, they had gone to buy new shirts, which now lay wrapped in paper on the floor of the Jeep, between his shoes. He saw a television camera held up to get a better view over the heads of the sword. The sword point would prick the base of the man's spine and the instant reflex of the man would be to extend his neck. He saw the flash of light, the *rakban* held high, before it fell. He heard the soft groan of many voices before the crowd began to thin, and then the corpse was dragged away. Another man carried the head by the hair. They would have had a confession and it would lie in a file; the bastards would play their dignity and not share. Sawdust from a plastic bag was scattered.

He told Mary Ellen that she no longer needed to look at the telephone office and instructed the driver to head on back to the embassy. He was now on indefinite posting in Saudi Arabia, which broke the Bureau's culture of not permitting agents abroad to put down roots. It was six years since he had last worked a home posting—Kansas City, truck hijacks across state borders—and every week he'd served there he'd filed a memorandum to the J. Edgar Hoover Building with his assessment of the current power play in Tehran. The resident agent in Riyadh had broken a leg playing tennis; Seitz had been sent back as emergency replacement and had resisted, ever since, with a cunning competence, suggestions that he come home. At his age there wasn't much to come home to. Who'd want a Farsi-speaking Iranian expert on their staff list handling the prosecution of drunk drivers in a federal Indian reservation; who'd want him in New Mexico? Who'd want him in Nome, Alaska? His Quantico class had scattered through the breadth of the Bureau. Some had pushed themselves, through TV appearances, towards celebrity status and gone after the Mafia big shots in New York and Chicago. Some were experts in the science of ballistics, or the analysis of footprints. Some were just worthy guys doing time in Los Angeles or Miami. None of them had made a life's study, as he had, of the Iranians. The great dread of his life was the arrival of the signal that would bring him home.

There was a message on his fax requesting his availability for a secure hookup. He glanced at it, felt nothing. Seitz had only old footprints to follow.

She broke the quiet. She threw back her head, and the auburn of her hair flashed. She threw a stone, savagely, ahead of her towards the tide line.

"Who are you?"

"I am, will be, Frank Perry. You never met Gavin Hughes. This time, I am not running."

"What did they say?"

She stared in front of her. Her eyes were red-rimmed. She allowed him to take her limp hand.

"For what I did, the consequence of my actions, the Iranians would kill Gavin Hughes. He disappeared, ceased to exist. A new name, a new identity, a new home. He would have been hunted, but the trails had dried out, were lost. I am not trusted enough to be told how the Iranians found my new name. What I was told—if the Iranians have the name, then in probability they've the location where I live. The men who came yesterday wanted me to move out, offered me a removal van, said—I quote the words—"There is evidence of danger." But I'm not doing it again, not running. This is my home, where you are, and our friends. I don't have the strength for more lies. I am staying . . . It's like I've drawn a line in the sand."

"But they're experts. They're policemen or intelligence people. Don't they know what's best?"

"What's convenient, that's what they know, what's cheapest and simplest for them."

"And you're right, and all their experience is wrong, is that what you're saying?"

"All they've done is send me a book about being sensible. It's not that bad or they'd have done more. I know these people, you don't. They look for an easy ride . . ."

"And me?"

"I don't know what it means, saying that I will stay, for you or Stephen. I do know it's better than running. I've done that."

"It hurts that you kept the truth from me."

"For fear of losing you . . ."

The sea was gray dark in front of them. The gulls hovered over them, screaming. Her grip on his hand tightened, and their fingers locked together.

". . . and I told them what was owed me."

Once before, he had asked for what he said was owed him. Nine months after they had cut him off, three months before he had met Meryl, exhausted by the loneliness of his life, he had taken the train from Croydon to central London, and walked along the river to the monolith building at Vauxhall Bridge Cross. He had reached the gate, been stopped at the glass window of the outer reception building, and he'd asked to see Ms. Penny Flowers. Did he have an appointment? He did not. Did he know that it was not possible to come off the street and ask to see an officer? He did not. He'd been told there was no procedure for such a visit. He'd said, "Do you want me to sit down here till you call Ms. Flowers? Do you want to call the police and have them cart me off, and me tell them what I did and what I want?" The call had been made from the reception desk, and inside ten minutes she'd been there.

She was slighter than he'd remembered her, and had seemed older than in the heady days when she'd bought him drinks and meals and made him feel that he mattered. She'd taken him to an interview room, and sat him down, and brought him a beaker of coffee, and looked at him with distaste. What did he want? He wanted to belong. Did he want more money? He didn't want money, but to feel that he was a part of something.

Did he want a job found for him? He didn't want to be found a job, but to feel some pride in what he'd done. She'd looked at him across the surface of the plastic-topped table and said, "You don't belong with us, Mr. Perry. You are not a part of us and never will be. On any given day there are, on our books, fifty men like you, and when they've outlived their usefulness, we forget them. You're past history, Mr. Perry." She'd shown him the door and told him that she didn't expect to see him or hear of him again, and he'd walked out into the winter sunshine the better for the crisp six-minute exchange.

He'd shrugged his shoulders, straightened his back, and stridden away. He had broken the link and believed his dependence on them was cut. He'd taken the train back to Croydon and reached the library in time to start his first trawl through the engineering magazines on the shelves. Turning the pages of advertisements, his mind had raced with opportunities and plans for a new life. For what he'd done, they owed him that new life, which her rejection had sparked.

Her eyes were closed. His fingers played with the ring he had given her. He did not know what more he could say, and he waited for her to tell him whether she would go or whether she would stay.

Classification: SECRET

Date: 31 March 1998

Subject: Gavin HUGHES (UK national)—assumed identity of Frank PERRY 2/94.

Transcript of telephone conversation (secure) between GM, G Branch, and Duane Seitz, FBI Riyadh.

GM: Hello, can I speak please to Mr. Duane Seitz?

DS: That's me.

GM: This is Geoffrey Markham, G Branch of the British Security Service.

DS: Pleased to talk to you, Mr. Markham. How can I be of help?

GM: You produced the name of Frank Perry—I'm sure you're a busy man, I won't go off on sidetracks.

DS: Sometimes busy, sometimes not so busy, I've all the time you want. Correct, I found the name of Frank Perry on a sheet of paper, burned . . . We had a raid down in the Empty Quarter. We got less than I'd hoped for. I sent the burned pieces of paper to our Quantico lab—not that anyone's had the courtesy to come back to me in two months . . . Sorry, I'm griping, it's been that sort of day. Is Frank Perry yours?

GM: When your people had drawn blank on the name it was sent to us. We have a Frank Perry.

DS: You have my full attention, Mr. Markham.

GM: Frank Perry is an identity given a man after it was considered his life was under threat from Iranian hit squads. Perry was formerly a British engineering salesman, Gavin Hughes. What I need to know . . .

DS: Come again, that name.

GM: Gavin Hughes.

DS: [Expletive].

GM: What I was saying, we are into threat assessment. I need to know where the name was found, in whose possession.

DS: You got him secure—of course you have.

GM: Actually, he's at home.

DS: What's his home? Is it Fort Knox? You got his home in a basement at the Tower of London?

GM: We offered to relocate him—he refused.

DS: [Expletive]. What did you tell him?

GM: He was told that they had his new name, that in probability they would have the location of his present home—that they might come after him . . .

DS: [Expletive]. *Might?* [Expletive].

GM: Please, explain.

DS: He's coming, he's on his [expletive] way—God knows why it's taken him so long. He is a top man, alpha quality. You'd better believe he's coming . . . What have you done for him, for Perry/Hughes? You got a unit of Marines round him?

GM: We sent him our Blue Book.

DS: Is that a Bible? Is that a joke?

GM: Not a joke, a sort of Bible. The Blue Book is a guide to personal security, sensible precautions . . .

DS: [Expletive].

GM: He should look under his car, vary his routes . . . The same as in any FBI manual.

DS: The top man—there was once a code name for him I heard of in Dhahran, it was, literal translation, the Anvil. My dictionary, that is (open quote) a heavy iron block on which metals are hammered during forging (end quote)—it's the entry below Anus—it's the same meaning in Saudi Arabic, where I've heard it, and has the same meaning in Persian Farsi. The people who go with him, what I've heard, they regard him as indestructible. To me, he's a hard man. Before you ask, Mr. Markham, I don't have his name and I don't have his face. What I have is a pattern of digital calls that we have failed to break into, but from which we get, when the computer is allowed time to work on it, locations. Before each hit he goes to Alamut. It's spiritual for him. He was there just over two weeks ago. That's why I say he's coming.

GM: Sorry, what's Alamut?

DS: You know about Vetus de Montania, the Old Man of the Mountain?

GM: Afraid not.

DS: You know about the Fida'is?

GM: No, sorry.

DS: So, you don't know about Raymond the Second of Tripoli, not about Conrad of Montferrat. [Expletive]. You don't know what was shown to King Henry of Champagne . . . It's about Alamut. If you don't know about Alamut, then, my friend, you're [expletive] with your threat assessment. [Pause.] Where are you located, Mr. Markham?

GM: G Branch, Thames House, Millbank, London—why? Shorthand is Box 500.

DS: Are you in charge of this guy's safety?

GM: I seem to be getting the donkey's load.

DS: Tell me, if the pressure grows on him, will Perry/Hughes crumple? In words of one syllable, if the crap comes thicker, will he accept the relocation offer?

GM: I wouldn't have thought so. He talked about home and about friends. He ran once, says he won't again. Why?

DS: How do I reach you?

[DS given my personal extension number, personal fax number. GM]

DS: I'll come back to you. Oh, Mr. Markham . . .

GM: Yes, Mr. Seitz.

DS: Forgive me, and it's not my style to patronize, but you sound to me to be at the bottom of the heap. At the top of your heap are the guys who know to what use was put the information supplied by Gavin Hughes on the project at Bandar Abbas. When you've been told that, I promise you'll be in a position to make a very fair guess at the threat assessment, and get Alamut into your head. Can I offer you some advice? My advice is go put some serious hardware adjacent to our friend . . . I'll get back to you . . .

Fenton read the transcript and his nails worried at his mustache. His brow was furrowed as if a plough's blade had cut it.

Geoff Markham stood in Fenton's room and looked at the vinyl floor, then at the ceiling, where the cleaners had missed a spider's web, then at the walls, which were bare except for the leave chart for the section, then at the desk and the photograph of Fenton's family. He thought the transcript made poor reading: when he had typed it up from the tape supplied him by the Grosvenor Square people, he had thought he came across as an ill-informed pillock, a kid in an adult world.

Fenton paced with the transcript.

Geoff Markham blurted, "Do you know about Alamut?"

Fenton nodded—as if it was basic for anyone working the Islamic road to know about Alamut.

"And do you know to what use was put the information supplied by Perry/Hughes?"

Fenton shook his head—didn't know, and had no wish to.

"What do we do now?"

Abandoning the rape of his mustache, Fenton laid down the transcript pages and picked up his telephone. He dialed his PA in the outer office, gave the name and extension number for the superintendent from Special Branch, held the telephone loosely against his ear, and waited.

Markham felt so tired. He wanted to be back in his own space and clear of Fenton's room, where there was, he thought, all the fun of a mortuary chapel. He had known bad times in Ireland, when the weight of responsibility had seemed to crush him, but hadn't known it before at Thames House. In his mind was the picture of Frank Perry. Defiant, bloody-minded, awkward, obstinate, like a vixen with cubs deep in the darkness when the hounds and the terriers came to her earth. It would be different at the bank—pray to God that he pulled it off at the interview—different and better. When he'd stood by the door in that gloomy living room, looking out of the window towards the rooftops and the sea, he hadn't quite believed that the threat was real. He could not conjure the image of a man, of alpha quality, coming. He headed for the door.

"I'll be at my desk, Mr. Fenton, I've got a mountain of work."

Fenton ignored him and told the superintendent, on the telephone, that they should meet, that they should consider a protection officer.

Markham's mountain was a missing man who had bought all-weather clothing that did not fit him and a guidebook, and a woman who had left the address recorded on the file with no forwarding details. He rang Vicky, said he was thinking about his interview, said he did not know when he would be clear—said it wasn't his fault, not anybody's fault.

The call came through as she worked at her keyboard, distracted her. She finished the entry, picked up the phone, and heard his voice.

She had been Gladys Eva Jones, only daughter of a train driver out of the Derby depot. She had been a plain girl, with poor eyesight, a love of mathematics, and a desperate loneliness. Her schoolteachers, perhaps out of pity, had concentrated sufficiently on her that she won a place at Nottingham University. She had clung limpetlike to gangs of fellow students, and she'd seen the efforts they'd made to avoid her. One night, second year, drunk in the union bar, they had told her to get "fucking lost" because she was so "fucking boring" and so "fucking ugly." She had gone to an abandoned lecture room to sob out her misery. She had been the girl found by an Afro-Caribbean cleaner, and she had wept on his shoulder. It was he, six years before, who had taken her to the classes of Sheik Amir Muhammad. She had learned the Five Pillars of the faith—the *Shahada*, the *Salat*, the *Zakat*, the *Sawm*, and the *Hajj*. She had recited the words "There is no deity but God. Muhammad is the apostle of God." In her last year at the university, she had gone to her lectures wearing the chador or the *roupush*. She had felt the protection of her faith, and the respect it gained from fellow believers, and had taken the names Farida and Yasmin. Her degree was mediocre, but she knew that reflected the prejudice of her examiners. She had been turned away by many potential employers, but that reflected the prejudice of the management who interviewed her, because she wore with pride her chador. Her mentor had been Sheik Amir Muhammad, her friend Yusuf Khan, and she felt herself to be safe in a world of enemies. She had not known she was under the watching eye of an intelligence officer from the Iranian embassy.

Three years after her conversion, when Yusuf Khan had appeared to abandon the faith, forswear the prayer meetings of Sheik Amir Muhammad, and had left their small group, she had been rocked. At that time, her own obedience to the faith had been total . . . Without Yusuf Khan's friendship, her own commitment to the faith had gradually weakened. She had the intelligence to be aware of the change, but she had tried her best to ignore the weakening. At night, alone, she could analyze the shifting ground on which her faith was based. She had wanted a place for herself, had wanted respect. At first, the white girl, she had been a prized convert and a focus of the sheik's attention, but new converts had come to the small redbrick mosque and she had sensed she was no longer the center point of interest. Even so, Farida Yasmin had still been shaken to the core when the sheik, with Yusuf Khan sitting silently behind him, had quietly told her that she could best serve the true religion if she, too, were to seem to walk away from everything that was precious and reassuring. She had not doubted them, she had been obedient to their wishes. She had felt undressed, dirtied, when she had gone for a job interview at a Nottingham insurance company, two years back, dressed in a skirt and blouse and not in the black chador. She said her prayers each day at the appointed time in the privacy of her new bedsit home and in the insurance company's lavatory, but the comfort of the mosque was now denied her.

For much of those two years she had been ignored; no contact had been made. At first she had been merely miserable, then resentful. The friendship of the mosque was in the past, and the present offered no warmth because she despised the other girls who worked around her. She had been given no explanation of why she had been recruited as a "sleeper," nor what would be expected of her one day, until six weeks ago. Arriving back at her one-bedroom flat from another day's humdrum work for the insurance company, she found Yusuf Khan waiting on the pavement for her. After she had telephoned the company and pleaded a family bereavement, they had driven north, and the following week they had gone to the Suffolk coast. She did not know who had instructed Yusuf Khan to contact her, but at last she felt a small sense of usefulness. Farida Yasmin, an unknown soldier of Islam, had just come back from the lavatory when her telephone had rung.

She hid her face from the other women tapping at their keyboards. The virgin Farida Yasmin always felt pleasure flush her cheeks when he spoke to her, because they shared the secret of their faith and the secret of their work against God's enemies.

"Tell me you're right, and it's not real."

"They try to frighten you . . . If you're frightened, then you're compliant . . . If you're compliant, then it's easier for them . . . what's easiest for them is when you run."

"If it was real, bad real . . . ?"

"What they want is convenience. I stood my corner and they backed off. Because they backed off, I can't believe it's bad real."

"What's going to happen?"

"I don't know. When I sent you out—God, I'm sorry, I was foul—a man came, a creepy little bastard. He came into our house and he looked around like he was wondering what sort of price he could get for everything that's special to us. He left a brochure of locks and bolts and alarm systems. We've to choose what we want and they'll be fitted. There's a pamphlet he gave me with all the things we have to do—it's like being sick and listing all the pills you should take and how far you should walk, that kind of thing. Look under the car with a mirror each morning, don't establish patterns over regular journeys, after dark go into a room and don't switch the light on till you've first drawn the curtains, look for strangers watching the house, and there'll be a panic button. You've got to make net curtains . . ."

"I hate net curtains."

"I said you hated them. Please, Meryl, we've got to have them."

"Why?"

"Because . . . because . . . net curtains absorb flying glass."

"It's not much, Frank, what we have to do."

"It's what he said."

"You want to know what I think?"

"I want to know if you're going to stay."

"You're brought up always to believe a policeman or an official. I think, as you said, it's a scare and they're doing what comes convenient. You've convinced me, Frank. They've got all the powers they want and if it was really serious I think they wouldn't have listened to what you said, they would have shifted you . . . It's my home too."

"And Stephen's . . . Are you going to stay?"

"I won't find another home."

"I won't make another home, not another home where there's love, where there's friends."

"I think you were right, Frank. It was just to scare you, so's you'd make it easier for them."

"Are you going to stay? Whatever you want, I'll do. I can make a phone call. I can have the removal van here tomorrow and we can pack the bags. No good-byes, nothing, scuttle out in the dark. Leave everybody who's important to us, no explanation. Fear all the waking hours, and no sleep because of the fear. Don't get to know anyone again, not ever, because you'll be moving on, running, rootless. I can make a phone call and it will happen, and it will be convenient for them . . . What do you want to do?"

"It's our home . . . If it were real they would have moved you. You'd have been kicking and screaming, but they'd have shifted you."

The wind was freshening and the sea lashed the beach stones. He wanted, so desperately, to believe her. To believe her was to be given courage. She held his hand.

He was in his cabin when the master brought him his one meal of the day, a plate of rice and boiled mutton, a bowl of spiced cooked vegetables, an apple, and a glass of fruit juice.

Only the master had access to the locked cabin. It was a woman's space, with bright decorative curtains, a cheerful woven carpet, and the photographs on the walls were of pretty views from home. The master's wife would have used the cabin as her dayroom, where she could sew and read and pray beyond the sight of the Iranian officers and the Pakistani crew.

As the master talked he ate calmly. The next night, out in the Channel, he would leave the ship. He did not hurry over his food, was at peace, as the master again reiterated the procedures that would be used. He knew they were planned with meticulous care. He had been told in the airless room high in the Ministry of Information and Security of the many people involved in tracking down his target, and the thoroughness of their work. Nothing had been left to chance.

He had been shown the photographs, and had been talked through the schedules. It was the way of his people and he had complete confidence in the plan drawn for him. It was the work of many effortful months, and his own role was simply to conclude it. Later, when the darkness had come around the tanker, he would again slip down the corridor and out onto the deck space, and he would walk far from the bridge lights, sit alone, and think of his wife, of the mission that had been given to him, and his homecoming.

When he had finished the food he passed the tray back to the master, thanked him curtly. Then he sat in his chair and studied the enlarged photograph of the face of the man he would kill. He had no cause for fear, he had been told that the man was unprotected.

Sergeant Bill Davies should have been watching his boy play football. But it had been a pig of a day, starting at half past midnight when Lily had thrown two pillows and a blanket down the stairs and screamed at him that the sofa was where he'd sleep or she was leaving.

Four bad hours of sleep, then out from home in southwest London and across all the bloody traffic streams to beyond east London. Half awake, jazzed to hell, he had been in the worst possible frame of mind for shooting. If he'd failed with the Glock and the H&K, failed to make the necessary score, then he was out on his arse for a month until the next slot came round, with his personal weapon withdrawn. He'd forgotten, until late the last evening, to tell Lily that he was in a shooting slot, that he wouldn't be there to see his elder boy, Donald, play central sweeper, and she'd screamed that it was the last straw, that he was more married to the Branch than to her.

He'd never been a crack shot, good enough on the Heckler & Koch, had the necessary score there, but he'd gone down the first time round on the Glock. He was the only one in the group who had failed with the handgun. They'd put him through it a second time. The instructors wanted to pass him, willed him to get the score, and the guys and girls from armed-response vehicles and Static Protection and Special Escort Group, they'd all rooted for him, but he had failed again midmorning. The instructors had told him to get a coffee in the canteen, that they'd try one last time before the lunch break. If he failed the last time, then he'd have to hand in the gun, and it would be a month behind a desk until the next chance. If they knew back in the office about Lily throwing the pillows downstairs and yelling about leaving, it could be handing in the gun for all time because they'd have said his emotional stability was unproven.

He took the isosceles stance, readied for double-tap shooting; walking squares, swinging to aim when the damn target swiveled, drawn-weapons position and shooting. The last shot, a nine-millimeter bullet, was on the line of the target circle in the figure shape, ten meters range. Some instructors said that on the line was failure and some said it was good enough. He had needed the last shot, and they'd given it him. He was thirty-seven hits out of fifty shots, the bare minimum. The bullet hole on the line had saved him . . . He'd sweated. There had been one little bastard, off an armed-response vehicle, arrogant sod, who had gained maximum score first time round and who had watched his final scrape-through with a smirk . . . Damn all use as a protection officer if he couldn't shoot straight. He'd been toying with a bacon sandwich in the canteen, his hands still shaking, when he'd been called to the telephone.

And the day hadn't finished with Bill Davies. The superintendent wanted him back in London, onto the Branch floor at Scotland Yard. A file was thrown at him. He'd been given two hours to digest it; should have been two days. He had speed-read it, "Techniques of Iranian Terrorism (Europe)," when he ought to have been on the touchline watching his son. Then they'd thrown him the principal's file and given him thirty minutes when it should have been a full day. And when he should have been at the flower stall at Victoria Station

shelling out for the biggest peacemaker bouquet they could put together, he'd been with his signed authority down in the basement ar-
mory, drawing the kit, the Glock, the Glock's ammunition, and the
heavier firepower. And there wouldn't be a call to a restaurant to re-
serve a corner table with lit candles.

The bloody awful day was coming to an end as he'd driven down
the narrow straight road into the village on the north Suffolk coast.

He sat on the concrete and metal bench on the green. Later, he
would find a bed-and-breakfast, but not before he had absorbed the
smell, pace, and habit of the village. He sat on the bench with his
raincoat folded on his lap and his Glock in his shoulder holster under his suit jacket as the light fell on his day. Bloody awful days went
with the job of protection officer and were commonplace in the life
of Detective Sergeant Bill Davies.

Frank and Meryl walked back into the village as the dusk shadows
thickened.

His arm was on her hip and her hand was against his waist. They
had clung to each other on the beach before turning for home.
Vince, coming back to the village in his van, saw them and played a
raucous fanfare on his horn. It was as if they were youngsters in love
and didn't care who saw them. Gussie, cycling back, stinking, from
the piggery, wolf-whistled.

They strolled past Rose Cottage and the dark, lifeless windows beyond the For Sale sign. Perry thought it wouldn't be long before
lights blazed there, like a new dawn for a new family. Maybe there
would be a new guy to drink with in the pub, a new friend for Meryl,
new kids for Stephen to mess with. Not that he and Meryl were short
of friends, and that was why they were staying. The cottage was
chilly and unwelcoming, and he hurried her on.

They kept up the contact. Dominic, sad and gay, rolled his eye-
brows gently and made a small grimace as he closed down his shop
for the day. The lie was dead. The vicar, Mr. Hackett, strode past
them, lifted his cap, and smiled. He held her, she held him, because
they needed each other and had nowhere else to run. They reached
home and squeezed through the gate because neither would release
the other.

A man was sitting on the bench on the green. He looked like a salesman killing time before yet another cold call.

In the kitchen, surrounded by his schoolbooks, Stephen saw them come in and the light spread in his eyes. The poison was gone. It was their home, their castle. Perry had convinced her that they had only tried to scare him so that it would be easier for them, and that the danger was not real. In the kitchen, in front of Stephen, he kissed her.

Back in Newbury, his wife used to complain to anyone who'd listen that her husband didn't notice women. On trips away and in the office he had never played around because the job consumed him. That first time he'd met Meryl, as he was trying to put some purpose back into his existence, he'd noticed her as a damaged kindred spirit. Getting his coat off the hook in the outer office where she sat, he'd seen her loneliness. It had been in her eyes and her careworn mouth, and he'd blurted out that since he might be coming back a few times they might as well get to know each other and he'd asked her for a drink. She'd hesitated and he'd apologized for his forwardness, and then she'd said there was time for a quick one when the works closed for the day. Their first drink and the attempts to find common ground had made them like a pair on an initial singles club meeting. It had been a strange chemistry, stilted conversation, but each recognized the wounded solitariness of the other. Dinners had followed, and pecks on the cheek, and both of them had realized that they needed the other to put some foundation into their lives. They'd bought the house on the green together, furnished it, and moved in. The first night there, with the wind on the windows, and Stephen in the next room, they'd slept together and loved each other.

It had been accepted by both from the start, that their previous lives harbored secrets. The ground rules were set: no inquisitions, no interrogations. She didn't ask where he'd come from, why he had no anniversaries, no relations sending him cards and letters. He didn't quiz her on Stephen's father. They buried their past under their new happiness and mutual dependence. He could justify to himself the cordoned-off areas of his life. He was a changed man. If anyone from the old Newbury office, a onetime colleague of Gavin Hughes, had met Frank Perry, they wouldn't have known him. But the past seemed now to rush around him, and he wondered whether an old lie was replaced by a new one.

At the last light of the day, going to get a storybook for Stephen from the living room, he paused and looked out of the window. The man in the suit, the stranger, with a raincoat loose on his lap, remained motionless on the bench on the green.

5

The door opened, and he held up his warrant card. In better times Lily had said it was a rotten photo that didn't do him justice; that morning, like as not, she would have said it flattered him. He was tall, had no surplus weight, with a pale face and cheeks drawn in under the bones. His nose and chin were overprominent, his hair was dark, cut short, and his light blue eyes were dominant. He said briskly, "Morning, Mr. Perry. I'm Detective Sergeant Bill Davies."

He could hear a child's and a woman's voice in the depths of the house. He saw Perry's jaw fall and then tighten. There was never a right time to start the process of protection. He thought of himself as a shadow cast over the principal's life; he could have come in the late afternoon as the family was preparing for supper and television, or in the evening when they were readying for bed, or early in the morning when they were starting a day at the breakfast table, but there was never a best time to arrive on a stranger's doorstep.

"They called you last night, yes? Sorry it had to be the duty officer, but my guv'nor tried to reach you in the afternoon and you weren't at home. Sorry it worked out like that."

God help anyone called by the night duty officer—the guv'nor, the superintendent, would have been familiar with tact, might have thought through what was appropriate to say, and certainly would have had the file to dictate his tone. But not the NDO. It would have been blunt and to the point—what the protection officer's name was, at what time he was arriving, and good night.

Perry swiveled, looked behind him, back towards the kitchen door and the voices.

Davies said, with confidence, "Just getting the lad off to school? It's Stephen, Mrs. Perry's lad, right? If you don't want me around for the moment, that's no problem, Mr. Perry. I can wait till he's on his way, and then we'll do the business. I've got my car here, I can sit there."

It was all about getting off to the right start. It didn't work if the principal refused to cooperate with the protection officer. He needed, from the beginning, to set the tone of the relationship. No call for diving in, breaking the routine of the family, jarring them, then having to mend fences because there was a lingering bitterness. Most principals, in his experience, were frightened half to death when he first came to their homes. The women were worse, and the kids were the big problem, always the headache. Best to go gentle. If his guv'nor had called there would have been a few crumbs of detail on why the threat had ratcheted up, but there'd have been none from the night duty officer. The principals were never given the full picture, not even senior persons in government, certainly not judges and civil servant administrators—and this principal, Perry, was only a civilian with a past and he would get no detail. The threat was not a matter for debate and discussion.

He had worked late into the night in his room at the bed-and-breakfast, and early in the morning before his breakfast, on the file and the village. He'd had the electoral list, the large-scale map that showed every house, digests of police and local-authority files on residents, and had written names against houses. Only one property, currently for sale, was unoccupied. With that mass of information digested, he had made the plan of how they would work together, him and the principal. "I'll be in my car, Mr. Perry."

Perry said, in a low voice, "My wife knows, the boy does not."

"That's not a problem. We'll let him get off to school, then we'll talk."

"He's being picked up, the school run, in about five minutes."

"You know where to find me, Mr. Perry."

There was a shout from the kitchen, from the woman, about the door being open. Who was there? Perry turned and yelled back into the depth of the house that he wouldn't be a moment. There was defiance in his face; there usually was at the start from the principals.

"I'll see you in a few minutes, Bill . . ."

"Detective Sergeant or Mr. Davies, please, and you are Mr. Perry and your wife is Mrs. Perry—it's the way we do it." He said it brusquely, coldly. There wasn't call in the job for familiarity. What they said at the Yard, in the SB protection unit, get too close and the principal starts to run the show. That would not happen with Bill Davies's principal. He had a job to do, he was a paid hand, and it mattered not a damn whether he liked or disliked the man. He would tell him later about the workmen and the technicians who would be crawling round the house by late morning, up the walls, through the rooms, in the garden. There was no soft way of making a start.

"The neighbors don't know."

"No reason why they should—we're used to discretion. The less they know, the better."

Perry frowned. He was a moment summoning up the question, then rushed it. "Are you armed?"

"Of course."

"Has the situation got worse?"

"The doorstep isn't the place to discuss it. When you're ready, come and get me out of the car."

The door closed on him. Of course he was bloody armed. Perry would have said all the brave things when the Thames House people had come on their visit and been rejected. Now he would be realizing where the brave things had led him.

Davies sat in his car. He had a good view of the house and the green in front of it, the road and the homes on the far side of the house, the sea. The car was from the pool. It looked like any other Vauxhall sold for company fleet driving, but it had the big radio with a preset console linking Davies to the SB's operations center, a fire extinguisher, and the box with the comprehensive first-aid equipment. In a metal container, reached by lifting the rear seat central armrest, was a compact case holding a Heckler & Koch submachinegun, with ammunition and magazines, and a dozen CS gas grenades. In the boot was an image-intensifier sight for the H&K, a monocular night sight, a bulletproof square of reinforced material, which they called the ballistic blanket, the gas masks, and the television monitor with the cables and the headset.

Bill Davies waited. By his feet was the lunch box given him by Mrs. Fairbrother at the bed-and-breakfast, and his thermos, which she had filled with coffee—black, no sugar. He had discarded the shoulder holster, left it locked in his bag in the room, gone for the waist-belt holster, and put his loose change into his suit jacket pocket; weight in the pocket so that the jacket moved decisively back if he had to draw his firearm fast. He saw the neighbor leave for work with his wife, bustling out of his weathered, brick-built house, before stopping and peering at him as he sat in the car. Finally, the child ran from the house and into a car.

From the doorway, Perry waved for him to come inside. Davies, of course, had a trained eye for descriptions: Perry was of average height, average build, with fair hair and a face with no particular distinguishing marks. He was ordinary and unremarkable, the sort of man who was easy to miss in a crowd.

He took his time, straightened his tie and checked in the mirror that his hair was in order, then eased out of his seat. He didn't hurry. He was not there to be at the beck and call of the principal. The Glock in the waist holster lapped against his hip as he walked towards the door. He would set the rules, start as he meant to go on. He went inside.

Perry said softly, "I told my wife that the threat wasn't real."

"Then you'll have to do a bit of explaining, sir."

When the engine pitch changed he was sleeping. He stirred in the hard bunk bed, closed his eyes again, aware of the swinging turn of the tanker. Then he wiped his eyes, dragged at the floral curtain, and peered through the porthole window. Beyond white-flecked sea was a horizon of dark land, browned cliffs, yellowed fields, and the grays of a town's buildings. In the sea, bucked and heaved by the swell, was a small boat, its blue hull lost, then found, as the spray broke over a garish orange superstructure. The small boat closed on the tanker. He was awake, he remembered.

The tanker slowed to allow the pilot's launch to come alongside, turning to shelter it from the bluster of the wind. He pressed his face against the weathered glass of the porthole and watched until the launch was under the sheer wall of the tanker's side. He imagined the pilot jumping across a void of water from the deck of his boat to the rope ladder cavorting from the bottom of the fixed steps, and if the pilot slipped . . . In the night, when he went over the side, his God would protect him. From his porthole window he could not see the pilot come aboard, but he watched the small boat heave away and head back at speed towards the land. He felt the turn of the tanker and heard the throbbing power as the engines regained cruising speed. By the time that the ship, guided by the pilot on the bridge with the master, rejoined the northern lane of the English Channel's traffic-separation scheme, he was asleep again. He needed the sleep because he did not know when next he would have the opportunity. He would sleep until the alarm on his watch woke him at noon, then pray, then sleep again until midafternoon, then pray, then sleep again until dusk, then pray, then ready himself.

"They bought it—I don't believe it, but it's authorized." The faithful Mary Ellen tore the paper off the fax roll. "That's just incredible. They swallowed it. You've got the clearance, you're on the freedom bird tonight." She laid the sheet of paper down in front of him. "Have you got enough socks?"

The special agent (Riyadh) of the FBI and his personal assistant sat beside each other and made a list of what he should pack and what he might need to buy in the embassy shop. She wrote down, and underlined, the names of the pills for his blood pressure problem.

When the list was complete, she made the airline reservation. "The authorization is for a week—is that OK? Book you to return in a week?"

He nodded agreement.

She chattered on. "Don't you worry about me. I'll be just fine. Be glad to get rid of you for a week. We're behind with our accounts, filing, all that stuff—might just get the place cleaned up. I'll have a great time here."

But he was hardly listening. Duane Seitz would not have paused to consider whether his personal assistant could cope with a week of his absence. His wife, Esther, was in Iowa, between Audubon, which had been his home, and Harlan, where she had been reared. She was in the world of cattle and corn, where she had brought up two daughters, and he hadn't lived with her, not really, for a few months short of twenty-one years. She had, with gentle firmness, refused even the move to Kansas City, and he had never asked her to travel with him to Riyadh. It did not seem to matter to him, or to her. He went home, to the old farmhouse between Audubon and Harlan, every leave that was given him and every Christmas. He wrote to his wife each weekend that he was away and never forgot a birthday. It was a detached marriage but it stayed alive.

He had lived his life for the study of Iran.

Those who did not know him, the embassy staffers who passed him in the corridors or saw him in the parking lot or at the ambassador's functions, would have reckoned him an academic, eccentric and gentle. They would have been wrong. He played the dangerous game of counterterrorism. It was a solitary, work-driven life, where victims held little relevance, where the requirement for victory was paramount.

Duane Seitz had a light, bouncing step as he left his office and went on down the corridor, cheerfully slapping the arm of the Marine at the grille. His stride was almost a skip of pleasure.

His purpose in life, through all of twenty years, had been to put a smoking gun into an Iranian hand. If the chance came, he would act with a ruthlessness unrecognized by those who did not know him well.

His finger hovered over the names he had written on his paper pad. Fenton stood over him.

Geoff Markham recited, "Yusuf Khan, disappeared off the face of the earth. SB have beefed up Nottingham from Manchester and Leeds, but they don't have him. He's not been home since he was lost, and has not showed at work. The one associate we have listed is Farida Yasmin Jones, the convert, but that's a problem because she's dropped out, doesn't go to the mosque now, and has moved out of her bedsit. I can't trace her electricity, telephone, and gas bills for a new address, like it's covering a trail and intentional—which is to me both interesting and worrying. The protection officer given to Perry hasn't called back to his coordinator. It's a slow haul."

"Keep pushing, keep kicking bums. I'll be at lunch."

He nibbled at the fringes of impertinence. "That's nice, enjoy it."

Fenton grinned. "I will. Need to get up to speed. I have a good feeling about this one. In my water, I've the feeling this might even be exciting. I'm preparing for a jump onto the learning curve."

His superior had been transferred from the Czech/Slovak/Romanian/Bulgarian desk only fourteen months before, which was why Cox had been able, effortlessly, to win promotion over him. Markham thought Fenton should have been on his learning curve a year ago. He stepped over the fringes. "I am sure that Mr. Perry would be pleased to hear that he's providing a bit of excitement."

"You want to make anything of this job? My advice, take the heat."

"I'll be here."

"Where I would expect you to be."

Markham did not look up. Fenton was going to the door, whistling happily, and he steeled himself. "Mr. Fenton."

The whistling stopped.

"Mr. Fenton, I know we're in unpredictable times, but I need to be out tomorrow afternoon, for one o'clock, be about an hour."

Fenton would have been looking at the photo on his wall of Vicky, the one where she wore the short skirt. He asked, "Going to get a little cuddle in, to see you through the day?"

"I am entitled to an hour at lunch, Mr. Fenton." Vicky would maul him if he didn't put his foot down. He said doggedly, "I'm not obliged to work right through a night, but I did."

"No call for claws, Geoff. If you can be free, then you will be."

"Sorry, Mr. Fenton, it's not 'if.' I have to be out of here for one o'clock tomorrow."

"Clock-watching, Geoff, does not fit the Service ethos. May be all right in a bank . . . but secret work, security work, makes a bad bedfellow with a clock face."

Fenton was gone. Geoff Markham sat at the console and hammered out the text, giant format, then printed it. He took a roll of Sellotape from his drawer and stuck the paper to the outside of his door.

"This Project is so SECRET even I DON'T KNOW what I'm doing."

The principal and his wife were subdued, out of sight, when the van arrived with the men from London. Davies jumped out of his car to meet them. He took the foreman down the narrow track at the side of the house and showed him the rear garden, the façade of old stone, and gave him the sketch map he'd drafted of the layout for the property and its interior.

Two more men were at the front now, unloading the cables and boxes from the van, and unhitching the ladders' stay ropes from its roof. He had his own key to the front door now, and took the foreman inside. He'd leave the kitchen, where the principal was with his wife, until last. The foreman hadn't wiped his boots and left a trail of wet earth round the rooms. They went through the house, and the foreman never lowered his voice as he discussed arcs of surveillance for the cameras, and the sighting of the infrared beams, and through which upper window frames they would drill the cable holes, and which ground-floor windows and doors should be alarmed. They came to the kitchen last. She sat with her back to them, didn't acknowledge them. Perry tried to make small talk but the foreman ignored him. It was usually like that, when the gear was put in, and there was no easy way of riding out the shock.

Outside, the ladder scraped as it was extended. The kitchen window darkened as a man's body settled on the lowest rung to test its reliability. The wife had her head down and her lunch half eaten in front of her.

Perry said, "I thought I had the choice on the new locks."

"It's a bit more than locks, Mr. Perry. It's cameras and infrared and tumbler wires and—"

"What's going on?"

They were always worse, more aggressive, in front of the lady, as if they felt the need to make a stand and pretend they were in charge. The principal was not in charge, not anymore, of his house, and certainly not of his life.

"I can't tell you, Mr. Perry, because I don't know—and if I did, I couldn't tell you."

He went outside. There was a light rain falling and the sky threatened more. Another ladder was up against the front wall, the cables dancing as they were unrolled. An electric drill was whining through the wood of an upper window frame. It wasn't the job of the detective sergeant to feel sympathy, but already, inside their home, their lives were being violated, and this was merely the beginning.

There would be some who would say afterwards that this had been the War of Fenton's Belly. They were the bureaucrats of the first floor (Administration—Sub-Branch Accounts), tasked with the study of expense receipts and entertainment bills. Five bills in a week for expenses and entertainment handed in by the head of Section 2, G Branch, and the handwritten demand for reimbursement. They would call, after the business was completed, for explanations and would receive only the vaguest information of what had happened, what had been at stake, and its outcome.

Harry Fenton would have preferred to walk on nails rather than go to Vauxhall Bridge Cross with an invitation to Penny Flowers to join him for lunch. He said it to whoever would listen, often enough, that the Secret Intelligence Service treated the Security Service as lesser creatures. He would not go cap in hand to Ms. Flowers for help and information. So, the first step on his learning curve was to offer a good meal to the senior Mideast (Terrorism) analyst of the Foreign and Commonwealth's research division. They ordered, and then she launched.

"Iran is on the move. Don't believe all that garbage the Americans peddle about a dark, bloodstained hand, Islamic and Iranian, behind every vicious little guerrilla war in the world, it's just not true. Iran is going modern. There've been fair elections, a new, moderate president, a breaking down of the taboos of Muslim life. Look, you want a drink in Tehran, you can get it—you'll have to be discreet, but you can have it. Only three, four years ago, you'd have had a public whipping to sober you up. The woman's role, in government and the civil service, is advancing fast. Women now have power, and there are fashion boutiques for clothes to be worn at private parties. They are modernizing at speed, and if it was not for the bloody stupid American sanctions, they would be going even faster towards a viable economic infrastructure—I'm a fan."

She chewed on the bread sticks with the same enthusiasm with which she talked. Fenton, watching her and listening, didn't think research analysts were overwhelmed with invitations.

"There is much greater internal stability now. They've wiped out the Mujahiddin-e-Khalq. Very few bombs explode in Tehran. The monarchist faction is gone. I accept that they are paranoid about opposition, and that'll last a bit longer, but if we break their isolation they'll get respectable quickly. The Americans forever bleat about state-sponsored terrorism when a bit of hush and encouragement will do a quicker job than a stick. We believe the importance of their guerrilla training camps is overemphasized. We think they offer more training in theological correctness than in bomb making. Every time a bomb goes off in America they shout about Iran. Remember the knee-jerk accusation that Iran was responsible for Oklahoma City? Ouch . . . Remember every American commentator insisting that Iran had knocked TWA 800 into the sea? Yow . . . Remember, Iran had organized the attacks in Saudi, but it's nowhere near proven. We think they give encouragement, financial support, offer a safe haven to dissident groups, but that is way short of controlling them. The Americans need an enemy right now, Iran is available, but the facts don't support the need."

She was gray-haired, severely dressed, with only a small sterling silver brooch for ornament, but there was a twinkle of light in her face.

"Of course, Iran has ambitions. Iran demands recognition as a regional power and believes she has the economic, cultural, and military clout to deserve that status. The current leaders detest the image abroad of a pariah state, and they say they received no credit for a statesmanlike neutral posture during Desert Storm. They deny they export revolution. They say that all they export is oil, carpets, and pistachio nuts. They say they practice good neighborliness. At the bottom line they cannot afford to offend the West because the West is the purchaser of their crude, and without that revenue the country simply folds. Actually, they rather respect the British, admire us, give us credit where it may not be due. They have a saying, "If you stub your foot on a stone you can be sure an Englishman placed it there." London's awash with Iranian dissidents but they're alive, aren't they? They're not being shot dead and blown up. We don't think they want to offend us, quite the opposite. Believe me, the shah was more neurotic about British intelligence and meddling than the present lot. The shah said, 'If you lift Khomeini's beard you will find printed under it, "Made in Britain."' Go to the trade fairs, go to the queen's birthday party at our summer residence, you'll find great friendship for the British."

They ate pasta. The end of the Cold War had been a career disaster for Harry Fenton. He was of the old school at Five—the abbreviated name that the insiders gave to their organization, Military Intelligence Desk 5, that had been founded to hunt out German spies in the First World War. The youngsters, the new intake, preferred the modern title of the Security Service, but to Fenton's generation it would always be Five. As a former tank squadron commander in Germany eyeballing Soviet armor, he had found it a straightforward move into counterespionage when soldiering lost its glitter attraction. He'd been on major spy investigations and found that work totally fulfilling. But the bloody Wall had come down, the enemy was now to be treated as an ally, and after years of dogged resistance, he'd been shuffled to the Islamic Desk. For the first time since that move he felt a frisson of excitement.

"Another hoary old favorite is weapons of mass destruction, which gets everyone in a proper lather. Our assessment goes against the grain. They're way behind in the production of a microbiological capability. Research facilities, yes, but they're not there. On the chemical front, and they have cause to develop such hideous weapons after the gassing the Iraqis gave them, they were making fast progress until five years ago. Then—we don't know why—everything seemed to stop. It was peculiar and I don't have the answer. They're back on track now but they lost several years.

"Top of the list for horror stories is the ayatollahs' nuke, makes the Americans wet their Y-fronts, but we think it's ten years away, that it was ten years away five years ago, that it'll be ten years away in five years' time. Yes, they have missiles for delivery, they can reach the Saudi oilfields, but they've nothing that matters to put in the warheads. Anyway, they're not idiots, they cannot compete on military terms with the Americans and they know it. They're not going to hit

Saudi and get a bashing they can't defend themselves from. Is this a disappointment to you? God, look at the time! My little white neck will be on the block when I wobble in smelling of your booze—as if it matters."

She nodded enthusiastic agreement when he pointed to the empty first bottle, then raised his hand to the waiter for another to be brought. She had lamb and he had veal.

"Bear with me. I'm getting there . . . As I said, the dissidents here are still alive. How long since we last expelled one of their IOs for sniffing round a target? Six years. OK, OK, there are plenty of disparate groups, factions of their intelligence agencies that are not under specific control, they moonlight, but not on a big one. Would they come into Britain and attempt to assassinate a guarded target? No. Absolutely not. Am I a killjoy? But I would urge considerable caution on you in the event that my assessment is wrong. Please, if I am wrong, don't go into the pulpit and denounce that country, because you would set back years of quiet diplomacy and cut the legs off those we believe are moderates. We're not dealing with school-brat vandals, who should be made an example of, but with a nation state we have to live with . . . Damn good lunch, thanks."

He walked back to Thames House and put his head round Cox's door.

He had, of course, a network of high-level contacts; he had been with a senior and respected official of Foreign and Commonwealth Office, and very illuminating it had been.

The eyes of Cox, the bureaucrat, beaded on him.

"Do they believe Iran is on the march, coming to Suffolk?"

"They don't, no—and if they are on the march, then the FCO pleads for a soft line."

"Difficult to take a soft line with an assassin."

Fenton boasted, "I've several more sources that I'll be milking. If there's more to know, I'll find it."

"The motivation that makes people fight in a holy war is that death does not represent the end of life for a human being . . ."

The words were in his mind. He had prayed for the last time that day, the fifth time, an hour and a half after dusk. He had slept well and was rested. He had eaten a small portion of the rice and boiled chicken brought him by the master. He had sat for many minutes on the lavatory in the corner of the cabin until he was satisfied that his bowels and bladder were cleaned, emptied, because that was important. He had stripped, washed himself with soap in the tiny shower cubicle that had been installed for the privacy and personal use of the master's wife. He had dried himself, then shaved.

"On the contrary, immortal life begins after death, and the kind of salvation that a man has in the next world is dependent on the kind of life he lives in this world . . ."

In his mind were the words of the ayatollah who taught at a college in the city of Qom. He stood naked in the cabin. The clothes he had worn when he had boarded the tanker off the port of Bandar Abbas, and on the voyage, with the wedding ring and the gold chain from his neck, were now folded in the cupboard with the chadors and *roupush* trousers left by the master's wife. He was a tall man, 1.87 meters. He was well muscled yet weighed only eighty-six kilos. His hair was dark, close, short cut, but with a neat parting that he combed to an exact line. He was pale-skinned for an Iranian, as if he did not come from the Gulf but from the sunbathed countries and islands of the Mediterranean; it was a reason he had been chosen. The texture of his skin was the gift of his mother, along with the jutting chin and the determination. From his father, he took his eyes, deep-set, shrouded in secrecy. He was thirty-six years old.

His English-born mother had been the daughter of an oil worker at Abadan, who had married the young Iranian medical student against the bitter opposition of her family. She had not wavered and had been cut off from all contact when her father and mother had returned to their Yorkshire home. There had never been reconciliation. She had embraced the faith, become a good Muslim wife. The determination of his mother to follow the road of her love lived on in the jaw shape of her son. Her husband, his father, had qualified as a doctor and they had settled in Tehran with their child.

He could remember the unannounced visitors coming late at night to the house, and the murmur of voices. As the blinds went down in the surgery room, he, the child, kept watch for the SAVAK thugs, the scum men of the shah's secret police. At night, behind the lowered blinds, his father treated the patriots who had been tortured by the SAVAK in the cells, and who had been beaten by the SAVAK in street demonstrations. He could remember when the SAVAK had broken into their home and taken his father away. He could remember when his father had come home, bleeding and bruised, and he'd learned to despise and hate the countries that had supported the corrupt shah and trained the SAVAK policemen. Now his parents were dead, suffocated in the rubble of their Tehran home after the explosion of an Iraqi Scud missile.

He stood naked. What he would wear that night was laid out on the tidied bunk bed. When the revolution had come, when the tanks were on the streets, and the rule of the shah was in its death throes, he had dropped out of school. Going forward with the Molotovs, running across open streets to retrieve those shot by the soldiers, he had been noticed. He had felt no fear and it was seen. When the imam Khomeini at last came home he was, at seventeen years old, given a Kalashnikov rifle and drafted into a south Tehran *komiteh*. He had been on the roof of the Alawi Girls' School when the last chief of the SAVAK was half hanged, cut down, beaten so that his leg bones splintered, mutilated with knives, lit by television lights, killed, and he had felt no pity. He had been inducted into the *pasdars*, joined with pride the unit of the Revolutionary Guard corps that safeguarded the imam at his simple home in Jamaran. He had gone into the embassy of the Great Satan, into the den of spies, into the rooms where the shredders had failed and the files on collaborators and traitors were to be found, and he had hunted them. The war had come. The military could not be trusted. The war with Iraq was his transient route from teenager to man. He had become an elusive, skilled master of the flooded death ground that was the Faw peninsula and the Haur-al-Hawizeh marshland. He had come home, his first leave in two years, to find the dried heap of rubble with the small tunnel through which the bodies of his parents had been extracted. After praying at their grave in the Behesht-e-Zahra cemetery, he had taken the next bus back to the front line.

The Scuds were fired with American help. American satellite photography was passed to the Saudis, who forwarded the images to Baghdad. The hatred grew. When the war was over and the imam had sued for peace and had spoken of taking a decision more deadly to him than drinking hemlock, when he had come home, he had been taken under the wing of a brigadier in the Ministry of Information and Security, as if by a foster parent. And his talents were let loose, and killings followed in his footprints. From what he had seen, suffered, experienced, survived, there was no place in his mind for fear.

He began to cover his nakedness. He wriggled into ankle-length thermal undertrousers, then a thermal vest. He struggled into the rubber suit. He had worn such suits in the probing fast craft they had used in the swamps of the Faw peninsula, and he had been in such a suit when he had first gone ashore on the coast of the eastern province of Saudi Arabia. He put his watch back on his wrist. Later, he would synchronize the time on it with the time on the master's watch. Later, the master would send a radio message of seeming innocence to his employer, the National Iranian Tanker Corporation, in Tehran, and his watch would be synchronized with a clock at the NITC, and the clock there with the master clock in the room at the Ministry of Information and Security where the brigadier waited. Later, the master clock would be synchronized on a secure voice link with the embassy in London. Finally, the intelligence officer at the embassy would synchronize his watch with that of the courier on the shore . . . Everything was planned to the smallest detail, as always. He waited for the master to come to take him to the stern deck. On his bare feet, below where the wet suit sealed his ankles, he slipped a pair of casual trainer shoes. He waited for the master and thought of his wife, Barzin, and their small home, and he wondered whether she missed him. They had no children—perhaps it was his fault and perhaps it was hers, but the doctors they visited would not tell them. She asked nothing of him except that he should serve the revolution of the imam. The tanker churned its way north up the Channel. He took comfort again from the words of the ayatollah from the college at Qom. He was Vahid Hossein. He was the Anvil.

It was a pretext, but the first, and there would be more.

The rain, as promised, had come on harder. Davies sat in the car. He didn't need to wind down the window and let in the damp air. He had the monitor screen on the floor in front of the empty passenger seat, and the headset over his ears. Two cables led from the car to a small junction box screwed to a side wall of the house. He was parked right up against the wall, filling the alley. He could see, in black-and-white on his screen, the neighbor on the front doorstep, and hear distorted speech from the button microphone secreted in the porch.

The pretext seemed innocent enough. "Sorry, Frank, for disturbing you. You got a Philips screwdriver? Can't seem to find one anywhere."

"Sure, Jerry, won't take me a minute."

"Everything all right?"

"Everything's fine. Just wait there, I'll get it."

He saw the neighbor's grimace. He'd have expected to be invited inside, but the principal had learned fast and left him at the door. The neighbor's eye line roved over the front of the house and checked the cables, the broken plants where the ladder had been, and looked into the camera. He wouldn't have seen the button microphone because the men from London were skilled in positioning them—had to be because not even the principal knew about the audio surveillance. People didn't mind outside cameras but they were generally difficult about microphones. He could hear, adequately, anything said in the front of the house, ground floor, and on the stairs; it was good technology and necessary.

"There we go, one Philips screwdriver."

"Brilliant."

"No hurry for it back."

"Great. Frank, Mary said you had a new alarm system fitted today."

"Yes."

"Something I don't know?"

"I doubt it, Jerry."

"Don't think me inquisitive, Frank, not me, but there hasn't been a burglary this end of the village in four years, not since the Doves' place. Mary said you'd put in the full works, chaps like chimps running up ladders. Friend to friend, what do you know that I don't, eh?"

"Just taking sensible precautions, Jerry. You're getting soaked."

"Frank, no pissing, who's that joker in the car?"

"I'm right in the middle of a bit of work. Bring it back when you've finished with it, no hurry."

The door closed and the neighbor retreated. He'd have been sent by his wife; neighbors always were. He'd report that he hadn't really learned anything. That wouldn't satisfy the wife, and she'd be round in the morning to beg a half pint of milk or borrow a half pound of flour. And they'd fret through the evening, the neighbor and his wife, about the cables and the camera, and whether a wave of thieving was about to strike their small corner of heaven.

The boy came home, and the woman who drove him gave Davies a grinding glance before she pulled away. He doubted this little place could survive without knowing every soul's business. His lunch box was finished, except for the apple he always kept till last. It would be another hour before Leo Blake turned up to do the night shift. He polished the apple on his sleeve and listened. He'd made his suggestion, how they should tell the boy. They might have been at the bottom of the stairs or just inside the kitchen. His mother did it. There were faint voices.

Frank used to work for the government abroad. He'd made some enemies. He did secret work, and it was still secret, and Mummy's secret and Stephen's. Frank's going to be protected by the police just for a few days . . .

"Are we going to have to go? Will we have to leave here?"

"No." Her clear voice. "There's nothing to worry about—we aren't leaving our home."

Davies put the apple core in his lunch box.

The evening had come.

The car was parked in a deep lay-by used in the summer by tourists for picnics. It was hidden from the road by trees and evergreen bushes. Yusuf Khan had reclined his seat and dozed. The small bedside alarm clock in his pocket, synchronized to the watch of the intelligence officer, would rouse him thirty minutes before it was time to move.

It was the most comfortable car seat he had ever sat in, a BMW 5 series with a 2.6-liter injection engine, high power, high technology, high luxury. His own, left behind in Nottingham, was an eleven-year-old Ford Sierra, 1.6-liter, underpowered and undermaintained; the carburetor had choked on the 150-mile journey to the northwest. They had needed to call out a mechanic to fix it and had sweated to get to the hospital in time to see the target, Perry, the car he used, and the logo of the salesroom that had sold it to Perry. Farida Yasmin's car was a nine-year-old Rover Metro, cramped and with a small engine, good enough to get them to the car salesroom in Norwich, where a story had been told and information received, and good enough to get them into and out of the village by the sea where the photographs had been taken that had lit up the eyes of the intelligence officer.

Yusuf Khan's car was unreliable, Farida Yasmin Jones's car was too small. The cash float given him by the intelligence officer included enough for him to hire a fast, reliable, comfortable vehicle when he had come off the train. It was fantastic, the BMW, but difficult to handle: once, he had been off the road and a tire width from a ditch because he had underestimated the speed into a corner. There was caked mud on the driver's-side doors. He didn't use the radio because all the stations on the pretune buttons played degenerate, corrupting music.

He imagined the man he had been sent to meet, who would come out of the darkness. The sausage bag was behind his reclined seat, on the carpeted floor. He felt a sense of pride that he had been shown such trust, and Yusuf Khan dozed, waiting.

He tried to concentrate, but the words mocked his efforts. They registered, then they blurred; their message was lost.

Markham sat on the rug in front of the electric fire in Vicky's apartment. She didn't like the word "flat," it was an apartment, but the problem with it was the size. Smart but small, as his was dingy and small. Neither's home was big enough for two, so he read the books she'd bought in her lunch hour and left for him in a neat pile. Everything about the room was neat, organized, like his Vicky.

Vicky was with a girlfriend at aerobics, and then they would be going on for a pizza. The books, they'd have cost her a small fortune,

were on business management, self-expression, leadership, and finance—he'd have gone down to a library and borrowed, if he'd had
time. He tried to remember what she had told him. For the interview
he was Geoffrey, not Geoff, his father was in banking, not a high-
street deputy manager out on his neck last year with downsizing, his
mother organized one of the princess's causes, wasn't a two-days-a-
week helper in a charity clothes shop; he was ambitious, he carried
ambition round in wheelbarrow loads . . .

But the thoughts strayed back to Frank Perry. There had been
enough of them in Ireland, bloody-minded Presbyterian hill farm-
ers, running beef stock over poor land, doing evenings in the part-
time military, who were threatened by the Provos' policy of ethnic
cleansing. The obstinate old beggars had stayed put and taken a sub-
machine gun out in the tractor cab when they went to muck-spread,
wouldn't have considered quitting and running. He'd admired their
courage.

What Vicky had drilled into him . . . He wanted responsibility.
What Geoffrey Markham wanted more than anything was the responsibility of handling the investment of clients' savings. Nothing
rash, but the careful placing of their money and the safeguarding of
their pension schemes. He was not frightened of responsibility. Nor,
if the markets slumped, of crisis.

And Geoff Markham couldn't cling to the interview's strands. Always bloody damn frightening when a player went missing, and
Yusuf Khan was missing—like he had been bloody frightened in Ireland when a Provo player disappeared and they had no word, had to
wait for the Semtex to detonate or the blood to drip on the pavement—and they had lost the trail of the girl who was the only associate thrown up by Rainbow Gold.

Wavering back with his concentration . . . And he expected to
work hard, play hard, had always believed physical fitness went
hand in hand with psychological stability—weekend hiking, after-
work weights and tennis . . . He was to decline the offer of a drink,
old trick, with a friendly refusal, and he was to be polite but not
smarm deference . . . And they shouldn't know it was the only short-
list interview in his locker. He was to wear the new tie she'd bought
him, and his best suit—but he could take the jacket off if they sug-

gested it, though not loosen the tie. And be sure to thank them for fitting him in during a lunch hour . . .

The interview was the next afternoon and he couldn't read the pages in front of him, or remember what she'd told him . . . Rainbow Gold was gone cold on them. Without this job there was no home for him and Vicky, no bright ambitious future. An armed protection officer was at Frank Perry's home . . . Of course Geoffrey Markham wanted a career in banking.

It might have helped relieve the frustration of his work if Markham had had a really good friend at Thames House. It had been better in the early days when the probationers had hung around together and made a social life inside their own restricted, secretive clan. He had no friends now. The probationers who had lasted were dispersed in the building and intersection friendships were discouraged. The society was a mass of hermetically sealed cells; it was not appropriate for East bloc personnel to fraternize with Irish or narcotics personnel—loose talk followed, the old hands said. The former friends were married off anyway, had babies, and didn't go to the pub after work but hurried home. He'd taken Vicky to one insider dinner party, which had been a disaster: she'd thought the men were underachieving and the women were little mice. Actually, thinking about it, the Fentons of Thames House were the lucky ones. They had no expectation of changing the world and used the system as a personal fiefdom for fun and entertainment. Set around with rules, regulations, and procedures, Geoff Markham believed himself a small, irrelevant cog. He would never matter and never be noticed. He wanted out.

He jolted awake at the sound of Vicky's key in the apartment door.

At the end of his twelve-hour shift Bill Davies handed over to DC Leo Blake, checked him through the inventory, took him over the camera controls, the radio channels, and the chart with the red lines marking the infrared beams.

"How is he?"

"Fine, so far."

"And her?"

"She's not spoken, not a bloody word."

"Come again—his call sign?"

"He's Juliet Seven."

"Bit light-handed, aren't we?"

"Maybe, maybe not."

Davies crawled out of the driver's seat and wished his colleague a good night with a wry smile. He saw Blake already pulling up the armrest in the center of the backseat.

In the small hours, and Davies couldn't blame him, Blake would be cuddled up with the cold grip stock of the H&K, what the trade called the Master Blaster. Davies had been promised that the next day he would be given a realistic threat-level assessment, but Blake, who was going to be alone through the night, wasn't waiting for it.

He drove back towards the bed-and-breakfast and the room where he would use one twin bed for the night and Blake would use the other for the day, and he'd have to square that with Mrs. Fairbrother, lie his way out of it. He'd have a shower, then find a pub in another village for his supper. It made it a proper bastard when there wasn't a decent threat-level assessment.

The master hugged him, gripped the thick rubber arms of the wet suit, kissed his cheeks, and pressed against his life jacket. The second officer and the engineer officer flanked him. He had not seen them since he had come aboard fifteen nights before. While he was kissed, the master went again through the timetable of the drop-off and the schedule of the pickup.

He broke free, stepped into the Zodiac inflatable, and settled on its floor of smoothed planks. The whole craft was only four meters in length and he crawled forward so that the engineer officer had the space at the back beside the outboard engine. The engineer officer reached out to him, squeezed his arm, and said that the wind was growing, which was good.

It was good, too, he had been told, that they were able to make the drop-off from the tanker when it was fully loaded and lower in the water. The master and the second officer turned the wheel of the crane, and the cable was drawn up farther on the drum. The four ropes from the inflatable to the cable hook took the strain, then lifted them. The pilot, on the bridge with the navigation officer, would have no view of the stern deck and the crane, and what the crane lifted.

They swayed up above the rail and then the crane's arm lurched them out into the darkness. They clung to the holding ropes of the inflatable. He had no fear. He was in the hands of his God, ten meters above the water. If the crude holds had been empty, it would have been a twenty-one-meter drop.

They went down the black-painted cliff of the hull slowly. The tanker was now past the *Bassurelle* lightship, close to the sand ridge that divided the Channel into the northern and southern traffic-separation schemes, and under the monitoring watch of the radar at Dover Coastguard to the west and Gris-Nez Traffic to the east. The tanker, on the pilot's direction, would hold steady course and steady speed at 14 knots and would arouse no suspicion from the men who watched the sweep of the radar screens. They bounced on the water, sank as the sea splashed over their feet, and surged up. As the cable tension slackened, the moment before they were dragged along and then under, the engineer officer unfastened the cable hook from the ropes. They were clear. The cable swung loose over their heads and clattered against the plate steel of the hull. They were tossed in the white foam water of the engine's screws and he did not understand how they were not dragged down into that maelstrom. The tanker ploughed on, a great bellowing shadow in the night.

He had been told that it was good when the wind increased and the swell was greater, and that British seamen used the word "poppling" to describe such waves. He knew the English language, had learned it from his mother, but he had not known that word. When the sea "poppled," it was impossible for the men watching the radar screens to see the signature of a craft as small as a four-meter inflatable. The outboard engine coughed to life at the second pull. Three kilometers back, they could see the lights of a following ship. The bow rose from the water as their speed grew.

They crossed the sand ridge. Higher waves there, more spray slashing them.

They approached the westerly funnel of the traffic-separation scheme. There was a line of navigation lights ahead. The engineer officer throttled back, paused, and meandered. The inflatable was lifted, fell, and corkscrewed in the waves before he was satisfied. He was like a kid crossing the wide freeway road going south out of Tehran for Shiraz or Hamadan, but waiting for the gap in the traffic, then running. The engine screamed, they bounced forward.

They went for the darkened space of the beach between the lights of New Romney and Dymchurch, near Dungeness. He could have gone by plane or ferry or on the train through the tunnel, but that would have exposed him to the gaze of immigration officers and security policemen. No papers, no passport photographs, no questions, no stamps. He saw, ahead, the white ribbon of the surf on a shingle shore.

The engineer officer, perhaps because tension now caught him, or because there were only sparse minutes before they parted, told of how he had been on the tankers when the Iraqi planes had come after them with Exocet missiles, and of the terror on other tankers when the missiles detonated and the fireballs erupted. He said that he hated those who had helped the Iraqi fliers, and he had reached forward, with emotion, grasped the hand offered him, wished his passenger well, and God's protection. In the last minute before they reached the beach, he told the engineer officer of a birthday party at a seashore restaurant and the bus that carried the guests there, a long time ago.

They hit the shore.

The bottom of the inflatable squirmed on the pebbled beach. He tore off the life jacket, the cold whipping his face. He slid over the ballooned side of the craft, into the water of a gentle, shelving beach. He ran forward, kicking his stride against the sea, struggling until he was clear. He heard the roar of the inflatable's engine. When he was at the top of the beach and looked back, he saw the disappearing bow wave of the inflatable. He was alone.

He walked forward blindly, then stopped and stood stock still against a small wind-bent tree trunk. Seven minutes later, on the hour, as if by synchronization, the brief, twice-repeated flash of a car's headlights pierced the darkness.

He couldn't sleep. Watched by the red eye of the alarm, he lay on his back.

Frank Perry knew that he had to live with the past because the consequences of his former life were inescapable. There was no dusty cloth with which to wipe clear the words written on the blackboard. The past could not be erased. He had attempted it. Quite coldly, he had changed his attitudes. The salesman, Gavin Hughes, focused on work, had never noticed the people around him. He was now more temperate and more caring. He had thrown himself into the life of the small village community, had time for people, and seemed to value their opinions, as if that hard-won popularity was a substitute for his past. He was, he knew it, a more decent man, and it was natural to him that he should help others with the experience of his engineering background, and cut the churchyard grass and attend meetings of the community's groups.

But in his mind the words stayed on the blackboard, and a new-found decency was insufficient to expiate the past. A man had been sent on a long journey, had traveled with a knife or a gun or a bomb, to kill him. Those who had sent the man would not know, or care, that Frank Perry was a changed man.

He heard the boy toss in the adjacent room, and he heard a car door opening, the sound of a man urinating, the door closing again. Meryl was silent beside him, staring at the ceiling. Like sinners, neither of them could sleep.

6

He went too fast onto the bridge and, too late, saw the twist in the road beyond it.

Yusuf Khan had met the man, stood in awe of him. He had come out of the darkness in response to the flash of the headlights, just as the intelligence officer had told him. He had babbled greetings to the man and tried to please him with the warmth of his welcome. Nothing had been given him in return. He had been told sharply, in good but slightly accented English, that he talked too much.

He was in a myriad web of narrow side roads and he was lost and did not wish to show it. The first light was already a smear in the east. He went too fast over the bridge unaware of the right-hand bend immediately beyond it.

First the man had peeled off his wet suit, then stood in his long-trousered underclothes and had clicked his fingers irritably at Yusuf Khan, who watched. He had been caught idle and felt keenly the criticism of the snapped fingers. He had dragged the newly bought clothes from the bag, and the man had cursed softly because the shop labels were still on them. Yusuf Khan had torn them off before handing them back. He had held the torch and passed the man the camouflage trousers, the tunic, and the thick socks. The fact that the new boots were not laced provoked another savage glance.

When he had set out the schedule in his mind, he had not expected that the clothes would be worn now; he'd assumed the man wouldn't be using them from the start. And he had not expected that the man would demand the opening of the tubular bag. With only the torch beam to guide him, the man had been meticulous in his examination of the weapons. He had broken open the mechanism of the launcher and examined each of the working parts, studied them, cleaned some with the window rag from the car, and reassembled it. Because it was only a small torch beam, Yusuf Khan had recognized that the man had worked virtually blind. He had leaned forward, anxious to please, held the torch closer, but had abruptly been waved back. The schedule had gone.

The man, in the fragile light, had then turned his attention to the squat form of the rifle. Yusuf Khan had never seen a man take apart a firearm, and was amazed at the seemingly casual way that the weapon disintegrated into pieces. Each round had been examined before two magazines had been filled, and the pressure of the coil tested. By the time he had started up the car his fingers had been stiff and his legs taut, and he had lurched through the manual gears. The sausage bag with the weapons had been on the floor behind him within the man's reach—as if, already, he was prepared for war, to kill. The man had leaned back in his seat and closed his eyes.

He was lost, stressed, when he came too fast over the bridge and into the hidden right-hand bend beyond it. As he swerved to hold the center of the road, the wheels failed to grip, and Yusuf Khan stamped on the brake pedal. At that moment the 5-series BMW was out of control.

The car slewed on shrieking tires across the width of the road. He saw the pole that carried telegraph wires. Short of it was the ditch, looming towards him in the headlights' glare.

Yusuf Khan saw everything, so clearly, so slowly.

Plunging into the ditch, the bonnet going down—the ditch throwing the back of the car upwards—the man's arms went up to cover his forehead, but he made no sound—the car standing on its nose— no fear on the man's face—the roof of the car impacting against the telegraph pole.

There was a wild pain in his leg, a fleeting sensation, as the car came down, crazily angled in the ditch. His skull hit the point where the roof met the windscreen.

Blackness around him, and peace.

. . .

The early morning was a precious time to Dominic Evans.

His partner, Euan, would be in the shop, cleaning the floor and the windows, stocking the shelves, putting out the ice cream sign, taking a list of the postcards that needed replacing.

Dominic loved his partner deeply, but he also loved the early-morning walk, on his own, out of the village and towards the Southmarsh. Left behind, in Euan's care, was his dog because the sweet little soul would disturb the glory of the early morning's tranquillity. He was forty-nine, had come to the village and bought the shop fifteen years back with the money from his mother's estate. For twelve of those fifteen years Euan had been his partner. He thought the villagers, with their Neanderthal minds, accepted him and did not jeer at him because he had integrated carefully and made it his ambition to write down the old history of the community. Through learning the history, explaining it, sharing it, he had won acceptance, and he was discreet. It was a good place to gain the sense of history's inevitability, to recognize the futility of man's efforts to combat the power of nature. In time the sea would claim all of it: everything that man had built would crumble off these soft cliffs and be lost to the waves.

In the half-light he walked past the narrow, silted stream that had once been a great waterway where skilled artisans built big ships. That summer, he would write a special pamphlet on the shipbuilding from Viking to Cromwellian times, publish it at his own expense, and lecture on it to the Historical Society. But that morning, each morning for a month, history did not intrude on his thoughts.

It was the miracle month of survival and navigation, the month when the birds completed the migration from the south seaboard of the Mediterranean and the west coast of Africa. Each morning in the dawn before the shop opened and each evening in the dusk after it closed, he went to watch for the arrival of the birds on the Southmarsh. That they came from so far, that they could find their way to this particular area of water channels and reed banks, was truly incredible to Dominic.

He settled on the damp ground, at his watching place. Usually he went to the Southmarsh, more rarely to the Northmarsh. There were godwits, warblers, and avocets, but they had not come from Africa, nor the shelducks, nor the geese. It was a few minutes from the time that he should return to the village and open the shop when he saw the bird he was waiting for.

The tears pricked in his eyes, and the sight made this gentle man cry out in anger.

The harrier flew low in tortured flight. A pair had come back to the Southmarsh three evenings before and their wing beat after the journey of thousands of miles was firm, true; they had left the next morning for a destination farther north. It was as if this bird flew on one wing.

For all his anger, for all his gentleness, there was nothing Dominic could do to help the bird.

It had come home, it was injured. The infection would be in the wound. It would die a starved, agonized death. He lost sight of it as it came down into the reeds.

He wiped his eyes. The harrier, *Circus aeruginosus*, rust and copper feathering, was the most beautiful bird he knew. It would be in pain, in hunger, in exhaustion, and he was helpless.

He went back to open his shop.

Vicky slept as Geoff Markham dressed. While he did so he played in his mind with the words she had written down for him, made sentences for them.

. . . I believe in the totally *ethical* use of finance . . .

. . . A bank, in my opinion, should never deny the *participation* of the investor in the handling of his or her affairs . . .

. . . Money is for the benefit of the whole of the *community*, not just for the wealthy . . .

. . . Finance stands at the *interface* of society and should be used to create general wealth and not narrow affluence . . .

Vicky had said that he must use the modern idiom, not the cobwebbed language of Thames House.

He put on the new tie she had bought, thin, woven, with brightly colored stripes.

The intelligence officer, in his Kensington flat, took the call. The number of the mobile telephone was jealously guarded and changed every month, and he assumed that the landline telephone was routinely listened to. A voice of great calm spoke of a traffic accident, gave a location of signposts a mile from the accident site, and quietly told of the need for help in moving onwards.

Deniability was the creed of the intelligence officer.

He took the number of his caller and rang off. He threw on basic clothes. He had not the time to consult Tehran, nor to call his colleague's apartment in Marble Arch. It was his decision, against every regulation of his service, that he should take a personal involvement in a situation of emergency.

Often, his Kensington apartment was watched. There might be a car, with the engine idling, on the far side of the road to the front lobby of the block or in the side street. He went out through the fire door at the back, past the janitor's little locked room and the waste bins. To further the creed of deniability, he ran for a phone box. He called a number, waited for it to be answered, heard the sleep-ridden voice, explained what had happened, ordered what was to be done, rang off, walked back to his apartment.

He believed he had not compromised the creed of deniability.

Blake told him that the woman in the house across the green had a big backside and didn't draw the curtains when she undressed, and that was about the limit of his overnight excitement. There were cat's footprints all over the bonnet and Blake told him that he'd had the brute inside with him until it had tried to get into his food box. Blake stacked the H&K back into the case and slotted it behind the rear-seat armrest.

Davies rang the front doorbell as Blake headed back to the bed-and-breakfast.

The door was opened by the wife, and from her eyes, it didn't seem that she'd slept. She led him into the kitchen. The boy broke from his cornflakes and stared at him. Davies thought he was looking for his gun, but he wouldn't have seen it in the waist holster underneath the fall of his suit jacket. She told the boy to go upstairs, get his books ready, go to the toilet, get his hair combed.

"Morning, Mr. Davies."

And it didn't look to him that Frank Perry, the principal, had slept any better than his wife. There was a dazed tiredness in his face.

"I don't need to trouble you for too much of your time, Mr. Perry, but you had rather an amount to take on board yesterday, and I'd like to confirm a few points."

"Wasn't the easiest of days I've known, but, what I've said to Meryl, it could have been worse."

"Always best to be positive, Mr. Perry."

"We could have run away—could have turned our backs on all this."

From what he had seen in her face, the hopelessness in the fall of her mouth, he thought the woman was deeply wounded and he wondered if Perry realized it. Not his job . . . He should have phoned Lily, should have spoken to the boys, should have . . . He was hardly qualified for marriage counseling, and it wasn't his job to try.

"What I want to reiterate, Mr. Perry, are the procedures, and for the correct application of the procedures I need your cooperation."

"And you should not forget that I worked for my country, Mr. Davies. I am owed protection."

They faced each other across the breakfast table. There was a tight, curled snarl at Perry's mouth.

He smiled, defused. "Of course, Mr. Perry. If I could just repeat . . . Please, you don't spring any surprises on me. You tell me who you are expecting as visitors, where you will be entertaining them. That will be very helpful to me."

"It's a village, Mr. Davies, it's not an anonymous damn city. Our friends call by, they don't make appointments, we're not an optician or a dentist."

He was generous. He knew that the snarl was from tiredness and understood the stress. Behind Perry, the woman watched him, her eyes never leaving him.

"And I need to know, Mr. Perry, your intended movements for the day. Are you going out? Where are you going? How long will you be there? Who will you meet? I need specific detail of your planned movements."

"Why?"

He reckoned they were sparring and wasting each other's time. He said it straight, brutally, "We have laid down procedures, they are based on experience. You are at least danger when in your own home. You are in the greatest danger when in transit. There are two points of maximum danger, when you leave your home and are exposed as you go to the car, and when you leave your car and walk into a building, particularly if that is a regular journey. You are in danger en route, if your journey is predictable. I told you this yesterday and I am sorry that you weren't able to comprehend it. The danger on the pavement, to the car and from the car, is from a sniper at long range or a handgun used at close quarters. The danger during a journey is from a culvert bomb with a command cable or remote detonation or from a parked car bomb. Get me? If it couldn't happen, Mr. Perry, I wouldn't be here."

The woman rocked on her feet, as if caught by a shock wind, but her eyes were never off him.

It was like he'd hit Perry in the solar plexus, and his voice was quieter. "You can't search half the countryside. What difference does it make if you know my routes?"

He said easily, "I can plan, in the event of an ambush, where to drive to, the nearest safe house—might be a telephone exchange, a government building—and I can have worked out where's the nearest hospital."

"Jesus."

"So, if you could just tell me, Mr. Perry, your plans for the day, then there are no surprises."

"Meryl's visiting this morning and she's got a class—"

"I'm not concerned with Mrs. Perry's movements."

Perry flared. "Doesn't she matter?"

"You're the target, Mr. Perry. You're the principal I'm here to protect. That's my instruction. Are you going out today?"

She had an antique furniture restoration class in the afternoon. Perry was committed to the school pickup.

"Can you cancel?"

"No, I bloody well can't. And I intend to live a life."

"Of course, Mr. Perry. Let's go over the route."

He was shown in by Fenton, and Cox was hovering behind. Markham thought the man looked as if he'd just stepped off the Ark.

"It's Mr. Seitz, Geoff, from Riyadh. You told him you did the 'donkey's load,' so he's come to offer you some oats. You're his liaison with us," Fenton said.

Markham stood. It was that sort of depressing morning where the pieces were obstinate and refused to slot. Nothing to report from SB's operations center on the target, Juliet Seven. There was no trace on Yusuf Khan from Nottingham. The associate, the woman thrown up by Rainbow Gold, had moved from the address listed for her electricity and telephone bills, but he had, small mercies, registration details for her car, about as common a small saloon as any on the road.

The American had close-cut gray hair, not brutally short, but done in a style that was, to Markham, old fashioned. His tie was from a similar bygone age, crisply clean but well used, a navy blue with a discreet motif. His shirt was new, first time worn. It was the suit that Markham noticed. The American was dressed in a brown three-piece herringbone, what a prosperous lawyer would have worn thirty years back in north Lancashire; the suit was old but cared for. Everything about the appearance of the American, except his eyes, gave an impression of tidy but mild eccentricity—there was nothing tidy, certainly not mild, about the darting and alive and penetrating eyes. Markham glanced down at his watch.

"I apologize, but I did tell you, Mr. Fenton, I have to be at an appointment over the lunch hour." And he added limply, "A family business appointment. I can't cut it and I can't be late either."

Fenton said, dry, "I hope the family business is important—Mr. Seitz has flown three thousand miles so that he can offer us the benefit of his experience. Bring him back to me."

Fenton and Cox were gone.

He shuffled, tried to tidy his desk space, merely confused the papers and his notes.

"Would you like a coffee, Mr. Seitz?"

"Only if you can put whisky in it."

"Can't," he said sheepishly. "At the donkey level it's not permitted to keep alcohol in the work area. I'd get a reprimand and it would go on my record."

"No problem. Where I come from it's a capital crime, Mr. Markham."

"In here I'm Geoff—please, feel free."

"Then you'll have to forgive me. It's my FBI training. We like to stay formal until we really get to know the other guy. Right now, Mr. Markham, and I'm sure you know it, you're sitting on the big one."

"Right now it's all ends, frayed and not tying. I don't know what I'm sitting on."

"OK, OK. The target, Hughes/Perry."

"We've call-signed him as Juliet Seven."

"OK, Juliet Seven. Is he still refusing relocation?"

"Yes."

"What have you done for him?"

"We have given him specialist police protection."

"They got howitzers?"

"They would have machine pistols and handguns."

"How many?"

Markham said, dispirited, "There are two, each doing a twelve-hour shift."

"Fuck."

"It's a matter of resources."

"Are you listening, Mr. Markham? This is the big one. I know him as the Anvil. I don't have another name for him. I don't have his face. He was in Alamut. Did you read, like I told you to, about Alamut? Of course you didn't. Donkeys don't have time to read, donkeys just get the shit piled on them. The Anvil was in Alamut—I hate that name, it's crass and comic book, but it's the name that's whispered in the souk, in the mosque, and in the theological colleges throughout Saudi Arabia, so it's good enough for me. The Anvil goes to Alamut, each time, before he travels for the hit. I know so little of him, but he's the best, and he's dedicated. That he goes to Alamut is important because it is the small window I have into his mentality. Please, Mr. Markham, when I'm talking to you don't look at your wristwatch. Right now he is traveling, and his target is your Juliet Seven.

"Before you rush away to whatever is important, take time out for a little history. Alamut is a few kilometers northwest of Qasvin, where there is a terrorist training camp run by the Iranian Revolutionary Guards corps. At Alamut, nine hundred years ago, Hasan-i-Sabah founded the sect of Assassins. The modern word is from the same root core as "hashish"—Western scholars believed the killers were drugged or they would not have gone forward against guarded and near impossible targets. I doubt they were drugged, they just weren't scared. For two hundred years the Assassins, the living cult of political murder, created terror from Syria down through Lebanon and Palestine and into old Persia because they had no fear of death, and worshiped the notion of martyrdom. He goes there, to what is now a few stones on a mountainside, unrecognizable as a fortress, to gain the courage that will push him forward. Pretty damn easy to guard against a killer who's looking to keep his skin intact, but pretty hard, Mr. Markham, to block the killer who has no concern for his own survival—and he's coming after your Juliet Seven. Maybe you don't believe me, maybe you need the Alamut case histories to crank up my credibility . . ."

Markham hated himself for saying it, but said it anyway. "Don't think I'm being rude, Mr. Seitz, but I really do have to go."

He was skilled at finding cover.

It was the skill that had dictated his survival in the floodplains around the Faw peninsula and the water channels between the reeds of the Haur-al-Hawizeh marshlands, and in the mountains of Afghanistan, and in the desert wilderness of the Empty Quarter, and in the forest near to the village in southern Austria. He could find cover and use it.

At the edge of a small group of trees was dense, thorned scrub. He had gone so quietly into the trees that he had not disturbed the roosting pheasants, and then crawled on his stomach into the depth of the scrub. A rat had passed within three meters of him and not seen him. If a farmer came into the field he would find no trace of him. The rain dripped rhythmically down on him from the thorn branches of the scrub. Beside him was the sausage bag. In it was what he had thought he could carry across country and still retain the speed of movement.

The cover was well chosen. He had a clear view across a hundred meters of grassland field to an open gateway, and through the gateway to the signpost at the crossroads. He waited. His stomach rumbled with hunger, but a few hours without food did not concern him: food was for sustenance, not for enjoyment. He waited.

He had seen a police car come down the road with a blue light flashing in the dawn, then an ambulance. His driver's pulse had been faint, the breathing erratic and gasping, the head wound bleeding. It had not been necessary to finish the man's life. He would not regain consciousness, would be dead by the end of the day. He had thought the man foolish, and had then corrected himself, because the man had achieved the state of martyrdom in the service of the faith. He should not think badly of him. The ambulance had come back through the crossroads with the bell going and the light brilliant against the dark rain clouds. Later he had seen a towing truck pull away the wrecked car.

There were only bruises and small scratches on his own body and he took that as a sign. His life was in God's hands. His work was God's work. God watched for him. There had been setbacks before, however thorough the planning, and he had overcome them. He would do so again.

He had waited three hours and fifty-one minutes when the car finally came.

It was a small car, old. He could not see the driver at that distance. It drove past the signpost and disappeared behind the hedgerow, then reversed back into his vision. The car stopped in the field gate. The brake lights flashed twice.

He breathed hard. There were times in the life of Vahid Hossein when his safety, his life, and his freedom rested in his own hands only, and God's. There were times, also, when he must give his trust to the intelligence officers who controlled him.

It had been written, "Once you engage in battle it is inexcusable to display sloth or hesitation."

He crawled from the thorn scrub.

"Take no precautions for your own life."

He hurried through the trees and the pheasants clattered in flight above him.

"He that is destined to sleep in the grave will never again sleep at home."

He ran along the hedgerow towards the gate. He reached the small car. He flung open the door and heaved the weight of the bag into the back. The engine was turning. He dived for the seat, slammed the door shut, and the car jerked forward. He swiveled in his seat.

He sat beside a woman.

He sat beside a woman with the skin of her face exposed, and her forearms, and the skin of her thighs above her knees and below her tight skirt.

He sat beside a woman whose body was scented with soap and lotion. He was aghast.

She said, "It's what they told me to do. They told me I should give up the clothing of decency. I'm sorry to offend you."

He stood on the pavement and looked around him. There were no concrete posts outside the building to prevent a car bomb being left under the façade. The building was glass-fronted, not heavy stone, with small, laminated windows.

He went inside and a pleasant young woman directed him to the lift. She had no guards beside her and there would not have been hidden guns within reach under her desk.

He came out of the lift and pushed through an unlocked door. There was no requirement for a personal security card.

It was what Geoff Markham wanted.

Long after the ambulance had gone, and after the recovery vehicle had towed away the wreck, the two traffic policemen worked with their cameras and tape measures. From what they'd seen it would go to the coroner's court and an inquest, and there were a hell of a number of questions to be answered—a young black paying cash for the hire of a BMW 5 series and not being able to handle it, writing it off and himself—and the technical investigation looked to be the best last chance of finding the answers.

The two traffic policemen stopped work for a sandwich lunch. One, after he'd eaten, the elder one, complained of his bladder and slipped through a hedge hole.

He didn't notice the canvas sack, rammed down into the base of the hedge, until he'd finished and was shaking himself. He would not have seen it if he hadn't been standing almost on top of it. He bent and pulled it open.

The traffic policeman shouted to his colleague to come, and bloody fast, and showed him a black rubber wet suit, a pair of trainer shoes, and some squashed sales dockets, before pointing down into the bag at the hand grenades.

She drove well, confidently. She was not intimidated by the heavy lorries. His own wife, Barzin, did not drive. He admired the way she drove, but he was ashamed that each time she punched her foot on the brake or the accelerator he could not keep his eyes from the smooth whitened skin of her thighs. She would have seen him flinch and flush.

"They called me when I was asleep, told me it was urgent. I just took the first clothes that came to hand—I didn't find any stockings. I suppose it's what you'd call bad *hejab*, yes?"

There was a mullah, he had heard, who had stayed inside his house for thirty years, never gone outside his house, never dared to, for fear that he would see a woman improperly dressed, bad *hejab*, and be corrupted . . . She kept in the slow lane of the wide motorway skirting London. Never in his life had he been driven by a woman. The diesel fumes of the lorries came and went, but constant in the car was the soft scent of soap and lotion.

She saw the twitch of his nostrils. "I went out last night with some girls from work. One of them's getting married next weekend. We went out for some drinks—no, I don't drink alcohol, but I can't tell them it's for my belief. I have to tell a little lie; I say I don't drink for a medical condition. They've told me to be like everyone else, and that way I can better serve my faith and the revolution of Iran. I have to use women's soap and *eau-de-toilette* if I'm to be like everyone else. They tell me that God forgives little lies."

Because of the persecution of his faith throughout history, her faith, it was acceptable for the Shi'a peoples to tell the *khod'eh*, the half-truth, in defense of the true religion . . . He believed, as did his wife, so Barzin told him, that the place for a woman was in the home and rearing children. She would be in their home, cleaning it, always cleaning it because they had no children to divert her. His mother had been different: dressed in good *hejab*, she had come out of her home to help his father on his sick visits. His wife, Barzin, only undressed in his presence if the room was darkened.

When she changed the gears, her body shook and her breasts

swung loosely, and he had flushed the most when he had seen the cherrystone shape of her nipple—he would have picked the fruit from a tree in the Albourz hills and sucked it, turned the stone on his tongue and cleaned it, then spat it out—and then he stared straight ahead at the spinning wheels of the vehicle in front, and the grinning idiot face of a child in the vehicle's back window.

She knew. "I had the call, I was out of my room in four minutes. I told you, I didn't have the chance to dress properly, decently. My name's Farida Yasmin."

It was said that the imam Khomeini, on the drive from his French home in the village of Neauphle-le-Château to the airport at Orly for his flight home and the triumphal return, had never looked from his car's windows onto the decadence of the Parisian streets, had kept his head lowered to avoid the sight of impurity.

"You've seen the man's photograph, Perry's? Of course, you have. I took it. You've seen the picture of his house? Yes? I took that as well. I think I'm to be trusted."

He jolted. Under the law that was the basis of the state, the *sharia*, the testimony of a woman was worth half that of a man. They were not of half value, the crucial photographs of the man and his house. She was beside him and her thighs were bare and her breasts bounced under a thin sweater. It was written that exposure of the flesh "without Islamic cover can invite foul looks from men and invite the devil's lusting." He was dependent on her.

She told him when she had seen the man and about his house. In the planning of an attack he had never before talked to a woman as his equal.

She looked into his face, caught his eyes. "What happened to my friend, to Yusuf?"

He said what he knew, and offered her no sympathy. She was strong. He had known so many who had died young, gone early to the Garden of Paradise. She looked ahead.

"You talk well, Geoffrey," the man said. "You say the right things, but I am not yet convinced of your commitment to them."

"We get a lot of sincerity these days," the woman said. "What we have to look for is when the sincerity is larded on like greasepaint."

Markham swallowed hard.

"Anyway, that's as may be, that's our problem to evaluate, not yours . . ." The man hesitated, as if for effect.

The interview had lasted twenty-five stilted minutes. He had used all the words that Vicky had written out for him, woven them into answers, and twice he had seen the little mocking glint in the woman's eyes.

"Let's press on. Let's explore a bit more . . . We're not with the Civil Service, we're not able to rely on government's safety net, we're in a hard, commercial environment. A man works for a company, does all that it asks of him, takes his work home and frets over it, is a good colleague—and a pimple-faced creep who knows nothing of anything hands him a letter of dismissal, without warning, and a second letter of redundancy terms, and he's cleared his desk and gone in ten minutes, on the scrap heap for the rest of his life. Could you be the pimple-faced creep and do that?"

The woman leaned forward. "Are you up to that, Geoffrey, screwing good employees' lives?"

He took a deep breath. "I've done it, I know about it. It got to be pretty much every day. I was in Northern Ireland, I ran informers—that's playing God. You make a mistake with an informer and you get him killed—it's not just killed like in a road accident, it's torture first with electricity and beatings and cigarette burns, and then it's the terror of a kangaroo court and then it's a bin bag over the head and a kick so that he goes on to his knees, and the last thing he hears is a weapon being cocked . . . They're not good guys, they're scumbags, and they're so damned scared that they get to lean on you like you're a crutch. You know how it will end and they do, but you don't let them quit. It's expensive when they quit, and they're damn all use once they're out of it. So you keep your player in place, and you sleep at night and put him out of your mind. It's your work and you don't worry about it . . . I've played God with people who won't be getting a good pension and won't have only their ego bruised—I've played God with men who'll have the back of their heads blown off and whose women will be spat on as the wife of a traitor and whose parents will disown them and whose kids will be ostracized for their lifetime. Does that answer your question?"

The bleeper went at his waist. The woman stared at him, her mouth slack. The man looked blankly down at his notepad.

He read the message: "MARKHAM/G—RE JULIET 7—GET BACK SOON-EST. FENTON."

He said, "I'm sorry, I'm called back."

The woman asked, "To play God?"

The man looked up from his notepad. "You'll hear from us."

Markham was out of the chair. "Thank you for your time."

He left the office and waved down a taxi.

He was dropped on the corner, and went into the building that had housed the last ten years of his life, past the desk where they had the hidden guns, through the security locks, and ran up the stairs with the laminated windows.

He came to the door of Fenton's office and heard the American's quiet voice. "You'll have a week, and you should take this as the first day of the week. In a week either he'll have reached his target and gone, or you will have him dead or in your cells. A week, not more, believe me. Your countdown, gentlemen, has started. And—can I say?—you've had the luck of a break the like of which I've never had. The question is, can you use your luck?"

The police, uniformed and wearing bulletproof vests, their hand-guns on their hips but their machine guns secreted in cases, filed into the cubicle area at the far end of the ward for the hospital's emergency cases. Away from the sight of the patients, close to the bed, they unpacked the cases, produced and loaded their machine guns. The nurses came and went, checking the purring equipment and dials on the rack beside the bed, and glanced at them with raw distaste. They found chairs and settled in. Their role, the guns across their laps, was simple. The problem was away down the corridor where the detectives met the duty physician and the arguments began.

He turned his head and saw the cottage with the For Sale sign, and thought what it would cost to buy and repair. It was the sort of home that Lily would have loved, and the village was the sort of place where the boys would have flourished. But it was an empty thought because his job was in London, and it was beyond the bounds of possibility that he could have afforded it. It was the sort of place that some high-flying bastard out of London bought as a second home, for occasional weekends, and they were the people he detested.

They were out of the village, and soon into the narrow roads. Davies had the map on his knee. Perry drove.

If there was just the one protection officer, the principal always drove. He had jerked his coat back so that the butt of the Glock was clear for his hand to reach. He had the road map open and on it were marked the regional hospital, fifty-two miles away, and the two local hospitals with Casualty and Emergency, twenty-four and thirty-one miles away; by now all of them would have been discreetly requested to hold plasma stocks of the principal's blood group. Also on the map were air force bases to the north and the southwest, and a telephone exchange in the destination area; all designated as safe areas of refuge.

"It's nice countryside—it's fabulous, isn't it?"

"Yes, it is."

Bill Davies knew the countryside round the prime minister's bolt-hole, Chequers, and round the Oxfordshire home of a onetime Northern Ireland minister, round the estate of a Saudi fat cat, and the countryside round Windsor Great Park, where the Jordanian king had a mansion. He knew about the countryside and loathed it. He called it a hostile environment.

They'd come out of the village on the one long, straight road and were now in the close, high-hedged lanes. His eyes were on the hedges, on the ditches, on the concreted culvert entries, on the trees back from the lanes. It was the nature of the job, and he regarded himself as professional and dedicated to it, that the warning time might be two seconds or three, and the principal wasn't trained to drive, wouldn't have known how to perform the bootlegger turn, wouldn't have known how to get to maximum speed. He'd half frozen just before the last junction, his hand hovering over the Glock, when they'd come to a Transit van half filling the road with the bonnet up and a man working on the engine. They'd had to slow almost to a stop before passing it. His eyes raked ahead.

"You get out into the countryside much, with your family?"

"Not often."

"You've got a family?"

"Yes."

"Boys, girls, both?"

"Boys."

"What age are they?"

"If you don't mind, Mr. Perry . . ."

He stared through the windscreen. He should have cleaned it. They all wanted to talk, to unburden themselves with their protection officer, and it was the route to disaster. He was not tasked to offer a sympathetic ear.

Ahead, there were men and warning bollards and a heap of excavated road tarmac. The road was clear beyond, but one of the workmen held the Stop sign facing them. Perry was slowing, but Davies shouted for him to keep going and they went through to a volley of rich local obscenities. Friends fell out, and the rule was to keep it as a job. The tools of the job were the H&K in its case with the magazine attached, at his feet, and the Glock on his hip. He loved the job. The pity was he might just love the job more than he loved Lily.

"How long have you been at it, doing this?"

"Quite a time."

"Good shot, are you?"

"Adequate."

"Don't you have to be better than adequate?"

"It's about planning, Mr. Perry, boring planning. Planning is the best defense against attack—if there is an attack, then the planning has failed."

"What do you know about the Iranians?"

"Enough to respect them."

It was final, and dismissive with it. What he knew, and wouldn't say, was that the Iranians were a different league from the Provos.

The Provos would back off from a guarded target, find something softer. He had studied the case histories of Iranian hits: not many killers made it away; for too many the reward was martyrdom. The message from the case histories would make any conscientious bodyguard nervous. He read all the detail he could find on political killing. It was his job.

They were outside a school, and in a line of cars waiting at the gate. It was a school like any other, an old brick turn-of-the-century building and a mass of raised prefabricated huts, like the school his children went to.

Parents were milling at the gate and inside the playground where kids ran and screamed, skipped and swarmed after a football. If he could, he went to Donald and Brian's school to pick them up, but it still wasn't often enough.

"Am I allowed to go and get them?"

"Don't see why not."

Sarcasm, like that was his defense. "You don't think I'll be shot?"

"Shouldn't think so."

He could have told him, but didn't, that the Irish were gold-medal standard at killing off-duty policemen, prison warders, and magistrates on the church steps or in hospital wards, or at the school gate. They had no qualms about blasting a man when he wasn't taking the necessary precautions.

He said he would come with Perry, into the asphalt playground, that they must lock the car because of the H&K, that he must have Perry and the car in his sight at all times.

They walked through the gate. The loose change clinked in his suit jacket pocket. Beneath it the holster was tight against his upper thigh. He hung back and watched his principal before turning twice, in complete circles, to observe the faces of the mothers and fathers, the grandparents, the kids chasing the football. He saw the way that men and women came to his principal, slapped his back, shook his hand, and laughed with him. The other boy, the one they were getting home, stood by the principal. They came round Perry like they were flies to jam and he heard the roar of the laughter.

A kid, would have been the same age as his Brian, kicked the football high in the air.

The swarm followed the spiraling ball.

He'd ring that night, find out how Donald's game had gone, when he'd done the shift with Juliet Seven.

The ball landed and bounced. The bounce would take the ball over the playground fence, out into the road and the traffic.

He jumped. It was his instinct to keep a bobbing, chased ball out of the traffic. He was grinning at his own athleticism, his back arched with the leap, his fingertips pushing the ball back towards the pack of kids. There was the lightness, emptiness, at his waist.

The gun, the nine-millimeter Glock pistol, fell from the waist holster. As he landed he snatched for it. It was beyond his grasp. It fell away from him. The gun clattered on the asphalt playground, cartwheeled, and came to rest away from the grope of his hands. The kids' shouts and yells died and the black shape of the Glock lay on the asphalt beside the white-painted lines of a netball court.

The parents' laughter and talk withered. He walked forward, half a dozen paces. He saw the rolling, abandoned football and the young, old, numbed faces. He picked up the gun and the screaming started. He saw the parents grabbing kids, going down onto the asphalt and sheltering them with their bodies, hugging them, guarding them. He held the gun in his hand, the tool of his job, and did not know what he should say. Perry stared at him, blank and uncomprehending. A great space was widening around him. Through a glass window, he saw the gray, lined face of the head teacher as she lifted the telephone. He put the gun into his waist holster.

The first cars were already charging away from the school gate. He took a deep breath, then strode towards the school building and the sign for the head teacher's room.

It took fifteen minutes to sort it. He showed his warrant card, made a telephone call to turn back armed-response vehicles and another to verify his identity for the head teacher. His explanation to her of his principal's need for police protection was economical and bland.

He walked back across the empty playground.

They were all gone, his principal's friends and their children.

He slipped down into the front passenger seat.

Davies said stiffly, "I owe you an apology, Mr. Perry. That was unforgivable, unprofessional. You are perfectly entitled to ring my guv'nor to request a personnel change."

"But I'm a beggar, Bill, so I can't be a chooser. What I'd get might be worse than you." The principal laughed, with a hollowed echo.

"Thank you. If you don't mind, it's Mr. Davies . . . I don't know what the consequences will be."

"None . . . forgotten . . . just a little dose of excitement. I have to tell you, I saw the gun. The gun was real, but it's the only part of anything that seems believable."

"It's all real, Mr. Perry, and you shouldn't forget that."

The mobile telephone went in his inside pocket. Could Bill Davies talk? No. When could he talk? In fifteen minutes. Would he call back soonest, when he could talk? In the guttering light they drove back to the village.

It was the second time he had asked the distance to the village—she said it was six and a half kilometers by road. He told her to stop, then told her when he would see her again at this precise place. He took her map, large-scale at four centimeters to a kilometer, and the sausage bag. There were trees close to the road and he went for them. He did not look back and he did not wave. Farida Yasmin Jones wondered what she would have to do to earn his trust and watched him until the trees hid him.

7

"Well, are you . . .?"

"God, it's not that simple."

"It's black-and-white . . . Are you going?"

"I'm trying to be sensible."

"Are you staying?"

"I said I wasn't going, I said I was staying."

"What, then, is the *problem*?"

The boy was upstairs. Davies had gone and Blake was in the car outside. They had come home. Perry had told Meryl that the policeman had dropped his gun in the playground. They had been responsible for a moment of blue panic. That was one problem. Davies had come to the front door fifteen minutes later with another problem.

"I want to stay."

"So stay."

"I don't want to go."

"So don't go."

"But I'm not told anything."

"Neither am I."

Davies had stood on the step. She would have seen the technique he used. He stood on the step, his body blocking the open doorway, and he had motioned Perry to stand back in the hallway. He had reached forward to the switch and turned off the hall light. Perry had been in the shadow, she behind him, their bodies protected by the policeman's. Davies had told them, calm and businesslike, that again he was offering his apologies for what had happened in the playground and repeated that Mr. Perry was perfectly entitled to request a change in personnel, and Perry had shaken his head.

Then the second problem was explained. Like a doctor at a bedside with a bad diagnosis to deliver, clearly and concisely, Davies had said that there was an upgrade in the threat-assessment level. The property was to be protected by armed uniformed officers; premises for them would be delivered in the morning; there would be additional personnel, mobile, assigned to the village. Davies hadn't said it, it was in his face, but they were going up the tough road; the easy road was to pack the suitcases. They had paced around the kitchen and worried at the problem. They had broken off the talk to eat with the boy before sending him upstairs, and starting at it again.

"What do they know?"

"They haven't told me."

"Why haven't they told you?"

"They don't explain. They never explain."

"What does it mean?"

His voice rose. "If you want to go, go."

"I don't want to go."

"Can we, then, leave it?"

"I'm just frightened. I'm frightened because we can't even talk about it. Is this our best effort at *conversation*?"

"Everything I know I've told you. Let's drop it."

"What sort of life . . .?"

"Better than running out of suitcases. It's home. It's our place. It's among our friends. So leave it or go."

He turned on the television. It was a quiz game and the audience bayed encouragement at the contestants going after giveaway money.

Bitterly, Perry wondered how many of them could have answered real questions. Where was Iran? What was the government of Iran? What was WMD? What was the requirement of mixing machines in the program for the development of chemical-agent warheads, and the requirement in the program for the development of ballistic missiles? What did they do with a fucking spy in Iran?

The telephone rang. The sound was suppressed by the shrieking of the studio audience. She heard it and jolted, but he didn't stir from his chair. He watched the ecstatic faces of the audience. The telephone rang a long time before she weakened and went to answer it.

She went into the kitchen, and it was silent.

He could not hear her voice.

He hated the game show, the moronic questions, the cacophony of applause.

The curtains were drawn, as the policeman had said they should be. He'd come into the darkened room and groped in the blackness towards the window and drawn the curtains, then groped back towards the standard lamp and switched it on. Before, they would not have drawn the curtains. Only their home tonight would have the curtains drawn. The drawn curtains separated them from the village, their neighbors and friends. Meryl had said that in the morning she would buy the lengths of net from which to make more curtains, and the boy had been told he was not to stand behind windows when the curtains weren't drawn, where he could be seen.

She came back into the room. She was biting her lower lip. She was pale.

She shouted, "Can't you turn that puerile bloody noise off?"

He hit the mute button on the remote.

"Who was it?"

"One of your friends."

"Who?"

"Emma Carstairs."

"What did she want?"

She spoke deliberately, but without emotion and without feeling. "Emma has dropped out of the school run with us. We won't be taking Sam, she won't be taking Stephen. Emma won't be coming to our house again, and Sam won't. It's dangerous to come to our house, your friend said, and she's not prepared to put Sam at risk."

"That's ridiculous." He pushed himself up from the chair.

"It's what she said."

He blustered. "I'll speak to her, and Barry."

She blocked his way. "She said she wouldn't speak to you. She said her decision was final. She said that if you rang her back she would put the phone down on you."

"The bloody cow."

"She said . . ."

"What did she say?"

"She said that it was selfish of us to expose others to danger, then she rang off."

"She's the only one, we're popular here, you see."

He heard, beyond the drawn curtain, a car's engine crawl by and wondered if it were the armed police. He felt the same chilly sweat as when he had come off the feeder flight and joined the emigration queue at Tehran for the international leg, as he had shuffled forward a small step at a time, dying to urinate, trying to appear unconcerned. He'd wondered then, as he did now, if the fear showed. The last time the sweat had soaked his shirt under his jacket as he had presented his passport at the desk. Behind the emigration official were always the penetrating eyes of the *pasdar* men, in their washed-thin uniforms, who leaned forward and stared in suspicion at the offered passport. When it was handed back, there was never a smile, no farewell joke, and he had walked away towards the departure lounge, his legs weak, fearing that they played with him and would let him go a few paces before the shout for him to come back. Each time as he'd slumped into the aircraft seat, before the engines gained power, before the steps were taken away, wondering whether they would allow him to settle before coming on board to heave him off, he'd felt the cold sweat, because he knew the fate of a spy in Iran.

Meryl had gone to the kitchen, and he heard her start to wash up the saucepans.

"Who's the PO?"

"An SB sergeant, Davies."

"He's useless. Who's on the other shift?"

"A DC, Blake."

"Next to useless. Who's in charge?"

"Box 500."

"Totally fucking useless—bloody lights, get on through."

Paget was driving the escort car, with Rankin beside him, through heavy traffic into the road junction as the lights changed to red. The prison van they followed had gone on, shouldn't have. The dozy beggar driving it should have checked his mirror, seen whether the escort car was clear to follow, but he hadn't. No bloody option for

Paget but to break the red light and follow across the junction. Rankin hit the siren button and the cars coming at them across the junction from right and left were braking and swerving to avoid them, all except one. The car heading straight for them was a battered old Cavalier with a toothy, gray-haired black at the wheel. They were two, three seconds from a disabling, side-on collision.

Rankin had his window down, the siren scream in his ears, and the H&K up. The gun was racked, bullet in the breach, and Rankin's thumb was resting on the lever at safe. As the escort team, they should have been right up behind the prison van. The guy in it was important, a drugs supplier and a bad bastard, on the daily run between the Old Bailey and the Brixton jail remand block. He had the contacts and cash resources to buy a rescue bid, which was why armed police escorted him each day from his cell to the court and back. The bullet was in the breach, Paget and Rankin were not there for the ride, and they knew it.

The old Cavalier was coming right for them, on target for the driver's door. If the bad bastard had bought a rescue, the copper-bottomed certainty was that the armed escort car would be isolated and rammed, taken out. Rankin was close enough to see, through the Cavalier's grimy windscreen, the gold teeth in the black's wide open mouth and the big mahogany eyes. Rankin's aim, held steady in the swaying escort car, was on the black's forehead. His thumb hardened on the safe lever.

If he shot to kill, the law was bloody vague. Section 3 of the Criminal Law Act, 1967, would back him if it were a genuine escape attempt and crucify him if it was only a traffic accident. They were on collision course and closing, and Paget was wrenching the wheel to avoid the old Cavalier, might succeed, might not. It'd take Rankin about half a second to depress the lever from safe and put a double tap, two bullets, through the man's forehead. He'd get a commendation if it was a rescue bid and a murder charge if it was not . . . And they were through, the junction cleared. Paget was accelerating like a mad idiot, wrong side of the road, to get back up behind the prison van, and in their wake, the old Cavalier had careered into a traffic bollard. The H&K was back on Rankin's lap.

"Where were we, Joe?"

No fast breathing, no taut hands, like it was a weekend run-out with the wife. "We were on about who was in charge, Dave—Box 500."

"What I said, totally fucking useless. Who's the principal?"

"Civilian, ordinary, an obstinate sod because they offered him the chance to bug out and he wouldn't."

"What's the opposition?"

"Iran—he's up the mullahs' noses."

"That's bloody choice, that's not clever. When do we get there?"

"Go down tonight, recce, take over in the morning from the half-arsed locals."

They had left a minor traffic accident behind them and were comfortably cozied up behind the prison van. Constables Joseph Paget and David Rankin were a team and inseparable. The driver, Paget, was a toadlike man, short and squat, bald with a thick Zapata mustache, and he had been changing the oil, checking the tire pressures, and valeting the interior during the long wait at the court, while his colleague had been given the new assignment's briefing. With the H&K resting loose on his thighs, Rankin was a wafer-thin willow of a man with a brush of cropped dark hair, the smooth-skinned complexion of a child, and a mustache identical to his colleague's. Anyone meeting them for the first time and noting their language and gait would have believed they made conscious efforts to ape each other. They were both forty-nine years old, lived in adjacent streets in north London, went on holiday together with their wives, and grumbled with each other like a married couple. They would retire on the same day. Both Joe Paget and Dave Rankin were considered expert marksmen. But they'd never done it. Been on the courses, been endlessly on the range, been on every exercise, but never actually done it. For all of their training and with a combined total of thirty-two years' service with firearms, neither had fired for real.

They saw the prison van go through the big gates of the jail, and swung away.

They stopped at a newsagent's and Paget went in. He bought three books of crossword puzzles, some soft drink cans, and two packets of sandwiches.

When he had come back up from the canteen and his supper, but before he went to Fenton's room to collect the American, Geoff

Markham took a single sheet of white paper and the roll of Sellotape from his desk. He fastened the paper to the outer face of his door, then scrawled on it, with a black marker pen, DAY ONE. The FBI man had said it would be over within a week. It was near to the end of the first day.

The American had gone off with Markham, and the fax purred onto Fenton's machine. He thought of Markham, like a worrying dog at the heels of a sheep as he'd rounded up the American, made sure he had his coat, gently chided him for fastening the buttons of his waistcoat out of kilter, and done them correctly himself. Sheep were stupid and willful, a bloody nuisance, and necessary . . . He read the fax from Special Branch operations.

Incredible, an eighth wonder, remarkable. SB had done a deal with the local force. Must have been the angle of the moon, or some such crap, for SB and a local force to have done a deal. He would have predicted an ongoing, entertaining dispute. SB would provide the close-protection detail and had liaised with SO19 of Scotland Yard for a static uniformed presence. The local force would offer armed vehicles to watch the single road into the godforsaken dead end and to cruise the area.

There was, had to be, a little scorpion's sting. At the tail of the message: "SB, on own behalf and that of local force, will negotiate with Security Service for budget funding during operation concerning Juliet Seven, with view to reimbursement of expenditure." It was the bare, basic level for protection, and it would cost a goddamn fortune, and the resources bucket was not bottomless. He pondered how to limit the extent of the commitment. He put on his coat, picked up his briefcase, and switched off the light in his room.

The budget ruled his life and would until the day he filed his application to join the Portcullis Society, until he joined the rest of yesterday's spooks at the Christmas reunion, reminiscing and carping about days gone by. The commitment could not be endless, and he cursed the bloody obstinate fool who had refused a most reasonable offer of help in moving on.

As if with a sudden afterthought, Fenton went back into his darkened room and dialed the home number of their duty solicitor. "Harry here, G Section, sorry to call you this late, Francis. Can I just run this past you? We have a man who we consider to be an assassination target. We've suggested he disappears and we've offered the means to do that. He won't take our advice, says he's staying where he is. Does the law provide us with powers to remove him forcibly from his domicile, against his will, and place him in protective custody? . . . I see . . . Assault, civil liberties, yes . . . Not on, eh? . . . It's just that these things are so bloody expensive. Thanks for your time, Francis, and regards to Alison . . ."

When he crossed the silent, deserted work area, Fenton saw the sheet of paper fastened to young Markham's door. DAY ONE.

There had to be a containment on the commitment or the operation would bleed his section dry. He went out into the night.

He had walked quickly along the hedgerows and into what the map called Sixteen-acre Wood and, from the safety of the trees, watched her drive away. With his back against a big trunk, Vahid Hossein used the last light of the day to study and memorize the map.

When darkness came and he could no longer see the trellised patterns of the upper branches, he had again moved forward.

The map was in his mind. He took a length of dead branch from the ground and used it as a blind man would. He had friends who were blinded in the marshes by mustard gas shells, and he used the stick in the darkness as they used their white wands in daylight. The stick told him where were the desiccated lengths of wood that he could have stepped on, broken, left a trail. He walked carefully from Sixteen-acre Wood into Big Wood, then onto Common Wood. From Common Wood he skirted open fields and then he sheltered by a road, and watched and waited and listened. The caution was instinctive. He had crossed the road and passed what the map called a tumulus but did not know what the word meant, and then he slipped into Fen Covert.

It was in Fen Covert that he first smelt the salt of the sea, and that he first heard the screaming.

The smell was soft, the same as the tang off the Shatt al Arab waterway and at the Faw peninsula. Then the screaming had come again.

At the Shatt al Arab and the Faw, when the salt scent had been in his nose, he had heard the screaming of a man wounded or gassed and left behind in the retreat. It had been his duty, then, inescapable, to go back into the marshes to find a man with a shrapnel-severed leg or with the gas droplets on his skin and in his eyes. He moved towards Fen Hill, catlike and quiet, where the scent was stronger and the screaming louder. Ahead of him, dappled by thin moonlight, was the open expanse called Southmarsh on the map.

At the slight slope of Fen Hill he angered himself. His mind had been on the scent and the screaming, and on the ribbon of lights that he estimated to be three kilometers away, when he set up a pheasant. If he had been among the marsh reeds of the Shatt al Arab or the Faw, he would have given his enemy his position. It would have been a fatal error. He stopped and stood motionless against a tree trunk so that his body made no silhouette, smelling the sea and listening to the screaming.

The distant sound of a car's horn, among the ribbon of lights, carried over the Southmarsh.

He found the rabbit, its throat caught by a snare. He did not use his torch, but felt it first with his stick and then with his hand. His fingers brushed the fur of the animal's back and then came to the restraining wire. The movement of his fingers, caressing it, had quietened the terror of the rabbit. He held it by the fur at its neck and loosened the fine wire. He could not see it, could only sense it hanging supine from his grip.

Because of his mistake in disturbing the pheasant, his anger and self-criticism, he felt a need to reassure himself. He killed the rabbit with a chop from the heel of his hand against its neck, one blow. He reset the snare and covered the ground where his feet had been with loose brushwood because at first light someone would come to check the snare. He pocketed the rabbit, dead and warm, and moved on.

He came to rest in the heart of a thick tangle of bramble on the edge of Foxhole Covert. Not for hunger, but to purge himself of his mistake, he tore a leg from the rabbit carcass, pulled the skin from it, and ate it. In his religion, rabbit was classified as *makroo*, a meat that was not preferred but one that could be eaten by a soldier in circumstances that were exceptional. He chewed on the raw sweet meat. It was important to him to feel no revulsion, to be strong. He chewed at the leg until his teeth scraped on the bone, then put the carcass beside him and the cleaned bone, and wiped the blood from his mouth. The act of killing and the eating gave him strength.

The sausage bag was beside him. Through the bramble branches he saw the close-set lights across the Southmarsh. He had the photograph of the house and the man. His hand, stained with the rabbit's blood, rested on the bag and sometimes found the shape of the launcher and sometimes the outline of the automatic rifle. He thought that it would be as easy for him to kill the man as it had been to chop the rabbit's neck and eat its leg.

He tried, lying on his back in the silence, to think of his wife, Barzin, and of the home that they shared, and of the rooms they had decorated, and of the possessions they had gathered together, and of the shy, darkened love between them, but the bare thighs of the girl in the car intruded and disturbed him. He could not shake from his mind the white skin of the girl and the outline of her breasts. Vahid Hossein tried, but he could not.

The bell rang three times.

Meryl said she would answer it. She said coldly that she didn't want to see him cowering in the shadow of the unlit hallway again when the door was opened. The detectives had said they'd use three short blasts on the bell when they wanted entry to the house.

Blake was at the door and seemed surprised that she opened it. His face fell a little when he saw her. She thought he would be one of those creatures who expected only to deal with the man of the house. Blake said, fumbling for the words, that there were more personnel down from London, uniformed, armed, and static, and that they needed to look over the house. She thought him supercilious. He did not ask whether it was convenient, but stood aside for them as they came out of the darkness. They shouldered past her as if she did not exist, and pushed the door shut behind them.

Frank stood in the living room doorway. She heard the names they gave him, Paget and Rankin. She grimaced, a bitter little smile, because neither asked Frank if it suited him, just said that they needed to walk round the house, look it over. They went together, as if there was an umbilical cord between them.

They wore blue-black overalls and webbing belts, on which were holsters and weapons and what she thought were gas canisters, ammunition pouches, and handcuffs. When they had been waiting for her to answer the bell, they must have been in the mud at the side of the road and the green, and their boots smeared it over her carpet. They seemed not to notice. They looked around the living room, at her furniture and her ornaments, as if they were all dross, and the glass cabinet where she put the china pieces she'd collected, and the pictures of the seashore, prints by the local artist that Frank had bought. She strained to hear the murmur of their voices.

"Have to get it taped up, Joe."

"Too right, Dave, nothing worse than glass cabinets."

"Have to get the pictures down."

"What you think of where the television is?"

"Not happy, should be back against the wall, right back."

"Shouldn't Davies have done this?"

"Should have, didn't."

"Pillock—I don't like all the stuff on the fireplace."

"Quite right. Let's do the windows."

The tall one, Rankin, went to the standard lamp and switched it off. She stood in the darkness and could sense the rising impatience of Frank beside her, could hear the sharp spurts of his breath. The curtains were pulled back. A faint glow eased into the room from the street lights on the opposite side of the green. She heard the scrape of their fingers on the glass and the window casing, then the noise as the curtains were yanked without ceremony into place. Only then was the standard lamp switched on again.

"Thought they were supposed to have been laminated, Joe."

"They haven't got round to it—the work order's in, be done by the end of the week."

"Bloody marvelous."

"I don't like that window, Dave, not without the lamination."

"Don't tell me, I've got bloody eyes. What is it, a hundred meters, to those houses? A sniper, piece of cake, or an RPG."

"What you say, Dave, piece of cake for a rocket launcher or a rifle. God, this place needs sorting out. Come on . . ."

They did the hall, the dining room, and the kitchen. Frank trailed behind them and she followed. She didn't have to ask. Everything that was glass, china, or pottery, everything that was heavy and un-attached, would shatter, fracture and fly, maim and wound. They said they needed to see upstairs. She stiffened. Frank muttered that they should go upstairs if that was necessary, but they hadn't waited for his answer and were already on their way up. There wasn't any more mud from Rankin's boots to dirty the carpet. They looked around her bedroom.

"Don't like the mirror, Dave."

It was the big mirror on her dressing table.

"Tape it over."

She imagined the mirror, where she made up, where she worked the delicate brushes before they went out for an evening, with pack-ers' adhesive tape crossing it.

"Look at all that loose stuff."

On her dressing table were the cream jars and the glass *eau-de-toi-lette* bottles, the vase of dried flowers, and the silver-backed hair-brushes.

"Have to get it boxed up, Joe."

She would have to rummage in a cardboard box on the floor for her eyeliner and lipstick. She imagined everything that was precious to her put away on the instructions of these men.

The pictures would have to come down, of course. The photo-graph frames would have to be put into the drawers, and she won-dered if she would be allowed to take out the photographs and stick them to the walls, if they would permit that. In the bathroom, at the back of the house, she couldn't have said they lingered on anything that was hers. They were merely indifferent to each item that be-longed and mattered to her. Better if they had lingered on them be-cause then the items might have seemed important. They went into the spare room and discussed what should happen to the pictures, the mirror, and the ornaments there. They paused on the landing outside the last door. It was as if they had kicked the fight out of her, and the resentment was flushed on Frank's cheeks, but neither of them protested. She could hear her boy's voice, making the noise of a lorry. They didn't ask her to go first, or Frank. The short one went in, the tall one behind him.

"Hello, sunshine—my word, aren't they brilliant?"

"Great lorries, sunshine, proper little haulage business."

"Just call me Uncle Joe . . ."

". . . and I'm your uncle Dave, that's a real good one, the Seddon Atkinson lorry."

"The Seddy's good, Dave, but the Volvo's fantastic."

"It's a great fleet, sunshine . . . No, sorry, don't touch."

"What's your name? Stephen? Well, Stephen, you mustn't touch what's on Uncle Dave's belt. It's gas, it's handcuffs, and it's the Glock . . . Like what? . . . He did what? That must have been fun, sunshine. You hear that, Joe? DS Davies chucking his Glock round the playground—that's nice to store away for when he gets all pompous. I expect it's time you were in bed, sunshine . . ."

The door was closed softly. They had come, she thought, effortlessly, into her family's life and brought with them their gas, their handcuffs, and their guns. And in the morning, her home would be prepared for defense against a sniper's attack and against the devastation of a rocket launcher's explosion. When they had gone outside, into the back garden, she went for the vacuum cleaner to remove the mud they'd left on her carpets, and before she started it up she heard Frank's voice.

"Don't ever do that again. Don't dare ever treat me and my wife like we're rubbish. We're human beings and deserve to be treated with decency and respect. This is our home, so show a bit of sensitivity when you come into it. Don't look at me in that dumb, insolent way, just don't. We live here. If that's not convenient, soft shit."

She didn't hear their reply.

When they'd finished in the garden and gone out through the front door, and it had been bolted and locked again, while she was in the living room with the vacuum cleaner, she heard Blake's voice.

"You shouldn't have done that, sir, bawled them out. They're at the end of a pretty long day. But don't worry, they won't take it personally, they're used to principals being stressed up. But you shouldn't have bawled them out, sir. One day you might depend on them to save your life, one day soon."

"This is not a zoo. You don't come here to rubberneck. It's a working area—you're causing disruption."

He'd been told but it had slipped his mind. It could have been the fourth time the detectives had confronted the duty doctor, but it was more likely to have been the fifth.

"I will say when you can talk to my patient—and it is the same answer as the last time, and the time before that. No. My patient is severely concussed, quite apart from the effect of the drugs alleviating the pain of a triple femur fracture. No."

They were at the end of the ward. Beside the door to the partitioned cubicle, Geoff Markham hovered a pace behind the two Branch detectives. The doctor was young, harassed, probably sleepwalking and on the edge of his temper.

"It is not my concern what my patient is alleged to have done, my concern is his health and welfare. I understand he has been neither cautioned nor charged. So, he is in my care, and I decide if he is to be questioned. My answer . . . No."

A policeman was sitting beside the bed on a hard chair, facing the door, his hands on the snub weapon resting on his legs, his face impassive. The second uniformed policeman sat outside the door, cradling his own gun, a wry smile flickering at his mouth.

"I tell you, it's bad enough for my patients to have guns paraded around, but right now they are trying, unsuccessfully, to get the rest they need. They are not resting, as they should be, because this ward is being treated by you like a high-street pavement. Just get out, go away."

Geoff Markham's fingers were locked together, clasped tight, flexing hard enough to hurt. He thought Seitz was somewhere behind him. The American had said this was the big and lucky break, but it didn't seem as if they knew how to use it.

"Just listen to me. You are interfering with the running of this ward. I will protest most strongly in the morning to the administrators about that interference. If the condition of this patient, or any other patient in the ward, were to deteriorate because of your refusal to accept my guidance, then I will make it my personal business to see you broken. Get off my territory."

There was a dull blue sheen of light in the cubicle. Geoff Markham thought, could have sworn to it, that he saw an eye glinting from the mound of white pillows. The head of the patient, the face that Rainbow Gold had identified as Yusuf Khan, was half hidden by the left leg raised in traction. The glint was momentary, but he'd seen it.

The patient now seemed unmoving, unconscious. The detectives turned away.

Markham said, "He's fooling you."

"You're a doctor? Familiar with this case history, are you?"

Markham persisted, "He's alert, listening. He's feigning."

"You're an expert on concussion? You know about the effects of pain-depressant drugs?"

"What I am telling you—"

"No. I do the telling on my ward, and I am telling you to get out."

Markham spat, "There could be blood on your hands."

"I doubt it."

"A man could be murdered because of your refusal—"

"Get out."

He had failed to exploit the break. The faces of the uniformed policemen were expressionless, as though they didn't need to tell him that he'd made a right idiot of himself. Geoff Markham turned angrily and walked up the central aisle of the ward towards the low light at the far end where the night sister sat at her table. The detectives were alongside and he could hear the soft pad of the doctor behind him. He saw the American sitting on a visitor's chair, in deep shadow, against a patient's locker. The patient was passing him a grape, and before he took it the American had his finger on his lips. Markham kept walking.

Beyond the ward's swing doors, there was a last snapped question: "How long?"

The doctor said that it might be two days and it might be three, or it might be a week, before his patient could be interrogated.

He walked on down the empty corridors. The Branch men were with him, said they were looking for a coffee machine. His footfall stamped to the stairs.

There was a fight in Casualty reception. A drunk with blood streaming from a forehead wound swung a fist at the security people. He didn't care and threaded his way past them.

He went to the parking area and his car.

He wished he smoked. He wished he had a hip flask. He wished he was warm and wet-sweaty with Vicky. He wished he worked for a fucking bank.

He sat in the car.

The wail of a siren approached, and he watched the staff gather at the door to meet it, the flurry as the stretcher was hurried inside.

He waited. He was cold, tired. He had seen how the bastard had watched them, listened to them, fooled them, and the first day of the week was ten minutes off its end. And he couldn't imagine why Seitz had found it important to stay behind.

He was slumped in self-pity, and wondered whether the bank would turn him down by letter or by telephone. Damn sure they wouldn't accept him. He wouldn't tell Vicky what he'd said, about playing God, or tell her how her buzz phrases had been sneered at . . . The American eased the car door open and lowered himself into the seat.

"First, thanks for being so on the ball and giving me space. You did well. Jesus, what depressing places hospitals are . . . You see, Mr. Markham, it's all about Alamut . . . the sort of places we'll all end in, not able to do a lot about it . . . Alamut is the key . . ."

Markham began to drive away, and had to swerve out of the path of another ambulance.

"I'd need convincing I did anything well. Right, Mr. Seitz, tell me why Alamut is relevant."

"If he had known Alamut, been there, then he wouldn't have talked to me."

Markham gasped, then laughed out loud. "Why, Mr. Seitz, did he talk to you?"

"The policemen were very cooperative, heard what you said, about blood and murder. One needed a piss, so the other took his place in the corridor."

"Why?"

"I guess he talked to me because I poked the tip of my pen into the middle of the three femur fractures."

"Didn't he scream?"

"He probably did, but I had my handkerchief and my fist over his mouth. He wanted to talk more than he wanted the poke of my pen—if he'd been to Alamut then he wouldn't have cared about the pain."

"What did he say?"

Markham drove recklessly fast on the open road.

"Hey, Mr. Markham, would you slow down, please? I don't want to be going back to that place on my back—ease it off, please. He said the guy came off a boat, and I told him we knew that. I hadn't a name, and neither had he. I hadn't a face, but he had. The face is interesting, it's pale-colored, it's what I imagine to be the edge of Caucasian, and there's no facial hair. English, English accent, not American. Tall but not exceptional, hair not black matte, didn't get the eyes . . . Age would be late thirties. He crashed the car because the guy sort of frightened him."

"Weapons?"

"He started to tell me—I think he was trying to talk about a launcher. Yes, he wanted to tell me the whole thing, I had the pen right in front of his face, but he didn't. I think he wanted to tell me, but he fainted."

"Associates?"

"The faint wasn't acted. He got another poke, but he was out cold, like Smoky Joe had hit him—and the law came back from its piss."

"So what do we have, Mr. Seitz?"

"Enough to think about. May I, first, educate you on Alamut? With education, you get to understand the Anvil, what he'll do, the sense of sacrifice, the danger he poses, the dedication to his orders. In the year 1152, Mr. Markham, two of the Fida'is were sent from Alamut to kill Raymond the Second of Tripoli, that's the port city in present-day northern Lebanon. Raymond the Second was the Christian crusader king. They chose the most public place in his city to kill him, where he would be surrounded by the maximum security. The place they chose was the main gate of the city. Imagine it, crowds, traders, travelers, guards, the greatest audience in front of which to demonstrate their power and their commitment. They stabbed Raymond the Second to death at the gate of his own city, and they would have known that within moments they would be chopped into small pieces by his guards. That's Alamut for you, Mr. Markham, that's what you're up against."

He pretended to sleep and made a pattern of his breathing.

Her breasts and stomach were against his back and his buttocks. They were naked in the bed, but for comfort's sake, not for loving.

Sometimes he heard the engine of the car parked beside the house, as if Blake boosted the heater. Sometimes he heard a car coming slowly by and stopping; then there were quiet voices and chuckled laughter. Sometimes there was the empty whistling of the wind, and the distant ripple surge of the sea on the beach.

If he pretended to sleep and his breathing was regular, then he hoped it would be easier for her to sleep.

He lay on his side with her warmth against him and he played the television's quiz game in his mind. The grinning show host asked the questions, and bright-eyed Frankie answered them.

Where was Iran?

"Iran, with a territory of 1.68 million square kilometers and a population estimated in excess of sixty million, is at a pivotal geopolitical position between the Middle East and the Asian subcontinent, where it cannot be ignored and is unlikely to be humored."

What was the government of Iran?

"Iran is ruled by Islamic clerics categorized as fundamentalist and conservative in the extreme, but the government has loose relationships with the organizations of the Revolutionary Guards corps and the autonomous private armies of clerics boasting vengeful actions against Western cultures."

What was WMD?

"Weapons of mass destruction, chemical and microbiological and nuclear, are all the subject of urgent research programs in Iran."

What was the requirement for mixing machines?

"The manufacture of the chemical air droplets to be included in the warhead, and for the lining material of the interior of the missile body that must withstand extreme temperature, requires dual-purpose mixing machines sold on fraudulently prepared export dockets."

What was the fate of a spy in Iran? What did they do with a spy in Iran?

"A spy in Iran is either hanged in secret on the gallows at the Evin jail, or hanged in public from a crane in a Tehran square and hoisted so high that the crowd can better see his death dance."

A final question. Had to answer correctly to win the holiday for two in Barbados and the new-fitted kitchen, the food liquidizer, and the wide-screen television. He squirmed in the bed.

What were the consequences in Iran of the spy's report on a military factory at Bandar Abbas?

"Don't know, can't answer, was never told, don't want to know, better not knowing."

To black, to the darkness of the room, and no prizes to carry away.

He took a point on the shadowed wall, stared at it. She was asleep. If he slept he would dream of the crane. She didn't know of the crane, and she slept. There was a small gale of laughter from the side of the house, and a car drove away. He was drifting . . . He had always rather fancied Emma Carstairs, and always thought she rather fancied him . . . drifting, but not sleeping. If he thought of Emma Carstairs, her bold smile, and her wriggling her hips to work off her knickers, her hands taking his to the buttons of her blouse, then he wouldn't sleep, and if he didn't sleep, then he wouldn't see the crane. He stared at the bare wall.

8

In the last minutes of the night he moved like a wraith.

He came off Fen Hill and kept inside the tree line, skirting the end of the marshland. The high winter tides, blown by storms, and the heavy winter rainfall had made the ground he covered into a swampy bog. The water was always above his ankles and sometimes above his knees, but he left no visible track of his advance, and he was hidden by the tree line. He left behind him the carefully concealed sausage bag and the weapons because, at this time, he had no need of them.

When he came to a small stream feeding the marsh it was necessary for him to wade up to his waist, the sediment clawing at his boots and his legs. The higher ground of Hoist Covert, the name he had read from his map, was ahead of him, and the faint outline of the church tower loomed beyond it.

He moved fast. Once he was out of the bog land and the marsh, he did not stop to unfasten the laces of his boots and empty out the stale dark water and the mud. It was all familiar to him. He crossed the ground as if he were again in the Haur-al-Hawizeh reeds. It gave him comfort to be on familiar ground. He did not move as a trained soldier would, working from instructions and manuals, but used instead the innate skills of a predator. He did not have to consider the dangers of silhouette, of breaking cover, of leaving a scented track behind him. It was natural to Vahid Hossein that he should go as a stalking animal searching for a prey.

He had kept a steady pace and broke it only once when he had seen a single man come with binoculars and sit on a bench between Hoist Covert and a path that led back to the church. He stopped then and checked the ground ahead of, behind, and to the side of the man and watched the traverse of his binoculars. He was only twenty meters from the man when he passed him, in scrub cover. He assumed that the man had come to the bench to watch for birds from the viewpoint that overlooked the marshes; it was a point squirreled in his mind for future attention.

He moved on past high fences and garden hedges and a sign marking a narrow worn path towards the village.

He climbed a fence and used garden shrubs to mask his movement. He crawled on his stomach through a gap in a hedge, lifted a length of chicken wire to go under it, and replaced it. Twice he was within five meters of a house and could hear voices inside, but he kept from the arc of light thrown from the windows. Once he stopped and retraced his steps because a back door opened and a dog, bouncing and barking, was put out to run on a patch of grass. He needed to know where the dogs were: they were a greater enemy than the people.

The houses he went by were of old brick. Some were the homes of artisans, with wilderness gardens stacked with rubbish bags and discarded kids' bicycles, as they would have been in south Tehran. Some were the homes of the affluent, with little tended squares of lawn, heaps of raked leaves, and the smell of dead bonfires, as there would have been around the villas on the slopes above Jamaran where the *tagt-ut-tee* lived, the idol worshipers who only pretended to respect the teachings of the imam.

It was for reconnaissance. It was to find the way in and know the way out.

He heard the noise of cars ahead, slowing and changing down through their gears. He was beside a fence and hidden by ornamental bushes from a small path. It was well timed . . . He had arrived at his vantage place when it was light enough for him to see ahead, and dark enough to preserve his cover. It was the few minutes of the point between night and day. He could not yet see the vehicles because bushes were blocking his view. He lay very still. A woman in a night robe came out of her door and he heard the clink of the bottles she carried. The light above her door flooded the path as she went to the gate. The empty bottles rattled onto the concrete and she went back inside, slamming the door behind her. He saw the lights of cars rolling across the houses ahead of him, and illuminating the open ground.

He crawled on. The photographs of the house and the target man were seared into his memory.

He heard the mutter of low voices as the engines of the cars were killed. The voices were indistinct.

On his knees and elbows he edged forward, and gently parted the branches and leaves of a garden shrub.

He felt the shake in his hands . . .

There was a police car, with two men in it, a dozen meters from him.

Beyond the police car was the open grassland of the photograph, and beyond the open ground were two more cars. Four men stood beside them. Two wore civilian clothes. The others wore blue overalls, and across their chests they carried machine guns on straps.

He felt the cold twist in his stomach.

Beyond the cars was the house shown in the photograph. All the curtains were drawn, and no light showed. He had been told the target was without defense, had no protection. He thought the men in front of the house were changing shifts. He watched. The car nearest to him started up, and the roving eyes of the marksman and the barrel of a machine gun peeped above the door and out through the opened window as it edged slowly away. One of the men at the house was stretching, arching his back, as if he had stayed the night in his vehicle.

The two men with the machine guns went to the door of the house in the photograph: he saw their wariness and that one covered the back of the other. When the door was opened there was no light in the hallway. It was professional protection. They went inside and the door closed on them. If he had come a few moments later he would not have seen the machine guns.

He had the photograph of the man and wanted to look into his face as he took the knife or the gun from under his coat: it was important that the man could see his face and the eye of vengeance.

He slipped away. He crawled through the hedgerow, pulled back the length of chicken wire, climbed the fence, and scurried in the growing light towards the scrub and the shelter of Hoist Covert.

He waded the stream, then staggered across the bog among the trees. It was not the threat from the machine guns to his own life that made his hands shake and his breath pant. He would be carried as a martyr to the Garden of Paradise; he had no fear of death from the bullets. It was the fear of failure. The brigadier, the man who loved him as a son, who had replaced his long-dead father, would be waiting in the office high in the building of the Ministry of Information and Security for news of his success. Vahid Hossein could not contemplate the cloud passing over the face of the brigadier if the message carried word of failure.

He came through the trees onto Fen Hill and stopped dead in his tracks.

He had seen the bird.

The beak, tugging, and the talons, clinging, were at the rabbit's carcass. He saw the raw wound on its wing. The bird was at the limit of its strength. Its beak was tearing at the fur but had not the power to rip it aside. It was less than five paces away. He saw the wound and the movement of ants in it, and the color of the flesh at the wing was not pink and pure but putrefied, like the old wounds of the men in the Haur-al-Hawizeh. The bird flapped the damaged wing and the good wing as if to flee from him, but the strength was not there and it only hopped, crippled, a few meters from the carcass. He knew the harriers from the Haur-al-Hawizeh and from the Shatt al Arab and Faw. They were often with them as they hid up in the marshes and watched for the Iraqis, waited for the darkness and the opportunity to probe into their enemy's defenses. He had grown to love them, to worship the beauty of their feathering. They were light, the harriers, in the darkness of the killing grounds. He dropped to his knees and crawled forward slowly to the carcass. The wound would kill the bird if it could not feed.

With his fingers, he tore little strips of flesh from the rabbit.

Vahid Hossein believed the hunger would defeat the bird's fear, and that the bird was his escape from failure.

He took the black felt pen and the clean sheet of paper to his door, ripped off the existing message, and fastened on its replacement. He scrawled the words. DAY TWO.

It was seven forty-nine. The traffic had not yet built up on the Embankment outside Thames House, but already they were at their desks. Geoff Markham had come in on the underground before the crush, but they had beaten him there. Cox was in to supervise the expansion. Fenton was huddled with the American, chuckling, as if they were conspirators. Gary Brennard was there from Administration (Resources), organizing the new team, their new consoles and new telephones. A red-haired woman, Markham recognized her from one of the Irish sections but didn't know her name, was sitting, scratching her head and wiping her eyes, looking like she'd been heaved half awake from her bed. There were two probationers and one of the old men from B Branch. They were in early, as if they feared they might miss the entertainment.

He'd slept in his own bed at his own place, and there'd been four messages from Vicky on his answerphone. How'd it go? Did you do all right? Was it OK? Did you do enough to get it? He went back into his partitioned office room. Overnight, in his own bed, he hadn't thought about the interview but about the American with his pen, and whether that constituted a criminal assault, whether it was a sacking offense, whether he was just too damn squeamish for the job. He'd make the call later in the morning. When the new team was bedded down, he'd ring Perry.

He wandered across the open work area towards the new cluster of desks and screens. He went by the woman with the red hair. She seemed tired and uninvolved, was flicking the pages of a newspaper—maybe nobody had told her, maybe they'd told her and she didn't think it mattered. Fenton's laugh was louder.

Fenton said, "Morning, Geoff, just hearing about last night—damn good."

He said it grimly. "What we did was illegal."

"Bollocks."

Fenton strode away.

The American sidled over to him. "Sleep OK, Mr. Markham? Not so well? Listen, it's a rough world and rougher when the stakes get high. You have to play hard if you want to win. Remember Alamut and then you can judge your enemy. Do it by the rules and your enemy will walk over you. They came out from Alamut, two of them in 1192. Their target was Conrad of Montferrat, who was the king-elect of Jerusalem. They caught up with him finally in the city of Tyre, present-day south Lebanon, but they'd stalked him nearly half a year. He was guarded close, had the best security of the day, and they beat it. They were dressed as Christian monks, the clothes of their enemy. They went right through the security and knifed their man to death. The way they did it, they condemned themselves, but they reached their target. Go legal if you want to—if you do, you won't win against cunning, patience, ruthlessness, dedication . . . Is there anywhere you can get decent coffee around here?"

She'd been up early to take the pictures off the bedroom walls, and had stacked them, glass down, behind the dressing table. Everything off the top surface of her dressing table had gone into the drawers. Then she'd crisscrossed the mirror with heavy adhesive tape. Frank had watched her from the bed.

She'd snatched breakfast, and dumped a plate of cereal down in front of Stephen. She was already late for the school bell.

They'd been changing the shift at home when she had left—nothing to say to her, nor to Frank, but the uncles had time to chat with Stephen about his lorries. She'd had to drag him away from them. On their shoulders they'd had machine guns on webbing straps. She'd thrust Stephen into the car and Frank had stayed inside.

Emma Carstairs had once told Meryl that she had best-friend status. They'd been to dinner there three months before. Emma Carstairs would have said to Barry, she thought, that Frank and Meryl Perry were the right sort of people for the village. Barry had put work Frank's way and joked about keeping things close, in a little Mafia. The loss of the friendship hurt badly.

Meryl hadn't faced up to telling Stephen why they didn't have Sam in the car now, had made instead a poor excuse about a grown-ups' squabble. She'd have to tell him properly, but later. Probably there would be things said at school, but she couldn't yet cope with telling him the complicated truth. A van was parked beside the road, and she saw a man reaching up to hammer a Sold sign across the middle of the For Sale board outside Rose Cottage. She wondered who'd bought it and what they'd be like.

She drove fast to the school and had to brake fiercely to avoid a car pulling away from the curb. Most of the kids were already in.

She frowned. Barry Carstairs drove a sporty Audi, provided by his building-suppliers company. It was parked outside the school gate, three vehicles ahead of her. Barry never did the school run. She kissed Stephen and pushed open his door. The child ran through the playground gate towards the door of the main building, where he was stopped by Mr. Archer, the deputy head. He had one hand on the child's shoulder, and with the other he was waving her to come to him.

Several of those who didn't have jobs with regular hours helped with the painting, the reading, and the lunches of the nursery class. She knew Mr. Archer, a little ferret of a man, and the talk was that he was slyly bitter at being ignored for the headship. She saw Stephen try to pull away from him, as the bell went inside. Archer's fist, clenched in the material of Stephen's anorak, restrained him. She stamped across the playground.

He didn't look her in the face.

"Mrs. Kemp would like to see you, Mrs. Perry."

"Why are you holding Stephen like that?"

He looked at the ground, then at the sky. "If you could go, please, to Mrs. Kemp's office."

"Why are you preventing Stephen from joining his class?"

"It will all be explained, Mrs. Perry. They're waiting for you."

"You're making Stephen late for class."

"He'll be in the common room—I'll be with him."

Kids knew. They always knew first. Stephen's face was blank. At home last night, he'd worked really hard at his writing, was proud of it, before he'd pulled out his lorries and the men had come to his room. His exercise was in his satchel with his lunch. She told him, ignored the ferret, that she'd sort it out, and fast. She stormed down the corridor, didn't knock, pushed her way into Mrs. Kemp's office.

From the door, her eyes roved over the faces. There was Mrs. Kemp, trim and gray-haired, the head teacher; Bellamy, overweight and everybody's friend, the self-appointed organizer of the PTA; Barry Carstairs, the smart-suited businessman who was going places, the chairman of the governors; and a woman with fiercely bobbed hair and a severe black trouser suit. The men were either side of the women, and they were all huddled close against the legs of the desk.

The head teacher's voice piped at her, "Thank you for coming in, Mrs. Perry. Please sit down."

"Why am I here?"

"Just sit down, Mrs. Perry, please. You'll know everyone here, except Miss Smythe from the county's education department."

She remained standing. "What's going on?"

The head teacher fixed her with a glance. "I am afraid I have something difficult to tell you."

"What?"

Bellamy grunted, "It's pretty obvious, Mrs. Perry, after yesterday afternoon."

"What's obvious?"

Carstairs tried to look somber. "There was a very disturbing incident affecting the school yesterday, Meryl, which cannot be ignored."

Her child, with the ferret's hand on his anorak, knew. Stephen was in the common room, and would be scared half out of his wits. She stood her ground and glowered. "So, which of you's queuing to use the knife?"

"That's not called for. We have a responsibility—"

"It's a responsibility we're not ignoring."

Barry Carstairs didn't look at her. He was playing with a pencil and he'd scribbled words on a pad, as if he didn't trust himself without notes. "This isn't easy for us. As chairman of the governors, after consultations with our head teacher and bearing in mind the feelings of the parents' representative, I have taken a most serious decision. Yesterday, your husband came to the school to collect Stephen. He was, we now know, accompanied by an armed bodyguard. It was not his intention that the presence of the bodyguard should be known, and that was an act of deceit. The bodyguard, after a grossly irresponsible incident with his pistol—an incident that could have led to the gun firing in a crowded playground—in the head teacher's hearing, spoke to the local police after she, quite rightly, had called them. In his explanation to the local police, he spoke of a threat to your husband that necessitates his constant protection from terrorist attack. We feel, after very careful consideration, that a threat to your husband represents, also, a threat against your husband's family—"

"You're blathering, Barry. Why don't you say what you mean?"

Carstairs pushed aside his notes. There was a curl of anger at his lips. "I was trying to do it the decent way. What Frank's done, what's in his sordid past, I don't know and I don't care. What matters is that his family is exposed to bombs and guns, in our school. The children and staff here are all threatened by terrorists. Their safety is paramount. Stephen, as much as his stepfather or his mother, could be a target. If he is a target, then everyone at this school is a target. He's out, he's no longer welcome here."

"You can't do that, not to a child."

The woman, Miss Smythe, leaned forward to intervene, and spoke with a low, intense voice. "We can do it, Mrs. Perry, and we are doing it. My department, after full consideration of the facts, has decided to back the governors' recommendation. We're foursquare behind them. As soon as is practical we will communicate with you on proposals for alternative education for Stephen, but I can't say when that will be. A thought, Mrs. Perry. Is it possible for Stephen to move away, stay with an uninvolved relative, and attend school elsewhere?"

"It is not. We are together, a family."

"Then he'll have to sit at home," Carstairs said. "I'm sure Mrs. Kemp'll loan you some books—but he's not coming back here."

"You are despicable. You are, Barry Carstairs, always have been, a second-rate rat, always will be."

"As of now, Stephen is no longer a pupil at this school. Take him home."

"And Frank thought of you, and your stupid wife, as a friend."

"Your problems aren't ours, they don't concern us, get off back home. And when you get home you should call for a removal van and take your problems away. You're pariahs, you're not wanted."

There was so much she could have said. Meryl thought, in that moment, that weeping and pleading would have shamed her. She eyed them with contempt and none of them could meet her gaze. Once before she had been through the business of shame, and she would not go there again. No begging, no cringing, not then and not now. Nine years before, she had resigned from the haulage business where she worked the logistics computer, four months after the Christmas party. Hadn't been drunk, incapable, before that party, or since. Too drunk, too incapable, to know which of the men had done it. It could have been any of the thirty-eight drivers, twelve loaders, three managers, and two directors. She would have needed DNA testing to learn which was the father of the embryo baby. She turned. Living with Frank, loving him, bringing up her child together had erased the shame. She left them behind her, the silence clinging in the room, and strode down the corridor to fetch her son from the common room.

They would be watching her from the head teacher's office as she led the child back across the empty playground towards the car; their faces would be pressed against the glass. She had shown them defiance, but by the time she reached the car the pain and the despair hit her.

With her boy beside her, she drove into the town center to buy the length of net from which she would make the curtains.

Classification: SECRET.

Date: 4 April 1998.

Subject: JULIET SEVEN.

Transcript of telephone conversation (secure using SB mobile at Juliet 7 location) between GM, G Branch, and Juliet 7.

GM: Hello? Mr. Perry? Good, got you. I'm Geoff Markham, I came down to see you with Mr. Fenton. 'Fraid I didn't make much of a contribution. This is a secure call. What I mean is, we can talk frankly. There's a bit to talk about . . . Are you there?

J7: I'm here. What is there to talk about?

GM: You appreciate my difficulty, the same as before. It's the same difficulty as Mr. Fenton had?

J7: You've a difficulty—very funny. Try your difficulty on me.

GM: The difficulty is that I cannot share sources of information available to us.

J7: Join the queue—nobody tells me anything.

GM: Let's try to keep calm. That way we make better decisions.

J7: What decisions?

GM: This is not easy. Frankly, the situation around you and your family has deteriorated, we believe.

J7: Spell it out.

GM: That's my difficulty. As I've already explained, I cannot—

J7: Because you don't trust me. Nobody [expletive] trusts me—that's why I intend to make my own [expletive] decisions.

GM: Please, please, listen to me. My judgment, based on information I am privy to, is that you and your family should relocate—

J7: Your judgment—you can shove it up your [expletive].

GM: I used the word "deteriorated"—I'm not using that word lightly. You should go—hear me out. We can make all the arrangements within a matter of hours.

J7: I provided information, and I am not trusted sufficiently to be told what use that information was put to.

GM: That, too, is one of my difficulties. I, too, am not need-to-know on that information.

J7: Then stop playing bloody errand boy and [expletive] well find out— Wait.

[Pause of 38 seconds.]

J7: Meryl's just come home. She took her son to school, and was told at school that they're barring the boy—[expletive] bastards. You think I'll run away because of the say-so of those [expletive] bastards? Think again.

GM: It is a situation of grave danger.

J7: I'm not running, not again. This is my home.

GM: Perhaps you would reconsider when matters are less fraught.

J7: I make my own decisions. I am staying. (Call terminated.)

The tanker, moored at the offshore jetty, had started to unload its cargo of 287,000 tonnes of crude. The master stood with his engineer officer on the small stern deck behind the tower of the bridge and accommodation block. The inflatable, covered by tarpaulin sheeting, was stowed beside them. They discussed a schedule. It was important for them to plan the length of time the tanker spent there for the crew to take shore leave, and the sailing time back into the English Channel. Time was critical. The great tanker should not reach the point in the Channel too early or too late to make the pickup. Neither man entertained the slightest doubt that he would be on the beach, and that an enemy of their country would, a few hours before, have been justifiably killed. They made calculations: because they had been delayed in taking their place at the offshore jetty it seemed unlikely that the crew would enjoy more than a few hours of shore leave in the Swedish port.

The restaurant was on no list in good-eating guides that Harry Fenton had ever seen, but it was where the Israeli had said they should meet. It was an unpredictable place for the Mossad station officer to have chosen, and one where it was unlikely his enemies would look for him.

"So, Harry, you are confused. You are confused because you have spoken with your foreign-affairs people, who are an apparatus of appeasement. They're telling you that Iran is misunderstood, more sinned against than sinning, and wants only to be permitted to take a rightful place in the affairs of that region. Allow me, because you are paying for this excellent food, to disabuse you of what you have been told and to further your confusion. Before he was killed, Rabin tried to alert the international community to the need to 'strike at this viper and crush its skull,' and he was a man criticized in his own yard as a peacemonger. They were strong words from a man vilified for attempting a deal with the Syrian, Lebanese, and Palestinian enemies. Why?"

They were in the farther reaches of east London, under railway arches and facing a line of boarded-up shops. It was small, dingy, and frankly, unclean, but the Israeli said the restaurant served the best Afghan cooking in the city. He ate with enthusiasm. Fenton was less sure.

"Why? Because we, in Israel, understand the real threat. We understand it while many in Europe refuse to open their eyes. Everywhere a bomb explodes or a bullet impacts we find the fingerprint of Iran. They pay for, equip, and train the Hezbollah in the Lebanon, and Hamas for the Palestinians. The bombs on our buses, in our vegetable markets, are placed by proxy but they are theirs. Yet what they're doing now is only a pinprick, Harry, in comparison with what they intend."

The Israeli pushed the cleaned plate away from him, wiped his mouth vigorously with the paper napkin, and laid the palm of his hand over his glass. Fenton masked the taste of the spiced baked vegetables and sauces with beer and was now on his third bottle.

"What they intend is to gain a triple arm of weaponry with which they may dominate the oilfields of the region. For the development of the nuclear site at Bushehr, and they already have small quantities of plutonium, they will beggar their own people and bankrupt the state. They are scouring the Asian continent for the necessary chemical agents for an independent poison-gas manufacturing industry. What is the work the scientific community of Iran is given? The means to deliver a warhead containing the most revolting disease known to man—anthrax, foot-and-mouth, any biotoxin, any of the peasants' weapons of mass destruction. Where are they putting these weapons and the missiles to deliver them? In tunnels. They bury them where they are beyond the reach of conventional attack. Only once have we been able to strike at such targets. Do you know how we achieved that, Harry, with whose help? Were you never told, Harry? If not, it's not for me to tell you."

The meat on the plates laid in front of them was unrecognizable as part of any animal Fenton knew. He assumed it had been a young lamb, ritually slaughtered. The thought of what had happened to it was sufficient to stifle his appetite.

"The Iranian program for the manufacture of weapons of mass destruction gives me, and the rest of our intelligence community, bad nights. It's the big picture. It's what the people of Israel will face in the future. The Mossad and the general staff have to plan the defense of our state against nuclear devices, against nerve gases, against toxins, but that is in front of us. The present . . . Ignore the denials, ignore the protestations of fluent, gentle diplomats who make your foreign-affairs officials feel comfortable. The present is that every attack abroad by the Iranian killer squads has the authorization of the highest echelons of government. It's only the appeasers who say otherwise. Government provides the training for the killers, the weapons via diplomatic pouches, the digital secure-phone links, the passports, the finance. Every operation abroad is laid before the foreign minister, the interior minister, and the defense minister sitting on the National Supreme Security Council. It is authorized, sanctioned, on one condition only. The condition? There should be no smoking gun in Iran's hand . . . Look in your files, Harry, it is there if you wish to see it. Is there something wrong with your food, Harry?"

Fenton had barely touched his meat, hardly eaten enough to offer a pretense of politeness. He grimaced, and signaled for more beer.

"If you don't eat, Harry, you'll just fade away . . . The Germans have done deals, appeased them, looked for the easy life—and the French, the Italians. They have submitted to the blackmail. They want to trade, they want to offer export credits, and they believe, if they are generous and restructure the debts, that the killer squads will stay off their territory. Prisoners are returned, investigations are stalled. Have the Germans helped you over Lockerbie? Have they fuck. What about all the killers the French have caught within their jurisdiction? No prosecutions. They appease. And you in Britain, Harry, on your little island, you do not believe that the problem of Iran is real. How can I say that? I say it because of what I see from my embassy window. You allow, unchecked, on your streets, flourishing, such organizations as the Hizb-ut-Tahrir, or the Young Muslims who provide the cheap charter flights to Iran, or the Al-Muntada al-Islami, who fundraise for the Algerian fundamentalist butchers who are in their turn trained in Iran. You allow it to happen, Harry. You refuse to recognize the cancer in your belly."

The Israeli declined coffee, which was a relief. What had been served at the next table, coughed and spluttered over, had looked like tarmacadam sludge.

"A great meal, Harry, and a great opportunity to talk with you. I say hit the bastards wherever you find them. It is the only language they understand. They are clever and determined, they are not to be underestimated. Good day to you, Harry."

He stood, the gold Star of David bouncing in the grayed hair of his chest behind his open-collared shirt.

Fenton finished the beer, then followed him out onto the street.

The Israeli tugged at his sleeve. "Remember what I said. To stop them you must crush the skull, crush it under your heel, crush the life from it. And then you have to have the courage to shout it to the world, and fuck the consequences. You got the balls, Harry, to tell the world you crushed the skull?"

The Israeli had said, deviously, that he had a man to meet. Fenton was abandoned.

He walked at least a mile before, thank God, he was able to flag down a taxi.

He told Cox that he'd been networking again. He dropped the name of the senior Israeli intelligence officer in London and saw that Cox was reluctantly impressed. He was tired and his feet hurt, and he complained that the Israeli policy position was in total contradiction to their own.

"I'm supposed to be learning but the pointers conflict. That's where we are, between a rock and a hard place. But I will press on."

"Of course you will," Cox said. "That's what you're here for, isn't it?"

The crane came across the green, past the Keep Off the Grass sign, the big wheels gouging a track on the rain-softened ground. Peggy stood on the far side of the green, leaning on her bicycle and staring.

The hut, the size of a large garden toolshed, had already been hoisted off the flat-top lorry that had reached the village in slow convoy with the crane, and now dangled from a cable under the crane's arm.

Frank Perry watched the crane's maneuvers from the dining room window, with Paget and Rankin. They had asked for, and been given, a spare blanket from the airing cupboard and had draped it over the polished table.

He'd said earlier, "I'm sorry about last night, what I said."

"Didn't hear you say anything, sir."

"Nothing to apologize for, sir."

A pleasant afternoon of watery sunshine threw sufficient glare to highlight the garish yellow of the crane and the rusty brown creosote seal on the planks of the swinging hut. The crane's engine coughed diesel fumes as it powered towards the gap between his house and the Wroughtons'. Davies edged his car clear to make space.

Behind him, Paget and Rankin were discussing kit. They seemed uninterested in the arrival of the hut. On the blanket, with their machine guns and the small black-coated gas grenades, with a book of crossword puzzles, was a kit magazine. They turned the pages and pored over the advertisements.

His face against the window glass, Perry peered at the crane's advance, and heard the scraping noise. He tilted his head, looked up and to the side. He could see that the hut swayed against the Wroughtons' plastic guttering. Wroughton was the deputy bank manager in the town, his wife was the surgery manager, and their twins were in school; a small blessing that they weren't there to see the destruction of the plastic guttering. The crane hoisted the hut higher, clear of the Wroughtons' guttering and roofing tiles. He imagined a crowd cheering as a man swung and twisted from such a crane. The crowd here was just Peggy, Vince, who was out of his van and watching with her, and Dominic, standing in the shop doorway. Paul held tightly to the leash of his dog, which yapped incessantly and strained forward on its hind legs. He could no longer see the slow swing of the hut, but could hear the shouts of the men guiding it. In Iran, from what he had seen on television when he was there, they didn't blindfold a man before he was lifted high for the crowd to see, and they didn't pinion his legs to deny the crowd the sight of him kicking.

Behind him, in low voices, Paget and Rankin talked through the brand names of windproof sweaters, thermal socks, and rainproof trousers. They sat huddled close beside each other. It was more than twenty minutes since the crane and the lorry had come to the village and they'd not passed comment on anything other than the advertisements in the magazine for kit.

He left them and went into the kitchen. Meryl didn't look up. She was at the kitchen table with her sewing machine, and her boy was feeding her the lengths of cut net. In the back garden more of the men from the lorry were laying heavy planks on the grass lawn, cursing because they were awkward to move and heavy. She'd spent half of last summer's evenings working at that grass, digging out the weeds to make it perfect. The kitchen, in spite of the long fluorescent strip light, was dark. She was looking at the window and he could see her teeth gnawing at her lower lip. The hut was being lowered past the window to the shouted instructions of the men, who eased it towards the planks on her perfect lawn. He'd heard that a man was left hanging dead for a whole day before they lowered the arm of the crane. The hut jolted, and the cable slackened. Davies was calling their names.

Paget and Rankin came through the kitchen. They had the machine guns, their rucksacks, their food boxes, their magazine, and the crossword book. The tall one tousled Stephen's hair. It was the first time Perry had seen the child half smile since Meryl had brought him home. They walked out through the kitchen door to inspect their hut. There was the roar from the front of the house as the crane backed out of the gap between the houses.

"Are you all right?"

"Yes." Her head was down, but her tone was aggressive. She fed the net onto the needle of the machine.

"I was only asking . . ."

"Why shouldn't I be all right? I've got you, I've got my home, I've got my friends. What have I to complain about?"

"Look, don't be sarcastic."

Davies rapped at the kitchen door. He was carrying his gear: the case with his machine gun, his heavy coat, a duffel bag for his sandwiches and thermos, a clean shirt on a hanger, and a pair of heavy boots. Through the window, Perry saw Paget and Rankin taking possession of their hut. They'd dumped their kit inside, and were supervising the linkup of the cables from the house. One of the lorry men brought them two plastic chairs and a kettle; another, a small television set and a microwave cooker. Outrage had been building with Meryl throughout the day, but she had held on to her control because of the men in her dining room. If Davies hadn't been at the door he thought she would have screamed. Everything around them was worse for her than for him.

"Yes?" He turned on Davies.

Davies said quietly, "It's been decided that I should be inside with you. It's not a matter of comfort or anything like that, it's about my safety when I'm sitting in the car. It's because of a reassessment of the security threat. The car is too vulnerable, that's the assessment now. The boys in the hut are behind armor-plated walls. They're certainly proof against low-velocity bullets and there's a good chance they'd stop high-velocity, but the car doesn't have that protection. They want me inside."

"I've been asked, again, to run away. I'm staying."

"I've been told that, Mr. Perry. That's your decision, not for me to comment on. But the car outside, with the new assessment, is too vulnerable."

The strangers were with them inside the house, and in the hut, which blocked the precious view of their garden. Later, the strangers would be all around them as the laminated plastic was fixed to the windows. It would be late in the afternoon, when Paget and Rankin were safe in their hut, when Davies was safe in the dining room, before the lorry rumbled away and the crane's wheels dug another track across the green.

And there was nothing he could do, except run. All his life he had made for himself the decisions that mattered. He had always been self-reliant: at school he, not his parents and not his teachers, had decided what subjects he would specialize in; at university, ignoring his tutors' advice, he had decided what branch of engineering he would concentrate on; at the company, his only employer, he had decided that the opening he wanted was in the sales division, and he had explored the tentative, difficult trade openings that were possible with Iran. First his wife, and then Meryl, had left decisions to him. He had never been frightened of backing his judgment, and now he was helpless and snared in a web. It was a new sensation to him. He couldn't, of course not, go out of the house and man a personal roadblock at the end of the village and check the cars coming in, and couldn't beat across the common ground beside the road for the people sent to kill him, and couldn't thrash around in the marshland. No action was open to him except to run. He was neutered, and the men were all around him, inside and outside his house, and they ignored him as if he were an imbecile and incapable of independent thought. There was nothing he could do but sit and wait.

"It isn't my fault."

She had come where and when he had told her to come. Farida Yasmin Jones hung her head, pressed her face against her knees. The damp of the evening was in the air. She had driven her car down the narrow lane off the wider, busier road, and after the bend that prevented it being seen from the road she had parked near to the track that led to the tumulus.

"I do not criticize you."

"You look as though you do—when I came with Yusuf there wasn't protection."

"Perhaps he lived."

"You said he'd die."

"Perhaps he lived and talked."

"Yusuf Khan would never talk."

"All men say they would never talk, and believe it."

"You're insulting him."

"He was stupid, he was like a child. He spoke too much and he could not drive—why should I believe he would not talk?"

"You've no right to say he'd talk. What're you going to do?"

He had come from Fen Hill and across Fen Covert and he had sat for close to twenty minutes hidden in bushes watching her before he had shown himself. After twenty minutes Vahid Hossein had gone in a wide loop around her to check that she was not followed, was not under surveillance. He had seen the men at the house with the guns. He had no trust in anything he had been told. There had been an Iraqi ruse in the marshland in front of the Shatt al Arab: an ambush would be set by a patrol; they would lie up and their guns would cover a raised pathway through the reed banks; a cassette recorder would play a conversation, men's voices, in the Farsi tongue; men of the Revolutionary Guards would be drawn towards the voices of their own people. Friends had been killed because they trusted what they heard. He had watched her. She had eaten mint sweets from a packet, and scratched the white skin of her legs above her knees, and looked frightened around her in the quiet. She had rubbed hard against the softness of her breast, as if there was irritation there. She had snapped her fingers together in impatience. All the time he had watched her. He had no trust in her and yet he was yoked to her.

"Think, plan."

"Think about what? Plan what?"

"Think and plan."

"Don't you trust me?"

"I have faith only in myself."

Her face was against the white skin of her legs and her hair cascaded over her knees. He thought that she might be crying.

"I'll do whatever you want."

"You cannot think for me and you cannot plan for me."

"Is that because I'm a woman?"

"Because . . ."

"What is your name?"

"You have no need to know my name. You have no need to know anything of me."

She gazed into his face and the half-light made shadows at her mouth and her eyes, but the eyes held the brightness of anger. "Then I'll tell you my name and everything about myself, because that shows you my trust. I take the chance, the trust, that you'll not talk."

"You believe that? You believe I would—"

She mimicked, "'All men say they would never talk, and believe it.'"

His hand went instinctively to her shoulder, caught it, gripped it to the bone. "You play a trick with me, a trick of words." He had felt her body, gazed into her uncovered face. He snatched away his hand and looked at the ground between his damp, muddy boots. He had been wrong: there were no tears in her eyes.

"I trust you," she said. "Before I converted, I was Gladys Eva Jones. I come from a town in the middle of England, not much of a place. My father drives a train. He's fat, he's ugly, he likes newspapers with pictures of girls without swimsuit tops, he dislikes me because I'm not a boy. My mother's empty, stupid, and she dislikes me because I'm not married and breeding—actually, the married bit

might not even matter to her, it's not having kids to push round in a
pram that upsets her. They both, equally, dislike me because I was
clever enough to go to university. It was the most miserable time of
my life, and I'd had some. I was nothing on campus, no friends,
lonely as sin. I met Yusuf and through him I went to the mosque of
Sheik Amir Muhammad, and I was taken into the true faith, and became Farida Yasmin and happier than I'd been in my life. I'd found
respect . . . I was asked to drop my faith, to hide it, to go to the hair-
dresser and beautify myself. I was told that was the way I could best
serve the memory of the imam. I was trusted. I was sent with Yusuf
to identify this man, Perry, at a hospital in the north of England
when he was visiting. His father was ill and the doctors thought he
might die. His parents didn't know how to call for him because he'd
cut all the family links when he changed his name. There was an appeal on the radio for him, using the old name, and it was heard by
Perry and by the people at the Iranian embassy, and it said where
the hospital was. We went there, Yusuf and I, but it was I who actually went into the ward and asked the nurse which patient was his
father. I saw him by the bed. We waited outside and noted the car he
was driving, and it was I who walked past it and took down the
name of the garage that had sold it. We went to the garage and I
chatted up the salespeople, gave them a story—I flirted, I did what
was disgusting for my faith—and I was given the address of the man
who'd bought it. I did all of that because I was trusted. Then I was
trusted enough to come down here, to Perry's home, to photograph
him and his house. And I was trusted, when Yusuf crashed, to drive
south, collect you, and bring you here. How much trust do you
need?"

He gazed at his boots, at the crossed laces and the mud.

She bored on. "Is it too difficult for you now?"

"What?"

"Because he is protected, is it too difficult?"

"You believe . . ." He had never before been interrogated by a
woman, then lectured, not even as a child by his mother.

"Are you giving up, going home?"

"No . . . no . . . no . . ."

She had angered him. She smiled as if his anger pleased her, as if
she had finally reached him.

"What are you going to do?"

"Think and plan."

"It's possible?"

"In God's hands, everything is possible."

"How can I help?"

He said, "I need bread and cheese and bottled water, and I need raw minced meat. Please, bring them for me tomorrow."

"Same time tomorrow—bread, cheese, water, minced meat—yes."

He pushed himself up. The damp of the ground had seeped through the material of his camouflage trousers, stiffened his hips. He stretched. She reached up with her hand. He hesitated. She challenged him. He took her hand and she used the strength of his grip to pull herself to her feet. The blood flushed in his cheeks. She rubbed the skin at the back of her legs as if to give them warmth. He looked away from her and began to brush the ground on which they had sat with sticks to lift the flattened grass.

"I don't know your name and you don't trust me," she said softly. "But you can't do without me, can you?"

9

"We're stuck with him."

"Don't know how we can shift him."

"Whichever budget it's coming out of will be facing a black hole."

It was where they found comfort at Thames House: a meeting around a table, an agenda, and a stenographer parked in a corner to record conclusions.

Barnaby Cox, once, had gestured discreetly to the stenographer with the palm of his hand, an indication to her that a particular area of discussion was not to be recorded for posterity; no hack trawling in future years through the archives in library would learn how information was extracted from a hospitalized patient.

Fenton was beside him. Next to him was the senior warhorse from B Branch, former Army with a history going back to Cyprus and Aden. Beyond him was Seitz, in his crumpled tweed suit and creased shirt, then the red-haired woman. Opposite Cox was the Branch superintendent with the maps on which were drawn the lines covered by the sensor wires, and the arcs watched by the cameras, and the fields of defensive fire . . . and Geoff Markham was isolated at the end of the table and watched and said nothing.

The agenda had covered the threat; the guarded prisoner; the evidence of the presence in the United Kingdom of a killer with the coded name of Anvil—good laughter at the top end of the table at that; the possibilities of putting a name to Anvil; the missing associate thrown up by Rainbow Gold—no laughter there because Rainbow Gold was a sacred Grail, cost an annual fortune, and was beyond criticism; and the mobile surveillance and taps on the movements and communications of the IOs at the Iranian embassy. The agenda had reached the transcript provided by Geoff Markham.

"The call, Geoff's call, wasn't authorized . . ." Cox fretted.

"All Geoff's done, not that we needed it, is provide further confirmation that Perry's a stubborn fool," Fenton said reassuringly.

"He should have cleared it first," Cox complained.

"The bloody trouble is, and Perry knows it, we cannot abandon him. If the Iranians drop him in the gutter, with half his head missing, they've won, and that is unacceptable." The Branch man gazed at the table.

Cox huffed, "Sounds as if he's deranged, all this rubbish about home and friends."

Fenton said, "I think we should call him up to London, with his wife, give him lunch and the treatment. Plant the doubts in him, scare the daylights out of her. Soften him up."

The Branch man relaxed and grinned. "Spell it out in words of one syllable that even an engineer can understand."

"A good lunch, a good wine, and a good dose of fear should crack him," Fenton pressed on.

"The cost of protection, with no end date, is simply unacceptable." Cox pummeled his hands together. "But I like what I'm hearing now."

Fenton rocked back in his chair, smiled broadly. "Get some photographs from the Germans, the French, a few of their corpses courtesy of the Iranians for her to look at while she's eating. Always best to go through the little woman—works every time."

"Right, agreed." Cox rapped his pencil on the table. "We're not criticizing Geoff for his initiative, he was following the agreed line. It's just that he didn't have sufficient weight in his punch. Handle it, will you, Harry?"

The stenographer scribbled briskly. At the far end of the table, Markham felt like a child brought in to the adults' dinner, not expected to contribute but to be washed, neat, and silent. The red-haired woman yawned. The American, who hadn't spoken since his precis of the hospital-bed interview, coughed.

Cox gathered up his papers and stood, content. "Thank you all for your time—the main priority, get him out. A good lunch and lashings of gore to help it down—Harry to make the arrangements. Thank you."

The American coughed again, in a more stagy fashion.

"Sorry, Mr. Seitz, have we ignored you?" Cox grimaced.

While they were on the move around him, Seitz remained still and sitting. "Just something I'd like to say."

Cox glanced at his watch, then said patronizingly, "Any further contribution you wish to make will be, of course, greatly valued."

Seitz smoothed the brush of his hair. Markham reckoned his hesitation was a good act. He thought the American was as hard as granite.

"That's gracious, much appreciated. It follows on from Mr. Markham's transcript. Quote, 'You think I'll run away because of the say-so of those [expletive] bastards? Think again. Get it into your head—I make my own decisions. I am not running away,' end quote. That's good, excellent, that should be encouraged. The best place for him is at home. What I would urge on you, don't give him lunch and wine and show him photographs, keep him where he is, at home. There are rare occasions, too few for my liking, when we have the chance to win. This is such an occasion . . . and I think you should take the opportunity as it presents itself."

Cox was back in his chair. The rest of them listened in silence.

"If you like, I am a surrogate child of Iran. Iran, my parent, feeds me, clothes me, provides my reason for living. Without that parentage I have no life. A child watches every move of its parents. So, I watch Iran . . . Iran is at war with the United States, with my government, and if you'd care to recognize it, at war with you too. The weapons they have are stealth, deceit, the probing for weakness. My government, and I believe rightly, calls it state-sponsored terrorism, and every year puts Iran top of the world list. The war, most currently, is being fought on Saudi Arabia's territory. Iran's war aim is, via destabilization, to bring down the government of the kingdom and replace the administration of an ally that irritates us with that of an enemy actively hostile to us. The road to destabilization is through the bombing of the United States' military infrastructure now settled in Saudi Arabia. They are trying to force us out, and if we go the kingdom falls . . . I don't have to give you the statistics of oil reserves in Saudi Arabia. That country is a vile place, a police state, characterized by medieval cruelty, but it is important to us— hear me, *important*. And it is a most challenging environment for an enemy to operate in. To survive there, to continue to kill, the enemy must be of the highest caliber. Our man rates up there. Each time he strikes he creates further government repression, which, night following day, creates further destabilization. He organized the bombing of the National Guard barracks at Riyadh, five Americans dead, and the attack on the Kobar Tower barracks, nineteen Americans dead. Three Americans killed on the road between Dhahran and Riyadh. A Saudi general working with Americans was targeted and killed last year. We had a chance to take him last month, and we missed him. Missing him hurt, because we categorize him as the principal terror criminal confronting us. He was called home from Saudi Arabia, and sent here."

Geoff Markham thought him masterful. Seitz's voice was never pushed; he used his hands only rarely and then for the supreme moment of emphasis.

"It bleats, cannot hide, cannot escape. It cries out, attracts the predator, is stalked by the predator. It is watched, dragging at its rope, by the marksmen in the hide. It is the tethered goat . . ."

Fenton's breath whistled in his teeth. The red-haired woman gazed at the American in fascination.

"If you go with your rifle into the bush or the jungle or the desert, then you have very little chance, the slimmest of possibilities, of finding your predator. But the predator has to be killed. So you get a goat. You put a stake in the ground and a rope around its neck. It will attract the predator. You tie the rope to the stake and you sit in your hide with your rifle, and you watch your tethered goat."

They sat in hushed quiet around the table as if, Markham thought, none of them dared to interrupt the bravado of the proposal.

"Afterwards, when you have shot the predator, you will receive the thanks of the community and you will walk with pride. You don't have to put the body on show. Others won't come, predators learn quickly, others will stay away. Forget your lunch, wine, and photographs. Leave Frank Perry in place, where the predator knows he can find him. Make the hide, put good men in it . . . You are lucky, so lucky, that you have a bait available."

Fenton and Cox spoke at once.

"That is fraught with danger."

"It's brilliant."

The Branch superintendent said there would be minimal risk to his people because the beast would have eyes only for the goat.

The red-haired woman chuckled, said nothing, but she patted the American's hand lightly.

Cox murmured nervously, "But the consequences of such action, they could be dire . . ."

"Not if the matter is handled with discretion. With the necessary discretion there are no consequences. But believe me, the necessary message will reach the Ministry of Information and Security—discretion avoids consequences."

"We'll buy that, if there's discretion," Cox said.

"I'll take responsibility for running it," Fenton rasped. "At the moment we're drifting. This way we have purpose."

"Our discretion is guaranteed, my word on it." Seitz spoke with sincerity. "It's what we'd do, if we'd had the luck that's given to you."

Geoff Markham wanted to ask, and didn't: how long would the marksmen wait before they fired? He held his silence. In the interests of a better shot, would they sacrifice the goat? The American had turned away from his audience and rubbed his smoothly shaven chin. Only Markham saw the satisfaction of his smile.

He hadn't asked his question because he already knew the answer, had seen it in their eyes. He slipped out of the room and left behind him the clinking glasses and the pop of a drawn cork.

Jerry and Mary Wroughton had lived in the next house with their five-year-old twins, Bethany and Clive, before Frank and Meryl had arrived in the village.

They were able to buy the house of pink stucco, with four bedrooms, overlooking the green, with upstairs views out across the sea because the bank offered favorable mortgage terms to employees. Without that they wouldn't have had a sniff at it, and with it Jerry had to be everybody's friend at work while Mary had to have a full-time job as a receptionist in a local surgery. In truth, they lived behind their front door as semipaupers. Appearances, for Jerry and Mary Wroughton, were deceptive and their poverty was hidden. To the outside world, they presented an aspect of cheerful, friendly affluence. Jerry Wroughton liked to be thought of as a bank manager, dropping "deputy"; Mary gave her job description as a practice manager, not mentioning the word "receptionist."

Just as Jerry, at work, acquired customers, and Mary, at work, acquired patients, so both, in the village, acquired friends. Friends went with the territory.

And they were, of course, careful in the acquisition of their friends.

Friendships, as with everything else in their lives, were planned. Friendships were useful, important, should not create stress. Friendships should not provide unpleasant or jarring surprises. Both hated surprises. They were close to the Carstairses, on good terms with the vicar, relaxed with the Fairbrothers, but their best friends were in the next house. There were never any surprises from Frank and Meryl Perry . . . not until that evening.

What Jerry and Mary liked about Frank and Meryl was that they listened. Jerry could talk all night round the kitchen table and Frank always seemed to find what he said interesting. Meryl was so kind, always ready to help out in a crisis, having the twins round if Jerry and Mary were kept out late, always prepared to shop for them if work was too pressing. They had never had any cause for complaint about their closest neighbors.

Vince, the vulgar little builder, had telephoned. Had they seen their guttering? Had they heard about the crane? What about the hut? Did they know about the guns? Would they be wanting him—cash, if they didn't mind—to check their guttering?

Coming home from work, Jerry Wroughton had seen the police car parked close to the junction on the main road at which the lane branched off to the village. He'd thought it was good to see them there, watching for thieves and speedsters, and yobs without tax discs or insurance. He'd driven down Main Street, had seen a second police car coming slowly towards him, and thought that it was high time decent, hardworking, law-abiding folk had proper protection. An empty car had been parked outside the neighbors'. He'd been tired, he'd wanted his tea, and he'd been sitting in front of the television when Vince had telephoned. He'd gone upstairs. From the back bedroom window he could see down into the neighbors' rear garden. He saw the hut and the policeman walking slowly round their lawn. The sight of the machine gun in the policeman's hands had sent Jerry Wroughton into the bathroom, where he had vomited into the lavatory. The killing zone was separated from his own property by a low fence of light palings. He rang Barry Carstairs, and then the fear was worse.

For the next hour, his wife doggedly insisted that it was his right to protest and told him what to do.

It was the worst surprise that had ever confronted Jerry Wroughton.

Her car had provided the lead they required.

It was a two-room flat, one room for the bed and the washbasin, one room for the easy chair, the television, and the cooker. The lavatory and the bath were shared with others on the floor below. The detectives had taken apart every drawer and cupboard, exposed every possession of Farida Yasmin Jones, and found nothing.

The Rainbow Gold file had carried an old address with neither a number nor a street for forwarding mail. The university records had failed them. The father had cursed and the mother had sulked, but they could not produce a current domicile for their daughter. The detectives hadn't a workplace and so had no national insurance number to feed into the computers. The driving license address had not been updated.

But they had the car's registration from the vehicle licensing files at Swansea. Four men, with the registration, had foot-slogged round the backstreet garages of Nottingham.

None of the possessions in the flat, scattered from the drawers and cupboard onto the floor, had produced what they searched for. The detectives had been told to look for evidence of commitment to an extreme fundamentalist Islamic sect, but the possessions were those of an ordinary young woman, one of thousands, working for an insurance company. They had her pay slips on the table.

A list had been drawn up of every motor repair yard qualified to issue an MOT certificate of roadworthiness. All they had was the registration of her car. To get into the garage's records, they'd had to promise that the evidence uncovered of VAT fraud and Revenue scams would be taken no further.

They'd rolled back the carpet in the living room, torn away the stuck-down vinyl in the bedroom, and prized up the floorboards with crowbars—each of the four detectives was familiar with failure, but it always hurt. They were sullen, quiet, surrounded by the debris of the young woman's life.

They had nothing to show that this ordinary young woman had clasped a new faith or had made a self-justification for a hatred of her own society.

The last chance was the entry hatch into the rafters of the building. They lifted the slightest among them into the space, with a torch to guide him. They could hear his body movements above them. As they made a play at tidying the flat, replacing the young woman's clothing, they heard his shout of triumph.

A suitcase was passed down through the hatch.

Laid out on the table of the living room was a leather-bound volume of the Koran wrapped in spotless white muslin cloth. There were the careful notes of a student, handwritten, listing the Five Pillars of the faith and their meaning, neatly folded clothes that they recognized, and the head scarves. At the bottom of the case was a packet of film negatives. The detective sergeant held them up towards the ceiling light.

"Well done, lads. That'll do nicely."

The darkness was his friend. But the quiet was a greater friend than the darkness.

Vahid Hossein sat cross-legged. He had heard a fox call behind him in the trees, and the shriek of an owl. He listened for each shift of the waterfowl, dippers and waders, in front of him. The bird was close. He did not need his eyes to see it: his ears had located it, and he knew it edged closer. He heard cars but they were a long way off. The only clear sound was of a dog barking in the far distance.

When he had come back to the place where the sausage bag was hidden, he had found that the bird had tried again to tear at the rabbit carcass and not had the strength. This time, feeling with his fingers, through the darkness hours of the evening, he pulled off small pieces of the bloodless flesh, slipped them into his mouth, and chewed to soften them, then tossed them towards the sounds of the bird. Each time he threw the chewed meat to the bird he drew it closer to him. By the morning, he would be able to touch it, smooth his fingers on its feathers. It was important to Vahid Hossein that he should win the trust of the bird through his help.

He thought of the marshlands at night and the bird. Later, when he was at peace, he would plan and think: he would put from his mind the white-skinned legs of the girl and the fall of her breasts, and make the plan. It was the same quiet he had found in the desert, in the Empty Quarter. His wife, Barzin, in their small house in the village of Jamaran, had a fear of darkness and of silence, and he could not change it: she would leave a light on outside the open bedroom door. It was harder, when he had left the desert and the Bedouin whose loyalty he had won, and driven on the streets past the barracks of the Americans, to make the plan and to think. The best times were when the quiet and the darkness of the Empty Quarter cloaked him, and he would be back there within two weeks to complete the plan and site the bomb.

If Hossein had lunged, he could have caught the bird—by the wing, the leg, or the neck—but he would have lost its trust. Then he could not help it. If he helped it, the peace would come. In peace he could plan and think.

The plan at Riyadh, for his last bomb, thought through by Vahid Hossein and accepted by his brigadier, had been complex. The adaptation of the petrol-tanker lorry to hold 2,500 kilos of commercial explosive had been carried out in the Bekáa Valley of the Lebanon. The explosives and the detonation leads had been loaded, the time switch had been fitted. The lorry had been driven into Syria, through Jordan, and across the Saudi Arabian frontier. Five days after leaving the Bekáa, the lorry had been parked fifty meters in front of the eight-storey residential block used by the Americans. The bomb had been set to explode and the driver had run to the backup car. It was a complex plan, but no thought had been given to the alertness of the sentry on the roof, who had raised the alarm as soon as he saw the driver run. Nineteen Americans killed, 386 injured, but many more would have died without that sentry's advance warning.

For that small mistake Hossein was blamed only by himself.

At peace, his mind clear and rested, in the darkness of the marshes, he thought of the time he should attack his target, now protected. At the change of the protection shift? In daylight, or at night? In the middle of the shift? At dawn, or at dusk? He chewed the meat and threw each piece nearer to his body, always luring the bird closer.

The bell rang.

He glanced at his watch. Blake would come to take over from Davies. But there had been only one ring, sharp and persistent, unlike the three Blake and Davies used. The bell went on, endless. Perry was watching television, the story of the renovation of a wildlife park in the Himalayas, the sort of program that made him forget where he was, what had happened to him. Stephen was sitting on the floor with his arm on his mother's knee. Meryl was sewing.

He didn't think, and stood up. The bell was still ringing as if a finger was jammed on it. He was in the doorway between the living room and the hallway when Davies came out of the dining room, pushing back the bottom of his jacket to reveal the pistol in the waist holster.

The last thing the lorry men had done, after the laminated plastic had gone over the windows, was drill a spy hole in the front door. Davies didn't seem fussed by the bell, took his time. The bell ring pierced the hall, too loud for him to hear what Davies said into the button microphone on his jacket lapel. Perry understood: the camera covered the front door, the monitor was in the hut. Davies was clearing the visitor with the men in the hut.

"It's your neighbor."

"That's Jerry, Jerry Wroughton—always on the scrounge. Probably wants—"

"Do you need to see him?"

"He's a good friend."

Davies switched off the hall light and unlocked the door. Jerry Wroughton's finger slackened off the bell button.

"Hi, Jerry, you in the business of waking the dead?"

Then Perry saw the clenched mouth, the quivering jaw—hadn't ever seen Jerry look so fatuous—and he smelt the whisky.

He'd been about to ask his neighbor to come inside.

He thought Jerry Wroughton was remembering what he had rehearsed, the mouth flapping without words as if the memory was slow coming. Meryl had said that Barry Carstairs had read off notes.

"What's the problem, Jerry?"

In the dark hall Perry went sideways as if to see his neighbor better, but Davies drifted across to stay in front of him, shielding him.

"Come on, Jerry, spit it out."

"What's going on? That's the problem. What's happening?"

The poor bastard, sent out into the night by Mary, had forgotten his lines. "Say what you want to say—that's our way, yours and mine—say it."

It came in a torrent. "I come home—I find you under guard. Police in your garden, police with machine guns. I talk to Barry Carstairs— you're on a death list, the kid's been put out of school because of the risk. Who's thinking about me, about Mary, about the twins? What's the risk to us?"

"Come on, calm down."

"*You*'re all right, you're bloody laughing! What about us? What protection have *we* got?"

"Jerry, you're upsetting yourself. Believe me, you don't have to. Just head on back home, sit in your chair, and—"

"You've got a problem, it's for you to fix it, it's not *our* problem. You made your bed, you lie on it."

He tried to be soothing and conciliatory. He thought he owed that to a good neighbor. Right, so Mary had primed him with drink and nagged, and Jerry had gone all pompous, but he was still a proper friend. He rocked on his feet and breathed deeply, which was what he always did to control a rising temper. "What are you saying, Jerry?"

"You've no right to bring your problems to our doorstep. Right now our children are sleeping a few yards from where you've got guns protecting you. Who's protecting them? Who's protecting Mary when she's in the garden at the washing line, when Beth and Clive are playing outside—or don't they matter?"

"There's been a professional assessment of what needs to be done. They'd have considered—"

Davies stood between them like a statue, impassive. He didn't contribute an iota of support.

"What good's that to us? We've done nothing wrong. We've done nothing to need protection. Whatever your quarrel is, it's not ours."

"If they come for me, they'll have the right address. Is that your worry? That they'll get the wrong house? No chance!" He laughed, couldn't help himself. The image came into his mind, so fast, of the turbaned mullah with the beard, carrying the assault rifle, knocking on doors in the village and going into Dominic's shop, calling up the ladder to Vince, into the pub, asking for directions.

He shouldn't have laughed. Jerry shook, quivering with fear and anger—just as Perry had, a long time ago. "All I can say, Jerry—and I don't get told much—is that I'm in their hands, and they're the experts. We're all in their hands."

"That's not bloody well good enough!"

"What *is* good enough?"

Jerry Wroughton stood his full height. Spittle bubbled at his mouth. It was the moment for which he had needed the cocktail of whisky and his wife's nagging. Davies was between them.

"You should leave—just go."

"Where?"

"Anywhere—just get the fuck out of here. You're not wanted."

"Since when? I thought you were my friend."

"Best thing you can do is go—be gone in the morning."

"I thought friends stuck together, in good times and bad. Don't you want to know what I did, why the threat's there?"

"I don't give a damn what you did. What matters to me is my family. I just want you out."

He didn't care anymore. There was a sickness in his throat, and he realized the shallowness of what he'd assumed was a valued friendship. There were plenty of other friends, with depth to them. He might just talk about it in the pub tomorrow, and they'd all laugh as he described the gutless, henpecked prig Jerry Wroughton. For long enough, on his own doorstep, he'd tried to humor the man. His temper snapped. "Go home and tell Mary that they offered me relocation and a new life. I chose to stay. I told them that this was my home, with my family and my friends . . . *Friends.*" He stabbed his finger past Davies's elbow, towards Jerry Wroughton's heaving chest. "Are you listening? *Friends.* I may not get support from you, when I'm up against the wall, but I'll get it from my true friends, and I've got enough of them. Meryl and I, we don't need you, either of you. Go tell her that."

The telephone rang behind him. He realized, at that moment, that he could no longer hear the television. Meryl would have turned the sound down: she and Stephen would have heard every shouted word.

He walked away and Davies closed the door behind him.

"He's a pathetic bastard."

"You called him a friend, Mr. Perry. You have to face it, people get cruel when they're frightened."

"I've friends here, believe me, real friends."

"Glad to hear it."

He picked up the telephone in the kitchen.

She was the only one left at the new cluster of desks down at the far end of the work area. The consoles were covered, the desks were tidied, all the lights were off except hers.

Geoff Markham came out of his cubicle and locked his door after him. The red-haired woman didn't look up from studying the illuminated green square and speaking soundlessly into a telephone. There was a ribbon of light under Cox's door, but the senior journeyman often did that—sloped off home and left his room lit so that the lesser people might believe he still beavered . . . Vicky was expecting him at her place for a verbatim of the interview, but Markham wasn't in the mood for an inquest.

He wandered towards the woman, towards the halo of light on her hair. He wanted to talk, wanted his feelings massaged. If she hadn't been there he would have gone out of the front doors onto the Embankment, sat on a bench, and stared into the river, watched the barges and the ripples. He waited until she put down her telephone.

"Hello."

She didn't look up. "Yes?"

"I just wondered—can I get you anything?"

"Are you the tea lady?"

"Can I help in any way?"

She said brusquely, "No."

"If it's not too secret"—he giggled—"what are you doing?"

"Pretty obvious, isn't it, or weren't you listening? The American's stuff was superb. Add light complexion to an English-speaking accent. It could equal the child of a mixed marriage. He's put at late thirties. A mixed marriage, maybe forty years ago. An Iranian marries an Englishwoman. That's what I'm looking for. It might be on file—if the marriage was over there, the FCO should have it because probably the consul would have been notified. If it was over here, then it's harder but possible. Is that good enough?"

He felt a rare shyness. She was older than him. With the white ceiling light bathing her face, he could see the first lines cutting her skin and the slight crow's-feet at her eyes. He couldn't face Vicky and her questions. He thought that, not so long ago, she must have been beautiful.

"Does that give you time for a drink, before they close? Sorry I don't know your name."

"I'm Parker."

It scratched in his mind. "Parker?"

"Cathy Parker."

"From Belfast?"

She turned away from her screen. She looked up at him and her glance was withering. "I am Cathy Parker, 'from Belfast,' yes."

"We used to talk about you."

"Did you?"

"The instructors used to lecture us about that bar, escape and evasion, the bar full of Provos and you taking them on."

"Did they?"

"It's a legend there, what you did in the bar."

"You want to know something?"

"Of course, please." What Cathy Parker had done in the bar up on the hill above Dungannon, East Tyrone Brigade country, when she'd been on covert surveillance, had been identified, taken by the Provos, was held up by the instructors as the single best example they knew of the will to survive. She was a legend. "Tell me."

She said, "It was all for nothing. What mattered was my tout. I lost him. I pushed him too far, and I lost him. Did the instructors tell you that? If you'll excuse me . . ."

"Have you time for a drink?"

"I have—you haven't. Hang around here and you'll end up pushing paper in triplicate, badgering night-duty archive clerks, errand running for those useless farts, sucking your bloody conscience, scrapping for a place on the promotion ladder. You'll be sad and passed over, and always have time for a drink. That what you want?"

"Where should I be?"

"Down there, where it's at, with the principal. If you don't mind, please, fuck off, because I want to get this boring crap finished with and get home. You shouldn't be whining around with has-been 'legends.' Get down there. Nothing is ever decided here—they think it is, and strut around as if they actually pull the strings. They don't. It's down there it'll be decided. Body to body, as it always is. Or is close quarters too tough for you? You're a lucky bastard to have the chance to be a part of it, if you're up for it."

Even while talking, she was dialing on her telephone. He spun on his heel and she didn't look up, as if she'd said everything that needed saying.

He paused by the door. He didn't knock, but he put his head round it and asked, "Can I come in?"

"It's your house, Mr. Perry," the detective said, droll. "You can go where you like in it."

It was all out on the blanket over the table, the Heckler & Koch, the bulletproof vest, a little cluster of gas grenades, the mobile phone, the radio, the thermos, the plastic lunch box, the newspaper.

"My wife's gone to bed."

"She's had a long day, sir," the detective said, noncommittal.

Perry shrugged. "We're not very good company for each other at the moment, I'm afraid."

"Early days, sir, takes a bit of time for us all to shake down. Never easy at the beginning, having us in the house."

"Do you mind talking?"

"Up to you, sir."

"It's not interfering?"

"You talk away, sir, if that's what you want."

The detective eyed him. Perry didn't know what he thought. He was a younger man with fair hair and a good suit, and he had the faint accent of the west Midlands. His jacket was off and he wore a shoulder holster on a heavy harness. He seemed not to notice when he straightened in his chair and it flapped against his body. Perry supposed that if you wore the thing the whole time, a holster and a gun, then you came to forget it.

"It's Leo, isn't it?"

"It's Detective Constable Blake, sir, or I'm Mr. Blake—you please yourself."

"Sorry."

"No offense, sir."

"I don't seem to get to talk much with Mr. Davies."

"We're all of us different, sir."

Perry stood in the doorway. "Sounds daft—I'm in my own home with my wife and I'm lonely. Late-at-night talk, you'll have to forgive me. I just need to talk, have someone talk to me. I'm not saying I want a shoulder to cry on, it's just talking that I need. I can't say it to Meryl. It's easier—and no offense—to a stranger, but already it's getting to me. But I made my bed, didn't I? That's what people say. Still, not to worry, there are good people here, in spite of tonight, and they'll see us through. Actually, being honest, the worst bit of all this is behind me. Believe me. A couple of months ago, I'm lying in bed, the radio's on for the news, Meryl's asleep, and I heard my old name. 'Would Mr. Gavin Hughes, last heard of five years ago, go to the general hospital at Keswick in Cumbria where his father, Mr. Percy Hughes, is dangerously ill.' I lied to Meryl as to why I was going out, I drove up there in a daze. I broke all the rules because I'd been told that I shouldn't ever try to reclaim the former life, and I went in to see him. The crisis was over. He was sitting up in bed. Me walking in made him cry, but he cried worse when I refused to tell him who I was now, where I lived, what I did. My mother told me to go away.

She said I was better gone if I couldn't trust my own parents. I came home. That day was worse than anything. There's three times since Mr. Davies arrived here that I've thought of telling that to him, but it never seemed the right time. I don't find talking easy with Mr. Davies."

He couldn't tell whether Blake was bored with the story or moved by it.

"He's a very conscientious officer, sir, one of the best."

Perry smiled ruefully, then forced himself to lighten the mood. "How is one officer better than another?"

"Planning, thoroughness, study . . . he's good at all that. There's an old principle in our job, sir—no such thing as complete protection. But if you do your work, then you're giving yourself a chance, and making a chance for your principal. Bill—that's Mr. Davies, sorry— he's good at planning and he's done all the studying."

"What is there to study?"

"Everything that's gone before, because you can learn from it. We had a half-day clear last year, and he marched me round central London, round five sites where there was an assassination attempt on Queen Victoria's life—he knew the exact place each time, the weapon, why she'd lived. He read about it so he could learn from it. We had a day clear in January, a course was canceled at the last minute, so he took three of us into the video room that SB have, gave us a screening. We had the killing of Sadat and Mrs. Gandhi, Mountbatten and Rabin. Each detail, what had gone wrong, where the security had fouled up—and the video of the shooting at Reagan, which was just diabolical for the protection officers, they did about everything wrong that was possible. You wouldn't want to hear too much about Sadat and Mrs. Gandhi, sir."

"Wouldn't I? Why not?"

A slight grin fluttered at Blake's mouth. Perry knew it was intended he'd snatch the bait.

"They were shot by their own bodyguards. Won't happen to you, sir—they were murdered by the people who were protecting them. Mr. Davies told me that Mussolini was paranoid about his protection people, gave them guns to wave about but kept the ammunition locked up. He studies what's happened, learns from it. He could walk you down the street, by the Hilton Hotel in London where the Israeli ambassador was shot, and talk you through it as if he'd been there—the PO did well, fired and hit the gunman, but it was still too late, his principal was critically injured, brain damage. We're always trying to catch up, we're told that their action is faster than our re-action, stands to reason. To give yourself a chance, what Mr. Davies does, you study and learn. It matters to him. The job matters too much to him, it's bad for his wife and kiddies, but it's good for you, sir. Can I say something?"

"Of course you can."

"Like, in confidence?"

"Please."

"Not to go further. We're all covering for him. It's a lousy bit of wife trouble. If the bosses knew how lousy they could pull him off the job. They don't let men with bad home problems carry firearms. When he lost the weapon in the playground, if you'd shopped him then, made a complaint, the bosses would have put the evil eye on him and the trouble bit might have surfaced. If you'd complained, he could have been out on his neck. You did well there, sir."

"Don't take me wrong but it's a comfort to know that other people have a bloody awful day."

"He told me—not easy for you, sir."

"Well, time for bed. I'm grateful. Thanks."

"You pretty down, sir, on the floor? Has Mr. Davies told you about Al Haig? No? Get him to—it's his favorite. When you feel low, like the world's kicking you, get him to do his Al Haig story. Good night, sir."

Perry turned for the door, then stopped. "There's something I don't understand. I was asked by the London people to leave, and I refused, we had a shouting match. They came back this morning, tried again, new life and a removal van, and again I refused. But they called this evening, it was all soft soap, and they accepted my deci-sion to stay. Why'd they change course?"

"Don't know, sir, couldn't say."

Perry went to the bottom of the stairs, and hesitated. "Can I ask you, Mr. Blake, in a live situation have you ever fired your gun?"

"Only the once. Two shots, stone dead, pints of blood on the pavement. Just happened to be there and just happened to be armed because I was going off duty. Before you ask, I didn't feel good about it and I didn't feel bad about it. I shot a beef bullock that had broken out of an abattoir pen and was running up a high street in south London. I didn't feel anything. Get him to tell you the Al Haig story. Good night, sir."

Frank Perry climbed the stairs, past the winking light of the security sensor, and went to bed.

10

"Hello—here already, Cathy? How's it going?"

"Getting there steadily, not there yet."

It was the Saturday morning. The early underground trains were empty, and Geoff Markham had reckoned that he'd be the first. There would only be lowlife in early on a Saturday morning. Cox was down in the country for the weekend, to be disturbed only with news of earthquake-shattering proportions. The warhorse from B Branch would be in charge, but not in before nine, and there'd be a probationer to answer his telephone. Fenton could be called at home.

Markham should have been driving with Vicky to see her parents in Hampshire. He'd still been smarting from the fracas with her when he had grabbed his coat and briefcase and fled the flat. He'd met the postman on the pavement and snatched his mail—bills and circulars, a couple of other envelopes, catalogues—and then hurried for the station. Vicky had said that her mother was cooking a special lunch; it had been in his diary for weeks. Her mother had invited friends in, and Vicky's brother and his partner were also driving up from London. After the few bitter words, and then the harsh silence, Markham had put the phone down on her and run. He could have stayed out of Thames House that morning, and that afternoon, and all of Sunday. He could have made an issue of it to Fenton, whinged about the hours he'd put in through the week. He hadn't. Instead he'd rung Fenton early, before he'd rung Vicky, and told him what he intended, gained the necessary clearance. Actually, he didn't think Vicky's mother thought much of him, didn't rate him as a good catch for her daughter; but Vicky was two years older than he, and there wouldn't be that many more chances of marriage coming her way, so he was tolerated.

Cathy Parker, the legend, was back at her screen, studying it with concentration as if he wasn't there.

In his cubicle, he checked the answerphone and there was the SB overnight digest to get through. He took a sheet of clean paper to his door, and used the black marker pen.

DAY THREE.

He went off on a wander down the corridor to the coffee machines. The building was hushed quiet. Weekends in Thames House were like a plague time. The corridor was darkened, every second light was off as a part of the newest economy campaign. The doors were shut. The notice boards for cheap holiday advertising, through the Civil Service union, for rentable cottages in the country and secondhand cars were in shadow. Perhaps he should ring Vicky's mother with an apology, but later, and maybe send some flowers . . . He swore softly: he hadn't the right change for two cardboard cups of coffee, only for one, and he didn't know whether she took sugar, whether she took milk. The first big decision of Geoff Markham's morning: milk and no sugar. He stamped back down the corridor, his footfall echoing past the locked doors.

The American was sitting opposite her now. He had a newspaper in front of his face and his chair was tilted back, his shoes on the table.

He felt a youngster's hesitation.

"I thought you might like some coffee."

She looked up. "If I want coffee, I am capable of getting it."

"I've brought a milk-and-no-sugar."

"I don't take milk in coffee." She was at her screen, typing briskly.

The American grinned. "Mr. Markham, I could murder for coffee."

Flushing, Markham slapped the cardboard cup onto the desk in front of him, spilling it.

"You're very kind, Mr. Markham. Miss Parker tells me you're going down to your Juliet Seven's territory?"

"Did she?"

"And I'd like to hitch a ride."

"Would you?"

"So's we get the hassle out of the system good and quick, may we just establish some minor points? If you had a problem getting out of bed, that is not a concern of mine. If you have a problem with working weekends, I don't, because I work every weekend. OK? You have been tasked as my liaison, and I think us going down to Juliet Seven's territory is a good idea, and a smile helps to start the day."

Seitz spoke with the same quiet, relaxed tone with which he had laid out the notion of the tethered goat—the image had stayed with Markham through the night. Seitz swung his shoes off the desk and reached for the coffee.

Markham said shrilly, "If that's what you want, then that's what you'll get."

He headed back to his cubicle for his coat, and the American trailed behind him.

"She is, Mr. Markham, a very fine young woman, a very attractive young woman . . . Ah, day three . . ." The American had paused in front of the door, and the smile rippled at his face. "I believe that we've four days remaining. He will move, and very soon. He will want to strike as soon as is practical. I assume, by now, he or his collaborators will have gone close for reconnaissance and he will already know that the target is protected. That will not deter him, only delay him. Don't get a comfortable, dangerous illusion into your head, Mr. Markham, that he will see the protection and back off. He has the spirit of Alamut, where it was all about blind obedience and discipline. Let me tell you a story about old times at Alamut . . ."

Markham snatched up his briefcase, shrugged into his coat, slammed the door shut behind him. He went fast, and sourly, towards the corridor. The American was at his shoulder.

"In the time of the Old Man of the Mountain, Hasan-i-Sabah, Alamut was visited by King Henry of Champagne. That was a big prestigious visit. Hasan-i-Sabah needed to put on a show that would impress the king with the dedication of the Fida'is. The show he put on was the death leap. Centuries later Marco Polo, on his travels, heard about it and chronicled it. Hasan-i-Sabah had some of his people walk to a cliff top, a high cliff, then jump off to their deaths.

They weren't pushed, they were volunteers. That's obedience and that's discipline. I'm telling you, Mr. Markham, so you understand better the commitment of your opposition. They just walked off the cliff because that's what they'd been told to do."

He held out his hand and felt the beat of the rain.

Vahid Hossein's arm was at full stretch. In his fingers was one of the last pieces of chewed rabbit meat.

The bird watched him. The rain made a spray of jeweled colors on its collar feathers and on its back. It was beside his hand and he saw the wild suspicion in its eyes. He thought the suspicion fought with its exhaustion and hunger.

Each time it hopped closer, he could see the darkening flesh of the wound under the wing and he knew the bird would die unless he could clean it.

He made small sounds, slight whistling noises, the cries he had heard long before in a faraway marshland, like a hen bird to chicks. The beak of the bird, with the power to rip at his hand, was beside his fingers and the chewed meat. He saw the talons that could gouge his flesh.

He had woken and crawled from his bramble den. The bird had been watching him and he'd taken comfort from it. Once again, he had skirted the marsh, cut through Old Covert into Hoist Covert, and crossed the river. For a final time, he'd gone over the ground he would use at the end of that day. He had approached the house from the side and had found a tree in a garden under which the grass was covered with a carpet of blown-away blossom. He had sat motionless in the tree for an hour. From it he could see the back and the side of the house, across three gardens. He saw the soft light in the hut and the curtained black windows. He watched the policemen, backlit when they opened the door of the hut, emerge and walk the perimeter of the garden, and he saw the guns they carried.

The car cruised past every twenty minutes, as regular as if a clock timed it. That night, he would return in the darkness at the end of the day, and he would use the rifle.

The harrier, in a darting movement, took the chewed meat from his fingers. He could have wept with happiness.

There was caked blood and yellow mucus on the wound.

Carefully, as if he moved forward on a target, Vahid Hossein took another scrap of meat with his free hand, chewed on it, and laid it on his wrist. The bird flapped, jumped. He felt its talons strike into his arm and then the prick of the beak as it took the chewed meat from his wrist.

The bird perched on his arm and, with great gentleness, he stroked the wet feathers on the crown of its head.

"It's Saturday."

"I really think, Mr. Perry, we should talk this through."

"It's what I do every Saturday."

"You have to accept, Mr. Perry, and I am picking my words with care, that the situation has changed."

"I haven't been out, not even into the garden, of my house in two days."

"Which has been sensible."

"I am bloody suffocating in here. Enough is enough, I go out every Saturday lunchtime."

"Mr. Perry, I am not responsible for the situation."

"Oh, that's brilliant. I suppose I'm responsible. Blame me, that's convenient."

It was another of those moments when Bill Davies thought it necessary to assert his authority. "You are, in my opinion, totally responsible. You told my colleague, Mr. Blake, last night about your reaction to a radio appeal that gave your former identity. Probably half of the adult population of the country heard that appeal, and the name of the hospital you were directed to. Don't you think that the Iranian embassy listens to the early-morning news bulletins on the radio, which follow directly after such appeals? I'm not a high-flying detective, but I'm bright enough to put that together. They'd have picked you up there, then hung on to the trace. It was your mistake just as the weapon in the playground was mine. Don't get me wrong, Mr. Perry, I'm not one of those people who'll say you've brought all this on yourself through emotional carelessness, but I know plenty who would. That was just to set the record straight—brought all this on yourself."

But the principal had a streak of obstinacy, which Davies found mildly attractive. Perry blinked, absorbed what he was told, gulped, then said, "It's Saturday, and I'm going."

"Your last word?"

"Last final word. I can't take it, another whole day, like a rat in a cage."

"I'll make the arrangements."

"What arrangements?"

"It's not straightforward, Mr. Perry, getting you out for a Saturday lunchtime drink, then back from the pub alive."

His principal had swung out of the dining room, and shut the door noisily, petulantly, behind him. Bill Davies sat again at the dining room table reading the paper. He'd rung home that morning, hoped one of the boys would pick it up, but Lily had. He'd tried to be pleasant, to make reasonable noises, and she'd asked him when he was coming home, but he couldn't answer her, hadn't been able to think of anything else to say. She'd put down the phone on him. In seventeen weeks he had had nine complete days off work, and for four of them he had been so tired he had slept through till midday. His marriage was going down the drain and he didn't know what he could do about it. He'd seen it often enough, with other guys, who all put on the brave front and moved out of their homes to shack up with barmaids and slags. Some were taken off SB protection, and some smooth-talked the counselor and kept the job and the firearm, had the meetings in parks and at McDonald's with the kids every third weekend, and they all talked about the new woman in their lives as if it were heaven. He could never find the time to think about it, he was too busy, too stressed. If it happened—*if*—Bill Davies would have two or three seconds to react, top estimate. Should his mind be on his wife, his kids, in those seconds he would lose his principal, *if* it happened. All the case histories he knew were about mistakes and distractions.

He pushed up from the table and went to the window. The dining room window was next on her list for net curtains. He stood back from the glass and peered out. He could see the neat homes, the tended gardens, the shop, more homes, and then the village hall with waste ground at the back.

It had been raining earlier and the road glistened; there was thin sunshine now, but the rain was threatening from the sea. At the end of the road, on the corner, was the pub. From the window he could see only the end gable of the building. He counted eighteen houses on the left side, between the house and the pub, and the parked cars, and fifteen on the right side, with the shop . . . At the shooting range they used was Hogan's Alley, a row of plywood houses, and in front of them were derelict gutted cars. Behind the plywood and in the cars were cardboard shapes that could jump into vision. When to fire, when not to fire, was the reason for Hogan's Alley. They used "simunition" there, paint-tipped nine-millimeter plastic bullets. The target might have a weapon or be holding a baby against her chest. No escape when walking Hogan's Alley: hold the fire and the instructor would tell you drily, "You're dead, mate, he got you." Fire too soon and you'd be told, "You killed a woman, mate, you're charged with murder." The road, the houses, the parked cars, was Hogan's Alley, all the way to the pub.

She came into the dining room and brought him a mug of coffee.

"That's very kind of you, Mrs. Perry, but you didn't have to."

"I was doing one for myself. You're going to the pub?"

"That's what Mr. Perry wants, so that's what we're going to do."

"It's not about a drink, it's about finding his friends."

"I appreciate that."

"He has to have his friends."

"Yes."

She was close to him. He could smell the scent and warmth of her and could see the worn-down strain at her eyes. It was always worse for the women. She held a handkerchief in her hand, pulling and worrying at it. Had he put his arm around her shoulder, then her head would have gone to his chest and he thought she would have wept. It was not his job to offer comfort. He thanked her for the coffee and began to make the arrangements to visit the pub at lunchtime.

They were at the last stages of the discharge of the crude. The weather at the offshore jetty was too fierce to permit his crew to work with paint rollers on the superstructure and hull plates of the tanker. The master's crew were employed on small maintenance jobs in the accommodation block below the bridge and in the engine housing; unnecessary work, but something had to be found for them. The master's greater concern, more than finding work for his crew and occupation for his officers, was the failure of the people in Tehran to provide him with a time for sailing. He still expected to leave the waters of the terminal port that night, but the coded confirmation had not reached him. The man who had gone over the side of his tanker was never far from his thoughts. It was not possible for the master to believe this man was blocked. He demanded of his radio technicians that they maintain a watch through every hour of the day. He waited.

"Hello—can you put me through to Theft Section, thanks . . . Hello, who's that? . . . Tracy, it's Gladys—yes, Gladys Jones. I've still got flu. Yes, that's what I heard, a lot of it about. I'm not coming in, not passing it all round . . . Yes, bed's the best place. Can you tell them in Personnel? Thanks . . . What? . . . Police? . . . What sort of police? . . . What did they want? . . . Thanks, Tracy, it'll just be something silly . . . Thanks . . . I'll sort it when I've got rid of the flu . . . No, I'm not in trouble . . . Bye . . ."

She pocketed the handkerchief through which she had spoken to give the sound of illness to her voice and put down the receiver of the pay phone. A woman beat her knuckles impatiently on the glass screen beside her. She felt faint, worse than if she had influenza. Detectives had been in that morning, a Saturday morning when only a half-strength staff worked till lunchtime, had searched through the drawers of her desk and asked where she was. If they knew her name they would know, also, her car. She staggered away from the pay phone, barging past the woman. She had been told there were four detectives. She was an intelligent young woman, she could assess the scale of the crisis that faced her.

But it did not cross the mind of Farida Yasmin that she should run, hide, and abandon him. He needed her.

Martindale kept the Red Lion in the village.

He was a brewery tenant. The brewery owned the freehold of the building; he must sell the brewery's range of beers; for that privilege he paid heavily in rental and the percentage in profits from sales, and still he was responsible for finding the resources to decorate and furnish the bars, and the purchase of the pictures and ornaments that gave the pub a slight atmosphere. Every penny of cash ever saved by him and his wife was now sunk in the pub, along with the bank's overdraft. It had been a mistake. The mistake had been in coming to the village on a warm, crowded August day two summers back, seeing the visitors parading on the beach and queuing for ice creams at the shop, and believing that he could do profitable trade where his predecessor had failed. He had thought the market was in visitors wanting cheap meals and fruit machines. But last summer it had rained in torrents and the visitors had stayed away. It had been their dream, through all the years they'd owned a corner newsagent's in Hounslow, to have a busy, pretty pub on the coast. Now the dream was going sour, and the bank manager wrote more often.

His winter trade was entirely local—not gin and tonics, not sherries, not whiskies with ginger, but the brewery's beers and lagers, on which the markup was least profitable. He had enough locals to make a darts team, and they came in wearing their work clothes to prop themselves against his bar. If he alienated his few regulars, he would not be able to meet the brewery's dues and keep the bloody bank off his back.

He quite liked Frank Perry.

Martindale owed Frank Perry. Frank Perry had helped him sort out, at minimal cost, the central-heating boiler in the cellar. If he'd gone to the trade it would have been maximum expense. The far side of the bar, the previous night, the talk had been of Frank Perry, the school, and the policemen with guns.

He scraped open the bolts on the front door, against which the rain lashed, and waited for his Saturday lunchtime drinkers.

"I'll look ridiculous."

Davies said firmly, "In matters of protection, Mr. Perry, please do me the courtesy of accepting my advice."

"It weighs half a ton."

"Mr. Perry, I am asking you to wear it."

"I can't."

"Mr. Perry, put it on."

"No."

Meryl exploded, "For Christ's sake, Frank, put the bloody thing on."

They were in the kitchen. The boy, Stephen, was in the shed with Paget and Rankin, out in the garden. It would be worse if the kid heard the parents rowing. Davies held the bulletproof vest.

"What does it matter what you bloody well look like?" she added. "Put it on."

His principal took off the anorak and scowled, but he'd been chastened by the fury of her outburst. She turned, went out, crashed the door shut after her, and they heard her stamping up the stairs. His principal dropped his head and Davies slipped on the vest. It was navy blue, Kevlar-plated, and the manufacturers said it was proof against a handgun's bullets, flying glass, and metal shrapnel. It covered Perry's chest, stomach, and back. Davies pulled the Velcro straps tight and fastened them. She came back in, carrying a grotesquely large sweater. Perry was foul-faced, but she just threw it at him. Davies kept a wry little smile hidden because the sweater fitted comfortably over the vest.

"And what about you?"

"What I do, Mr. Perry, is not your concern."

"I hope you find them," Meryl said.

"Find what?"

"What you're looking for—I shouldn't expect too much."

Perry led, followed by Davies.

He held his radio up to his face and told Paget and Rankin that he was leaving the location in the company of Juliet Seven. Through the front door, the wind and rain whipped at them. They walked briskly. The house was now a gloomy bunker, and he thought it was precious for his principal to get out of it. Davies's eyes raked each of the front gardens to his right and left, and the parked cars. Since he had given the instruction, the unmarked mobile had gone up and down the road seven times between the house and the pub. It was what it took to get a man his Saturday lunchtime drink. They had started at walking pace, then they jogged. Davies held the hem of his jacket so that his Glock in the waist holster would not be exposed. The rain came on harder, and they ran. Going to the pub was an idiotic, unnecessary risk.

Before he had left the bed-and-breakfast, a call to the duty officer had told him they were now categorized as threat level 2: *The principal is confirmed on a death list, the enemy intend to kill the principal; the security coordinator does not have the method or the time at which the attempt will be made.* Davies knew it by heart.

He had done protection officer on threat level 2 years back when he had guarded the secretary of state for Northern Ireland, but he had never been with a principal categorized as threat level 1. As they sprinted across the car park in front of the pub, he was thinking that it would be worse for her, left behind in the bunker, lights out, curtains drawn.

They reached the porch. Davies used his sleeve to wipe his face, then smoothed his hair. He heard laughter from inside, and canned music.

In front of him, the principal stiffened momentarily, as if gathering his nerve, before shoving open the door.

A man was leaning against the bar, talking.

Perry said, almost diffident, "Hello, Vince."

Another younger man at the bar stopped laughing.

"All right, then, Gussie?"

Another man, older, was perched on a stool.

"Good to see you, Paul."

Round the corner was a larger bar with more drinkers. Davies wasn't concerned with them. He stared around him at the fruit machines, tables and chairs, reproduction photographs in sepia tint on the walls, and bits of ship brass, the smoking fire burning wet logs. The story had stopped, and the laughter; the older man held his glass against his privates and beer was frothed on his lip. The landlord was a skinny, whey-faced weasel with a cigarette hanging from his mouth. Davies thought it a pitiful place. Everything around him was fake. He noticed a chair at the side of the bar, away from the drinkers, where he could face the door and also see round the corner.

"What's it going to be, Mr. Davies?"

"Orange juice, thanks."

He eased down into the chair.

The west Middlesex whine of the landlord's voice cut the silence. "Before you go asking, I'm not serving you. Far as I'm concerned, the sooner you turn round and get back out of here, the better."

"Oh, yes, very funny. Mine's a pint, and an orange juice, thanks."

Perry was fishing for coins in his pocket. Davies glanced down the blackboard on which was chalked the menu for the day—sausage and chips and peas, burger and chips and peas, steak and chips and peas . . .

"I'm not having you in here—it's within my rights. I'm not serving you."

"Come on, a pint and an orange juice."

"You want it spelled out? I am not serving you. I've my custom to think of. That man with you, he's carrying a gun. I'm not having that on my premises, and I'm not having you. Got it? Bugger off."

Davies stood up from the chair, saw the stunned shock spreading on his principal's face and the cold hostility of the men he'd called Vince, Gussie, and Paul, and the landlord's smirk. His principal clenched his fists and the blood flushed his cheeks. Davies kicked back his chair and strode towards the bar. He caught his principal's sweater and propelled him out through the door, left it open, let the rain spatter in. He heard the laughter behind him.

The rain ran on Perry's face. He seemed dazed and in shock.

"I thought he was a good man—ignorant, a bore, but a good man . . . Jesus, I just don't believe it."

Davies said, "Let's get the hell out."

"Can't credit it, the bloody man . . . When I was low, last night, didn't think I could get lower, Blake said I should ask for the Al Haig story."

"When you're further down, that's when you'll get the Al Haig story."

They were standing in the middle of the road. Away ahead, wipers flailing, headlights on, was the unmarked car. There was a sign, Public Footpath, to the left. Davies took the principal's arm and headed for it. They walked between the banks of nettles and brambles, stepping over the dog shit, towards the rumble of the sea. They crossed a wooden bridge. The rain was in his hair, in his eyes, weighting his jacket, wrapping the sodden trousers against his legs. He radioed the Wendy house and told them they were going to the beach.

The marshland began a thousand meters to his right. They scrambled up the loose, tumbling stones of the seawall, clawing their way to the top into the teeth of the wind and the rainstorm. The tide was out. The pebble- and shell-pocked beach ran down to the sea in front of them. Beyond the tide line were the white-crested waves, then the shroud of the mist. His principal shrugged his arm clear. They walked together. The rain plastered his hair across his forehead, and Davies shivered in the cutting cold of the wind.

His principal stopped, faced the sea and the emptiness, sucked the breath into his lungs, and shouted, "You bastards, you fucking bastards! I thought you were my friends."

"What did he do?"

"Why do you need to know?"

"I have to know what he did, and the consequences of it, otherwise I cannot evaluate the reality of the threat."

"Didn't anybody tell you what the end game was?"

"Nobody's told me, and nobody's told him."

Geoff Markham drove. It had taken an hour of the journey to clean the detritus from his mind. Only when they were out on the open road did he begin to push.

"Why ask me?"

"I believe, because you are here, that you were a part of it."

"You need to know?"

"Unless I know, Mr. Seitz, I cannot do my job."

The American sighed. "It's not a pleasant story, Mr. Markham. It's about greater and lesser evils."

One of the room's walls was covered by the big-scale maps.

The largest showed western Iran's seaboard, the Gulf, the eastern coastline of Saudi Arabia, and the Emirates. A second map showed a city plan of Bandar Abbas and the road going west-northwest, past the docks, past the Hotel Naghsh-e Jahan, towards Bandar-e Khoemir. Tilted against the opposite wall were two display boards on which were pinned the photographs of selected personnel from the bogus petrochemical plant. Although it was early on a bright morning, the blinds of the room's windows were drawn. Hanging in front of them was the blown-up satellite photograph of the manu-facturing plant. They waited. They had received the call from the air-port, which told them he had arrived safely off the flight. They smoked, sipped coffee, and nibbled at biscuits. In the room were two men and a woman from the Secret Intelligence Service, three Amer-icans representing the Agency and the Bureau and the military, and the two Israelis. They waited for him to be brought to the discreet back door, normally used as an entry and exit point for kitchen staff and vetted cleaners. If it had not been for the most recently received intelligence briefings, none of the men and the one woman in the room would have countenanced the plan that was now set in place. They made desultory conversation. None would willingly have given such a pivotal position in the plan to a low-grade engineering sales-man, but it was accepted that the choice was not theirs. He was the access point. Only he could tell them whether the plan could be launched or should be aborted. They waited in the room, just as offi-cers of the Israeli Mossad waited in secrecy in the American huts of an Egyptian air base with the pilots who would fly them south, just as the officers and crew of a United States Navy fast patrol boat waited off the Emirates port of Sharjah. All of them waited for the arrival of the one individual who could give them the information required to launch or abort. He was led in. He was wan, strained, swaying on his feet with tiredness. His hands trembled as he gulped orange juice.

They all knew the risk he had taken. They let his nerves steady. He was sat in a chair and he told them, in a stumbling monologue, all that he knew about the restaurant, about the bus, about the invita-tion list to the celebration meal. When they had finished with him, teased out of him the precious information on which the plan de-pended, he was taken out by Penny Flowers to be told of the new life offered him. After he was gone, after the final assessment of his in-formation, the cipher messages were sent and the mission was launched.

·   ·   ·

"What do you mean—the 'greater evils'?"

"Try the missile program."

"Five years ago—yes?—how far along that line were the Iranians?"

"We were getting a mess of reports on the warheads but all contradictory, on when they'd be ready with nuclear, chemical, and microbiological. We could handle that, live with it."

"Explain that, Mr. Seitz."

"We thought we had a little time, but not with missiles."

"They weren't contradictory on the missiles?"

"Very clear, very precise. Without missiles, warheads don't count. They were up to speed with the missile program, maybe two years away."

"You cannot launch a warhead until you've a missile."

"Go to the top of the class, Mr. Markham. We needed to buy the time, to slow the program. But the installations are underground, bombproof, have air defense, with an army round them."

"Enter Juliet Seven."

"He gave us the way in. We couldn't reach the hardware, so the option we had was to go for their personnel."

The director was in the front of the bus, a double seat to himself. Behind him sat the project managers, the scientists, and the foreign engineers. He was relaxed and felt a sense of happy satisfaction. Behind him he heard the gentle, joking banter of the men who had made possible the advancement of Projects 193, 1478, and 972, and the babble of Farsi, Russian, Chinese, and the North Koreans' dialect. It was a worthy occasion, the retirement party for his colleague who controlled Project 972, and he had personally taken time to oversee the arrangements in the restaurant, down to the detail of the menu that would be served and the music that would be played. He rocked contentedly in his seat. He had believed, ever since his education in mechanical engineering at Imperial College, London University, that a happy team was a productive team.

The bus sped down the narrow road beyond the docks and left the city behind. He was lighting a cigarette, the flame close to his nostrils, when the driver stamped on the brake. He saw the man peering ahead. Through the cigarette smoke and the windscreen, a red light waved in the night's darkness. The bus slowed as the driver pumped the brake. He leaned forward, to make out a shadowed figure behind the light, and then a road-works emergency sign. He disliked lateness and glanced at his watch. He saw, thought he saw, a figure pass beside the bus carrying something, but could not be certain. The barrier was pulled aside and the bus powered on past the man holding the light. He eased back into his seat. Above the cackle of accents and laughter, the director heard the single thud from the side of the bus behind him and twisted instinctively towards the source of the noise. The last thing that registered clearly in his mind was the sight of the wall of fire coming like a torrent in spate through the bus. In the final moments of his life, the fire surged against his clothes, the skin of his hands and face, and beating in his ears were the screams of the scientists and foreign engineers. Trapped in the bus, with the flames and the screams, they had no possibility of escape.

"The personnel were burned to death? Christ."

"We delayed the program."

"But the missile factories were the same the morning after."

"Not the same. Yes, pieces of metal remained in underground workshops, but the team was gone. Take the team away and you screw up the project. Men matter. It's simply not possible to fly in replacements and carry on as if nothing had happened."

"The missile program was the greater evil?"

"In three years they would have had the capability of striking against any country in the Middle East, including Israel—even the possibility of reaching southern Europe. We bought five years."

"What was the lesser evil?"

For three consecutive days the satellite photography showed the skeletal shape of the burned-out bus. On the first day the movement of rescue workers retrieving bodies could be clearly seen from the enhanced pictures, with fire engines and ambulances. Radio Tehran carried reports of a tragic road accident in which twenty-four men involved in the petrochemical industry had died. The next day the photography showed a small group of forensic experts, identified by their white overalls, crawling through the gutted bus, and Radio Tehran made no mention of the accident. On the third day the pictures beamed from the satellite showed the bus being loaded onto a flattop lorry, and Radio Tehran's bulletins had brief reports of local funerals. By that third day, the United States Navy fast patrol boat had returned to normal duties, and the United States Air Force had flown five agents of the Mossad to Israel—and the life of Gavin Hughes had been painted out.

"Twenty-four men killed—did I hear right, Mr. Seitz? Is that what you're telling me? I can barely believe what you're saying."

"What you heard—a program was delayed."

"That was the greater evil?"

"Their weapons of mass destruction threatened our interests."

"And what the hell was the lesser evil?"

"The involvement of Juliet Seven—Gavin Hughes. The mission was done skillfully, and they had a poor forensic infrastructure. It was days, going on two weeks, before they could confirm the initial suspicion of sabotage, and by then Gavin Hughes had ceased to exist."

"I'm damn near speechless, it was pure savagery."

"We were looking after our backs, and we did it well."

"You were involved?"

"To a small degree, liaison—yes, I was involved."

"Did you consider the human misery—the widows, the children?"

"We considered the effect of the missile program. I don't really find emotion helps me get through the day."

"What about the little, awkward matter of state-sponsored terrorism?"

"Not applicable."

"If the Iranians kill one of their Kurds in Berlin, wherever, or a man anywhere in Europe who's planning murder, mayhem, in Tehran, we shout, scream, recall ambassadors, impose trade sanctions. We call it state-sponsored terrorism."

"Correct."

"If we roast twenty-four Iranians—"

"We call it looking after our backs."

"Forgive me, but that is mind-bending hypocrisy."

"You are driving too fast again, Mr. Markham."

"And if the Israelis go into Jordan to murder an activist?"

"That is justifiable self-defense. You should slow down a bit, Mr. Markham. I would suggest to you that the prime objective of an intelligence agent is to further by clandestine means the objectives of the taxpayers who put food in his stomach and a roof over his head."

"I believe in morality."

"I don't get to mix with people who use that word often . . . That's a better speed, thank you."

"I hope you sleep well at night."

"I sleep excellently, thank you. If we all talked about morality, Mr. Markham, none of us would finish a day's work."

"You used that poor bloody sales engineer."

"What the lady, Miss Parker, said, your work took you to Ireland. Unless you were completely useless at your job, I would have to assume that you 'used' people, were competent at running agents, manipulating them, exploiting them. Then you let them go . . . They did a job of work for you . . . Did you go and see your superiors and complain about your unhappiness at the ethics of running informers?"

"When does the marksman shoot, Mr. Seitz?"

"I beg your pardon?"

"Does the marksman shoot as the predator approaches the tethered goat, or when it's on the goat?"

"He shoots when he has the optimum chance of a clean kill. It's nice country out here. It's a little bit like Iowa, minus the sea, of course . . . ."

"Thank you."

"For what?"

"For telling me."

"Do you feel the better for it?"

"I'm devastated . . . but—yes, I'm the better for knowing it."

"Would your Juliet Seven be the better for knowing it? Will you tell him?"

"I don't know—I feel like throwing up. He was betrayed, treated like shit."

"I think we're going to hit the rain, which is a shame . . . Listen,

Mr. Markham, we went to a hell of a lot of trouble to do your Juliet Seven a favor. The Israelis could have machine-gunned the bus and left their calling card, bullets and grenades. We insisted on the fire and gave the Mossad the hardware, which guaranteed slow, difficult progress for the Iranian investigators. We bought your man time for his disappearance. He should have been safe, beyond their reach—I imagine, if you ever have the chance to look for it, it was his error that led them here. We did enough for him. Do you think there's time to stop for a pork pie and a beer?"

The beach seemed endless, stretching to the horizon where the cloud was poised over the gray stones of the wall behind which was the marshland. The wind and rain beat relentlessly on their backs.

Not until they turned for home did his principal start to talk. Davies stayed a pace behind him.

"Look at this place. It's as good as dead, it's condemned. Everything here is for nothing. The sea rules and eats at the place, like it's rotten and decayed. Seven hundred years ago this place was alive. It had a great fleet for trade, fishing, and boatbuilding. The Saxons, the Vikings, and the Normans settled here, where we are now. It had wealth. Their boats sailed after fish as far north as Iceland and they traded as far south as Spain and east to the Baltic. The sea killed this place, that same sea. In January 1328, there was a storm and a million tons of sand and stone was washed across the river mouth. The wealth went and the land began to follow it. The sea has the ultimate power. It eats at the cliffs and at the beach every minute of every day. Right here, where we are, it's a yard a year. Up the coast, not far, it's four hundred yards in the last five years. The fucking place, and everyone who's here, they're all doomed. Little people, fucking pygmies, living their lives, thinking they can change things. They've bulldozed seawalls, concreted the base of the cliffs, put in groins and breakwaters, but it doesn't make a damn of difference. The sea keeps on coming. A couple of miles down the coast was the tenth biggest town in England, five churches, built by people who thought that they'd last forever. Now they're all gone into the sea. They were pygmies then and pygmies now. The sea cannot be resisted. We're all dead here, doomed, we have no future. We build little houses, little gardens, make our little lives—and for what? For fucking nothing. People paid masons to carve gravestones so that the lives of their fathers, mothers, brothers, sisters would be remembered, but the stones are under the sea, like they'd never existed. We worry about the present but we're just too small. The future is the sea coming in, taking, snatching, in spite of our little efforts to protect ourselves. There is nothing we can do because there is no defense . . . Will you tell me, when do you think the bastard will come?"

In the distance on the seawall, wrapped in a dark anorak and waterproof leggings, watching them, facing into the thrust of the wind and the drive of the rain, was one of the policemen from the unmarked car. He cradled his gun close to his body, as if to protect himself against the onslaught of the gathering storm, now and in the future.

What Davies, drenched wet and frozen, had been told was that the killer would come soon, but he didn't say it.

11

Geoff Markham didn't like to drink in the middle of the day and had sipped a fruit juice. The American had washed down the pork pie with a dark pint from a wooden barrel and there had been salad with the pie. In the car, the onion was still on Seitz's breath.

Markham hesitated before turning at the signpost to the village. A cattle-carrier lorry swerved past him and gave him a long blast on the horn. It was all as he remembered it. Ahead of him was the high water tower, the dominating feature, and the American gazed at it with a sort of awe but didn't speak. Beside him, flanking the road, was a small car park and a sign—"Toby's Walks: Picnic Area." Away to the right was Northmarsh, to the left were wide, flat fields covered with half-moon pig shelters. He swung the car onto the minor road. Of course it was the same. How could it be any different?

The American smiled apologetically and murmured that he needed, and badly, to relieve himself.

Markham drove into the car park of the picnic area and saw what was different. There were two men in an unmarked car, uniformed, wearing Kevlar vests and silly little baseball caps. But there was nothing silly about the barrel of the Heckler & Koch aimed at him through the open side window. He braked. Seitz said that he couldn't have lasted much longer, and dived for the bushes. Markham held up his ID card for the policemen to see and sauntered towards them.

He introduced himself and said the American had bladder problems. He asked them how it was. The aim of the gun was no longer on his chest. He was told that they had the registration and the make of a car to look for, and it was all right in daylight.

"What's that mean?"

The policeman grimaced. "It's a sod of a place after dark. So quiet. Last night, before the changeover but after it got dark, we saw this shape in the bushes. Bloody near crapped myself. Seemed to be watching us. I got the gun on it, then two dogs came out. It was a woman walking her dogs, in the dark, like a bloody ghost, proper turn it gave me. It's Toby's Walks here. She asked, all straight-faced, had we seen Toby? She was serious—had we seen Toby? We asked the old biddy, who was Toby? You know what? He was Black Toby, Tobias Gill—no lie, it's what she said—and he was a black drummer in the dragoons who got pissed up, went looking for a bit of fanny, and brought her up here. He was found, Black Toby was, the next morning, drunk and incapable, and she was beside him, raped and strangled. They took him to the assizes and then carted him back here to hang him in chains. It was two hundred and fifty years ago, and the old biddy said he liked to walk round here, rattling his bloody chains. It's that sort of place. After what she'd told us, we heard every bloody bush move last night, every bloody creak of every bloody tree . . . She meant it. She was really surprised we hadn't seen him."

The American came out of the bushes and was pulling up his zip. Markham didn't laugh at the story. Out there a shadowy figure was moving in darkness among cover, silent, without the rattling of chains, towards a target and a place of death. He felt the cold wind coming off the sea and shuddered.

They climbed back into the car and he drove on.

Of course it was different, and for some it would never again be the same.

Markham asked the American what he wanted to see, and Seitz's finger jutted towards the church tower. The rain had come on heavily while they'd stopped for lunch, but now had eased into a fine, persistent drizzle. He could see the first houses of the village and the church tower looming above them. He was unsettled. It wasn't only the policeman's story of the ghost of the black drummer, it was also what Seitz had told him of Alamut, a place of death, and a bus ride out of Bandar Abbas, a place of carnage. And he remembered what Cathy Parker had said and asked. It would be decided down here, at the village, body to body, as it always was, at close quarters, and was he tough enough?

He felt inadequate. It was no longer about people like himself, rated as intelligent, educated, and thoughtful. It was about guns and nerve: this was a power play. Seitz pinched his arm and pointed to the parking lay-by at the side of the church.

At the near end was a fine squat tower, perhaps seventy-five feet in height, with wide walls of flint facing. Behind it were the nave and the high chancel windows and between them were stout yellowed stone buttresses. Beyond the church was a ruin, once finer and larger than its neighbor but now roofless and with the rain coming through the clerestory windows. Markham asked the American what he wanted to do, and was told he wished to go inside. He had a fascination for churches and a total respect for the quality of the architects and craftsmen who had built them, but the ruin disturbed him—death so close to life. He pushed open the church door. There were a few lights in the dull dim interior, as there had been in the weekend corridors at Thames House that morning.

A clergyman came towards him, a gaunt, fleshless-faced, older man. Markham thought Seitz was following him. He offered his hand in friendship and lied, said that he often diverted on a journey to see a worthwhile church. He heard the aged squeak of the hinges of a small door to the side. A smile lit the clergyman's face, as if few came to see his church. The flowers were already in place for Sunday's service, the only brightness stretching towards the altar and the stained glass of the arched window behind it. On the walls were the carved plaques remembering the dead.

The clergyman said, "There was an older church, of course, but that's gone, flooded by the sea first time round, then washed away. The origin of the building here is fifteenth century, and a magnificent building it would have been. But the village died. There were four altars here, now there's just the one. Once we had a bell that weighed three-quarters of a ton, but the community sold it off, in

1585, because they were dying from deprivation and hunger. It's so good to meet someone who's interested—my name's Hackett."

Markham looked around him, past the old carved-stone font, and could not see Seitz. If he had been alone in the church he would have said a short private prayer for those who'd been in the bus.

The clergyman droned on, "Disease, poverty, fires, all decimated the population of the village—I sometimes say that this is a place without a present, only a past. That's how it feels here sometimes."

He was in the bath. Meryl had made them undress at the back door, had insisted on it. Davies thought by now that Perry would have told her of the disaster in the pub, would have come up with an explanation as to why they had come back sodden, with sand caking their shoes.

She came into the bathroom.

Davies had hitched his wristwatch to the cold tap and was allowing himself five minutes' defrost time. The holster and the Glock were within reach on the floor, with the radio. She had brought two of Perry's dressing gowns to the back door.

There was no knock, and no hesitation or apology. He sat upright and hunched forward to obscure his waist, hips, and groin from her. Meryl carried a heap of folded clothes. Her face was expressionless, like those of the nurses had been while he couldn't wash himself, sponging his privates after he'd broken his ankle falling from a ladder when trying to get through a back window to plant a bug. There was a towel on top of the clothes. They could have been left outside the door, and she could have shouted to him that they were there.

She laid the towel and the clothes on the chair beside his head. Davies stared straight ahead and wondered how close she was to the edge of her sanity. It wasn't his job to prop up the morale of his principal, let alone that of his principal's wife. He felt himself to be the crutch on which she leaned. It was nothing to do with his personality, his warmth or his wit. It was because he had a Glock nine-millimeter pistol in a holster lying on the bright pink fluffy mat beside the bath. She came into the bathroom, where he was naked, for comfort from him and from his gun.

The wristwatch showed that his time was up. He had not the heart to tell her that he could not be her friend. He reached for the towel, hid himself clumsily, stood up in the bath, and began to dry himself.

He thanked her for bringing him the clothes. She went out of the bathroom and closed the door after her. She had not said a single word.

Duane Seitz paused, took his handkerchief, and mopped the sweat off his forehead. He swayed, clung to the rail, and climbed again. He had a horror of heights, but beyond the horror was a cruel sense of obligation. He had to climb the tower. He went up the narrow, worn, spiraled steps; if he had slipped he would have plunged. The door at the top was bolted and the bolt rusted. He couldn't move it. He balanced on a smooth, worn step, then heaved his shoulder into the door. It gave, pitching him forward through the doorway onto the small square floor of the tower's top.

The wind snatched at him. His coat was lifted and his tie was torn from his waistcoat. The drizzle made his eyes smart.

He looked around him and clung, with both hands, to the low, crenelated wall.

From the vantage point, he gazed down over the village.

His hair was ripped to a close tangle. He could see the road that was the one point of entry into the village and the lanes off it, the clusters of homes, and the patchwork shape of the green. He saw the house, and the roof of the small wood hut behind it. He saw the endless, disappearing seascape.

The house, its position, was of small interest to Duane Seitz. He sank to his hands and knees and crabbed around the square floor space, never dared to look vertically down.

There were the marshlands.

Dull, yellowed, reeds and dark-water channels between them, the marshlands were to the south of the village behind the seawall, and to the northwest. Reached by the one road, the village was an island surrounded by the old reeds, the dark water, and the sea. He estimated that each of the great marshes was a full three thousand meters long and a minimum of a thousand wide. He saw the thick cover of trees around the fringes of the marshlands, the tracks between the marshlands and the village.

In spite of his fear, without thinking, he straightened his back, lifted his head, and his nostrils flared. He snorted the air into them.

He was satisfied.

He had posed the questions and had answered them.

He crawled back towards the flapping door. He took a last look at the marshes and saw the gulls, white specks, meandering above them. He wedged the door shut after him and came down the spiral steps with his eyes closed.

He heard the clergyman's voice. "Everything went, the bells, the lead, the best-cut stones. Sad, but inevitable. They have a history, the native people of this community, of great suffering. It makes for a cruelty and a self-sufficiency. The original church was lost because survival took precedence over principle."

Seitz walked out into the rain and the wind. Markham came after him.

"What do you want to do now?"

"Go back to London."

"You don't want to see the house, at least drive past it?"

"No."

"You don't want to meet the protection officer?"

"Thank you, he'd be a busy man—well, he should be, he wouldn't want 'tourists.' No."

"Actually, you hitched a lift with me. I had a day planned down here. I needed to see for myself."

The interruption brooked no argument. "Are you a marksman? I don't think so. Are you expert at drawing defensive perimeter lines? I doubt it. There's nothing for you here. Don't sulk, Mr. Markham. You're a good driver—always do what you do well."

Markham unlocked the car, held the door open for him. Seitz felt aged, tired, cold. The tone of Markham's voice was resentful, the teeth of a saw on a buried nail. "So, back to London. I hope it's been a worthwhile exercise for you, Mr. Seitz—above and beyond lunch."

"It was worthwhile. Can we have the heater on full, please? He's there, Mr. Markham. I saw where he is. It was like I could smell him."

The bird ate the minced meat, stabbing down with its beak in quick, urgent strokes.

Vahid Hossein had led her to the small clearing among the bramble and thorn, at the edge of the marsh, where the grass was short from the rabbits' feeding. Farida Yasmin did not know whether he had brought her there out of a sense of boastfulness or he wished to share with her.

His fingers were long, gentle, and sensitive. She was behind him, within reach of him. He had sat her down, told her not to move, and whistled into the late-afternoon light. The bird had come from close by, had materialized over the dead reed fronds, with a labored flight. Now he stroked its head feathers with his fingers, and he used her handkerchief to clean the wound. The bird permitted it. She hoped it was not a boast but the demonstration of his wish to share with her a moment so precious. His fingers moved on the feathers, soothing the bird, and pried into the wound, and she saw the peace on his face.

It was as if, that day, she had slipped from the mind-set of Farida Yasmin Jones. The identity of her faith was discarded, as a snake's skin was shed. That day she had—she knew it and it did not trouble her—reverted to the world of Gladys Eva Jones.

She had stolen a car.

Any kid from her comprehensive school knew how to steal a car. It was the talk in the canteen at lunch, and in the grounds in mid-morning break, and on the bus going home. She had listened in disgust, years before, as boys, girls, had talked through the theory of how to do it, and she had remembered what she had heard. She was a thief, had broken the rule of the faith as it had been taught her, and she did not care. In the parking area beside the small railway station where the London commuters left their cars for the day, she had felt a raw excitement—and it had been so easy. The hairpin into the lock of the blue Fiat 127—because all the kids always said that the small Fiat was the simplest to take—and the stripping of the covering, the marrying up of the ignition wires. She was a thief; a few seconds' work with a hairpin and she was no longer the virtuous Farida Yasmin who could recite the Pillars of the faith, pages of the Koran, and had once been the favored pupil of Sheik Amir Muhammad. She had not felt shame, only excitement.

She watched him, watched his fingers on the bird, watched the rifle lying half out of the sausage bag on the far side of him, and the excitement was a toxin in her bloodstream. It was now a part of her. She recognized that it had nothing to do with the Islamic faith to which she had dutifully converted.

For all her teenage and adult life, Gladys Eva Jones had craved to be noticed, to be valued. He had listened thoughtfully when she'd told him that the police had been to her workplace, and had nodded his quiet appreciation when she had described the theft of the car. She sat and watched him, the bird, and the gun. She knew what he planned to do that night, had even seen the man he would kill and could remember each feature of that man's face. The excitement the knowledge engendered in her was a liberation. At last, Gladys Eva Jones was a person of importance. The sensation was as fresh as morning frost to her, compared to the dull tedium of her parents' home and the shunned, shut-out existence at the university. Her hand hovered over the hair at the back of his head. She thought of the empty boredom of Theft Section at the insurance company, and she stroked the hair on his head with the same gentleness as he caressed the feathers of the bird.

Her hand trembled, as if she sensed the danger of what she did.

The bird flapped away in heavy flight, and his eyes followed it, watching its wing beat.

Soon he would be gone with the rifle, and she would wait at the car for him to return. He needed her, and the knowledge of it gave her the confidence to slip her hand down onto the skin and bristly hair at the back of his neck . . . She knew the man who would be killed that night, and the house where he would be killed, and the excitement coursed in her.

There had been an older boy in her street who had a .22 air rifle. It was fired on wasteland where a factory had been demolished. Many times she'd gone after him to the waste ground, and hung back, had never quite had the courage to ask him if she could fire it. She'd dreamed at night about the chance to hold the rifle, aim it, and fire it. One summer evening the boy had shot a pellet against a passing bus, and the police had come and taken it away so she'd never had the chance. But for the lonely, unpopular girl, the rifle had stayed in her mind as the symbol of the boy's power. On the waste ground, with his friends, he swaggered when he carried it. The dream from childhood was roused. One hand still stroked the hair at the back of his neck, but her other hand moved in slow stealth behind his back until her fingers touched the weapon's barrel, which protruded from his bag. She felt its clean smoothness and the tackiness of the grease, and her fingers slid on the oiled parts. She imagined it against her shoulder, and her finger against the trigger, and she touched the sharpness of the fore sight, and she thought of the sight locking onto the chest of the man in the house on the green. Her hand moved faster, but more firmly, on the nape of his neck, but her fingers glided in gentleness on the cool metal of the rifle's barrel. He could see what she did, but he could not snatch the rifle away from her because that movement would frighten the bird.

She said, very quietly, "I should be with you."

"No."

"I could help you."

His free hand had moved to hers. She felt the roughness of his hand covering it. She would be with him, following him, and sharing with him. She had, in truth, no comprehension of the thudding blow of the rifle stock against a shoulder, or the ear-splitting noise of the discharge and the soaring kick of the barrel. She only understood the power that the rifle offered. The pain was in her hand. Relentlessly he squeezed her hand down onto the sharp point of the fore sight, crushed it until she struggled to remove it. His eyes never left the bird. He freed her hand and she quietly sucked the blood from the small, punctured wound. She kneaded the muscles at the back of his neck.

"I go alone," Vahid Hossein said. "Always I am alone."

"I am here to give you anything you need," Farida Yasmin whispered.

Meryl heard the impertinent, lingering blast of the bell.

She was in the kitchen, locking the legs of the ironing board, with the heap of washed and dried clothes in a basket at her feet. She started for the door to still its insistent shrillness. It surprised her that Frank had not gone to answer it. She heard the voice of Davies, the detective, speaking into his radio in the hall. Stephen was with her, at the kitchen table, methodically writing in his school exercise book. In spite of it all he was doing the weekend work that his class teacher had set. That was her next looming problem: Monday morning, and no school. Frank shouted down from upstairs that he was on the toilet. Davies was at the door, waiting for her to come, and assuring her that the camera had picked up one of the village people. She switched off the iron.

All Frank had told her was that Martindale, the bastard, would not serve him.

Davies opened the door, and she saw Vince, smelt his beer breath. She was behind Davies.

"It's all right, Mr. Davies, it's Vince. Hello, Vince—God, don't say you've come to start on the chimney."

Vince was the most fancied builder-decorator in the village. There were others, but he was the best known. He was a great starter and a poor finisher, but those with a leak or a slipped tile or the need for a sudden repainting of a spare bedroom for a visitor knew they could rely on him. And he was a popular rogue . . . The Revenue had looked at him twice in the last seven years, and he'd seen them off.

He was in a constant state of dispute with the parish council because of the builders' supplies dumped in the front garden of his former council house, now his freehold property, behind the church. Anyone who could lay a hand on a Bible and say they would never have a rainwater leak or a slipped tile or the need for fast redecoration could call him a fraud, a bully, a botcher. There were not many. Small, powerful, his arms heavily tattooed, he was everybody's friend, and knew it and exploited it. What Vince believed in, above all else, was the quality of his humor. He had no doubt that his jokes made him a popular cornerstone in the village.

Meryl tittered nervously. The mortar was coming out of the brickwork on the chimney. It was just something to say. "Surely you're not going up there?"

"Actually, I've come for my money."

"What money? Why?"

"What I'm owed."

"Frank paid you."

"He paid me two fifty down, but there was more materials—I've got the bills." He was routing in his trouser pocket, dragging out small, crumpled sheets of paper. "I'm owed nineteen pounds and forty-seven pence."

"You said it was inclusive, for Stephen's bedroom, everything for two fifty."

"I got it wrong. You owe me."

"Then you'll get the extra when you come to do the chimney."

"If you're still here, if pigs fly, if—"

"What does that mean?" He'd been in her kitchen. She made him four pots of tea each working day and gave him cake. She'd left him with the key when she'd gone out and he'd been working in the house. She'd trusted him. "What on earth are you talking about?"

"If you haven't moonlighted—going, aren't you? I'll be left, owed nineteen pounds and forty-seven pence, and you'll be gone. I've come for my money."

She choked. "I can't believe this. Aren't you Frank's friend? We're not going anywhere."

"No? Well, you should be. You're not wanted."

She stuttered, "Go away."

"When I've got my money."

The detective moved without warning, stepping forward two, three paces. He caught at Vince's collar and had him up onto his toes. When the fist came up Davies caught it as if he was handling a child. He twisted it hard against Vince's back, pivoted him round, and marched him back down the path. She heard everything Davies said into Vince's ear.

"Listen, scumbag, don't come here to play the fucking bully. Go back to that godawful pub and tell them that these people aren't leaving. And don't ever bloody come back here."

With a jerk of his arm, the detective pushed Vince down onto his knees in the roadway, forced his face into the deepest and widest of the puddles, and kept hold of him until he stopped struggling, lay still in submission. Davies released him and stepped cleanly back to watch Vince crawl away.

She leaned against the wall beside the door. Davies came back in and closed it quietly behind him. She hadn't noticed it before but Frank's trousers were too short for him and his sweater was too tight. She put her hand on his arm.

"Thank you—I don't suppose you should have done that."

"I don't suppose I should."

"Frank would have called him a friend—he went up on the roof in a storm last winter."

Very gently he took her hand from the sleeve of the sweater. She didn't look into his face, didn't dare to. She looked down at his waist and the gun in the holster.

"What you have to understand, Mrs. Perry, it's all totally predictable. It's not peculiar to here, it would happen if you lived anywhere. It would be the same if you were in a suburb or a city street. It's what people do when they're frightened. Maybe you'll find someone out there who has the guts to stand in your corner, and maybe you won't. What you have to remember, they're ordinary people, people you'd find anywhere. You can't expect anything else from them."

The lavatory flushed upstairs.

"I'll get the ironing done. How long will it be till they come for Frank?"

"Thank you, the stuff's a bit tight on me."

He disappeared into the dining room. In the kitchen her Stephen was still doggedly writing in his exercise book even though he would have heard each word Vince had said to her. Outside, the night was coming and the curtains were tightly drawn against it. Vince had always been so good with Stephen, had made him laugh. Would they come that night for Frank, or the night after, or the night after that? She shook and tried to hold the iron steady.

In a vile temper, Fenton returned to Thames House from his lunch. It should have been lunch and shopping with his wife, if the wretched man had not canceled lunch for Monday and insisted his only opportunity was Saturday. Fenton had bartered with his wife: lunch with the academic and then shopping, with her having access to the full range of his plastic.

He came up to the third floor, was told there was nothing new of note, then went into his office to shed his coat and spill his micro tape recorder onto the desk. The lunch had further confused him, and the expensive shopping had wounded him.

He had not used this source before, but the file said he was sound.

The academic was white-haired and ginger-bearded, a professor of Islamic studies at a minor college at the university, had a face lined like a popular ski run, from Sudan. The confusion, from the soft-voiced lecture, had fueled Fenton's temper. He listened to the tape again.

"What distresses me is the hostility of the Western media and the Western 'orientalists' towards the Islamic faith. They are servants of imperialism. They stigmatize, stereotype, and categorize us, and any scholar of the faith of Islam is labeled with the title of 'fundamentalist.' There's no denying it is a term used with hostility. If we judged Christianity by the excesses of the Inquisition, or if we took the Fascist elements in Zionism to reflect the faith of Judaism, you would be horrified. If we talked always about apartheid and Nazism as examples of Christian belief, you would rightly criticize us—but when a zealot hijacks an aircraft he is labeled an Islamic fundamentalist. If a lunatic shoots children in a school, do we call him a Christian fundamentalist? You live by a double standard. You follow slavishly the American need to have an enemy, and you plant that title, without the slightest reason, on the faithful of Islam."

They had been in the students' canteen, a dreary cavern of a building. They'd collected salads and fruit juice from a self-service counter, not a bottle of wine in sight, and the academic had persistently questioned the woman at the till to be certain there was no alcohol in the vinegar that accompanied the salad.

"You distrust us in your midst, even those Muslims who are British citizens. Our colleges for converts in this country are monitored by the security forces—why? Because we are different, because we live by other criteria? Is it that you fear believers and the standards to which they dedicate their lives? A Muslim will not steal from you, will not seduce your wife, will not go to prostitutes, and yet the strength of our decency is regarded as a threat, so we are harassed by the political police. Everything you talk about involves this threat, but it is a figment of your imagination. We are not drunk in the street and looking for violence, we are not hooligans. Would a virtuous young woman, an Islamic convert, join in a criminal conspiracy of murder? The very idea is preposterous and shows the depths of your prejudice."

Fenton had listened and toyed unhappily with his lettuce leaves, probably left over from the previous week's catering. They had a table to themselves. He had attended the Royal Military Academy at Sandhurst, not university, and when his eyes wandered to the students sitting around them, he'd felt a sense of disgust.

"You have made a growth industry in the study of the Islamic faith, but the work is shallow. You seek to vilify Iran, to cast that great nation and its people in a mold of the 'medieval.' I tell you, Mr. Fenton, where there is the *sharia*, the law of Islam, you would find it safe to walk in the streets. It is a code of fairness, charity, and decency. Yes, there is a death sentence. Yes, there is very occasional amputation—and the flogging of offenders—but only after the most rigorous examination of the felon by the courts. I venture to say that there are many in the United Kingdom, so-called Christians, who yearn for the punishment of the guilty. But to suggest as you do, Mr. Fenton, that the legally elected government of Iran would seek clandestine vengeance abroad is just another example of a warped and closed mind. Let me tell you—if a *small* incident or a *trivial* event occurred, if you made from it a fraudulent link with Iran, if you danced to the American tune, if you made lying public statements, then the consequences could be most grave. Do you dance to that tune, Mr. Fenton? Are you acting now as a lackey to those Islamophobic elements of the American establishment who wish to block the return of more normal relationships between Iran and the United States? A false and deceitful move would lead, Mr. Fenton, to the most desperate of consequences. Of course, I do not threaten you but I warn that your irrelevant and decadent country would be at war with a billion Muslims throughout the world. I do not think you would wish that."

So, earnestly, at the end of a meal that left him hungry, he had fled the canteen.

With a deep sigh, Fenton switched off the tape recorder he had worn under his jacket. The two roads split ahead of him, and the directions they took were opposite and irreconcilable.

Was Islamic Iran a force for good, which he was too bigoted to appreciate, or a force for evil, which made a sewer of the streets of his country? He did not know which road led to truth. What he did know was that Abigail Fenton had punished him for her missed lunch with the price of a new handbag, a dress, and a matching twin set.

He rang Cox in the country and hoped he was disturbing him. He told him what he had learned. Whichever way they twisted was fraught with problems. Cox said his confidence in Fenton's judgment was, as always, total. He'd always thought of Cox as a time-serving, networking fool; now he began to doubt that opinion.

He wandered towards Cathy Parker. "I'm confused, Cathy."

"Goes with the rank, Harry."

"I don't know whether it's real—can't quite bring myself to believe it—the threat."

"Best, Harry, as the actress said to the bishop, just to lie back and enjoy the ride. Do you want to be told?"

"If it'll blow some clarity into a fogged old mind . . ."

"Bollocks, you're loving every minute of it."

He grinned. She laughed and started to map it out, what they had. A man had come in from the sea. A car had crashed, the man had moved on. An associate was missing from home but photographs had been found of a target and a location. Between each point she rapped her pen on the desk, as if to alert him, then her face lightened.

"I've found a marriage, 1957. The daughter of a British oil engineer to an Iranian doctor. There's a cousin down in Somerset . . ."

"What'll that give you?"

"Who knows? Might give me a face. I don't like to see you confused. Confusion is like hemorrhoids, Harry, embarrassing for you and therefore bloody unpleasant for the rest of us. I'm making it my business, by hand, to swab away your confusion."

"Do you believe in it, the threat?"

"I'd be a right idiot if I didn't."

"And the tethered goat, do you believe in that?"

She laughed into his face. "I'm just the bottle washer—it's your responsibility, Harry, not mine. You volunteered."

The blue Fiat 127 was behind a hedge, hidden from the road. Brought up in the provinces by a family without military or criminal links, she had compensated for her lack of experience in such areas by the simple application of common sense. Using basic logic, she had thought through each of her moves. The car was the right color to avoid attention; the station, with commuters not coming back from London until the middle evening, had been the right place to steal it from. Her own car was abandoned in woods: she had unscrewed the number plates and buried them under fallen leaves. It would be days or weeks before it was found, reported. She had done each thing sensibly, and even if he had wanted to he could not have criticized what she had done.

She sat in the car, in the silence, in the dark, and her mind wafted between her two contrary worlds: Farida Yasmin, or Gladys Eva. He would now be making the final checks on his rifle and would be smearing mud on his face. She shuddered and tried to pray to his God, her God, to protect him. When she tried to pray, she was Farida Yasmin Jones. The man was guarded. Under her sweater, she was running her fingers over the skin of her stomach, as he had caressed the bird's feathers, as she had stroked his hair. The man was guarded with guns. It was the first moment that she had considered the realities of the guards, the guns. She thought of him shot, bleeding. As her fingers moved faster, pressed harder, she was Gladys Eva Jones. She thought of herself, waiting and alone. She thought of the boots on his neck where her fingers had been, and the pools of blood. Soon, he would be moving off, tracking beside the marshes towards the lights of the village.

Geoff Markham had crossed the orbital motorway and was coming through the dirty sprawl of east London's streets. Seitz had slept on the open road but the jerking drive through the traffic had wakened him, and he talked.

"Pathetic, really, a sign of age, that I can't climb a narrow staircase without a palpitation. I'm fine now, I'm warm, and I've had my necessary sleep. I owe you an explanation—why a hundred miles driving out of London, a quick climb of the church tower, and a hundred miles drive back has not been a waste of your time."

Markham stared into the weaving mass of cars, vans, and lorries, in heavy concentration.

"I am not a criminologist, or an academic, most certainly not a clinical psychologist. I detest those shrinks who charge fat fees for profiling. I am simply, Mr. Markham, an aging foot soldier of the Bureau. I have been in Tehran and Saudi Arabia for the last twenty years of my working life. I said, because I know those places and those people, I could smell him. It's not vanity, it's the truth."

Markham drove past the brightly lit shopwindows festooned with bargain stickers and kept his silence. He had noted that not a word of sympathy had been expressed by the American for Frank Perry and his family, as if there were no room in the job for compassion.

"My tools of trade, Mr. Markham, are intuition and experience, and I value them equally. Actually, there is little that's complicated. We are told he is late thirties. He would have been eighteen or nineteen years old when the ayatollah returned from exile. Then comes the war with Iraq. The military are not trusted, the principal fighting is given to the fanatical but untrained youth of the Revolutionary Guards corps. They fought with a quite extraordinary and humbling innovativeness and dedication. They made up the rule books of combat as they went along. Any man, given the responsibility for a mission of this importance or the importance of the bombings in Riyadh or Dhahran, would have come through that route."

He saw the men who carried the clusters of shopping bags and the women who pushed prams, and the voice in his ear dripped the story of a world they would not have comprehended. Markham would be joining the great uncomprehending masses because he did not believe he had the ability to affect events.

"Most of life is a linked chain. Think about it—the Iranians could not match the quality of the Iraqi weaponry that had been provided by the Western powers. They had to learn to improvise and fight where that hardware was least effective. They chose the most unpromising ground. You won't have heard of these battles, Mr. Markham, but they were of primitive ferocity. Fish Lake and the Jasmin Canal, the Haur-al-Hawizeh marshes, the Shatt al Arab waterway, and the Faw peninsula. The battleground for the best of the Revolutionary Guards corps was water and reed banks. By choosing to fight on such hostile and difficult territory, they nullified the sophisticated equipment of their enemy, and that's why I had to climb to the highest point, the vantage position. I am not ashamed to say it, I was on my hands and my knees, petrified. I surveyed the battle-ground, and all I could see was water and marshes. It's where he would be, it is why I said it was like I could smell him . . . Don't waste fuel by sending up helicopters with infrared, the Iraqis did that, and don't waste people's time by commissioning aerial image-intensified photography, they did that as well. He will be hiding there and an army wouldn't find him. But he has to come out, Mr. Markham, and then, God willing, you shoot him."

One day, before the end of the week, he would tell Seitz, insist on it, that he was Geoff, that he was a colleague and not a stranger. He didn't know whether the formality of the American was old-fash-ioned Iowa courtesy or the patronizing talk of a veteran to a young-ster. But as the bright lights of the city reflected up into his eyes from the roadway, he listened to every word and believed it. He thought the American brought as much soul to the business as he did when he played a board game with Vicky. It was, actually, distasteful, and near to being disgusting.

"You are a polite man, Mr. Markham. You haven't interrupted my rambling—and polite enough to humor me by driving slowly. But if you had been less polite you would have interrupted to ask the ques-tion that is most pertinent. What sort of man is he? Let me tell you, he is a child of the revolution. When you were chasing girls, Mr. Markham, he would have been on the barricades facing the bullets of the shah's army. When you were studying at college, he would have been learning to survive against heavy artillery barrages and mustard-gas bombing. When you were playing at war in Ireland, he was killing with expertise in the harsh environment of Saudi Arabia . . . He will be a man who has never known youth, gaiety, and mis-chief as you have. He will be a man without love."

Ahead of them was the Thames House building, and the light was going over the river.

"It's been a great day. I've said all I can—my part in this is just about played out. Would the Tower of London be open tomorrow? Esther would be upset if I didn't send her some photographs of Lon-don history. There's not a lot of history in Iowa . . . I won't be going down there again, not till it's finished. I don't believe in second-guessing the experts. It's in their hands now, the people with the guns. Remember what I said, a man without love, a man who won't walk away . . . I'll go down again if there's a body to view. I'd like that, if it can be done inside my schedule."

Markham swung the car down into the basement car park. He turned off the ignition and stared to the front, before turning to face Seitz. "Can I ask something, no, several things?" he said briskly.

"Haven't I given you the chance? I'm sorry. Fire away."

"It may sound like an idiotic question, Mr. Seitz, but do you think you change anything? Do you believe you do anything that's honorable and worthwhile? Do you care about people? Have you ever considered walking away and picking up work where there's something finite at the end? Is it a decent job?"

Markham looked into the American's old eyes and saw the light flash in them.

"That tells me you're thinking of bugging out . . . It's not for me to offer persuasion either way, but I don't think you're the sort to drop out. I've been through the bad times when it's just filing paper and getting a cold ass on a surveillance stakeout, and there's no big picture to tell me it's worthwhile. I've done that. I hung on in there. I got a grip and I hauled myself up, and I thought whining was poor sport. I believe in what I do. I think I serve my country's interests. There's plenty of places back where I come from that have banks and real estate offices and insurance companies where I could have gotten work—and I think it would have been slow death. But I'm a selfish man and I love what I do, and I aim to keep on doing it . . . If they threw me out tomorrow I might just go find a veterinary surgeon and ask him to put me down. I can't think, Mr. Markham, of a better thing that a man can do than to serve his country and not have it bother him that no one knows his name and no one will ever learn what he did."

Seitz had reached for the door handle.

Markham said, "Thank you."

"I've met your principal. I was at the meetings that evaluated the information he gave. He's a tough, proud, able man. Don't make a judgment on me because I'm not modern and emotionally incontinent. I hope, sincerely, he makes it through this. But I'm honest with you, my country's interests are paramount to me. You can't go soft on this. I have to tell you, I have very little respect for quitters."

Only later were they able to put together the sequence of events.

They were all trained men, but their memories were hazy and fuddled. On one thing they were all agreed, Dave Paget, Joe Rankin, Leo Blake, and Bill Davies, the speed with which it happened, so *fucking* fast.

Dave Paget and Joe Rankin sat in the Wendy house, the door shut tight against the cold. It was fifteen minutes to the end of the twelve-hour shift. They were both, wouldn't have admitted it, knackered. When they cared to look at it, the television screen alternated between the view of the back garden and the view of the front approach to the house; on the console, the lights indicating the state of the sensor beams were steady on green. Joe Paget was finishing the last of the sandwiches and muttering about where they would go to eat, where they'd find a new pub because last night's meal had been a bloody disaster. Dave Rankin flipped the pages of two magazines simultaneously, survival kit and holidays, talking to himself about thermal socks and about which month had the best weather in Bournemouth and Eastbourne, was engaged in a mindless interior dialogue. A red light on the console bleeped, indicating that a sensor beam was broken at the bottom end of the garden. Joe Paget said it was that bloody fox again, and Dave Rankin said that Bournemouth was as good as Eastbourne if it was out of season. Something moved, on the screen, at the far end of the garden . . .

Leo Blake tried to slip quietly past the sitting room door of the B-and-B but was ambushed by Mrs. Fairbrother. How long were they intending to stay? They were not the sort of trade she was used to. Did he realize how inconvenient it was to have him sleeping in their house through the day? She had a shrill, moneyed voice, and the bark hadn't been lost with the change in fortunes. He said that he didn't know, ducked past her, and hurried out to his car . . .

Bill Davies was reading his newspaper in the dining room, the radio and the Heckler & Koch resting on the blanket covering the table. He was warm, had an electric fire on two bars, and clean. Meryl had ironed his shirt, his underwear, and his socks, and had at-

tempted to press the creases out of his suit. Only his shoes were still
damp and they were filled with the sports section of his newspaper.
He had his feet up on the table. The television was on next door, in
the living room, and they were all there. He glanced down at his
watch; Blake would be relieving him in five or six minutes. His radio
crackled to life, jolting him from the newspaper . . .

Dave Paget and Joe Rankin were both numbed into silence. The
first call out to the house was the warning; now they stared at the
screen and were checking for the confirmation. Paget was very pale,
Rankin was sweating. Their machine guns were hooked over their
necks and shoulders. Red lights began to replace green lights on the
console. Twice the camera caught a movement, and twice lost it—
somewhere down at the bottom of the garden, where the shrubs
were and the greenhouse. It wasn't like Hogan's Alley and it had
fuck-all, sweet fucking nothing, to do with the shooting range. What
the hell should they do? Quit the Wendy house? Crab towards the
end of the garden where the beams were broken and the movement
showed? Shout? Activate the bloody floodlights? Run for the house?
There was no fucking instructor to tell them what to do. They saw
him on the screen. He was coming up the side of the garden, a
blurred white figure. They saw the rifle, outlined against a gray
furred background, then it was gone. Paget swore, and Rankin gave
the confirmation into the radio . . .

It might have been the rain, and the maintenance on the pool cars
was worse than last year, when it had been worse than the year before, but it took Leo Blake an age to start the damned engine. He sat
in his car and revved, long enough for the curtain behind him to
part, and he saw Mrs. Fairbrother scowling at him. Bloody car, and
he'd have some bloody words for the maintenance people . . .

Bill Davies burst the door open into the living room. The advertisements were playing between the soaps. The machine gun dangled free on its strap and thudded against his body. He was shouting.
They sat frozen. Perry was in his chair holding his coffee mug, Meryl
had her needlework on her lap, Stephen was on the floor with his
computer game. He was shouting, and they did not respond, and he
was shouting louder. He grabbed his principal and hauled him up
from the chair and the coffee flew in the air and down to the carpet.

He was dragging his principal, helpless, like a sack of sand, out into the hall. The radio was blasting in his earpiece, and she hadn't come and neither had the kid. He snatched open the door of the cupboard under the staircase and pitched his principal inside. Perry cannoned against the vacuum cleaner, the brooms, the boots, the kid's old pushchair, and the junk. He went back, shouldn't have done, for her and the kid, broke the drill they practiced. The principal should have been his only priority. He caught her arm and the kid's wrist—she was screaming, and the kid—and he threw them in the cupboard against his principal. He crouched by the door. God, if they would just stop screaming . . .

Joe Paget stayed at the console and watched the screen. Dave Rankin ducked out of the Wendy house, launched himself onto the lawn, rolled, then crawled towards the kitchen door and the cover of the water butt. Each had the selector off safety, had gone to single shot; each had one in the breach; each had the finger on the trigger guard. Joe Paget told Dave Rankin, face microphone to earpiece, that the Tango was out of the beams, off camera. Where was the bastard? Where the fuck was he? . . .

Leo Blake was going down the drive when he switched on the radio. He heard the chaos on the net, and the gravel spewed out from under his tires . . .

Bill Davies had his principal buried deep in the cupboard and the kid was in there behind him. But the woman was still screaming. He held her, he had to. With one hand he aimed his machine gun at the front door, with the other hand he clutched her to him. He held her against his chest to stifle the screaming, and she sobbed hopelessly . . .

Joe Paget said that the Tango had gone up the side of the house, would be on the neighbor's patch, and the front was not covered. Dave Rankin swore, said he'd try to cover the front. His breath was heaving and, to Joe Paget, he was damn bloody close to going incoherent. Coming across him and Dave Rankin was Bill Davies crying out for cover at the front, and the woman's sobs were across everything. And the unmarked car at the main road was playing bolshie and saying they weren't supposed to move off station, and the unmarked car that was cruising was more than two minutes . . .

Leo Blake came round the corner by the village hall and, with the green ahead of him, had to swerve to miss an old man with a terrier . . .

Bill Davies heard the shoulder hammer into the front door where there was a new lock and an old bolt, and held his hand over her mouth and tried to muffle the sobbing that would pinpoint for the Tango where they were. The door sagged . . .

Dave Rankin fell into the cold frame at the side of the house, crashed through the glass, sprawled, and lost the momentum of his charge . . .

Leo Blake drove straight across the grass of the green, wheels spinning, skidding, hit a young tree, and flattened it with its post. He swung his wheel and had the front of the house in his full lights, and saw him . . .

Bill Davies heard the door splintering . . .

For a flickering moment, Joe Paget saw him again, white against gray, then lost him as the car's lights blacked out his screen . . .

Leo Blake had the Tango in his lights. He could see the man's camouflage combat gear, his mud-smeared face, and the assault rifle. The man, as if it was his final desperate effort, threw his weight against the door. Blake shared the Heckler & Koch with Davies, and now only had the Glock in a shoulder holster. He'd forgotten it, its presence there was clean out of his mind. He dazzled the Tango with his lights. The Tango had the rifle up, aiming towards the car, but couldn't see through the lights. Blake knew the rifle, had fired the same weapon on the range, knew its killing power. He thought his last best chance was to charge the man with the lights on full beam. The Tango thrust an arm over his blinded eyes, then ran. The man sprinted, full stride, along the track in front of the houses. There was a moment when the back of the Tango was in front of the car, and then the man tried to sidestep towards the cover of a hedge. Clutching the wheel, Leo Blake felt the jolt as he clipped the Tango, and he was past him. The car surged on, spun, turned the full circle. Leo Blake saw, lying on the grass, the Kalashnikov. He switched off the engine. He tried to be calm, to report what he had done, what he had seen . . .

Bill Davies held the woman, his hand still over her mouth. The sound of bitter argument on the soap played from the living room through the hall and into the cupboard. He said it was all right, he said it was over, and he realized that he had no shoes on . . .

Joe Paget sat motionless in front of his console and watched the green lights of the unbroken beams . . . Far away, Dave Rankin heard the splinter crack of a fence breaking, as if it were rotten and gave under the weight of a man. He walked out of the front garden and across the grass to the Kalashnikov, cleared it, and made it safe . . .

Leo Blake sat in his car and tried to slow the beating of his heart. He put the window down, for air, and the stench came to him, from the hedge, of old stagnant mud . . .

Bill Davies took his hand from Meryl Perry's mouth . . .

Dear Geoffrey,

It was good to see you in person and hear you at first hand—if we had any doubts about your suitability or your readiness to take responsibility, then you most decisively struck them out.

My colleague and I are, therefore, very pleased to be able to offer you employment with the bank. You would start in our Pensions/Investment section, where we would monitor your progress before deciding where in our operations you would sit most comfortably. Our Human Resources section is currently drafting a letter setting out a proposed salary structure along with bonus emoluments, which you will receive on Monday. If they are acceptable, please let me know when you can start with us—the sooner the better as far as we are concerned. We would wish you to resign from your present employment at the earliest opportunity.

Sincerely,

The letter was under her buttocks.

It was Vicky's reward.

It was creased and crumpled, and her thighs gripped his waist, and her ankles locked against the small of his back.

The drink made her noisy.

She had cooked for the two of them, something Mexican. His absence at lunch with her mother was forgiven, and she'd drunk most of the bottle he'd brought round. Shyly he had shown her the letter that had lain unopened all day in his briefcase. She had left the plates, the empty glasses, and the finished bottle on the table, and taken him and his letter to her bed.

Wasn't he clever, wasn't he brilliant? Wasn't the future opening for them?

He was too tired to enjoy it, but he pretended. She grunted and squealed and kept him inside her long after he was finished.

When would he resign? When would he be shot of the bloody place?

It was as if Vicky had given him a present . . .

His pager bleeped on his belt. His belt was in his trousers, on the floor by the door, where she'd pulled them off him.

He prized open her thighs and fell off her.

All he wanted to do was to sleep, and to forget the one-road village, the prey and the predator, the high church tower that overlooked the marshlands. He crawled to his trousers and read the pager's message. MARKHAM G./RE JULIET 7—FAILED HIT—GET BACK SOONEST. FENTON. He started to dress. She lay on the bed, limp, her legs apart. He pulled on his underpants, his trousers, shirt, and his socks. The letter still peeped from under her buttocks. He pulled on his shoes and knotted the laces. He went to the bed and tried to kiss her mouth, but she turned her head away and his lips brushed her cheek.

"It's the last time you do this to me, the last bloody time. You're not running back to them again, like they're your bloody mother."

12

Bill Davies had clung to the pillow in the bed. In his dream mind Meryl had been with him through the night.

The pillow was the principal's wife. He had held her close against him in the doorway of the cupboard under the stairs when her body had shaken with the sobbing, and he had held the pillow against his chest. The pillow had been soft, vulnerable, needing protection.

He had slipped out of the house before Mrs. Fairbrother was downstairs, an hour before his wake-up call. He had driven away from the village, out past the church, to the woodland by the car park and the site. He had pulled up an oak sapling from the ground, wrenched it up from the sandy soil, and had found a pile of posts for fencing that had been left by the foresters, and taken one. He had thrown the sapling and a post into the boot of the car.

He waved grimly to the men in the unmarked car. They'd be the same shift as had been on last night, and the beggars had played by the rule book and said they weren't permitted to leave their station. He'd have them. Later in the morning he'd burn them when he could get his guv'nor on the telephone. It would have been shades of hell for that family, but the unmarked car had followed the rule book, and the family could have died because of it. He shook his head sharply, as if to block the memory, and started up his car.

He pulled onto the road and had to brake sharply. He'd damn near run into the back of the van. At snail's pace it was going towards the village. He was about to hit the horn when he realized the implication of the painted words on the back of the van.

"Danny's Removals. Nothing too large or too small. Go anywhere, anytime." And there was a London telephone number.

The removals van was lost and trying to find an address in the village. Why hadn't Blake radioed him, or his guv'nor telephoned him? He wondered whether they'd already gone, with their suitcases, and whether the van was just to pick up their furniture and possessions. They could have bloody told him, after everything he'd done for them. He beat his fist in frustration against the steering wheel. He'd been in charge of the security, and it had so damn near gone wrong. Was he responsible for the family running? Momentarily he shut his eyes, lost sight of the big back doors of the van. He'd thought Perry had the balls to stick it out, even if the wife hadn't. A van meant that Perry was going, or had gone . . . He felt limp, washed through. He thought that he had failed. He couldn't blame them for going, not after last night. He thought the bastards had won. The bastards were not a man with an assault rifle, but the men in the pub, the neighbor, the people at the school. The bastards, the friends, had won the day.

A man ran out from a hedge ahead, looked like a lunatic on the loose, and waved frantically to the dawdling van. He was wearing a raincoat, under which the hem of a nightshirt showed and bedroom slippers. The brake lights flashed.

Davies saw the For Sale sign onto which the Sold board had been nailed. The man was pointing to the narrow driveway of the cottage.

He stopped and breathed hard. He thought it was his tiredness that had made him react so fast and so stupidly. He waited while the van maneuvered into the driveway of Rose Cottage, then powered away down the empty road. He realized, then, how much the family meant to him.

In the half-light of the Sunday morning, Bill Davies used the short-handled spade from the boot to hack out the broken tree on the green and the snapped-off post that had held it.

The broken tree, an ornamental cherry, was in bud and would soon have been in flower. Last night, the wheels of Blake's car and its chassis had miraculously cleared the small plaque commemorating the planting of the tree by the parish council as a mark of respect for the dead princess. He dug a deeper pit and planted the oak sapling in the cherry tree's place, then used the back of the spade to hammer down the stolen post. He tossed the broken tree and the snapped stake behind the water butt at the side of Perry's house.

Where there had been a cherry tree there was now an oak sapling; where there had been a stake there was now a post. He used the point of the spade to scuff up the grass and cover the tracks of Blake's tires. He folded away the spade.

A teenage boy was working down the far side of the green with a bicycle-load of newspapers.

Two cars went down the road at the side of the green and plumed exhaust fumes behind them.

He shivered in the chill of the morning and wondered if she had slept or had clung to her husband, his principal. And Bill Davies was satisfied . . . The evidence of the night action was erased. He had told them, in London, in his interim report, of the highly professional defense of his principal and his principal's family. He had written in a stuttering hand, then controlled his voice to hide its quaver as he'd dictated a brisk litany of lies. They might just believe it in London. He looked across the green and the roofs of the houses towards the watery low light growing on the sea's horizon line. He looked at the house and the drawn curtains on the bedroom window, and he wondered how they would be . . .

He was walking to the front door when the neighbor spilled out from the next-door house.

"A word, I want a word with you."

Wroughton, the neighbor, was in a dressing gown and slippers. His hair wasn't combed and he hadn't yet shaved. Davies saw the wife behind him, half hiding in the hall's shadows.

"How can I be of help?"

"What happened here last night?"

"I'm not aware that anything happened."

"There was a car . . ."

"Was there really?"

"And shouting."

"Must have been a television turned up too loud."

"Are you telling me that nothing happened here last night?"

"If there's anything you need to be told, Mr. Wroughton, you'll be told it."

He stared into the neighbor's eyes, challenged him, then watched him back off and go back inside. Bill Davies could be a quality liar and a good-grade bully. He saw the woman's face at the window beside the door, smiled cheerfully at her, and waved. A man with a high-velocity assault rifle had been, in the darkness, a few feet from where that woman, her husband, and children had lain in their beds and listened to tire screams and panicked shouts. There were enough complications in Bill Davies's workday without added responsibility for the neighbors. He felt the burden of it, and stamped up the path to ring the bell. The previous week, he would have sworn it couldn't happen, that he would be emotionally involved with his principal's family.

Blake told him that a dog team had arrived three hours earlier, found a trail through the gardens down the green, across rough ground, and had lost the trail in the river. Apparently there was no blood on the trail. The dogs had worked the riverbank, Blake said, but had failed to regain the scent. A van had come an hour before and collected the assault rifle.

How were they, in the house? Blake shrugged. They were predictable.

What was predictable? They were on the floor.

Would they get off the floor? And again Blake shrugged, as if it wasn't his concern, but the woman had cried in the night and twice the man had come down the stairs and poured whisky, swigged it, and gone back up. They'd had the kid in the bed with them.

Was Blake, ten hours later, sure he'd hit the man? Blake was sure and, to emphasize his certainty, led him to the car and showed him the sharp dent in the paint work over the near-side wheel.

A small car, a city runabout type, came towards them. Instinctively, his hand slipped inside his outer coat and rested on the Glock.

He saw a young man at the wheel, his eyes raking the ground ahead as he approached. Bill Davies thought he was looking for the evidence of what had happened in the night, but there was nothing for him to see. It was like the aftermath of a road accident when the fire brigade had hosed down the tarmac, the traffic police had swept up the glass, and the recovery truck had towed away the wrecked vehicles.

The car stopped. The window was lowered. The young man, stubble on his face, tie loosened, held up an ID card. Davies thought he had been up all night.

"I'm Markham, Geoff Markham, I'm the liaison from Thames House. Are you Bill Davies?"

He nodded, didn't bother to reply.

"Pleased to meet you. They're singing your praises at our place, up to the rafters. I mean, it was a quality defense of a target. We'd have expected unadulterated chaos, but what you did was brilliant. There's a big meeting this morning, up at secretary-of-state level, that's why I'm here, for liaison. There has to be an evaluation of how the target will take the pressure—waste of time, really, because your report indicates exceptional calm. We'd have reckoned they'd be screaming and bawling and packing their bags. What was it like?"

Davies tried a thin smile.

"Well, it's what you're trained for, yes? We understand the dogs lost him on the way to the marshes going south . . . I'll talk to your principal later, when I've had a walk about the place and found somewhere to bed down. Hope I won't be in your way. There's talk of putting the Army in to flush him out, but that's for the meeting to decide . . ."

"I won't have it, I can't accept it." The secretary of state flexed his fingers nervously, ground the palms of his hands together.

"We should be there, we've the expertise." The colonel had driven from Hereford through the dawn hours.

"Out of the question, there has to be a different way."

"Special Forces are the answer, not policemen."

Fenton was there with Cox, at the side of the secretary of state but a step back from him. It amused Fenton to see the politician writhe in the confrontation with the stocky, barrel-bodied soldier. He understood. The Regiment's commitment to Northern Ireland was reduced: the colonel was touting for work for his people, and for justification of their budget.

"With the military and their backup, all their paraphernalia, equipment, we escalate way beyond any acceptable level to government."

"Policemen cannot do it, Counterrevolutionary Warfare Wing should be deployed," the colonel demanded.

"The military going through those marshes, like it's a pheasant beat, a foxhunt, ending in gunfire and a corpse. That's an admission of our failure."

"Then you take the risk on your shoulders for the life of this man, and for the lives of his family—we can do it."

The colonel wore freshly laundered camouflage fatigues and his boots glowed. Fenton and Cox were, of course, in suits. The politician was of the new breed, dressed down for a Sunday morning in corduroys and a baggy sweater. At Thames House, they harbored no love for the Special Air Service Regiment. The gunning down by plainclothes soldiers of three unarmed Provisional IRA terrorists— in daylight, in a crowded street—in Gibraltar had been, in the opinion of the Security Service hierarchy, simply vulgar. Each time, the moment before he launched himself in speech, the secretary of state glanced at Fenton and Cox as if they might offer him salvation, and each time both men gazed away.

"It would smack of persecution. We have close to two million Muslims in the country, the effect of a military gun-club drive could be catastrophic for race relations in the United Kingdom."

"Do you want the job done, or don't you?"

"Those relations are fragile enough. Even now we're walking a tightrope between the cultures. Deployment of the Army against what is probably a single individual, and his inevitable death, would create dangerous tensions, quite apart from the effect on international dialogue . . ."

The colonel thwacked his fist into the palm of his hand. "The idea of sending policemen into those marshes, that sort of terrain, against a dangerous fanatic, is preposterous."

"Another way, there has to be."

"No. My men have to go in for him."

The politician rocked and reached out to his table to steady himself. Perhaps, Fenton thought, he saw an image of camouflaged soldiers dragging a body from the water of those hideous marshes that bordered the road going away from the godawful place. Perhaps he saw an image of young Muslims barricading streets in old mill towns of central and northern England. Perhaps he saw an image of a British diplomat being pulled from his car by a mob in Tehran or Karachi, Khartoum or Amman. Every politician, every minister of government he had ever known, was traumatized when the men came from the dark crevices at the edge of his fiefdom, did not confide, demanded free-range action, and dumped on the desk a sackload of responsibility. The colonel had his finger up, wagged it at the secretary of state as if he prepared to go in for the kill.

". . . there is no other way."

It was Fenton's moment. He enjoyed, always, a trifle of mischief. He looked at Cox, and Cox nodded encouragement.

Fenton smiled warmly. "I think I can help. I think I can suggest an alternative procedure . . ."

He had been there through the night and all of the day before. The necessary stillness and silence were as second nature to him.

In that time he had eaten two cold sausages given him by his mother and not needed more.

He sat motionless, sheltered by a rock from the worst of the wind. He was a thousand feet above the small quarry beside the road where the police waited, two hundred feet above the escarpment of raw stones and weathered tree sprigs where the eyrie was. He had his telescope and the binoculars but he did not use them; he could see all that he needed to see without them. There was only the wind's light whistle to break the silence rippling around him; it was an hour since he had last whispered into the radio the police had given him, and the birds at the eyrie were quieter now.

When the egg thieves came to the mountains the police always called him because, as they told him, he was the best.

The anger burned slowly in the young man's mind . . . When he had climbed to his vantage point, using dead ground, never breaking the skyline or making a silhouette, the birds had been frantic at

the eyrie, wheeling and crying. It was impossible for the young man
to comprehend that a collector would hire people to come to the eagles' eyrie to take eggs, and harder than impossible for him to understand that those same eggs, a pair of them, would be valued by
the collector at a figure in excess of a thousand pounds. The notion
that the collector would hide the dead, smooth eggs away from
sight and keep them only for a personal gratification was impossible for him to believe . . . He loved the birds. He knew every one of
the nine pairs that flew, soared, hunted within twenty miles of
where he now sat.

The previous afternoon he had seen the decoy come down the
mountain. It was intended that the movement should be seen.
There was a routine and he had learned it. The eyrie would be hit
in darkness. A pair of men would climb to it with the aid of passive
infrared goggles, and would lift the eggs. They would move them
down a few hundred meters and hide them. They would be clean
when they reached the road and their car. A decoy would go on to
the mountain the next day and appear to make a pickup, would
search in the heather or among boulders, would seem to lift something, and would then come down. Were he stopped and arrested,
the decoy, too, would be clean, the surveillance would be blown,
and the eggs abandoned. If the decoy were not stopped, then a man
would come for the pickup the following day. The pickup man had
gone close in the misty dawn light to a group of hinds, had been
within thirty yards of them and not disturbed them, had been good.
But he had disturbed a solitary ptarmigan, and that had been
enough for the young man at his vantage point. He had followed
the pickup, his eyes needling on him. He had seen him lift the eggs
from a hiding place and start, with great care, to come down from
the mountain. He had told the police over the radio where he
would reach the road.

The mountains of this distant corner of northwest Scotland, their
eyries and the vantage points, were the young man's kingdom.

He was Andy Chalmers, twenty-four years old, employed to shoot
hinds in the forestry plantations for ten months of the year, and to
stalk stags for the guests of the owner of his estate—Mr. Gabriel Fenton—to shoot during the remaining two months of the year. He was

the junior by twenty years of the other stalkers of the neighboring estates, and in that small, close-knit world he was a minor legend.

If he had not been exceptional, he would never have been allowed near Mr. Gabriel Fenton's guests. Were it not for his remarkable skills at covering ground in covert stealth, he would have been relegated to renewing boundary posts and hammering in staples to fasten the fencing wire. He was surly with the guests, had no conversation, treated wealthy men with undisguised contempt, made them crawl on their stomachs in water-filled gullies till they shook with exhaustion, snarled at them if they coughed or spat phlegm, and took them closer to the target stags than any of the other stalkers would have dared. The guests adored his rudeness and insisted on him accompanying them when they returned in subsequent years.

He watched the distressed wheel of the birds above their thieved eyrie. Many times the pickup, from cover, searched the ground above and below him for evidence that he was identified, and failed to find it. There was little satisfaction for Chalmers in the knowledge that the police waited in the small quarry beside the road. The life warmth of the eggs was gone and the embryos already dead. The pickup disappeared into the tree line that hid the quarry and the road.

The radio called him.

The wind blustered against him and rain was shafting the far end of the glen.

He looked a last time at the birds and felt a sense of shame that he could not help them.

He took the direct route down, using a small streambed. The cascading icy water was over his ankles, in his boots, and he felt nothing but the shame.

He came to the quarry. They were big men, the police out from Fort William, and they towered over him, but they treated this slight, spare, filthy young man with a rare respect. They thanked him, and then led him into the trees and pointed to the yellowed yolk of two eggs and the smashed shells. The pickups always tried to destroy evidence in the moments before they were arrested. He looked at the debris and thought of the fledglings they would have made, and of the sad, aimless flight over the eyrie of the adult birds. He started towards the police car where the shaven-headed pickup sat handcuffed on the backseat, but the policemen held his arms to prevent him reaching the door.

He was told there was a message for him at the factor's office.

Peggy was a cog in the wheel of the village's life. She thought of herself as a large cog, but to others in the community she was of small importance. She didn't care to acknowledge that reality. Her husband, dead nine years from thrombosis, had been a district engineer with the water authority, and within a week of burying him she had joined every committee that gave her access. Her loneliness was stifled by a workhorse dedication to activity. Nothing was too much trouble for her: she hustled through the hours of the day, out with her bicycle and her weathered bag, on her duties with the Women's Institute and the Wildlife Group and the committee for the Red Cross. She had a checklist of visits to be made each week to the young mothers and the sick and the elderly. Dressed in clothes of violently bright colors, she believed herself popular and integral. What she was asked to do, she did. She was happily unaware that, to most of her fellow villagers, she was a figure of ridicule. She had no malice. She had a loyalty. On that Sunday morning she was tasked by the Wildlife Group to perform a duty which would also feed the curiosity, inquisitiveness, on which she lived.

Frank Perry could see, side on, the slight wry grin on Davies's face, and his hand sliding away from under his jacket. It wasn't anything Perry had seen before: Peggy's coat was a technicolor patchwork of color, and her garish lipstick matched none of the coat's hues.

"Hello, Peggy, keeping well? Yes?"

Peggy stared past him, a sort of disappointment clouding her features.

"Not too bad, thank you," she said severely.

Peggy's disappointment, he thought, was that she hadn't spied out an armored personnel carrier in the hall, nor a platoon of crouched paratroops. She was on her toes to see better into the unlit hall. Perry wondered if she'd noticed the new tree and the new post, the tire marks; she probably had because she missed little.

"How can I help?"

"It's Meryl I came to see—Wildlife Group business."

"Sorry, you'll have to make do with me. Meryl's still upstairs."

The unmarked car cruised behind her and Davies gave it a small wave as if to indicate that the woman in the dream coat was not a threat. There were two more cars in the village that morning . . . Perry was unshaven, half dressed, and he had left Meryl upstairs in bed. She had been crying through half the night, and only now had slipped into a beaten, exhausted sleep.

Peggy blurted her message. "I was asked to come, the Wildlife Group asked me. Meryl was doing typing for us. I've come for it. I've been asked—"

"Sorry, you're confusing me." But he was not confused, just wasn't going to make it easy for her. "Your next meeting's not till Tuesday. She'll have it done by then, she'll bring it with her."

"I've been asked to take it from her."

"By whom?"

"By everybody—chairman, treasurer, secretary. We want it back."

He was determined to make her spell it out, word by bloody word. "But it's not finished."

"We'll finish it ourselves."

He said evenly, "She'll bring it herself to the meeting on Tuesday."

"She's not wanted there. We don't want her at our meeting."

The day after he, Meryl, and Stephen had moved in, Peggy had brought a fresh-baked apple pie to the house. Of course, she'd wanted to look over the new arrivals, but she had brought the pie and talked about infant schools for Stephen with Meryl, the better shops and the reliable tradesmen, and introduced her to the Institute. She had made Meryl feel wanted . . . He didn't curse, as he wanted to. He saw that the grin had chilled off the detective's face.

Perry said quietly, "I'll get them. Would you like to take the stuff for the Red Cross? Have they decided that Meryl is a security risk too? It'll save you two visits."

"Yes," she said loudly. "That would be best."

He went inside. Meryl called down to him to find out who was at the door. He said he would be up in a moment. He went into the kitchen. Last night's supper plates were still in the sink, with the whisky glass.

He took the folders from the cupboard where Meryl kept her typing and flipped through them. There was the scrawled handwriting of minutes and deliberations by the group and the committee members, the chaotic mess that had been dumped on his Meryl. Her typed pages were clean, neat, because trouble was taken over them, because care was important to her. As he turned the pristine, ordered pages of her work, his resolve began to founder. Because of him, his past, his betrayal, and his damned God-given obstinacy, she suffered. He turned the pages of her typing—prize lists, outings, letters of thanks to guest speakers—all so bloody mundane and ordinary, but they were the necessities of her life . . . Like an outcast, he felt the touch of plague.

There was a church, St. James's, outside the next village down the coast, which had been built on the site of a lepers' hospital. Dominic had told him that when the church was built, a hundred and fifty years back, the laborers digging the foundations had found many skeletons, not laid out as in Christian burial, but in rejected disarray. When the first sore appeared, suppurating, and the first bleeding, and a man was sent to the lepers' place, had his friends still known him? Or had they turned their backs?

He gathered Meryl's pages back into the folders and took them to the front door, reaching past the detective to hand them to Peggy.

She dropped the folders into her bag.

So much he could have said, but Meryl wouldn't have wanted it said.

"There you are, Peggy, everything you asked for."

He knew that by not cursing, not swearing, he destroyed her. Her chin shook, and her tongue wriggled and spread the lipstick on her teeth. "I was sent. It wasn't my idea. 'You're with us or you're against us,' that's what they said. If I'm against them I'm shut out. Doesn't matter to you, Frank, you can move on. I've nowhere else to go. It's not my fault, I'm not to blame. If I don't bring those papers back, I'm out. I'm a victim, too. It's not personal, Frank."

She ran to her bicycle.

He let Davies shut the door on her, and climbed the stairs to the bedroom. There was never a good time for telling a bad story. She was wiping the sleep out of her eyes.

"I don't want to tell you this, but I have to. Peggy came to take away your typing for the Wildlife Group and the Red Cross. She's going to do it herself. We are not wanted . . . I could have thrown it all at her face and made her grovel down in the road to pick it up. I didn't. I know what I'm doing to you." He paused and drew a breath. "They say he's still out there. He may be hurt, but if the injury isn't severe, he'll come again. They say the dogs found a scent, then lost it . . . Peggy's going to do the typing herself."

She screamed.

The shrill staccato burst of her scream filled the room. She convulsed in the bed.

The scream died and her eyes stared up at him, wide and frightened.

Still in his pajamas, Stephen was in the doorway, holding a toy lorry and gazing at him.

He told Stephen that his mother was unwell. He tried to hold him but the boy recoiled. He left the bedroom, where there were no lights, no pictures, where the glass of the mirror on the dressing table was scarred with adhesive tape. He walked slowly down the dark stairs, as if descending into the lower reaches of the bunker.

He stopped at the dining room door.

"How much worse does it have to get?"

"Does what 'have to get,' Mr. Perry?"

"How much worse does it have to get before I'm told the Al Haig story?"

"A bit worse, Mr. Perry."

He hung his head. "And how much worse does it have to get before I say I'm at the end of the road, before I'm ready to run, quit?"

The detective, sitting at the table, the machine gun beside his hand, looked up keenly. "That door was open once, but not anymore. I think it was on offer a bit ago, but it's not an option, Mr. Perry, not now."

Cathy Parker had used one of the sleeping hutches at the top of the building to catch four hours' rest. She came down to the floor. Fenton was there with Cox. She riffled through her papers for the address in Somerset. It would be a good drive; she'd enjoy the blessing of being clear of Thames House.

She might have time to call in for tea or a sherry with her parents afterwards. Fenton was talking, convincing.

"You worry too much, Barney, you'll go to your grave worrying. You heard what the American told young Geoff, this man is essentially a civilian. He is not military, doesn't have the mind- set of manuals. He will think like a civilian and move like one. You don't put the military in against him, you put another civilian there. If it had been the military, then you've lost control—and that's something to worry about. God, the day I side with a politician is a day to remember."

She walked past the grinning Fenton, and Cox, whose face was an enigmatic mask, and paused at the closed, locked door. She took a pen from her handbag and made a decisive line through the writing on the sheet of paper fastened there. She wrote boldly, DAY FOUR, and moved off down the dull-lit corridor.

The Iranian crude was off-loaded. The tanker was buoyed up, monstrously high above the waves rippling against its hull, riding to its anchor. The radio message had still not been received.

Perplexed, the master called the terminal authority, reported a turbine problem, and requested that a barge come alongside to take his crew ashore. He did not understand why the order to make the rendezvous had not reached him.

All day Peggy had anticipated the opportunity to call on the new people who had moved into the cottage on the opposite side of the road to the church. It was a dingy little place, only three bedrooms. Old Mrs. Wilson, now in a nursing home, had always said the damp in the walls of Rose Cottage had wrecked her hips. The ride home had settled her after the confrontation with Frank Perry, and she'd collected the pie, wrapped it in tinfoil, and balanced it under the clip on the rack over the back wheel of her bicycle.

She had hoped to be invited inside, but she had had to hand over her welcoming gift on the step. A man had answered her sharp rap at the door, wispy-haired, slight, raggedly and dully dressed, and seemed to be astonished that a complete stranger brought an apple and blackberry pie to him.

He said his name was Blackmore. There were half-emptied packing cases in the hall behind him. He told her no more about himself than his name. A woman came down the stairs, picked her way between the rolled carpets and the boxes, but the man did not introduce her and awkwardly held the pie he had been given.

Peggy chattered . . . Her name, where she lived, the societies and groups in the village . . . The woman had a sallow skin, a foreigner, perhaps from the Mediterranean . . . The bus timetable, the early-closing day in the town, the best builder in the village, the walks, the milk delivery . . . Neither the man nor the woman responded . . . The layout of the village, the pub, the hall, the shop, the green—and they should not go near the green because of the disgraceful attitude of the people who lived there, endangered the whole community, protected by guns, showed no respect for the safety of the village . . . The man shrugged limply as if to indicate that he had work to be getting on with, and passed the pie to the woman behind him.

When she reached out her hands to take it, Peggy saw, very clearly, that the woman had no nails on the tips of her fingers and thumbs. Peggy's nails were painted sharp red to match her lipstick, but where the woman's nails should have been there was only dried, wrinkled skin.

She came away feeling that they were uninteresting and unlikely to contribute to the life pulse of the village, and that her pie was wasted on them.

"Show me."

She had waited all through the night in the car, huddled in the passenger seat. As she had waited, her mind had been churned with the torment of her split identity. The quiet had been broken by the owls, and once a fox shadow had passed close. She had sat, hunched, cold, and waited. She remembered Yusuf's kindness, and the calmness of the teaching of Sheik Amir Muhammad, and the strength given her by the conversion to the Muslim faith, and she thought of the confidence that the name Farida Yasmin had brought to her. It was as if the old world, the existence of Gladys Eva Jones, demeaned and diminished her. Again and again, alone, she murmured the name that had given her strength and confidence. Without it, she was base and trivial. The old world was lustful and cheap, the new world proud and worthwhile.

"Show the wound to me."

Through the night she had listened for the crack of distant gunfire and she had heard only the owls.

As the hours had slipped away, so her anxiety for him had increased, nagging and worrying at her, until she could no longer bear the loneliness of the vigil. She had felt an increasing sense of disaster breaking. In the dawn light she had left the car and tried to trace the route he had taken her the day before. In Fen Covert, she'd avoided fallen dead branches, stepped lightly on the leaves and not scuffed them, kept wide from the path, as he'd shown her, and she had heard the baying of big dogs. Then she had walked more quickly and her anxiety for him had been at fever point. Across the marshes, beyond Old Covert, she had been able to see right to the tower of the village church. The early sun gleamed on the river that ran from the marshes, and by the river were the dogs.

Behind the dogs, controlling them, were the handlers. Behind the handlers, guarding them, were the marksmen with the guns on which the bulging telescopic sights were mounted. They hunted for him. They had not killed him, and the knowledge of his survival brought pricking tears of happiness to Farida Yasmin's cheeks.

"You don't have to be shy but you have to show me where you are hurt so I can help."

While the sun had risen and the clouds had gathered off the sea and chased it, the dogs had tracked back on the riverbank, then searched away from it, and she'd known they'd lost the scent. When the cloud had crossed the sun, and the grayness had dulled the marsh reeds, she had seen the handlers call off the dogs. But she had taken note of where the marksmen settled, where they watched from after the dogs had gone. She had kept in the trees. She had gone into the woodland of Fen Hill.

Because of what she had endured, the anxiety, her anger snapped. "Fine, so you won't show me where, so you don't want help—well, get up, keep walking, turn your back on it, go home. Don't think about me, what I've done."

If it had not been for the bird Farida Yasmin would not have found him. It had lifted off, flapped away, cried, then circled the bramble clump into which he'd crawled. He had seemed to be sleeping, which had amazed her because his face was furrowed in pain. She had wriggled on her stomach into the back of the thicket and been within arm's reach of him when he had woken, jerked up, slashed his face on the thorn barbs, gasped, grabbed at her, recognized her, and then his eyes had closed, his body had arched as if the pain ran rivers in him. He had told her of his failure, of the car, the lost rifle. The words had been whispered and his head stayed down.

She whipped him with her hissed words. "Because of you—what I've done for you—I've police waiting for me. I'm on the line for you. Are you staying, or are you going? Are you going to let me treat your wound, or not?"

The rent was at the side of his fatigue trousers. The car must have caught his hip and upper thigh, ripping the seam of his trousers at the pocket. She had seen the long distance he had come, from where the dogs had lost his scent to Fen Hill. He could not have come that far with a broken femur or fractured pelvis.

Farida Yasmin thought the failure would have hurt him the worst.

Her hands trembled as she reached for his belt, unfastened it, and dragged down the zip. It was hard to pull down. The trousers were sodden wet. She crouched low above him, under the roof of bramble and thorn, then pushed her arm under the small of his back and lurched his buttocks clear of the ground. He didn't fight her as she dragged the trousers down towards his knees.

She saw the mottled purple and yellow bruising.

She saw the hair at the pit of his stomach, the limit of the bruising, and the small contracted penis. He stared up at her.

Her fingers, so gently, touched the bruise and she felt him wince. She tried to soothe his pain. She told him of the dogs and where the marksmen were. She told him what she would do and how she would help him. Her fingers played on the bruising and caught the hairs and she saw him stiffen. It was where her fingers had never been before. His breathing came more slowly, as if the pain lightened. It was what the girls had talked about in the schoolyard, and in the coffee shop at the university, and in the canteen at work, and then she, the virgin, had thought their talk disgusting. Her fingers caressed the bruising as his fingers had stroked the neck of the bird.

The voices were soft, atmospheric, metallic, coming over the monitor.

"I don't know whether she can take it, not much more."

"I have to assure you, Mr. Perry, that your security is constantly under review."

"If I'd known, realized, what I said to you and that jerk who came with you, what it meant, Geoff—what it would do to me and, more important, what it would do to her . . ."

"There are now two more ARVs—sorry, that's armed-response vehicles—in the village, four in total, and eight highly trained men. That's in addition to Mr. Davies and Mr. Blake, and the men in the shed. You should see it, Mr. Perry, as a ring of steel dedicated to you and your family's safety."

In the hut, the speaker was turned down low. Paget was eating sandwiches, Rankin watched the screen and flicked between the images of the rear garden and the front door, while they listened to the two men talk.

"You've bloody changed your tune. Why?"

"There are questions I cannot answer."

"That's convenient."

"You have to believe, Mr. Perry, that everything that should be done is being done. Look, take last night, a professional and expert defense—"

"Are you serious? It was fucking chaos."

After the handover and the debrief, Joe Paget and Dave Rankin had been up into the small hours going through, in exact and minute detail, every moment of the alert. Had the camera given them a target? Why was the next garden not covered by the beams? Why had they not moved the cold frame from the side of the house? They had been close to bloody disaster, Rankin had said, maybe a few seconds off it, and Paget hadn't disagreed.

"That's not the way Mr. Davies reported it."

"What the hell do you expect him to say? Grow up. Get real! She can't take the punishment, not much longer."

"We've made our commitment, Mr. Perry."

"When I told you and that jerk we were staying, it was because I believed we were among friends. That's the worst."

"Don't you read newspapers? It's how people behave when they're afraid—each week it's in your newspapers. A family have a child recovered from meningitis and they're about to fly back from a sunshine holiday, but the other passengers won't travel with them for fear of infection. They're bumped off the flight, no charity. How many examples do you need? A blind lady wants, a couple of years ago, to move into a seaside block of apartments, but the other residents organize a petition to have her blocked because they've convinced themselves that she'd be a fire risk because she's blind—fear again . . . Those east of England villages that have a USAF base for a neighbor, they'd all done damn well out of those bases for four decades, had made money and made friends. All very cozy, until those bases are used by the aircraft that attacked Qaddafi in Libya. Pretty fast change of mood—get the Yanks out, the Yanks are danger, the Libyans could bomb us as a reprisal. What price solidarity then? . . . The nicest thing you can say, when fear's around, is that people are pretty damn fickle with their loyalties. Everybody says they wouldn't behave like that. Don't believe them. It doesn't matter where you are. An American Navy ship shoots down an Iranian passenger aircraft, and it's a mistake, but the Iranians don't accept apologies and bomb the car driven by the captain's wife on some smart street in San Diego. The detonator was incorrectly wired. She lives, but she's chucked out of her job, she's a pariah and might endanger others. I can reel them off. It's a herd mentality. The fear makes them vicious, dictates they turn on the victim. It's human nature, Mr. Perry . . ."

There was the squeak of the planks at the door of the hut. Rankin swung, Paget gulped on the last of his sandwich. Meryl Perry was in the doorway.

On the speaker was Markham's metallic voice. ". . . I suppose it's because so few people, these days, ever get really tested that they're so scared of the unpredictable."

Her tone was dead, flat, like her eyes and the pallor of her cheeks. "I hope I'm not disturbing you, I came for Stephen's tractor."

Paget remembered her screams over the detective's radio, and Rankin had heard them as he had tried to get round the house and fouled up in the cold frame. Paget scrambled to kill the speaker. Rankin groped under his chair and found the boy's tractor.

"Do you always listen to us? Is everything we say, Frank and I, listened to?"

13

At that moment, Meryl hated them.

"Do you hear everything? What I say to Frank, what he says to me, are you listening? Is that how you spend your days?"

She could hear the rising pitch of her own voice. Paget wiped old crumbs from his mouth and looked away from her. Rankin passed her Stephen's tractor. She snatched it. To her, they were huge, dark shapes in the baggy boilersuits with the big vests over their chests. They were older than she, older than Frank, and they seemed not to care. Standing at the door before they'd known she was there, she'd seen one of them grin at the smooth reassurance being dished out to Frank.

"You get a big laugh out of what we say. Do you snigger when you hear us in bed? Not much noise when we're in bed, is there?"

Her control was gone. Meryl was over the edge. They would think her hysterical, stupid, or just a woman. They would wonder why she didn't just shut up, start the ironing, do the dusting, make the beds. She squeezed the tractor in her hand, tighter, hurting herself. Nobody told her anything. The wheels fell off the tractor. When any of them talked to Frank, and she came close, they stopped, and Frank cut short what they'd said. She was not included, not need-to-know, just a woman who was a nuisance.

"How long are you here? Forever? Is that my life, forever, having you listening?"

The short one, Paget, said quietly, "We're here, Mrs. Perry, till Wednesday night. That's the end of our shift."

The tall one, Rankin, said gently, "Thursday morning's a lieu day, Mrs. Perry, then we start our long weekend."

"Actually, Mrs. Perry, we'll have clocked up twenty-eight hours overtime in the week, so they won't mess with our long weekend."

"Then we're on the range for a day—not an assessment, just practice."

"After that, we might come back and we might not. We're always the last to be told where we're going . . ."

Rankin took the tractor from her, then crouched to pick up the wheels. The tears were filling her eyes. She thought they were indifferent as to whether they came back to this hut, this house, her life, or were assigned to another location. Rankin had the tractor wheels back under the toy's body and Paget passed him a small pair of pliers. She was just a makeweight woman who had lost control. She turned and leaned against the wall of the hut, her eyes closed to pinch out the tears. When she opened her eyes, the picture was in front of her—three or four inches from her face. It was hazy, a gray-white image of the bottom fence of her garden, the apple tree and the sandpit Frank had built for Stephen. The shape of the man they sought stood out and the silhouette of the rifle.

Her voice was brittle, fractured. "What'll you do when you drive away from us for your long weekend?"

"We were thinking of going fishing, Mrs. Perry, off the south coast."

"You get a good rate on a boat this time of year, Mrs. Perry."

Paget smiled. Rankin gave her back the repaired tractor.

She smeared the tears off her face. "Will you stand in front of us, before you go fishing, in front of Frank and Stephen and me?"

Rankin said, "I won't lie to you, Mrs. Perry. We're not bullet catchers. I don't expect to get killed on the say-so of a fat-cat bureaucrat sitting in a safe London office. If the opposition, him . . ." He gestured harshly towards the picture Sellotaped to the wall. ". . . if he wants to die for his country then I'll willingly help him along, but I don't aim to go with him. If he wants to end up a martyr, famous for five minutes, that's his choice. I'm here to do the best that's possible, and Joe is, and that's as far as it goes. If you don't like it, then you should get your suitcase down off the top of the wardrobe . . . That's the truth, Mrs. Perry, and I'm sorry no one told it you before."

"Thank you."

She turned for the door. The cloud had covered the sun and her home; what was precious to her seemed both drearily mundane and terrifyingly dangerous. She held the door handle for a moment to steady herself.

It was Joe Paget who called to her. "I'd like to say something, Mrs. Perry. We didn't do well last night, but we learn. It won't be like that again. We'll kill him if he comes back, and that's not just talk." He paused. "You should get back in the house and make yourself a fine pot of tea. I don't know him or anything about him, but I'll shoot him, or Dave will. You can depend on that, we'll kill him."

The husband stared belligerently at the sofa as Cathy Parker wrote briskly in her notebook.

His wife spoke: "I wouldn't know anything about her, except that when my aunt died I had the job of sorting through her papers. My uncle had passed on three years earlier. It was a sort of surprise to find any reference to my cousin, but she'd written two or three times a year to her mother, my aunt. I say it was a surprise because my uncle never spoke of Edith, it was like she didn't exist. My uncle was an engineer with the Anglo-Iranian Oil Corporation, based in Abadan. I think they lived pretty well, servants, a good villa, all that. He just couldn't accept that his nineteen-year-old daughter should fall for and want to marry a local. Ali Hossein was a medical student in his early twenties. My uncle did all he could to break the relationship and couldn't, and gave up on Edith. He didn't go to the wedding and forbade my aunt to go. He just cut her off, pretended there had never been a daughter, an only child. I don't think he ever knew that my aunt kept in touch with her . . ."

She was a neat, fussy woman. On her lap were old letters and a small bundle of photographs held together by a frayed elastic band.

"It was a traditional Muslim wedding. She must have felt very alone with just Ali's relations and friends. Her letters, over the years, were sent to a post office near where my uncle and aunt lived in their retirement, up north, and my aunt collected them. It was a sad little bit of subterfuge but necessary because my uncle's hostility never lessened, not till the day he died. The letters stopped coming in 1984 and my aunt, in the following months, badgered the Foreign Office to find out why. She made up excuses to be away for a whole day, and went to London and nagged the diplomats for information. Eventually they told her that Edith had been killed in a rocket attack in Tehran, and she never told my uncle. But it's their son, Edith's and Ali's boy, that you want to know about?"

Cathy Parker was quiet. It was the photographs she had come for, but it was her way never to appear eager. She let her informant talk.

"He was called Vahid. I think Edith had a sense of guilt about the way she and Ali brought him up. Ali was involved in dangerous politics, he was even arrested and beaten by the secret police, and Edith supported him to the hilt. The child, Vahid, was left to himself, and it wasn't a surprise that he became a tearaway, a street hooligan. He was involved in demonstrations, in fighting with the police. Myself, I'd have been horrified, but Edith wrote of her pride in the boy's determination. After the revolution, when that awful man, you know, the ayatollah, came back and there were all the executions, public hangings and shootings, the boy went into the military and was sent away to the war with Iraq. He was at the front line when Edith and her husband were killed by the rocket."

Behind their heads Cathy Parker could see an ordered, well-tended small garden. Their bungalow was on the outskirts of a small village west of Chard in Somerset. She thought how difficult it would have been for this elderly woman, reading the letters, to understand the world of revolutionary Iran, but she made no show of sympathy.

"I wrote to him, after I'd gone through the letters, to tell him there were blood relations alive in England, but the only address I knew of was the house where his parents had been killed. It was pretty silly, the house would have been destroyed by the rocket, and I never had a reply. So, why have you come from London and why is the Security Service interested in Edith's boy? You're not going to tell me, are you? . . . He's a nice-looking lad—well, he was a nice-looking lad in the last photograph, but that was taken a long time ago. He'd be thirty-seven now. Would you like to see the photographs?"

The bundle was passed to Cathy Parker. She flipped through them, feigning indifference. They were what a daughter would have sent to her mother. It was the usual progression: a baby, a toddler, a child in school clothes, at a picnic and kicking a football, a teenager. Only the last two pictures interested her: a young man holding a Kalashnikov rifle and posing with others in ill-fitting fatigues at a roadblock, and the mature man he'd become sitting hunched and dead-eyed in the front of a small boat with water and reed banks behind. She didn't ask, just put the last two photographs into her handbag.

"A good-looking boy, yes?"

Cathy made her excuses. She had seen the dead, aged, and cold eyes of young men in Ireland, and seen the misery they could inflict. She thanked Vahid Hossein's aunt for the photographs that might help to kill him.

Andy Chalmers was driven to Fort William in Mr. Gabriel Fenton's Range Rover.

He sat, truculent and quiet, in the front seat, with the dogs behind him. The light was going down to the west of the big mountains and the sea loch as they approached the station.

"Don't take any shit from them, Andy. I've said it before and I'll say it again—do it your way and the way you know. They'll be superior and they'll treat you like dirt, but don't take it. You're there at Mr. Harry's invitation, there because you're bloody good. You may be a kid but you're the best stalker and tracker between here and Lochinver, the best I've ever seen, and my brother knows that. Don't let me down. There'll be plenty there who'll want you to fall on your face in the mud, and fail, and you're going to disappoint them. I thought I was useful, in the Radfan up from Aden, but I hadn't a half of the skill you're blessed with. Mr. Harry's out on a limb for you, that's his degree of trust. Take care, Andy. Find this bastard, and if you bring me back his ears, then I'll have them mounted and hung in the hallway—that's a joke, you understand, a joke . . ."

He trailed, from the Range Rover, behind his estate owner into the station and he jerked his dogs to heel. It would be the first time in Andy Chalmers's life that he had left the mountains that were his

home. Mr. Gabriel Fenton collected the first-class ticket, return, and
the sleeper reservation, pointed through the doorway to the waiting
train, cuffed him cheerfully on the arm, and left him. Chalmers
walked towards the platform and heaved the dogs after him, ignoring the scowl of the attendant and the amusement of other passengers, before picking up his dogs and climbing on board.

"Please, Mr. Fenton, you have to listen to me. I've just come from
that house. Believe me, it's horrendous in there. We've created a
monster, and I'm not overstating the case here . . ."

There was a secure line in the newly created crisis center at the
police station in the town of Halesworth, twelve miles inland from
the village. Down the line Fenton told Geoff Markham he was suffering an attack of melodrama, should pull himself together.

"You're not here. If you were here then you'd understand. Let me
tell you, it's dark, there's hardly a light on, they're bouncing round off
their furniture. she's the problem. Sometimes it's hysterical weeping,
sometimes it's just sitting, withdrawn. She's traumatized. He'll follow her, he thinks he's going to lose her—he's got the guilt bad, keeps
saying it's all his fault. It'll be worse in the morning because the kid
doesn't have a school to go to. They're near to quitting. We're cruci-
fying this family, and he's close to demanding a safe house, a new
identity."

Fenton told Geoff Markham that his job, down there, was to keep
Frank Perry in place.

"That may seem reasonable enough in London, Mr. Fenton, but
viewed from where I've been today, it seems poorly informed rubbish. I am trying to stay calm, of course I am. What do you suggest I
do? Do I tell him what use was made, in Iran, of the information he
provided, how much blood there is on his hands? Do I tell him about
a tethered goat? That'll really get to him, Mr. Fenton, too right . . .
I'm not losing it, Mr. Fenton, I merely try to explain the situation
confronting me."

Fenton told Markham that policy dictated Frank Perry should
stay there.

"What do I do? Lock him in the bloody broom cupboard?"

Fenton told him to get Perry's friends in and get the bottles out.

"If you only listened to me, Mr. Fenton. The friends have all quit the ship, they're jumping off the decks. All right, most of their friends. I'm planning to meet the vicar in the morning, seemed a decent man. I thought if the village saw the vicar with him that might spark some conscience . . ."

Fenton told him to take the Perrys out for the evening, splash out on a smart meal, no expense spared, to sweet-talk them and relax them.

"I'll do that, Mr. Fenton, I'll book a table for tonight for them and a busload of police—should be a really jolly evening. I'm sorry to have troubled you at home . . . Maybe we can find a restaurant that serves boiled goat."

Donna should have stayed the extra year at school. At eighteen she was already as much on the shelf as the tins of beans, sweet corn, and quick-cook curries that she stacked at the supermarket in the town. She was trapped and she knew it. She wrote in a child's laborious hand for jobs in hair salons and with beauticians, but most of her letters were ignored and a few were rejected in three lines. She was unskilled and unqualified. In the village, only Meryl Perry had time for her and gave her the old magazines with which she could dream of smart salons and bright beauty shops where rich women would come to her for advice, gossip about their private lives, and offer her respect. Only the Perrys cared enough to fuel the dream, and she broke the boredom of home, and her parents, forever sitting in front of the blaring television, with little pockets of relief when she stayed with Stephen while Frank and Meryl were out for an evening. They picked her up, they dropped her back, they gave her a small sense of importance.

He came in through the door, murmured his request to Davies, took a big breath, and strode into the kitchen.

Markham said brightly, "I think we need an evening out, Frank. It's time for a splash on my masters' expenses, to cheer ourselves up."

Sausages were frying on the stove. The packet of instant mashed potato was ready at the side. Perry looked at him, astonished.

"We're going out, enough of being shut up in here. We're going out to drink a restaurant dry, to murder their menu. No argument, no hesitation, and I'm picking up the tab."

Perry asked, hesitant, "Where are we going at this time on a Sunday night, who'll have us?"

"We leave that to Bill. He's the expert, spends half his time getting his principals into restaurants that say they're full." He tried to laugh.

Meryl asked, flat-voiced, "Who's going to look after Stephen?"

He turned and saw her blank, reddened eyes. "I'm sure you've a regular baby-sitter. Let's get a call to her, we'll collect. Don't you worry about the detail, Mrs. Perry, just get yourself ready and let us take the strain."

Perry said, "I'm not sure—"

"Yes, you are, Mr. Perry. It's what's going to happen."

Meryl said, "I don't know that I want to go out."

"Yes, you do, Mrs. Perry. It's what's best."

He manipulated them, they danced for him. He had boasted to the man and woman at the bank that he was prepared to use people in the interests of policy, and here he was, doing it. Meryl Perry was lifting the frying pan off the cooker and muttering that the sausages would do for tomorrow, and that she'd already fed Stephen. Perry was at the telephone and scanning the list above it for Donna's number.

Bill Davies leaned through the doorway and said the local police had given him the name of a place, but it was twenty-two miles away and they'd have to shift themselves. He'd called the restaurant and he'd organized people to check it out. Markham thought she looked so cudgeled, so damned helpless. He asked her gently if she wanted to change, and wished that Harry bloody Fenton were here to see her. Meryl went out and he heard her deadened step up the stairs.

"Do you have a girl, Frank, to come in?"

"Thick as two planks, but decent and loyal—Meryl's been great to her and she's fond of Stephen." Perry lifted the phone and dialed.

Two cars were pulling up outside—Blake coming to take over inside the house and the change of shift for the hut. Markham drew a sigh of relief: at least he had achieved something. His mind flipped back to London: the letter would be at his flat in the morning, with the terms of employment. He would ring Vicky later—if they survived the meal—and ask her to go round and collect it, to read it to him. Once he'd resigned they would boot him out of Thames House so fast his feet wouldn't touch the ground. How would it be, a year later, ten years later, when he walked down the Embankment and went past the bulletproof windows and the concrete bollards? Would he feel fulfilled, streaming with the commuter hordes into the City? He had played God before, with agents' lives, and was playing God now. He wondered how it would be playing God with savers' investment accounts and pension holdings. If he hadn't met Vicky, he would know sweet nothing about investments and pensions. He heard the anger in Frank Perry's voice.

"What do you mean, you're not coming? Is it you can't come, or *won't*? It's nothing to do with your father, nothing to do with anyone but yourself. Listen here, we've been damn good to you. We're about the only bloody people in this place who have been. I thought better of you."

Perry's hand trembled as he tried to return the telephone to the wall fitting. Then he took a pen and scratched out Donna's name and number from the list on the wall. Over his shoulder, Markham could see the list. Donna was inked out along with most of the others. There were pitifully few names and numbers left unscathed.

At the kitchen door, Bill Davies took the radio away from his face. "Dave Paget and Joe Rankin will stay on. They've had kids themselves, God help the poor blighters. They can do child minding."

Meryl came down the stairs.

If her eyes hadn't been red and puffed, Markham thought, she would have looked marvelous. The poor damn woman had made the effort. He noticed Bill Davies take her hand and murmur something in her ear, but he didn't catch what was said. When they'd gathered in the hall, the detective told Paget and Rankin that there were sausages and mashed potato on the stove for their supper. The two men, in their boilersuits and vests, with their pistols hanging from their waists, thanked him balefully.

Blake came through the front door, carrying five fire extinguishers. He dumped them down noisily, then went to the car again, retrieved a heavyweight blanket from the boot with a box of gas grenades, and staggered back into the house. Markham thought it predictable that there should be more fire extinguishers inside, one for each room; the additional bullet- and shrapnel-proof blanket was for draping over a chair to make a wider protective barrier; the gas grenades were standard. But he wished that Meryl Perry hadn't seen them.

She asked where Donna was, and was told.

She wasn't given time to think about it. She was made to run to the open car door, her heels clattering down the path. There was an escort vehicle in front and another behind. Their front windows were down and Markham could see the machine guns. Well done, Harry Fenton, another great idea. As he helped to hustle her through the gate and pitch her into the car, he thought it was all, already, unraveling. Bill Davies came after him and seemed to be shielding Perry.

Markham drove. Beside him, the detective sat awkwardly because he'd twisted his body so that his hand could rest free on the pistol in his waist holster. Off for a night out with friends—well done, Harry bloody Fenton.

The helicopter had been over at last light, and Vahid Hossein had gone into the water at the first sound of its approach. Long after it had disappeared he had returned to the marsh shore. He lay in the darkness in the depth of the cover.

The policemen who watched the marsh, from the village side, on the higher ground of Hoist Covert and East Sheep Walk, had been replaced by fresh men, and he had noted their positions.

The harrier was close to him but he could not see it, could only hear its movements as it scratched in the ground for the last scraps of meat.

The girl had come to the rendezvous point in the late afternoon, bringing food and ointments for the bruising. She had been withdrawn, subdued. When he had told her what she should do the next day, she hadn't argued.

He was curled up on his side in the bramble thicket to keep the weight of his body off the bruising. The skin was bared at his waist and hip, and he could feel the soothing cool of the ointments. He'd

thought she wanted to smooth on the ointments herself and he'd refused her. He could not allow himself to be dependent on a woman.
He heard the sounds of the bird and tried to shut from his memory
the softness of her fingers, seeking instead to recall the sight and
touch and feel of Barzin, who was alone in their bed in the house at
Jamaran . . . Each time he summoned the image of her and the
touch of her hands, the image dissolved and was replaced—always it
was her fingers, the girl's . . . He called to the bird.

The bird was his truest friend, and would not corrupt him. It did
not challenge him, was his equal. His love of it did not make him
weak.

When it was finished and he was home, he would never talk to
Barzin about the bird. She would not understand. He was alone; he
was in darkness; he was sodden wet from immersing himself in the
water, sucking his air through the reed tube he had fashioned, when
the helicopter had circled overhead. He spoke soft, gentle words to
the bird, hushed so as not to frighten it, told it what he was planning
to do.

Vahid Hossein shifted slightly so that he could reach out with his
hand beyond the tangle of thorns. The bird pecked at it as if he
might have held a last piece of rabbit flesh . . . A lack of patience had
caused him to make mistakes: trying to break into the house without
sufficient preparation; taking the assault rifle . . . He criticized the
bird for its laziness—it should hunt, it was strong enough now . . .
He should have taken the rocket launcher, it would be the RPG-7
next time, he told the bird. His fingers found the neck and crown of
the bird's head and smoothed the silky feathers. He hoped it would
hunt in the dawn light and that he would see its power and beauty as
it dived to kill.

He trusted the bird as his friend.

They sat at a corner table.

Frank Perry was drunk. "What did I do?"

The restaurant had cleared, and he had taken on a drunk's aggres-
sion. "Will some bugger tell me what I did?"

The principal was in the angle of the corner, his wife was to the
right of him, and the detective to the left, with a clear view to the

door. Markham had his back to the room. The evening was a disaster, he thought, of titanic proportions.

Perry snatched at the bottle and poured again. "I've the bloody right to know what I did."

One of the cars was out at the front with its driver, but its passenger sat with his gun across his knees close to the glass door. The other car was at the rear of the car park, covering the outer entrance to the kitchens. A policeman was sitting by the swing doors through which the waiters had brought the French food. The customers who had been there when the late party had stampeded in, seven of them, at three tables, had stuffed themselves, gulped their drinks, paid up, and were long gone.

Perry swilled the wine, the most expensive on the list. Drops dribbled from his mouth and ran on his jaw. "Why can't I be told what I did? Why won't any bastard tell me?"

Meryl hadn't spoken a word through the meal. Twice, after wiping her lips with the napkin, she had dabbed her eyes. The detective's contribution had been to ask for various condiments to be passed him. The waiters had brought the coffee and retreated to the kitchen.

Frank Perry belted his hand on the table. "Right, no one tells me, then we're off. We get the hell out and that's that, end of story."

The principal was trying to push back his chair but he was wedged in the corner. Then he tried to shove the table forward, driving it into Markham's stomach. Bill Davies was snapping his fingers at the policemen by the main door and the kitchen swing doors, and they were adjusting the straps that held their machine guns and mouthing into their microphones . . . Geoff Markham thought how it would be on the telephone that night to Harry Fenton. He'd failed, the principal was running. The failure would be the marque to end his career at Thames House. However many years he lived, decades, he would be dogged by that failure . . . He took out his wallet and extracted a credit card. The owner came hurrying—God, he'd be glad to see the back of them—and took it. He straightened his tie, then rammed the table away from him, trapped the man.

"You want to know?"

"I've the bloody right to know!"

The bill was waved under his nose. It must have been prepared and ready. Without checking it, he scrawled his signature on the docket and took back the card. He waved the owner away, gestured for him to retreat and give them space.

"What did I do?"

There was at Thames House, and it would be the same at the bank, a culture against honesty. No advancement ever came from telling it as it was. He was hemmed in at work, and it would be the same in the future, by men and women who weighed their words for fear of giving offense. It had been the same at home, and the same at university. He had drunk nothing but carbonated water, he was utterly sober. For the first time in his life, Geoff Markham thought the moment had come for sheer honesty, the whole truth.

He spoke quietly, "You were a second-rate salesman. You were a grubby little creature on the make. You were into illegality, fraudulently writing out false export declarations for Customs and Excise. You were greedy, so avaricious for the commissions you were getting that the chasing of the money became more important to you than that your wife was screwing on the side and your marriage was gone—"

Perry swung a wayward fist at him and missed the target, Markham's chin, but hit the bottle's neck and toppled it.

"You were on a fast ride and going nowhere, but the greed held you and you wouldn't back off. To hell with the wife opening her legs, the money kept rolling in, and then, one day, comes the morning after, the dawn hangover, and there's a call from a lady, and most persuasively she's asking for a meeting. You thought you were in control until you sat down with Penny Flowers. Do you remember her, Frank? I hope you do, because where you are now is down to her. You dangled from her little finger . . ."

In the background, romantic piano music played serenely. The wine stained a path across the tablecloth from the toppled bottle.

"She was asking you for a little bit of help—and if you didn't care to do so, she was offering you a big bit of a prison sentence, like seven years—and of course, you chose to help. When you walked away from that first meeting with Penny Flowers you'd have thought you could handle it, without breaking sweat, and you were wrong.

She's a tough bitch, but you know that now. You don't get clear of Penny Flowers's claws. It starts easily enough, always does. It's the classic way, Mr. Perry, of agent handling. Did she tell you that she liked you, that you were really important? She would have regarded you as cheap dross, because that's the way all controllers regard all agents."

The wine stain reached the edge of the table and the first drip fell into Meryl's lap.

"At first, it would have been sketch maps of the plant, then character profiles of the prime personalities. After that, it's documents, later it's photographs with a supplied camera. Cheap dross you may be, but not an idiot. You understand now that you're into espionage, and you know the penalty in Iran for espionage. The sweat's started. The sweat becomes colder each time you fly there, and you're looking over your shoulder because it only takes one mistake to alert the security there. Each night in your hotel room, you'd have wondered whether you'd made that mistake. But you couldn't shake clear of Penny Flowers, and there was always one more trip back, always one more question she wanted answered . . ."

Frank Perry stared into Geoff Markham's face, and in his eyes was the fear, as if he lived it again.

"You told Penny Flowers, just happened to mention it, that they'd changed the schedule for your next meeting, brought it forward a week—she'd not have looked that interested, it's a handler's skill never to seem interested in what an agent says—but she'd have probed deeper, done it in easy conversation. If you'd understood the way a handler works, the few extra questions, and always the studied indifference, then the alarm bells would have rung. Just before you flew to Iran that last time you would have known it was the danger time. A debriefing the night before you traveled, not just Penny Flowers but hard-faced bastards telling you what was wanted. It was about a party, yes, a celebration dinner for heads of section?"

Frank Perry, grim, sobering, nodded.

"You would have gone back the last time, to all those people who welcomed you. I doubt you slept on any of those nights because you'd have been going over every question you'd asked—where was the party, who was going, when was the bus leaving?—and wondering if the mistake had been made. They were the heads of section for the chemical-warfare program, and the designers of the warhead. They were the big people in the big picture, and you were just a bloody ant by comparison. Your only importance was that you had access . . . They'd have hanged you, not so that your neck broke but so that you strangled and kicked the air . . . I couldn't have done it myself, Mr. Perry, I wouldn't have had the courage. I would have crumpled with the fear. I sincerely admire what you did. I don't mean to embarrass you, but I haven't ever met anyone of such raw bravery . . . Do you still want to know?"

Frank Perry mouthed his answer so softly that Markham couldn't hear it.

"The Jews do the dirty work for us. They understand about survival better than we do. They won't, again, go naked into the sheds and have cyanide crystals drop on them. They are, in modern jargon, *proactive*. The Israelis wouldn't have needed much persuasion because those warheads could fall on them. A squad was put on shore after being ferried across the Gulf. They landed up the coast from Bandar Abbas. They intercepted the bus on its way to the restaurant. A piece of charity fell off Penny Flowers's desk, probably the only time it has. What happened to the bus was an *accident*, you understand me. It created confusion and bought you time to build a new life before the Iranians realized the enormity of the crime and at whose door it lay . . ."

The music played on. Markham felt so sorry for the man.

"The bus was stopped, then burned. It was made to look, before a detailed examination produced the truth, like an accident. There were no survivors. The director, the engineers, the scientists all died in the fire."

Frank Perry jerked the weight of his body up, his lips gibbering, but he could not speak.

"You wanted to know. It is why the Iranians will hunt you, track you, try to kill you, and all those with you. There'll be files on you that are stacked high enough to eat lunch off. They will never forget you. What you did was buy time. I'd like to say that the time was well used, that the program was seriously delayed. I can't—I don't know. I don't know whether the time you bought with your courage, Frank, was well used or was frittered . . . but I recognize your bravery because it humbles me."

Meryl was crying quietly. Markham pulled back the table and let Perry stagger to his feet. The rain had started outside and the street glistened. He took Perry's arm gently and steadied him through the door and across the pavement. Davies held Meryl close to him. Her dress, from the spilled wine, was stained red like a wound. Markham thought it was what Perry was owed, and he was glad he'd done it.

He climbed the stairs slowly.

It had been a distressing evening for Simon Blackmore. Two months earlier, a surveyor had checked Rose Cottage and described the damp as minimal. Late that evening, without an appointment, a man who described himself as a builder and decorator had prized his way into the cottage. He called himself Vince, and explained that he always dropped by on new people moving into the village. He'd walked around and pointed out at least half a dozen places where the wallpaper peeled and the plasterwork was stained, tutting and frowning at the cost and his schedule. But the work needed doing, *must* be done. He'd spoken of Mrs. Wilson's rheumatism and laid the blame for it on the damp. He'd settled immovably at the kitchen table with a mug of coffee. They were both so tired, exhausted from the unpacking of boxes, but they had listened with courtesy as he'd talked of the village, his lifetime home, and his central place in it. And he'd told them, as if it were a kindness to them, that they should keep away from the green at the far end of the village because there were armed police there, guarding a family that no one in their right mind wanted to know . . . "But they've got the message, there's no-one'll speak to them, they'll be bloody frozen out of here." It had been an age before he'd finished his coffee, insisted that he would send in an estimate for necessary work, and left.

Simon went up the stairs and into their bedroom, where Luisa was undressing. They hadn't yet unpacked the shades for the ceiling bulbs. The garish, harsh light fell on his wife and highlighted the old burn marks on her breasts and stomach before the nightdress covered them.

. . .

The train hammered on the track, jerking and rolling.

Andy Chalmers lay on his side on the bunk bed, on the clean white sheets and the blankets. He had not undressed. His dogs, alert, were curled against his body and gave him warmth. Behind him, distanced, were the birds and their eyries on the crag cliffs, and the bog heather uplands where the deer grazed, and the mountain lochans that held the small brown trout, and the glens that were home to the plovers and wheatears and curlews. Ahead lay an unfamiliar terrain.

Andy Chalmers came south, to track a man.

14

He was into Thames House early, had limped from a photo-develop-
ment kiosk to the building, shown his temporary accreditation at reception, and hobbled into the third-floor work area. His feet were
blistered from a long day's walking; the deep bath and the salts in it
hadn't lessened the pain.

Duane Seitz had walked, the previous day, right round the Tower
of London—the Jewel Tower, the White Tower, Traitor's Arch, the
grass-centered square where the state's enemies had been beheaded, and all the places of death and imprisonment. Once he'd
giggled, attracted attention, because he'd wondered why his Saudi
friends hadn't bought the whole damned place—lock, stone, and
axe—and transferred it to Riyadh. He had gone round on a tour, led
by a costumed guide, then gone round again, on his own, and taken
a whole roll of film. From the Tower of London he had walked to
St. Paul's Cathedral, then hiked through the Sunday empty streets
towards the Palace and Parliament. Twice in the day his attention
had been distracted, and he'd reached towards the emptiness, the
lack of weight, on his belt, and grinned to himself because it was so
strange for him to be without a sidearm on his hip. It was a part of
what relaxed him, and it was hard for him to remember the last
time that he hadn't carried, not needed to carry, a personal weapon.
When he was half dead, and on the third film for Esther, he had

weakened and taken a taxi back to the embassy's service flat and the bath.

A probationer told him that his office in Saudi Arabia had called, that he should ring back. The young man fixed the secure link for him because Duane Seitz was adept at demonstrating technological incompetence when the situation necessitated. He listened to the distant, tinny, concerned voice.

Mary Ellen burbled at him, asking about his domestic arrangements, and he wondered whether she was missing him.

"It's been hellish hot here, Duane, 110-plus Fahrenheit, and the cooling system in here's zapped again, it's awful. One of the visa-section guys went out in the parking lot Saturday and cracked an egg on the paving to see if he could fry it. He couldn't, the egg dehydrated. Seriously . . ."

He saw Cathy Parker come in. She had a bounce in her walk. She stopped in front of Markham's door and scribbled through the writing on the paper stuck to the door. She wrote, boldly, DAY FIVE.

"What I thought you should know, Duane, we had a briefing, at short notice, from the Agency people. There was a big hassle about me being admitted in place of you. Was I cleared for a briefing by the Central Intelligence goddamn Agency? Ambassador, heads of section, and *me!* They are such seriously pompous people. Anyway . . ."

She sat beside him and laid a closed envelope on the table.

"You still there, Duane? Look, the guy said that the Saudi intelligence people admitted to him that the 'outsider hired guns,' you know what I mean, came in during the last *Hajj*, with all the pilgrims, and are still in place inside the Magic Kingdom. Also the Army's come clean and said that four—believe me—four eighty-one-millimeter mortars have been stolen from one of their bases up north. How can you defend against that sort of scenario? A dump truck pulls up on the median just outside of a major enclave of ours, the tarp is pulled back, the rounds fly, and the Agency say they could have chemicals in them . . . and the Agency have gotten the name of your pal, Duane, *A* is for Anvil, away now but coming back . . . The commercial attaché—you know, that idiot—had to be told why one man was so important, why they'd wait for one man's return before launching. He seemed to think that quality men, like Anvil, came off a production line as if they were General Motors products. He was put right. When Anvil comes back it's time to go into the shelters, that's what the Agency people are saying. There's real fear here, those mortars and the name of Anvil. It sort of, kind of, makes you shiver . . ."

Beside him, Cathy Parker pulled two photographs out of the envelope. He saw a young man holding a Kalashnikov rifle at a roadblock of Revolutionary Guards, and the picture was lifted away. The second photograph showed an older man in combat fatigues with his back to the water and the reed banks. She reached again into the envelope.

"I came away from that briefing and, I tell you, I was spooked. Well, that's it. I'll meet you Wednesday night off the flight—oh, sorry, how's it going? Nowhere? I'll cook you supper Wednesday night. Would you have done better to stay here? There's someone at the door. Bye."

He replaced the receiver. A slow smile was spreading across Cathy Parker's face. She took a blown-up picture from the envelope. He recognized immediately the work of computer enhancement, the aging process, a fattening at the face, a thickening at the neck, more lines at the eyes, shorter hair with bleached, graying, thinner lips. She took a pen from the table and wrote, in big capital characters, the place of birth, Tehran, the date of birth, 7/28/1962, the name, only the goddamn name, Vahid Hossein. He gazed at it, then at her and into the brightness of her eyes. He kissed her on the mouth, kissed her hard.

What they would have noticed, everyone else in the work area, Cathy Parker kissed him back, lip to lip.

Fenton was gathering up his coat, saying he had a train to meet, but he paused long enough to lead the applause and to call for a copy, posthaste, to be sent to Geoff Markham.

Duane Seitz stared down at the face, at a stranger who had become familiar, and could still feel the taste of Cathy Parker's wicked, groping tongue.

"Why isn't he coming?" Sam Carstairs howled.

His mother, distracted and trying to put on her makeup for the day in the solicitors' offices, told him not to worry his head with such things.

"He's my best friend. Why isn't he coming to school?" the child bellowed.

His father, trying angrily to put the papers together that he'd been working on the previous evening, told him it was none of his business.

"If he isn't ill, why isn't he coming to school?" In a tantrum, little Sam started to rip pages from the book they'd bought him only the week before, and stamped on them.

If Emma hadn't caught his arm, Barry would have hit his son. The row had gone on since the child had woken and sensed the tension. It was convenient for neither of them to take Sam into Halesworth for school. Emma, the legal executive, was in court that day with the senior partner, and Barry had the annual sales conference. It was the sort of day when they could have relied upon Meryl Perry's help: she was always prepared, with a smile, to alter the schedule of the shared school run. Sam and Stephen had always been close friends, good for each other. Barry grabbed the child by the collar of his school coat and frog-marched him to the car. Emma had said her job was as important as his; because of the row she'd be late meeting her senior partner, and he'd be bloody late at the conference. He put Sam into the back of his Audi, then ran back to the house because he'd forgotten, damn it, his briefcase.

Emma was throwing on her coat in the hall. "We've done the right thing, haven't we?"

"What on earth do you mean?"

"With Frank and Meryl." Until that moment, through all the weekend, neither had spoken of it, as if it were forbidden territory. "They must be so isolated, without friends."

"Their fault, not mine."

"You don't think that we should make a gesture?"

"What did she call me? A second-rate rat? What sort of gesture do I make in response to that?"

"I suppose you're right." She touched her hair in front of the mirror.

"Of course I'm right."

"Please, tell Sam in the car why they're not our friends any longer. He doesn't understand, hasn't a clue, why he's lost his best friend. Please do it, Barry."

"You wait, a week after they've gone we'll have forgotten they were ever here."

He set the alarm, she locked the house, and they ran for their cars, to live their busy lives.

Ten minutes earlier, Geoff Markham had gone out into the parking area behind the town's police station. The arrival time had been given them in the crisis center and others had drifted after him to stand in the light rain and wait.

Aside from Markham, glancing at their wristwatches, were a uniformed superintendent and the inspector from the Branch, detectives and the people who manned the radios and the computers; away in the corner of the car park were the military from Special Forces, denied involvement but permitted standby status. They were all out in the rain to see the arrival of the Scottish tracker. The local uniforms would have thought they were best equipped to search their own area, had the feel for it. The detectives from London, and the Branch, would have thought they had the trained surveillance specialists, had the necessary expertise. The military would have thought they owned the territory of stalk and track, had the right to crack the problem. They were all interested to see the man dragged out from the north by Five, the man given the job that should have been theirs. Geoff Markham felt an atmosphere around him of acid curiosity edging on malevolence.

The car, big, black, and sleek, driven by a chauffeur, swept into the parking area and braked hard. All eyes were on it.

Harry Fenton pushed himself out of the front passenger seat, mischief in his eyes. He called a cheerful greeting to the watchers. It was his show, and that mattered to him. He caught Markham's glance, and there was the slightest, faintest wink of his eye, then he opened the rear door.

The dogs came first. They were squat, scurrying creatures, held by leashes of fodder-bale twine, bright orange. They yapped.

He came after them, wriggled clear of the car.

What Markham had expected was an old man, ruddy and weather-skinned, a man with the lore of the countryside in his face and a lifetime of experience in his eyes.

He was small. He looked barely out of his teens. His visage was pale and his cheeks and chin were speckled with light stubble. His build was slight, looked as if the wind could blow him away. More than that, he was filthy.

The gathered audience gazed at him with astonishment.

At ten paces Markham could smell the dank dirtiness of his clothes. He wore boots, khaki trousers, and a tweed coat, all liberally smeared with mud; Markham thought the coat was a bigger man's castoff. Its buttons were gone and it was held tight at the narrow waist by the same twine. The man stood beside Fenton and glowered at them.

A titter of laughter rippled behind Markham.

An old man, Markham thought, would have merely ruffled feathers, but this pallid, grimy, stinking youth disjointed noses. The dogs, heaving at their leashes, coughing, had seen a police Alsatian—God, and the little verminous bastards would probably try to roger it if they were free—but the young man grunted at them, almost inaudibly, and they sat at his boots, their teeth bared. He didn't back off from the laughter but stared back at them. They were, Geoff Markham thought, the most frightening eyes he had ever seen.

From the backseat of the car, the chauffeur was lifting out sheets of newspaper and shaking the mud off them.

Fenton strode to Markham. He said, in a loud voice as if to be certain he was generally heard, "What a stink. Had the window open all the way down—I thought I was going to throw up. Like being shut in a cellar with a well-hung duck. I'd like you to meet Andy Chalmers, Geoff. It's your job to see he goes where he wants to go, has what he wants. I see that his appearance creates amusement. I want to see that amusement wiped off their faces and shoved far up their backsides. Got me? You'll brook no obstruction from any bastard in a clean shirt or I'll break his bloody neck—and yours. I've lunch to be getting back to. Keep to the windward of him. Good luck, and good hunting."

Fenton was gone, without a backward glance. The car swept out of the parking area.

The theater over, the uniforms, the detectives, and the military trooped back into the police station. Geoff Markham thought that if the young man failed it would be Fenton's neck for breaking. As the car disappeared down the road, he realized that no bag had been dumped with the tracker and his dogs.

"Damn, your bag's still in the car."

"Don't have a bag."

"Clean clothes and so on."

"Don't have a bag."

Markham laughed out loud. Who needed clean socks, who wanted fresh underwear, who had to wash?

"Do you like something to eat?"

"No."

"Do you want anything?"

"No."

"What would you like to do?"

"Get there."

There had once been ambition in Mr. Hackett's ministry, but that was long gone. He existed now in this coastal parish, believing his congregation and his community were beneath his talents, on a diet of godless weddings, hurried funerals, and a continuing anxiety about the maintenance of the fabric of his church. His welcoming smile, his proffered friendship were shams. He was lonely, he was bitter; his wife lived away and the fiction that explained her absence involved her need to care for an elderly, bedridden mother, but she had left him. He lived out his life in the village, kept trouble from his door and the bishop off his back, and waited for retirement, blessed release. The ambition of the Reverend Basil Hackett, then an inner-city curate on a fast-promotion track, had ended twenty-seven years earlier in the north Welsh mountains when he had taken a party of deprived children, with volunteer helpers, from their Manchester tower blocks for a camping holiday. It was the sort of expedition blessed by bishops, the sort of trip that was good for advancement . . . and an eleven-year-old boy had died in a fall. Such a long time ago, but there was no forgiveness in the file that passed from bishop to bishop each time he had applied for subsequent promotion. The file held the muted criticism, unspecified but hinted at, of the police evidence at the subsequent inquest—why had the child been alone, why had the child not been better supervised?

His career had never recovered, and the bitterness lingered still. Its target was sometimes the bishops, who did not seem to understand the problems of watching over eighteen hooligan youngsters, but most particularly the police. That bitterness verged on detestation. When he should have been explaining the circumstances of the accident to his bishop, and comforting the bereaved parents, he had been incarcerated in a bare interview room in the police station at Conway, treated like a felon, quizzed relentlessly by men seeming determined to find inconsistencies in his account. The career gone, ambition fallen, he had moved from Manchester to mid-Devon, then taken this Suffolk parish. It was a blighted life, no fault of his own, and empty.

They were in the village. If Geoff Markham spoke, he won a grudging response. If he didn't speak there was silence.

Did he want to go up the church tower, use it as an observation point? A grunt, a shaken head. Did he want to take a look at the house? Again, a similar response.

While he had driven, Chalmers had spread across his knees the map on which a red-ink line marked the trail the police dogs had found, and the riverbank where they had lost it. By Chalmers's boots, the dogs chewed noisily at the car's floor mat. Markham was pretty damn certain that one, maybe both, had peed during the journey.

The smell reeked through the car. He stopped near to the hall, down the road from the green. Chalmers's brow was furrowed in concentration as he studied the detail of the map.

A young woman with a guidebook was sitting on a bench, her back to them. An older woman was coming out of the shop with a wheeled shopping bag. He ignored the slow life of the village around him and busied himself with putting new batteries into the second radio, then checked the transmission between the two . . . Shit, the stress snatched at Markham. Hadn't rung Vicky, and he didn't know the terms of employment offered him. Hadn't spoken to Bill Davies, didn't know whether they were still on their feet or down on the floor. Hadn't remembered the picture. Chalmers eased out of the car, took a little of the smell with him, but not enough. The mat was chewed and puddled and he seemed not to notice. Markham took the picture out of his briefcase, locked the door after him.

"Sorry about that—sorry I didn't give it you earlier—you should have had it before."

He didn't know why he should be frightened into abject apologies to this stinking kid. He passed over the picture. It was the first time he had seen anything other than hostility in Chalmers's eyes. He had once been to a boxing match, when he was at college, for a middleweight title. He remembered the first sight of the men when they had come into the ring with the hype blaring over the loudspeakers, and it was supposed to be a grudge match. There had been no hate in their eyes, only respect, and the fight had started. Each had done his bloody damnedest to batter the other to the canvas. The bout had been brutal and merciless, and he'd hated it.

He took back the picture, and they walked away, following the map's trail.

Chalmers unpicked a piece of cotton thread from a strand of barbed wire topping a garden fence and said that the man wore a camouflage tunic.

Where the path narrowed, Chalmers stopped, hunched down, and studied the ground beside the path's mud. Half under squashed nettles, a bootprint was just visible. Chalmers said the man was size eleven, and added casually that he was hurt, handicapped.

They were beside the river. Chalmers unhooked the twine from the dogs' throats but cooed softly to them. They stayed at his heel.

Ahead were the marshes. The gray cloud was low on the reed beds. The rain spat on their faces. Chalmers gestured to his right, a contemptuous short motion of his arm, and Markham saw the movement of the policemen in bushes away on higher ground. The marshes stretched ahead to the mist line and the far, dull shape of the trees. There was the slow thunder of the waves on shingle beyond the seawall.

"Get lost," Chalmers growled.

"When'll I see you?"

"Sometime, when I'm ready. Go away."

Geoff Markham walked back down the path alongside the river.

He turned once, looked round, and the path behind him was empty.

Bill Davies flushed the downstairs lavatory and came back into the hall. Nothing for him to do but drink coffee and ruminate on the catastrophe of the evening before, which he'd been doing all morning. Perry had been looking like chilled death when Davies had come in first thing to relieve Blake and was now pacing the living room. Meryl was in the kitchen, quiet, and she'd only been out the once, to hang her washed dress on the line. Paget had been with her, scanning the bottom fence all the time she'd pegged it up, and the rest of the clothes from the machine. He heard a sudden clatter of sound from the kitchen and knew that with a numbed mind and clumsy fingers she'd dropped a plate, broken it. He glanced out through the window, through the new net curtains. There was a spit of rain misting the glass but he saw the tall, wiry man's clerical collar. He moved aside the curtain for a better glance. Mr. Hackett's name hadn't been scratched off the list by the kitchen telephone.

It was reflex, not thought through.

He spoke on his radio to the hut, said he'd be outside, to the front of the house.

He went out into the light rain. He ran across the green, past the new tree and the new post, towards the clergyman.

"Excuse me."

The man stopped in midstep, turned, the wind catching his graying hair.

"Excuse me—are you Mr. Hackett?"

"He is me." A piping voice and a thin smile of greeting.

"Please, have you a moment?"

"A moment for what?"

"I'm with Frank and Meryl Perry."

The caution clouded his face. "Which means you're a policeman, which means you're an armed policeman. Why would you want a moment of my time?"

Why? Because Frank Perry was told last night of his responsibility in the death of a coachload of Iranian military scientists. Because he had drunk two bottles of wine and been sick twice. Because he and Meryl were at home alone, and needed a friend.

"I just thought, if you'd the time—it's rough for them. A visit from a friend would help."

The clergyman took a step forward. "I have appointments. People are expecting me."

Bill Davies caught his arm. "What they need, please, is for someone to show them some charity."

"Be so kind as to take your hand off me. Another time, perhaps . . ."

Davies's hand was shaken off, and the clergyman quickened his stride.

"You are a leader in this community, Mr. Hackett."

"I doubt it, but I do have a filled appointments diary."

"Your example is important. Please, go and ring the bell, go and smile and make some small talk. Better still, walk up this road with Meryl Perry, with Frank—we'll protect you. Show everybody here that they have your support."

"Another day, perhaps. But I cannot promise."

"They need you."

"There are many who need me. I don't know your name and I do not need to, but we did not ask for your guns to be brought into our community. We did not ask for our children and our women to be endangered. We are not a part of whatever quarrel Frank Perry is enmeshed in. We owe him nothing. He should go—what he owes us is his departure from here. I have a wider responsibility to the majority. I do not condone the ostracism of this family, but I cannot condemn it. But we are a God-fearing and law-abiding community, and I doubt that observance of God's teaching and the rules of society have brought Perry to his present situation. In your search for a friend to Perry, I suggest that you look elsewhere."

"Thank you, Mr. Hackett, for your Christian kindness."

"Good day."

Bill Davies walked slowly back to the house.

The Italian owner of the restaurant, from Naples, eyed the many-layered stomach of the German and murmured, with quiet discretion to Fenton, "The full menu, Mr. Fenton, not the two-course luncheon special?"

They were eased into their seats, and immediately the German ordered decisively, as if to feed himself for the rest of the week. Fenton's guest was from the BfV, attached to the embassy, an old hand at counterterrorism and a friend of sorts. As was his habit, Fenton set an agenda. He was confused, he admitted, and in search of enlightenment. The Foreign Office preached appeasement of Iran, the Israelis demanded they be beaten with lump hammers, the Islamic movement claimed there was American-inspired unwarranted hostility towards the Muslim world. Where lay the truth?

The German talked and ate, drank and smoked.

"So, you have one of their excrement loose on your territory, otherwise it would be sandwiches and Perrier in your office. You wish to know how seriously to take that threat. My government, as you well know because you have leaked your criticisms, has taken a conciliatory attitude towards Iran, has rescheduled debts, has given out visas, has pushed for stronger trade links, and has still provided the venue for Iranian assassins to meet their targets. It won us nothing, so we have considerable experience of their tactics. That is what I should talk about—our experience of their murder tactics?"

A heaped plate of antipasti was followed by a wide, filled bowl of pasta with *funghi*. The German left his cigarette burning. The smoke made Fenton's eyes smart.

"They aim to be near, to kill at close quarters. But the beginning—the beginning is from the top in Tehran, from the peak of government, and the authorization for the allocation of hard-currency funding and the provision of weapons through diplomatic pouches. A trusted man is appointed and he will be backed by local sympathizers, but he takes the responsibility for success or failure. He will have no contact point with his embassy, there is the creed of deniability. He will not be helped by diplomats or intelligence officers. Our experience is that the trusted man is most hard to capture or kill. It is the sympathizers who reconnoiter and drive the cars who sit in our prison cells. It is a great triumph to take or eliminate the trusted man—if you can do that, you will have my sincerest congratulations."

When the steak was brought, the German took the majority of the vegetables, the greater part of the potatoes, and lit another cigarette.

"What is he like—the trusted man? I tell you, very frankly, he is the same as the people in our Rote Armee Faktion, the same as the people in your Irish groups. The less you know of him, the more impressive you will believe him to be. Our ignorance lifts his reputation. He is dedicated, fanatical, he is skilled, he is prepared for martyrdom, he is elusive—that is what ignorance tells us."

The German chose ice cream with pistachio flavoring, and asked the waiter to bring a double portion.

"But I have seen them, I have interrogated them. I have been with them in the cells and explained with politeness that the rantings of their government and the shouting mobs outside our legation compound in Tehran will not affect the length of a prison sentence. I have talked with those men of the Bundesgrenzschutz who have dragged them from cars at gunpoint, spread-eagled them on the road, laughed about shooting off their testicles. The trusted man, then, is the same as you or me. You know, at Fürstenfeldbruck, at the air base, at the time of the Olympic Games, we killed five of the Palestinians of Black September, and three surrendered. Did they then wish to die, go to the Garden of Paradise? Did they, hell! They knelt and wept for mercy. When the Italians, our esteemed friends, eventually capture a capo of the Mafia, he is the same. He has been a killer on a grand scale, perhaps murdered a hundred men and consigned their corpses to the Gulf of Palermo or acid vats or concrete construction pillars, but when he is arrested, when he faces the guns, he fouls his trousers. They are very human—invincible when free, pathetic when taken. You should not be intimidated by the trusted man."

Espresso coffee was brought, and small chocolates. The German cleared them, and stubbed out a cigarette in the saucer.

"Perhaps, when they leave their country, when the mullah's words are still fresh, they believe they are a sword of Islam, a soldier of the faith. My experience, they forget . . . So soon they are like all the other killers. They are, I believe, addicted to excitement, adrenaline is their narcotic. I said to you that they wished to be close, to see the fear in their victim's eyes, so they will try to use a knife to cut a throat, or a handgun from a meter. They are disturbed people and they will not gain the same excitement from a bomb or from a rocket attack. The bomb and the rocket are the last option, but will not provide the same excitement. If you take this trusted man, go into his cell, try to talk with him. Then I believe you will be sincerely disappointed at what you find."

When the wine was finished, they drank brandy. Fenton had the cigar box brought for him.

"He will be a lonely man. He will seek the admiration of the sympathizers, but will not share with them. He will have the paranoia of the isolated. He is nauseatingly sentimental. Above everything, he will seek praise, always he will want that praise . . . I think, also, he wants the body of a servile woman, not an equal because that would frighten him. What is most dangerous about him, he is terrorized by the thought of failure—he wants to go home, of course he does, but to praise and adulation. I think, to a psychologist, he is a rather tedious, pitiful figure. Let me know what you find."

They left the table, eased into their coats.

On the pavement, the German caught Fenton's arm and whispered close in his ear, through a fog of cigar fumes.

"But hear me. Ali Fellahian, who controls the trusted men, who sanctions their journeys, was invited by my superiors to visit us. For some of us it was a shameful day in the history of our Service to play host to a criminal, and our lips bled because we bit so hard on them to maintain our composure. He took our hospitality and he threatened us. We were left with no area for misunderstanding the economic and diplomatic consequences of publicizing the activities of his killers on our territory. Should you destroy or capture this piece of excrement now bothering you, you should consider very carefully the implications of triumphalist statements . . . A wonderful meal—we should do it more often."

Fenton took a taxi back to Thames House.

Cox was poring over a leave chart, but pushed it away.

Yes, Fenton told him, lunch had provided a most valuable opportunity to quiz a distinguished German antiterrorist officer. He had gained a good insight into the mind of their enemy. But how much further forward were they? Fenton gazed at the ceiling and found no relief there.

"What worries me, whichever way we jump will be the wrong way."

"I did hear you, Harry, unless my ears deceived me, take responsibility . . ."

At the nearest point the bird was a hundred meters from his cover, at the farthest it was two hundred meters. It was a hunter, and quartered the stretch of water and reed bed between. The sight of it made him lose the ache in his hip. Through his care, the bird could fly, could hunt . . . Many times, in the Haur-al-Hawizeh and off the Faw peninsula, he had watched these birds flying overhead. When they flew, hunted, had no sense of danger, he knew no enemy approached him. The pain in his hip was lessening, and he thought that by the next morning he would have regained his mobility and be strong enough to go back for his target.

The bird flew in long, slow lines, still handicapped but able enough, glided, the gold and brown of its neck bent to study the land below—and it dived. In a sudden moment, the wide wings were tucked in, and the bird fell. When it came up, flapping hard for height, he saw the flailing legs of the prey, held in a talon's grip. The bird, the wild creature, came back to him and set down on the grass in front of his cover. He saw the last writhing movements of the frog as the curved beak hacked at it. The bird ripped at the frog's carcass until only scraps were left.

In the life of Farida Yasmin, no one had ever told her she was *important*.

With her guidebook to the village and the neighborhood around it, she had sat on the bench, read it and reread it, then read it again so that the words danced on the pages and no longer had meaning.

No one had ever told her she was *valued*.

From the bench she had walked to the beach and gazed out at the sea. She had been alone on the sand and shingle, and had seen the faraway boats that hugged the horizon line. The next day, or the day after, the next night, or the night after that, farther down the coast, the tanker would divert towards the shore and a small boat would run from it, would collect him. She would be left behind, abandoned.

She had walked through the village, as far as the church, then turned and retraced her steps and come back past the pub, the hall, and the shop where she had bought postcards that would never be sent and a salad-filled bread roll, and the green. She had stood on the far side of the green, the guidebook opened, and looked around her.

She saw the cars come and go from the house. She saw the detective at the door, and the armed police, huge men in their bulging vests. She watched the pattern of their day. Earlier, the detective had run from the house and had spoken with a priest. She couldn't hear what was said, but the body language was of rejection. She noted the camera above the door at the house, and believed as the afternoon darkened that she saw the red wink light of a sensor . . . She wanted his body under her, in the position she had seen on television films. She wanted to ride over him, dominate him, and hear him cry out that she was important, valued, essential, and critical, as no one had ever done. Before he went off the beach into the small boat and out to sea to board the tanker, she wanted the memory of it. What would happen to her then, afterwards?

No one had ever told her that she was *loved*.

Not her father, the bastard, and not her mother, the bitch. Not the kids at school or at college or at any time afterwards. Love was the black hole, without a bottom, without light, in her life. From the bench she saw the villagers coming on foot and by bicycle and in cars, as the afternoon faded, to the hall. Ordinary people, and they didn't seem to notice her sitting on the bench with the opened guide-book, ordinary people who ignored her. She stood, stretched, wiped the rainwater off her forehead, and shook it from her shoulders. The lights of the pub were on, the first cars were scraping the gravel, and there was the first laughter. She wondered how long it would be before the ordinary people, gathering in the pub and the hall, knew her name and her importance.

She went away from the house. She thought she'd seen his shadow pass the window, and she determined that she would be there to witness it when the rocket was fired. She drifted slowly up the road towards the side lane near the church where her car was parked.

"I've said all I want to say about her, and that's too much. she's never coming back here again. If she showed up at the door, I'd slam it in her face—too right I would . . ."

Cathy Parker watched him. She leaned against the kitchen door as Bill Jones stamped out into the narrow hall for his coat and his train driver's satchel. He was a big man, two stones overweight, and she thought it was the blood pressure that reddened his face when he spoke of his daughter. The last thing he did, before glowering at her and barging out of the front door, was to hook a football scarf round his neck. He went out to drive a train from Derby to New-castle, and back. Cathy Parker's own parents had wanted her to be a pretty and feminine girl, and she'd fought hard against it; Bill Jones would have wanted his daughter to be a boy, with him at home matches, sitting alongside him in the workingmen's club, fol-lowing him into train driving.

"What's she done with her life? She's screwed it, and now she's screwing us."

Annie Jones was a small woman, grimly thin in face and body, with prematurely graying hair. She hadn't spoken while her husband had badmouthed their daughter, and Cathy didn't think she'd have spoken when the detectives had come to the house to search through the few personal things that Gladys Eva Jones had left there before the links were cut. Cathy made a pot of tea while the mother sat at the kitchen table. She had no difficulty in drawing the woman out: it was a skill that went with her job.

"We tried to love her, but God knows, it wasn't easy. She didn't want for anything—we haven't money, but we gave her what we could. It didn't satisfy her. You see, Miss Parker, we were never good enough for her, and nor was anyone else round here. She went to the university—Bill won't admit it, but he was proud. She was the only kid in the street that had got to university. I thought if she hadn't friends here she'd find them there. Perhaps the people she met there weren't good enough either. The few times she came back, the first year away, I could see how lonely she was. There's not much here, but you don't have to be lonely, not if you'll muck in. Gladys wouldn't do that, nor at the university neither. I think she was always pushing for more control of people, but it was so obvious that they didn't want to know her. It's not nice to say this about your daughter, but she's a stuck-up bitch. Bill can't talk to her, but it's the same for me. I tried but she never came near to halfway to meet me. Then she went into that religious thing. She came back once after she'd joined them. Don't get me wrong, I've nothing against foreigners having their own religion, but it wasn't right for her. She came back in her robes, her face half covered, and some of the kids in the street gave her some lip. She's not been back since. Do you know where she is now? Do you know what she's doing? She's in real trouble now, isn't she? Or you wouldn't have been here and the detectives wouldn't have come. She wants to belong somewhere special, wants control, wants people to talk about her. Is she going to get hurt? Please, Miss Parker, try to see she doesn't get hurt."

Cathy left her sitting at the kitchen table, staring out of the window above the sink at the songbirds wheeling around the hanging sack of nuts.

Once, on a course with the German GSG9 antiterrorist unit, she'd heard an instructor bark at the recruits about to practice a storm entry to a building, "Shoot the women first."

She drove away from the mean little street, headed for the motorway and London. The instructor had said that the women were always more dangerous than the men, more likely to reach for a weapon in the last critical seconds of their lives when there was no hope of survival.

She was wondering whether Farida Yasmin was a help to the Iranian or a liability.

Cathy thought of the girl, confused and willing, blundering forward with the man. Farida Yasmin craved a little spot where the sun shone on her, but Cathy didn't think she'd find it. A talent of Cathy's was to make instant assessments of the people she investigated: Farida Yasmin was unimportant and she would write only the briefest of reports on her visit; the girl was a loser. But there was nothing she could do to prevent her being hurt, and she felt quite sad.

She knew about loneliness.

. . .

"If we don't make it, it will be the fault of all these wretched boxes. But thank you for the thought. Luisa and I have always been interested in wildlife."

Simon Blackmore went back to his wife in the kitchen. They had been washing the plates, cups, mugs, saucers that had been wrapped in newspaper by the packers. The man at the door had said his name was Paul, that he was on the parish council, that he was the man to fix any little difficulties confronting them, was always pleased to smooth the way for new arrivals. He'd told them there was a meeting in the hall that evening of the Wildlife Group, with a talk on migration from a warden of the Royal Society for the Protection of Birds. Then, he'd asked whether Luisa typed, and had explained how the group had lost its typist: "The most selfish people I've ever known here, and I was born in the village. The worst sort of incomers. The sort of people who don't give a damn for the safety of those they live among." Simon Blackmore had seen the way that the man had looked at his wife's wrists, at the slash scars across the veins.

"What you're being offered, Geoff, sweetheart, is 63 percent more than you're getting now. It's fantastic. On top of that there's the in-house bonus scheme, the private medical thing, there's guaranteed three-star minimum accommodation when you're working out of London, business-class flights into Europe. You'll be on at least double the pittance you're getting now at the end of the day. Your pay at the moment is actually insulting, they don't deserve people like you. The sooner you're gone, the better. Get your letter in straightaway. Write it tonight. I stopped off in the travel agent's on the way from your place. They said Mauritius or the Seychelles are great—I'm talking honeymoons, sweetheart. As soon as you're back from that dump—tomorrow, day after tomorrow?—let's get tramping round some property. Call me. Love you."

Geoff Markham heard her blow kisses down the telephone, and cut the call. His mind was too distracted to make the calculation of a 63 percent increment on his existing salary. He was thinking of the young man out at the rim of the reed beds, and of the firm certainty of his gaze, watching the marshlands.

. . .

"And him, too." Frank Perry stood by the telephone in the kitchen. "Gutless bastard." He stood by the telephone and read the lengthening list of scratched-out names.

Bill Davies shrugged. "I suppose I shouldn't have done that, cut him off your list—sorry."

"I don't go to church, can't bear listening to his dreary sermons."

"I just thought, given the circumstances—I thought it would help if he showed support."

Perry turned to the detective. He was beaten down, gray-faced. The hand resting on Davies's shoulder shook as it grasped at the jacket, held tight to it. "Was I out of order last night?"

"Not for me to comment."

"I can—just—take it. Meryl can't. She's drowning. One more thing, one more, another bit of chaos, she'll go under. How long?"

"I'm not supposed to talk tactics or strategy."

"Bill, please."

The detective thought his principal was close to defeat—and that was not the policy. He'd done them all: he had stood with the Glock on his hip beside cabinet big shots and foreign leaders and turned IRA informers, and he had never felt any sense of involvement. He thought that whatever he said would go back to Meryl Perry.

"There's a fair bit going on, don't ask me what. We're beefed up, most of which you won't see. It was said at the beginning that our Tango couldn't last—hostile ground, lack of resources, your location—more than a week."

"What day are we?"

"We're at Day Five."

A tired nervy smile played at Perry's mouth. "What's the Al Haig story?"

Davies laughed out loud, as if the tension were lifted. "Monday, right? Getting to the end of bloody Monday. It's appropriate . . . United States Army general Al Haig was in Belgium on a NATO visit. The sort of trip where there are convoys of limousines about a half a mile long. A security nightmare. The convoy's hammering along a main route—of course, the search teams have worked over it. But they missed a culvert. In the culvert was a bomb, handiwork of a leftist anti-American faction. The detonation was a fraction late and, anyway, it malfunctioned. The car, armor-plated, didn't take the full force, kept on going, and the escorts. In the culvert had been enough explosive to bounce Haig's car right off the road and make a crater fish could have lived in. Al Haig said, "I guess that if we can get through Monday then we can survive the rest of the week." It's about hanging on in there. We've about got through Monday, Mr. Perry."

"I can hold her for two more days—if nothing else breaks her first."

It was the end of the day, and the quiet was all around him. The bird sky-danced, displaying for him its regained flying skills.

But there was the quiet.

He no longer watched the bird, no longer took pleasure from the extravagance of its flight. He watched the geese and the swans, the ducks and the wheeling gulls, and he looked for a sign, the quiet playing in his ears.

They did not stampede, they did not skim the water with flailed wings to take off in panic, they did not shriek as they would when disturbed. They were quiet, as if they were warned.

Vahid Hossein could see the positions of the policemen on the far side of the marsh, on the higher ground. He had no fear of them. He knew where they were. They would have thought they were still un-noticed, but he saw each movement of their bodies as their legs, backs, hips, shoulders stiffened and they shifted their bodies for re-lief . . . There had been an Iraqi sniper on the Jasmin Canal who used the SVD Dragunov 7.62-caliber rifle with an effective range of 1,300 meters. He was never seen, and he had shot eighteen men in three weeks. A prisoner had said afterwards that a mortar's shrapnel had hit him as he went to his firing position on the banks of the canal in the early morning. It was luck that a random shell had killed him. The birds on the Jasmin Canal were always quiet in the hours before the sniper fired. He sensed the presence of a watcher. He felt a new atmosphere. He believed himself now—and he had only the evidence of the quiet—to be challenged. A slight frown of apprehension had settled on his forehead. At the fall of the day, as the wind quickened and trembled the reed heads, he made his plan to go into the water, away from the bank, towards the place he had seen yesterday deep in the beds of old gold reeds and near to the central water channel.

He could not see the watcher, could only sense the new quiet that had settled around him.

15

Sitting with the damp of the ground seeping into the backside of his trousers and with the warmth of his dogs under his jackknifed legs, in his vantage point, Andy Chalmers listened to the night sounds.

There was no moon, no break in the rain cloud.

He was behind thick cover: if there had been light he would not have been able to see the reed beds and the water channels. It was possible that the man had an image intensifier, night-vision equipment; he would not give him the chance to identify his position. Chalmers did not need to see the land around him. Instead he listened.

There was the quiet, the rumble of the sea on the shore, the call of a distant fox. A policeman two hundred meters away stifled a cough and another one four hundred meters away stood to urinate. He was still, he was silent. When the fox called, his fingers felt the hackles rise on the necks of his dogs and he soothed them where they lay.

If the man was there, Chalmers knew he would hear him.

The wind that came from the west had turned, which pleased Chalmers. It scudded off the distant trees and fields, and came across the marshland riffling the leaves and branches behind which he sat. He could control *sight* and *sound,* but not the body odor of *smell.* Sight, sound, and smell all carried great distances over open ground at night, but in the high mountains where he worked, he regarded smell as the worst of the stalker's enemies.

He had left the keys to his caravan, where he lived at the back of the senior keeper's cottage, with Mr. Gabriel Fenton; the few coins from his pocket had been abandoned on the train; he carried nothing of metal in his pockets. It was his routine to make the owner's guests discard everything that could clink, rattle, rub together, before he started the stalk. His dogs were as still and silent as himself. There would be no sound for his prey to hear and no noise to disturb the birds in the reed mass.

The wind was as he would have wanted it and would carry his smell away from the man, if he was there. An American, a guest of his owner, had once brought foul pungent creams with him on a stalk and believed they would block the man smell that a stag might scent. Chalmers had made him strip and douse himself in a stream to wash the stuff off him; a French guest had rolled in sheep droppings, and that also was useless. The only possibility of hiding man smell from a target stag was to keep the wind in the stalkers' faces. He had not yet smelt the man, if he was there.

He sat and wrapped himself in his patience, let the night hours drift, and he listened.

He could sit still, silent, but he did not doze, did not allow himself to edge towards sleep.

If he had dozed, slept, then he would not have heard.

In the cold, the rain, and the quiet, Chalmers set himself games to play with his memory so that his senses were never less than alert.

Memories of stalks with guests of the owner, and clients who paid for a day what he earned in two weeks . . . The guest from Holland who had failed at the start of the week, in the disused quarry, to put six bullets out of six, with a telescopic sight, into a four-inch target at a hundred meters—he had refused to take him out. Mr. Gabriel had backed him, and the guest had been sent to thrash a river for salmon. The guest from the City of London, with new clothing and a new rifle, good on the target shooting in the quarry, who had been led for five hours towards an eight-year-old stag with a crown of antlers, been brought to within eighty yards for a side shot. He'd given the guest the loaded rifle, the Browning .270 caliber, cocked it.

He'd been on the telescope, on the beast, and the bullet had struck its lower belly. It had fled, wounded. He had told the guest he was a "bloody butcher," and had been out half the night and all of the next morning with his dogs to find the beast and limit its misery.

Chalmers was encouraged by the quiet of the reed banks: there should have been movement and spats over nesting territory and the cries of the birds.

The client from Germany who had demanded to shoot the stag with the greatest crown spread of antlers, but that beast was only six years old and in the prime of its breeding life. The client had hissed the sum he was paying and what he needed as a trophy. Chalmers had told him that if he "showed no respect for the beasts" he could go back down to the glen with his rifle unused. The man had crumpled then, whined about the money, and had been led forward to shoot an old beast at the end of its life. They'd passed within fifty yards of the younger stag as they'd moved towards the target beast, and at the end the client had thanked him for the best stalk of his shooting days. Chalmers had walked away from him because he acknowledged neither gratitude nor praise.

He thought the quiet was because the man was good, was among the birds in the reeds and on the water, and was still.

The guest, panting and unfit, had been in dead ground and had pulled a packet of cigarettes from his pocket. Chalmers had snatched the cigarette from the guest's mouth. He'd made the stalk last ten hours, two of them crawling against the rush of a stream-filled gully. Finally, when the beast was seventy yards from them, he'd told the guest, "You're not fit to shoot, you're a bloody ruin," and hadn't given him the rifle.

The memories kept the cutting edge to his senses. The birds were too quiet. He knew that the man was good and that the man was there, in the marsh.

He waited, patient. He felt a respect, brother to brother, for the man out there, in the water, the same respect that he felt for the big beasts he stalked and tracked.

"We've lasted through Monday."

He'd had to feed the boy and himself. He'd heated the last of the precooked meat pies in the fridge, and taken the remaining tub of ice cream from the freezer. He'd found a science program on the television for Stephen, and they'd eaten off their laps. He'd taken the trays back into the kitchen, and gone upstairs. She was on the bed, in darkness. He sat beside her.

"They say he has a week. He can't endure more than a week. It's closing round him. We're on the fifth day. We have to hang on in there . . ."

"Where is he?" Fenton asked.

"I don't know." Markham's voice, distorted by the scrambler, echoed back at him. "I only know that he's sitting out there in the bloody bog."

"Have you called him, has he sit-repped?"

"I wouldn't dare to call the ungracious little beggar, I'm only the fetcher and carrier—I reckon he'd garrote me if I disturbed him."

"Doesn't he know the importance of continuous contact?"

"He knows it if you told him it."

"Geoff, does he realize how much is riding on his back?"

"That, too, I expect you told him. I'll call you when he deigns to make contact. Bye, Mr. Fenton."

Fenton shivered. He was alone but for the company of a third-year probationer who watched the telephones. It was always late at night, when an operation was running towards climax, that he shivered, not from cold but from nerves. In the day, surrounded by acolytes, the confidence boomed in him. But Parker had gone, the American with her, and the elder of the probationers, and the old warhorse from B section. Cox had left early to prepare for a dinner party. It would be the end of him if the boy, Chalmers, failed. He would be a casualty, washed up, sneered at, shown the early-retirement door.

Halfway across the world was another man who would be sweating on the fear of failure. He did not know what an office high in the Ministry of Information and Security would be like, but he seemed to sense that man shivering in the same sweat as dribbled on his own back. He had talked of control but late at night, he reflected, there was not a vestige of control for either of them. It was always like that, never different, when the little people took charge and the power of the high and mighty was stripped from their hands . . . He would sleep at Thames House that night, and the next, sleep there until it was over . . . Because he had volunteered to take responsibility, the career of Harry Fenton lay in the grubby hands of Andy Chalmers.

"Home is where we are. Home isn't about people, isn't about things. Home is where you are, and Stephen and me. There isn't anything for us here. You said home was about friends—but there aren't any, they've gone. Anywhere we are together is home. I can't take it, not anymore."

She lay with her back to him. Her voice was low-pitched and flat calm. Perry thought she was beyond weeping.

It was coming to the end of a complex day for the intelligence officer. The demand for information, clarification of a situation, from Tehran led to his walking along the corridor with the flowers on his arm and the grapes in his hand, one among many visitors.

The brigadier in Tehran had insisted. The intelligence officer, nervous, wary, had left his embassy office in the middle of the day. He had not seen a tail but always assumed one followed him. He had driven to the home in west London's suburbs of a colleague from Visa Section, parked outside the front of the house, been greeted at the door and invited inside. Without stopping, he had gone out of a back door, crossed the rear garden to the gate, tracked along an alley between garages, and taken his colleague's car. He had driven to the offices and yard of the car-hire company at the extreme of south London, and asked about a BMW rented out to Yusuf Khan. A shadow of hesitation crossed the young woman's face, and he had eased his wallet from his pocket. A hundred pounds, palmed across the desk, in twenty-pound notes had lightened the shadow. He was shown, hurriedly, a photograph from an insurance file of the wrecked vehicle. He was told of the hospital where the injured man was treated . . . Did she know about a passenger? The police had not spoken of one . . . It was already early evening by the time he reached the hospital. After checking for the location of Delivery/Postnatal, he headed for the casualty ward.

He was another visitor, one of many who anxiously came to see the sick, the injured, and the maimed. He had the flowers and the grapes, as if they guaranteed him admittance.

He walked slowly down the center of the ward, through the aisle between the beds, scanning the faces of the patients.

He seemed lost and confused but none of the harassed nursing staff came forward to help him.

A corridor was ahead of him, signs for the fire escape, and to the side a trolley carrying resuscitation equipment. He took a risk because Tehran required it of him. He edged forward with the fool's smile on his face.

Only when he was beside the trolley did he see the policeman with the machine gun on his lap.

"I am looking for my sister and her baby."

There was a door with a glass window in it. Behind it a second policeman was reading a magazine that half hid the bulk of his firearm. He saw the bed, and the bandaged head of Yusuf Khan.

"Not here, no babies here—thank God."

"This not the place for babies?"

He gazed at the bandaged head, the linking tubes, the opened eyes. The head shook, the tubes wavered, the eyes blinked with recognition.

"Absolutely, pal, this is not the place for babies."

He saw the tears gathering in the eyes, and he thought he saw a trace of guilt flicker there.

"I must ask again."

He walked away. He had seen what he needed to see. He laid the flowers and the grapes on the ward sister's desk. When he left his colleague's house in west London, he sped back to central London and his office at the embassy, with the urgent report to be sent by secure coded communication to Tehran locked in his mind.

"Is that what you want, a van coming to the front door? All those bastards out in the road watching. You want to give them that satisfaction? Your things, everything that's personal to you—your furniture, your clothes, your pictures, your life—paraded for them. They'll spit at the car as it takes us away. Is that what you want?"

His hand was on her shoulder and his fingers massaged Meryl's bones and muscles. She never looked at him and she didn't speak.

The brigadier was a careful man. If his back was to be protected, it was necessary for him always to be careful. He was that rarity in the service of the Ministry of Information and Security, an intelligence officer who had made the transition from the previous regime. He had crossed sides. The majority with whom he had worked as a captain in the SAVAK were long dead, hanged, shot, butchered, for their service to the shah. But three days before the mob—the street scum from south Tehran—had entered and sacked the SAVAK offices on Hafez Avenue, he had taken a suitcase of files from his workplace and made contact with his enemy. The files were his credentials. With them were his memories of names, locations, and faces. In the confused days that followed he was, to the new men of Iran, a small, treasured mine of knowledge. The names of former colleagues, the locations of safe houses, and the faces of informers all had tripped off his tongue as he bought himself survival.

The new regime, of course, was innocent in the matters of security and counterrevolution. The changecoat prospered as his colleagues died. When the captured Americans from the embassy protested that they were not employees of the Agency, the changecoat could identify them. When the Mujahiddin rose in revolt against the imam, he could put faces to names. He had been promoted to major and then colonel in the Vezarat-e-Ettelaat Va Amniyat-e Kishvar, and now held the rank, in the VEVAK, of brigadier, but he was too intelligent, too cautious a man to believe that his position would ever be secure and above suspicion. A few detested him, a few more despised him; the majority, those who knew his past, were wary of him.

The protective screens with which he surrounded himself were the zealot's commitment to the new regime, coupled with a total, ruthless efficiency. No word of criticism for the mullahs in government and influence ever crossed his lips, no mistake in his planning of operations was ever admitted. If the mildest words of criticism were ever spoken he would be denounced and pitched from his office. There were many, and he knew it, who would clamor to fire the bullet or tighten the noose around his neck.

Vahid Hossein had been like a son to him . . . The communication from London was on his desk. The hot, fume-filled night was around his high office. Tears and guilt meant betrayal, were evidence that a coward, Yusuf Khan, had talked. It was his hope, alone in the cigarette-smoke-filled office, that the man who had been like a son to him would be shot dead.

It would be worse if the great tanker, which was the pride of the fleet, were intercepted as it slowed in the shipping lanes to launch the inflatable, was boarded and impounded. He weighed the possibilities open to him, then wrote an instruction for the VEVAK officer who worked as an official at the building of the National Iranian Tanker Corporation. The ship was to sail in the morning. There was to be no attempt at a pickup.

For his own survival, to avoid an inevitable fate, he cut the link to Vahid Hossein. He did not hesitate.

"I want to go shopping, I want Stephen to go to school, I want you to go to work, I want us go walking—I don't want, ever again, Frank, to see a gun. I want to be happy again. There's nothing left for us here."

Downstairs the television droned on, under Davies's tuneless whistling to himself. There was a muted cackle of laughter from the hut at the back, and the revving of the engine of the car at the front to keep the heater going. Everything they listened to, all around them, was sourced by the guns.

"Please, I'm begging it of you, please . . ." Perry's voice quavered to his wife's silence.

The cups and saucers for the coffee, the biscuit plates and the glasses for the fruit juice had been stacked on trays and carried away into the kitchenette area. The chairs scraped the wooden floor as the audience settled. Gratifyingly, the hall was almost filled, but the Wildlife Group always attracted the village's best response.

Peggy was busy rounding up the last of the lost crockery. Emma Carstairs was fussing with the blinds, checking they would keep out the nearest glow from the street lamp. Barry fiddled with the beam from the slide projector and called for Jerry Wroughton to move the screen fractionally. Mary was helping to maneuver Mrs. Wilson's wheelchair into a better position to see the screen. Mrs. Fairbrother sat aloof in the front row, Mr. Hackett behind her, and Dominic and his partner talked softly. There were more than fifty present, a good turnout on a bad night; the numbers of village regulars were augmented by a few who had driven from Dunwich, a carload from Blythburgh, and more from Southwold.

Paul clapped his hands for attention and the chatter died. "First, well done for coming on a filthy night. Second, apologies that we won't be having minutes from the committee's last meeting and can't hand out the usual list of summer speakers. I reckon most of you know the problem we've had with getting things typed up—any volunteers?" No hands were raised, but there had been a growl of understanding at the mention of the *problem*. "Third, my pleasure in welcoming Dr. Julian Marks from the RSPB, who is going to talk to us on the subject of migration. Dr. Marks . . ."

To generous applause, a longhaired man with a gangling body, his face tanned by weather, stepped forward.

Dr. Marks said loudly, "I'm taking it I can be heard. Everyone hear me at the back—yes? Excellent. I want to begin with a thank-you, two, actually. Thank you for inviting me, but more important, an especial thank-you from the RSPB for your last donation, which was an extraordinary amount from a village of this size and reflects a very caring and decent community. Fund-raising on that scale marks this village as a place of warmth, a place of overwhelming generosity. Now, migration . . ."

The lights faded.

The beam of the projector caught the screen.

Few in the hall's audience saw Simon and Luisa Blackmore slide soundlessly into empty seats in the back row; none present would have known of her fear of crowded, bright-lit rooms.

"You know, living as you do alongside those wonderful empty marshlands, the most beautiful of the migratory birds, the marsh harrier . . ."

"You're protected, and Stephen, and me."

"He was at the door, he was only trying to break down the fucking door. With a gun to kill us, in our home—"

"It can't happen again, I promise—it's what they've told me. You can't move for men here, everywhere, protecting us."

Meryl twisted on the bed to face him. Her arms were around his neck. She had his promise and clung to it.

Gussie, in the summer months, dug gardens in the village when he had finished at the piggery, then went home for his tea, then to the pub. In the darker winter months, when he couldn't use the evenings to turn over the vegetable patches at the Carstairses' and the Wroughtons', and at Perry's house, he went straight home from the pig farm for his tea, then to the pub. After the pub, his mother, his younger brothers and sisters already gone to bed, he sat in the chair, master of the house, and read the magazines he bought in Norwich, stories about combat and survival, and he dreamed. He sent away for mail-order books and reckoned himself expert in counterterrorism, low-intensity warfare, and the world of the military; he should have been listened to in the pub. His father was gone, living the last four years with some tart in Ipswich, and he was the breadwinner for the family. He had his tea when he wanted it. Home revolved around him and his earning power. He believed, as the wage earner, that he was the equal of any man he met in the pub. But he never found, quite, the popularity he thought he deserved. His life, with the other workers in the pig fields, with the people in the cul-de-sac where he lived, or in the pub where he propped up the bar each evening, was a constant search for that elusive popularity. Stories never heard through to the end, jokes never quite laughed at, his opinion rarely asked . . . He was big, well muscled, could throw around the straw bales on which the pigs slept with ease, and because of his size he had never known fear.

He had not told her that the option was withdrawn, no longer existed. Perry said it again in her ear as he held her. "It cannot happen again."

"Because if anything else happened . . ."

"It won't, it can't."

"Anything . . ."

. . .

Gussie was the loudest. Gussie was the one drinking fastest, talking the biggest talk.

More pints of strong beer were passed across the bar by Martindale. Two hours they'd been going, and the talk was in the drink. His wife, the timid Dorothy Martindale, had called him back from the bar, into the doorway. Why did he allow the swearing, cursing, drink talk? Because without these people they'd be at the wall, tramping to the bankruptcy hearing, that was why. She'd gone back upstairs to the flat over the bar.

The till rang again. They were the only customers he'd have in that night: everyone else was in the hall.

Vince said, "What I'm reckoning, if the bastard's still here when summer comes, the season starts, we can kiss good-bye to visitors."

Gussie capped him. "No bloody visitors. No money. Need the visitors."

Donna said, "Something's got to be done, some bugger's got to have the balls to do something."

It was all the custom he had, and all he was likely to have if the visitors stayed away because armed police were combing the village. Who'd let kids run round? Who'd sit on the green with a picnic or go walking on the beach? Most important, who'd sit on the bench outside the pub with a warm pint and crisps for the kids? Who'd be there if the village, when the season came, was a gun camp? He'd be finished if there were no visitors, and the others with him.

Gussie shouted, "They got to know they're not wanted, got to know it straight—and they're going to."

Vince wanted a plate of chips.

Martindale left the bar and went upstairs to ask his wife to make a plate of chips. He could charge a pound for a plate of chips. He apologized to her, but they needed each pound going into the till. He'd told her, when they'd started in the pub, that it would be a money trail, and now he was grateful for the money earned by a plate of chips. He went back down to the bar and Gussie wasn't there. He thought Gussie had gone to piss, and his glass, half full, was on the bar counter. He seemed not to hear the complaining whine across the bar. The bank's letter was in his mind, and the letter from the brewery that stated he was underperforming.

Martindale saw Gussie through the front window, crossing the car park and weaving. He was carrying a light plank, one of those the builders had left when he'd said he couldn't afford for them to complete the work on the outside lavatories. Martindale watched him lurching away into the darkness, beyond the reach of the lights, the plank on his shoulder.

He held her. Meryl had his promise, and the tension of her muscles ebbed. She lay soft against him. He heard the brief triple ring of the bell, then Blake's voice and Davies's wishing him a good night. Davies said, Frank heard it, that the "bloody place was quiet as a grave." He heard Blake settle in the dining room, and check the machine gun they shared. If he hadn't given his promise, she would have taken down the suitcase from the top of the wardrobe, and left.

He had been stifled in the house. Ahead of him was a meal alone in a pub, then the suffocation of the room in the bed-and-breakfast.

Bill Davies walked past his car. He had to think, had to be alone. There was no escape from the need to call home. There were enough of them gossiping in his section for him to know the talk of a marriage going down. Some said that, actually, they felt the better for it when it was over. A few said, in a bar with drink, that when it was over the loneliest time in their lives began. He had to steel himself to talk with Lily in the hope that she would let him chat to Donald and Brian. It would probably be like the last time, silences and refusal, then the challenge as to when he was coming home, to which he had no answer, then the purr of the cut call. He had to think, had to walk, had to know what he would say.

The rain lashed down.

The road in front of him, towards the hall's lights and the pub's bright windows, was empty.

There was a shadow of movement at the side of the road, beyond the throw of the lights from the hall, and he thought it would be one of the old idiots who took their dogs out, sunshine or rain, and was sheltering against a tree or a hedge.

He wrapped his heavy coat closer round him. His shoes and the trousers at his ankles were already soaked.

He would say, "I love you. I love my boys, our boys. I want to be with you. I want to share my life with you . . . I am a policeman, I carry a Glock pistol, I protect people who are under threat . . . I cannot change. I can't go back to chasing thieves, seeing kids across roads. I have to live with it, you have to live with it. Living with it, Lily, is better for both of us than splitting. Splitting is death. Death for me, death for you, death for Donald and Brian. Anything is better than us meeting on the doorstep on Saturday mornings, if I'm not working, and you looking at me like I'm dirt, and letting the kids out with me for four hours, a football match and a McDonald's. Give it another chance . . ."

The words jangled in his mind, and he was so tired. He had been sitting for twelve hours in the dining room of the house with his flask of coffee and his sandwiches, with his Glock and his machine gun, with his newspaper, and listening to them. He was trying to put Lily forefront in his mind, and his boys—and they were second best to Meryl Perry. Lily wouldn't understand about Meryl Perry, wouldn't . . .

The shot blasted out.

He froze. There was no pain, no numbness, and he was standing. The shot had missed.

He spun—but they didn't do pitch-darkness practice at Lippitts Hill. They did daytime firing or were under the arc lights in the shooting gallery.

He was reaching under the heavy coat, under his jacket, for the Glock. He had it out of the holster. He was turning, aiming into the blackness in front of him.

He was screaming for control, for dominance.

"Armed police! Throw your weapon down! Show yourself!"

But he was in the light, and the rain was in his eyes, and he couldn't see a target. If there had been anything to aim at he would have fired, not shouted. Finger on the trigger guard, like they taught —where was the bastard?

"Get forward, to me, crawl, or I shoot—I fucking shoot. Weapon first, then you! Move."

Bill Davies had never had his gun out before, never drawn it for real. Now he saw the movement . . . His finger slipped from the guard to the trigger. Not simunition in Hogan's Alley, not on the range. His finger locked on the trigger, and he began to squeeze. He blinked, tried to focus on the aim into the darkness.

A plank fell towards him, bounced twice, and came to rest at his feet. There was a whimpering in front of him, and an identifiable movement. He had the aim on it, and his finger was tightening.

"Come out! Come out or I shoot!" Davies bellowed at the blackness.

The shadow came, with it a whining cry. The young man crawled on his knees and elbows towards the light.

Davies knew it was over. He had been so shit scared and it made him angry. He saw the slack mouth of the young man and the terror in his eyes. He had seen him in the pub. They used planks in Ireland—kids and women used to stand in darkness, put their weight on a plank end, wait for a patrol to pass, then heave up the other end of it to let it smash down on tarmac or paving, its sound the replica of a bullet firing. They did it to wind up the soldiers. It was sport. He had been at the edge of firing . . . It was unnecessary but he caught the collar of the young man and dragged him across the road, out into the street light. He threw him flat on his stomach, drove the barrel of the Glock into his neck, put a knee into the small of his back, and, one-handed, frisked him. He could smell old beer and new piss. He had been at the edge of killing a drunk who'd played a game. He stood high over him and used his foot to turn him over. He saw the big stain where the young man had wet himself and the scratches on his face from being dragged over the road surface. The man made little noises of terror, and Davies realized he still covered him with the gun.

He shouldn't have, but he kicked the young man hard in the wall of the stomach.

"Go on, get back to your mammy. Tell your mammy why you pissed your trousers. Ever try it again, you're dead."

The young man scrambled to his knees, then to his feet, then lurched away sobbing. Davies watched him as he ran towards the hall and the pub's lit windows.

He walked back to his car outside the house and slumped in the seat. He didn't know why he hadn't made the final squeeze on the trigger that would have killed the kid, and his whole body shook. He knew he would make no phone call that night.

• • •

". . . wildlife is a jewel we are fortunate to see. The brightest of the jewels, making the incredible journey to and from west Africa each year, coming back to us, to our place, each spring, is the marsh harrier. We are a privileged people. Thank you."

The applause burst around Dr. Julian Marks. The lights came on. They had all heard the shouting in the road, had all turned in the half-light under the projector's beam, looked at the door, and seen Paul slip busily out. Barry Carstairs, attention elsewhere, led the applause. He was about to offer their thanks to the speaker when the swing doors burst back open.

The silence fell. Paul shouted, "It's Gussie, the police nearly shot him. It was the detective at the Perrys'—he had his gun on him, and then he kicked him to shit. I thought he was going to shoot him. Christ, we all know Gussie, he's hardly Brain of Britain, but he was damn near killed!"

There was a stampede to the door. The crowd surged past Simon and Luisa Blackmore and out into the night. Many were in time to see Gussie staggering across the brightly lit forecourt of the pub.

Jerry Wroughton said, the rain running on his face, "This nonsense has gone far enough."

Forgetting her reservations of the previous morning, Emma Carstairs said, "It's time somebody did something."

Martindale saw him first and dropped the glass he was drying.

Vince turned on his stool.

Gussie stood in the doorway, gasping for breath. His hair was plastered down on his forehead and his eyes showed stark terror, his face laced with bloody scratches. They could all see the dark patch at the crotch of his jeans, and the rips at the knees. None of them laughed.

Gussie stammered, "He was going to kill me—the man at the Perrys', the cop, he had his gun on me. I was only joking him, but he was going to shoot me. I thought I was dead, and he kicked me. I wasn't doing anything, it was a bloody joke."

Vince stood his full height. The drink gave him the stature and the courage. "Don't know about you lot, but I don't think those bastards have got the message. Myself, I'm going to see they get it. It's time the shits were gone . . ."

When the first rock hit the window, Meryl woke. Half conscious, she heard the cheer. She groped for Frank in the darkness beside her, but he wasn't there.

There was another crack of breaking glass and another cheer. She pushed herself off the bed, and heard Frank's voice, frantic, calling for Stephen, and the rush of feet through the kitchen below her, and into the hall. He'd promised her, she'd had Frank's promise.

She went to the top of the stairs. The bell rang, three bleats. Blake had a vest on, the gun drawn. Paget was in front of him. Paget did the door and Blake covered him. As it was opened, she heard the shouting, the obscenities, heard her name and Frank's, clearly. Davies squeezed through the half-opened door, and Paget slammed it behind him. More rocks, maybe half bricks, and perhaps an empty metal dustbin, clattered against the door.

She was at the top of the stairs and they had not seen her.

Blake yelled, "What the fuck is going on here?"

Davies was leaning against the hall wall and the water dribbled from his coat onto the paper. "It's about a bloody moron."

"What's half the fucking village got to do with a bloody moron?"

"I was walking. The bloody moron did me with a plank—I thought it was a shot. I bloody near fired. Christ, I had him in my sights. He was just drunk. I roughed him. If it's not happened to you then you wouldn't know what it's like. Bloody hell."

Bill Davies looked up the stairs and saw her. It was as if the panic cleared off his face, and the tiredness; his expression was a mask. He said calmly, as if she'd heard nothing, "Everything's under control, Mrs. Perry. There's been an incident, but it'll be over in a moment. Please stay upstairs, Mrs. Perry."

"Where's Stephen?"

"Stephen's with Juliet Seven—sorry, with Mr. Perry. Stephen's fine . . . Please, stay upstairs."

They didn't want to know about her. As far as they were concerned, she was just a woman. She heard the murmur of the voices of Davies, Blake, and Paget, and she caught the name Juliet Seven, and the words "safe area," and mention of "sector two" and "sector four"; her man, her home, and her garden. There was a window at the front of the landing at the top of the stairs, beside the airing-cupboard door. She peeped past the curtain. A little tableau was laid out below her. For a moment there was quiet, as if they regrouped, reconsidered, as if the fainter hearts ruled. They were all there. On the green, the village kids were at the front and behind them were Vince and Gussie and Paul, and others she recognized who worked on the farms or had no work or took the small fishing boats with visitors and sea anglers. Farther back, half hugging the shadows, were Barry and Emma Carstairs, Jerry and Mary Wroughton, and Mrs. Fairbrother. Deeper into the shadows, but she could still see them, were Dominic and his partner, and the vicar. She knew them all.

Paul came from the blackness, holding out the bottom edge of his coat to make a basket. When he loosed it, stones fell to the road.

The kids scrambled for the stones, snatched them up, and hurled them against the walls of the house, and the windows and the door, and the cars parked at the front.

She saw hatred.

She had seen such mobs on television—flickering, contorted faces from Africa and Asia, and from the corners of Eastern Europe, but theirs was an anonymous madness. These faces she knew, and the faces of those who stood back in the shadows and watched.

There was a flash of light in the far blackness, then the light lit the torso of a youth. She recognized him. He was from the council houses and helped carry ladders for Vince. He held a milk bottle and the cloth stuffed in the bottle's neck was lit. The crowd roared approval. There must have been fifty of them, maybe more. The youth ran forward, past Mrs. Fairbrother and Mr. Hackett, past Dominic, past Emma and Mary, Barry and Jerry, past Paul and Vince, Gussie and Donna, and his arm arched to throw the bottle.

She heard the pandemonium in the hall below, then the bolt scraping open and the key turning.

Through the window, she saw Paget go out, crouch, fumble at his belt, then throw his missile. The youth dropped the bottle and turned. It splintered and the conflagration of fire burst where he had been. The gas canister detonated. The wind took the gray-white

cloud past the light of the burning petrol and into the black darkness. She heard the choking, the coughing, and the screamed pro-
tests.

They had gone, all of them, to the cover of darkness.

This was not Ireland, or Nairobi, wasn't Guatemala City—this was
her home.

The fire guttered, the gas dispersed, shadowy figures moved in the
darkness. The two mobile cars were now drawn up to make a barrier
in front of the house.

The argument raged in the hall below her, Frank and Bill Davies
in spitting dispute. She was not supposed to hear. Then . . . Frank
propelled Stephen across the hall and up the stairs before shrugging
into a vest.

Davies wrenched open the door. She held Stephen and felt the
blast of the cold air. She crouched.

Frank was outside with Davies and Paget. She could not see them.
She was down on the floor and clinging to Stephen, holding his head
against her and pressing her palms over his ears. He would be on the
step, shielded by the bodies of Davies and Paget, protected by their
guns and their gas against his friends, her friends.

He had to shout. To be heard across their low front fence and the
grass, heard into the deep shadow, Frank had to shout.

"It's all right, you fuckers, you can go home. You can go home and
be satisfied that you've won as much as you're going to win. I
promised Meryl . . . Do you all remember Meryl? You should remember Meryl—she did enough for you lot. I promised her that nothing
more would happen. I was wrong. I had forgotten you, all of you. I
can't see you now, any of you, in the dark, but, please, stay and listen.
Don't creep away on your stomachs. Don't pretend it didn't happen.
You will remember tonight, what you did, for the rest of your lives. If
you're still there, if you're listening, then you should know that you
have won a little victory. You have broken my promise to Meryl.
She'll be going in the morning, and taking Stephen with her. She'll be
trying to find somewhere to stay. She'll have to ring round, people she
hardly knows, or check into a hotel she's never been to. Everyone she
reckoned was her friend is here, so it won't be easy for her to find
somewhere. Not me, though, not me . . ."

The tears streamed on her cheeks and fell on the hair of her child's head.

"You're stuck with me. Before tonight, I might just have gone with her, but not now. Your victory is that you've driven out a wonderful, caring woman, and her child. You don't win with me. I'm a proper bastard, your worst fucking nightmare, an obstinate sod. What I did, why there's the threat, I provided the information that killed a busful of men. I was prepared to betray a busful of men—so, what happens to you is low down on any relevance scale to me. I don't care what happens to you, and I'm staying. Got that? Can you hear me? When you next go to church, put money in charity boxes, when you next volunteer for good works and good causes, think of what you did tonight to Meryl. But the cruelty doesn't work with me . . ."

She could not hold back the tears.

"You see, you don't frighten me. I'm not frightened of yobs with stones. Where I was, for what I did, if I'd been caught there, I'd have been hanged until dead. That's not a trap under the gallows, and quick, but a rope from an industrial crane, and it's being hoisted up, and it's kicking and strangling and slow. There's not a few drunks watching, not a few cowards, there's twenty thousand people. You understand? Being hanged from a crane frightens me, not you . . ."

She lay on the floor beside the door of the airing cupboard, clutched her boy, and squeezed her hands over his ears.

"I bought some time. I'm told I delayed a program for the development of weapons of mass destruction. The warheads would have carried chemicals or microbiological agents, might have been nerve gases, and might have been something like anthrax. You, of course, wouldn't have known the people targeted by those warheads. They would have been Saudis or Kuwaitis or the Gulf people. They might have been Israeli Jews. When you're so selfish, when you live complacently in an island of your own making, you wouldn't think of the millions of other souls who exist around you. Are you happy?"

She heard the hoarseness of his voice.

"There is a man who has been sent to kill me. He is somewhere, out there, in the darkness. I know very little of him—but I know about his society, his culture. He is a Muslim, a child of the Islamic faith . . . He would not understand you. From his faith and his culture, he would believe that my community has closed ranks around me, not isolated me. I can find more love for him, the man sent to kill me, than for you, my so-called friends."

She heard his last shout into the night.

"Are you there? Are you listening?"

The door slammed behind him. The key was turned, the bolt rammed home.

16

He felt puny, insignificant, and unimportant.

Geoff Markham walked beside the stream that wound ahead of him between the sea and the Southmarsh. Behind him it skirted the village before drifting inconsequentially into Northmarsh. The wind was up and had blown away the rain.

He was unimportant because he had not been telephoned the night before. He had been killing time at a piano recital twelve miles away, in another town; he had sat in ignorance at the back of a half-empty, drafty Baptist hall. His mobile telephone, of course, had been on, but the call had not come. A trifle of life would have been injected into the performance if his telephone had bleeped, but it had not . . . Davies had told him, an hour earlier that morning, of the night's events. He had seen the scorched grass where the milk bottle had ignited and seen the smoked slivers. Near to the new tree was the small patch of burned ground where the gas canister had detonated. Only an unimportant junior liaison officer would not have been telephoned. Davies had told him what was going to happen that day—not asked him for his opinion, but told him. He had stormed away.

He was unimportant, he realized, because he did not carry a gun. The guns were what counted now. He was drawn towards Southmarsh. The guns ringed the marshland, just as they were around and inside the house. It hurt him to feel the minimality of his importance. And no communication, either, from the little stinking bastard with the dogs. Markham didn't know where he was, what he did, what he'd seen—and couldn't call him for fear of compromising his position.

There were two letters in his pocket. They were not typed up, or remotely ready for sending, but they were drafted in his handwriting. He thought, later, he would go to the police station and find a typewriter and envelopes. He had drafted the letters after the recital, back at his guest-house accommodation. Fenton had said, down the phone, fifty minutes earlier, "We're not a marriage-guidance operation, Geoff. If she wants to go, then I'm not going to lose sleep over it. But he stays, whatever. If you have to chain him to the floor, he stays." He walked towards where the little verminous bastard was, not that he would see him, but where he would breathe the same air.

The two drafted letters were in his pocket.

Dear Mr. Cox,

I write to inform you of my resignation from the Service. I am taking up a position with a merchant bank in the City. I would like to express to you, to Mr. Fenton, to colleagues, my appreciation of the many kindnesses that have been shown me. My future employers wish me to start with them at the earliest possible date and I look for your cooperation in that matter.

Sincerely,

and

Dear Sirs,

I have received your letter setting out my terms of employment and find them most satisfactory. Accordingly, I have resigned from my current employers by the same post, and have requested the earliest possible date of release. I much look forward to joining your team and will advise you, soonest, of when that will be.

Sincerely,

Once they were typed up they could go in the afternoon post, and then Geoff Markham would no longer be unimportant. He walked on the path, turned a corner, and could see, past a wild clump of bramble, the mass of the reed banks, the dark water channels, and a ruined windmill that had no sails. The bright light played on the dead reed tips, and the birds flew above the muddy banks.

"I wouldn't go any farther. If you don't want a bollocking from a police thug, I'd stop right there."

He spun. To the right, a few yards from him the man sat on a weathered bench. Markham recognized him but couldn't place him. A dapper little man, thinning hair and a nervous smile, with binoculars hanging from his neck.

"Quiet, isn't it? Wonderful. But there's a policeman ahead with a vile tongue and a big gun." There was a chuckle, like that of a teenage girl but from the soft full lips.

"I'm watching the harrier. It's a joy to behold . . ."

The man pointed. Markham saw the bird, cartwheeling in awkward flight. He squinted to see it better. It was more than half a mile away, and its colors merged with the reed beds. It was far beyond the windmill, over the heart of the marsh. He could see swans, geese, and ducks on the water, but this was the only bird that flew, and strangely, its motion was that of a clumsy dancer.

"Incredible bird, the marsh harrier—it migrates each spring from west Africa to here. It would have been hatched on Southmarsh, and then in the first autumn of its life it flies all the way back to Senegal or Mauritania for the winter. Then, come our spring, it returns. Comes back to us. I find that wonderful. Two thousand miles of flight and our little corner of the universe is where it returns to."

He remembered where he had seen the man. He had bought a sandwich two days earlier at his shop. Dominic Evans's name was over the door. That morning, Davies had given him, snarled them, the names of those who had been in the half shadow, who had not intervened—he was one of them.

"It comes back to us. Its trust makes for a huge responsibility. It can rely on our care and kindness."

"A pity, Mr. Evans, that Frank and Meryl Perry can't rely on that well of *care* and *kindness*."

"What's remarkable—this bird came back last week, and it was injured. It had been shot. I didn't think when I saw it last week that it could survive. It's flying, not quite at full strength yet, but it's hunting and it's getting there. It's almost a miracle."

"I said, Mr. Evans, that it was a pity Frank and Meryl Perry cannot rely on your care and kindness."

"That's not called for."

"It's the truth."

"What do you know of ultimate truths?"

"I know that you were there last night, one of those who stood back and let the mob have its bloody vicious fun."

"You feel qualified to make a judgment?"

"I make a judgment on those who skulk at the back, don't have the guts to come forward."

"That's mighty high talk."

"I'm talking about cowards who know what is right, and stay silent."

"Do you want to know?"

"Do I want to hear a string of sniveled excuses? Not particularly."

"I am not proud of what happened."

"Frank and Meryl Perry need someone from among you bastards to hold out the hand of friendship."

"I don't know your name. You're another of the strangers who has invaded our little place. Till you came, we were just ordinary people living hidden and unachieving lives, we were like everybody else, everybody anywhere. We were not challenged . . . I don't know your name but, *stranger*, I am homosexual. Queer, got it? I live with my friend and I love him. But I am discreet . . . I do not cause offense, I do not draw attention to myself. If I did, then in this little place I would be labeled a pervert. I buy tolerance with my work as the village historian. I can tell you where the old shoreline was, and the old churches, and the old shipyard, all that stuff, but at least I take this place seriously. If I were blatant I would be ostracized . . . Yes, I should have spoken up for Frank and Meryl. I like them, but I'm a coward. Yes, I'm ashamed. So, yes, I go with the tide. But it's like the sea and the history here. It makes for a sense of futility. Little gestures against the strength of the sea, over many centuries, have proved the worthlessness of man's efforts. We bow before the force of the inevitable."

Markham stared out over the marshland, and the peace that set-tled on it.

"You won't be here when this is over, stranger. We'll be left to pick up the pieces, and you'll have moved your caravan on—where you can make judgments on other ordinary people. Is it satisfying work? You sneer at me because I didn't, publicly, offer my hand in friend-ship to the Perrys. Let me tell you—no, listen to me. Twice, in the night when I wouldn't be seen, I've put my coat on and determined to walk to Frank and Meryl's door, and each time I failed to find the courage. Will you tell them that I'm ashamed of my cowardice?"

"No," Markham said icily.

He cursed himself for his cruelty. The man was gone, stumbling away. He wondered how he would have been if the challenge had faced him. The warm sun was on his face. Geoff Markham watched the flight of the bird and he had no sense of what was remarkable, what was a miracle.

Davies brought him a mug of coffee.

Perry had lifted his plans out of the chest's bottom drawer in the sitting room and carried them into the dining room. He had asked Davies if he minded the intrusion and the detective had shaken his head. It was only a small job, a problem with the air filtration on the production line of an assembly plant in Ipswich. Davies had moved his machine gun and the spare magazines across the blanket over the table to make room for him, then headed for the kitchen.

It was the first time that Frank Perry had taken out some work in a week. Only a small job, which wouldn't pay more than a thousand pounds, but it was his little gesture of defiance. He had noticed that Davies didn't ask before going to the kitchen to make coffee, and he thought the detective was at home now, comfortable, in their house.

Perry thanked him for bringing the coffee. Meryl was upstairs, packing.

She had slept alone.

Poring over the workshop plans, tracing the course of the filtra-tion pipes, Perry reckoned out where the new motor should be placed, and what power it must have to create the necessary airflow down the pipes to the unit. There were two more consultancy jobs in the drawer, one larger than this and one smaller, and after that there was nothing. He was tapping out calculations and jotting the numbers while she packed.

The ceiling beams and floor planks of the old house creaked under her weight above him. She was in Stephen's room. He didn't know how much she intended to take, everything or the bare minimum. If she took everything, cleared the child's room of clothes and toys, then she was going forever.

She had called Stephen in from the hut, and he'd come reluctantly—his days were now split between the television and the hut. He'd noticed that, just as he had noticed that Davies was now more comfortable in the house. He had not asked how much she intended to take because he had not dared to hear the answer. The footfall moved above him.

She would be in the gloom of their bedroom. She had left the child on his own to pack his toys.

Perry heard the thud as she pulled down the biggest of the cases from the top of the wardrobe, and then another. He stared down, doggedly, at the plans for the new filtration unit.

"Are you all right, sir?"

"Why shouldn't I be?"

"Where's she going?"

"Haven't the faintest idea."

"She has to go somewhere."

"Her mother and father died in a coach crash, and she's never spoken of any relatives. She's no friends where she came from . . . We only have each other. We thought it was different."

"Shall I book a hotel?"

"That would be best."

"Where should the hotel be?"

"How the hell should I know?"

Davies slipped away, left him. Perry swore. He had made a bloody mistake, had missed a bloody decimal point. He ripped up the sheet of paper on which he'd written his calculations, threw the pieces to the carpet, and started again . . . She'd be packing the blouse he'd bought for her last birthday, and the diamond cluster ring with a central sapphire that he'd given her last Christmas, and the underwear she'd shown him when she came home from Norwich three weeks ago; everything that mattered to her, and to him, would be going into the suitcases. He corrected the positioning of the decimal point. It was the principle that mattered. He would not surrender. Why did no one understand that he had to hold on to the principle?

Davies came back in. Perry saw the smudge of lipstick on his collar, the damp patch around it, and knew the detective had *comforted* her.

"How much is she taking?"

"Not too much, not too little."

"How long is she going for?"

"Not for me to say, sir."

"Where is she going?"

"An hotel in London—I've said I'll book it."

Davies asked him if he'd like a refill of coffee, and Perry nodded. He was wondering, when she was in a hotel in London and the detective was relieved from the duty, when a new man had come to replace him down here, whether Davies would see her, seek her out.

His fingers smacked clumsily against the keys of the calculator.

It had been her idea.

Simon Blackmore held tight to Luisa's hand.

He had had the same idea, but it was she who had articulated it.

They walked through the village with purpose.

Either they did it or they left. They both knew that and did not have to speak it. If they had not started out on their walk through the village to the house on the green, both of them would have gone to the garage beside the cottage and brought out the empty packing boxes and started to fill them. They would already have rung for the van and telephoned the estate agent, and they would have gone.

Separately, when they had first seen the cottage, they'd each thought the village was a small corner of heaven, a place of perfection for them. But as Luisa Blackmore had said, pulling on her coat before the start of their walk, a place in heaven had to be earned.

It was a fine morning. The sunshine played on the tiredness of her face, and on his, and on the brick walls of other cottages where the honeysuckle and the climbing roses were already budding. The light shimmered off the neatness of lawns cut for the first time that year.

They went past the pub, not yet open, and the empty car park, and saw the landlord grunting as he maneuvered beer kegs from the out-building to the main door. The caretaker's bicycle was leaning against the wall of the hall. A young woman sat on the bench and read a book. The shop was open. The builder went by in his van, the man who had told them about their damp problem, and they had seen him the night before, and he waved to them as if nothing had happened in the darkness. They went on to the green, towards the house.

All the time they walked, on the road and on the green, Simon Blackmore held his wife's hand on which there were no fingernails. Her coat cuffs hid her wrists and the old marks of razor slashes. Under her coat, across her breast, was a thick scarf, and under the scarf and her blouse were the burn scars. He supported her. It was necessary to give her support because of the knee injury from long back.

They came to the front gate. They were watched, eyes strip-searching them, by the policemen in the car at the front. They were within the vision of the camera on the wall above the front door. Simon Blackmore squeezed hard on his wife's hand and rang the bell.

They waited. The camera's image would be watched. The police-men in the car would be reporting. He was middle-aged and frail. She limped, and her face showed harmless exhaustion. Nothing about them was threatening.

The lock turned.

The policeman wore a bulletproof vest over his shirt and his hand hovered near to the pistol in his waist holster. Two bulging suitcases were in the hall behind him. His expression, cutting his eyes and mouth, was of contemptuous hostility.

Holding his wife's hand, looking up at the policeman, Simon Blackmore drew a deep breath. He said, "We heard him speak last night. We were in the crowd but not of it . . . We haven't met him, we're newcomers, so he won't know us. He said his wife would leave but that she had nowhere to go, and that she would need to find an hotel. We live at the far end of the village, near to the church, at Rose Cottage. It's only our third day here. We have come to offer the lady, and her child, a place in our home, a refuge."

Surprise clouded the policeman's face. He told them to wait there, on the step.

He came back a couple of minutes later, after a hushed conversation inside, and said they'd be visited, and he told them that the Perrys were grateful.

They walked home.

"Do you think she'll come, Simon?"

"I don't know, but for both our sakes, I hope so."

The bird flew above him. It glided with him as if escorting him.

Vahid Hossein moved, very slowly, through the reed banks. Sometimes the bird would wheel and fly back past him, and sometimes it would hover over him. The wing beat seemed stronger each time it flew. In the depths of the marsh he went so carefully to be certain that he did not disturb the nesting birds. When he waded the mud clogged up to his knees and he had to use his strength to drag himself forward through the reed stems. When he swam, the weight of the rocket launcher and the missiles on his back pushing him down, he did so with great caution. He was never in the open water. He never broke the reed stems.

He sensed that a man watched for him.

When he rested, exhausted from the mud and the weight of the launcher in the bag on his back, he was relieved to realize that the bruised hip now caused him less difficulty. In the cold of the water there was no pain, and the restriction on his movement was less marked. He was sufficiently fit to go forward, to move against the target.

Only when he was near to the shoreline, when it circled over him, did he talk softly to the bird. He was in dense reeds and he moved them aside singly, and he passed close to geese.

"I wish you well, friend, and I regret that I did not find you at the Jasmin Canal or at the Faw marshes or at the Haur-al-Hawizeh. There were good birds there, but they were not your equal. I would have been grateful there, friend, for the comfort of your company— as I am grateful here. I will remember you . . ."

Vahid Hossein did not believe it stupid or sentimental or childlike to talk to the bird.

"Will you remember me? I think so. You will not forget the man, the soldier, who cleaned your wound and fed you. I believe that when you come back next year, from wherever you go in the cold winter, you will look for me."

In his exhaustion, Vahid Hossein did not recognize the danger to him of rambling and incoherent thought. He was weakened and hurt, and he did not know it. He dragged himself across the mud of the shoreline, through the last of the reed stems. He was still and gasped for breath.

"Good-bye, friend, look for me, search, do not forget me."

A sparrow flew away, cheeping, as he scrambled the few yards for the cover of the trees and undergrowth on Fenn Hill to meet Farida Yasmin. They would shout his name in the streets when he was home. He did not feel the exhaustion. He had the love of the bird and believed himself supreme.

The great anchor chain rose from the sea. The power of the huge engines edged the tanker away from the mooring buoys. Its cargo gone, the deck of the tanker and the bridge were high above the water.

It would be a long climb . . .

They would have sailed two hours before but for the late arrival back on board of seven of his crew. They had claimed they were lost ashore, and the master had believed they smelt of women's bodies. They always went with whores when allowed ashore, and they were all good Muslims, and they brought back on board foul magazines that would be thrown into the sea when the tanker, days later, reached the Straits of Hormuz and the last leg for home. They would make full speed, 24 knots, and be near to the port of Rotterdam in the late evening, where they would collect the pilot before sailing into the separation zone. They would reach the waters off Dungeness in the hour before dawn the next morning. It was still possible for his instructions to be changed and for him to pick up the man under the cover of darkness, lift him off the beach.

But it would be a long climb for the man, if his orders were changed, on a bucking rope ladder, from the sea to the deck and safety.

. . .

Farida Yasmin sat on the bench and watched the muted life of the village pass her by. She could see the green and the far end of the house. Today, the police cars cruised more frequently on the one road. She had been through the village twice, gone to the sea twice, and up to the church. She hated those times, when she was away from the bench, when she could no longer see the end of the house, but she thought it important to break any pattern she set. She should not spend too long on the bench. A woman with a brightly colored coat had come and sat with her and had talked about the village. She seemed lonely and bored, so Farida Yasmin had smiled sweetly and fed the questions that had kept the woman talking. The woman had been with her for an hour. It was a valuable hour. In the police cars, going slowly by, the men would have seen her listening earnestly, and would have thought she belonged. While the woman had talked, looking at her with interest, smiling, laughing with her, Farida Yasmin had been able to see the end of the house over the stupid bitch's shoulder. She glanced, too often, at her watch. Time was passing. She sat on the bench and she thought of the smooth skin of his body, the discoloration of the bruising, and she held her fingers against her lips because the fingers had touched his skin and hair and the bruising . . . But she had nothing to tell him that would help him.

"Excuse me, miss."

Under his cap, he had a dull, pudgy, middle-aged face. Below his face was the top of the bulletproof vest against which he held his machine gun.

"Hello." She made her voice calm, pleasant.

The car was parked behind her, and the driver watched them. It was bright daylight and she had no weapon; he was protected and armed.

"Can I ask what you're doing, miss?"

She grinned. Imperceptibly, she opened her legs, and she straightened her back to emphasize the fall of her chest. "What you wish you could be doing, officer, letting the rest of the world take the strain."

"You've been here a long time, miss, doing nothing."

"My good luck, to have the time to do nothing."

A small rueful smile slipped his face. He'd have seen the shape of her thighs and the outline of her breasts, as she'd intended.

"So what are you doing here?"

She still grinned, but her mind raced at flywheel speed. It was the moment at which she was tested. It came to her very fast, and she clung to it. She had no time to consider what she said. She must follow her instinct. There might be an old photograph of her, but she believed she looked sufficiently different.

"I'm at Nottingham University—we're doing a study on rural problems. I chose here. Didn't I do well?"

"You don't seem, if I might say so, to have done much studying."

"Watch me tomorrow, if you're still here, officer. You won't see me for dust."

"What's your name, miss?"

"I'm Carol Rogers. Geography at Nottingham."

"Do you have identification, Miss Rogers?"

"I don't, actually. I left everything like that where I'm staying, in Halesworth—does it matter?"

She'd given the name of a popular girl, a right bitch, at the university. The policeman could take her to the car and sit her in the back, and radio through the details and wait for confirmation of her identity. If Carol Rogers was still at the university, going after a master's, and was called from the library, then Farida Yasmin had failed. If she failed, when the light shone into her face and the questions hammered her, she might break as Yusuf had broken. Her hand touched her breast. She thought it was just routine, that he was doing his job and was undecided.

"Don't you have anything—driving license, cash card?"

The voice boomed from the car. "Come on, Duggie, for Christ's sake . . ."

He turned away and walked back to the car. When they drove past, he looked at her hard. She bit her lip. She wouldn't tell him that she had been questioned. She thought of her future, when he had gone; anxiety about the future had gnawed increasingly at her through the day. She would be hunted, and looking over her shoulder, always waiting for a policeman to ask her for identification. But she could not leave the village, not while she had nothing to tell him that would help him. And then the pride flushed in her because she had come through the first test of her skill.

Davies ended the call and he finished scribbling notes on his pad. They were waiting on him. The principal had his arm around his wife's shoulder.

Davies said, "Two officers in uniform went round to see them. Maybe they hit the door a bit hard, but it took Blackmore five minutes to get her to come out of the kitchen and talk to them. They got it out of her eventually, who she was and what had happened to her. It's not a pretty story. Control ran it through the computer. They're what they say they are . . . I don't know whether it's the right place for you or the wrong place. We couldn't have you visit there, Frank— nor you, Meryl, come back here. You'd be a mile apart, but it might as well be a hundred. It's your decision, both of you. You'd stay there, Meryl, until the conclusion. I think we're close to that, hours from it, but I don't know, and I don't know what's afterwards. I can't tell you how long is 'afterwards' . . ."

Perry said, "Listen, afterwards I'll go in my own time. Of course I'll go. But it's not them, the people here, who decide when."

Davies said quietly, "They check out. He was British Council in Santiago, capital city of Chile. First posting abroad for Simon Blackmore. He would have been running a library at the embassy, bringing out the odd slice of Shakespeare, chucking British culture around, and finding a girlfriend. It was late in 1972. The girlfriend was Luisa Himenez, and she wasn't suitable for a young fellow from the British Council—not at all, left-wing political, the ambassador wouldn't have liked that, one little bit. In 1973 there was a military coup that deposed and killed the neo-Communist president, Salvador Allende, then a roundup of sympathizers. She went into the net, she'd have been screened first in that concentration camp they set up in the football stadium, then faced the heavy stuff. The interrogators—probably we trained them, we usually did—gave her a hard time. 'A hard time' is an understatement. Blackmore would have badgered his ambassador for action, and that would have been a waste of his time, and then he went direct to Amnesty International. By his efforts, she was adopted as a prisoner of conscience.

There are very few who get to that status, and sometimes it can make a small difference. The military were bombarded with letters, it meant hassle for them. For her, it reduced the chance of the old one-liner 'died of medical complications.' Without Simon Blackmore's efforts she would have disappeared into an unmarked grave. She was quietly released four years later when the government was whipping up interest in a trade fair. Before she received prisoner of conscience status, the interrogators had tortured her—no fingernails, did you notice? Did you see her walk away, limping? They broke the ligaments in her right knee, and surgery wasn't on offer. There are slashes at her wrists, attempted suicide when she thought she was going to break. Oh, what we didn't see, she's got burns on her breasts, which they used as an ashtray . . . The Blackmores have experienced persecution and isolation, which is why they're offering a hand of friendship, and they can't be frightened anymore. Their understanding of living and suffering is different from what you've found here. But, Meryl, I can't tell you what to do, go to them or go to a hotel. They might be right for you, they might be wrong. It's your decision."

He came to the hiding place.

Andy Chalmers hadn't slept in the night, nor in the day.

He could control tiredness, had contempt for it and for hunger, but he had biscuits in his pocket for the dogs. In the night he had listened to the silence, and in the day he had watched the flight of the bird.

To stay awake, and keep alert, he had chosen to concentrate his thoughts on the big birds of his home under the mountain slopes. The bird he watched was half the size of the eagles, pretty and interesting but without majesty . . . If he had been home, that day, he would have gone to the eyrie on a crag face of Ben More Assynt, scrambled on the scree, then climbed and taken cut hazel branches from down beside the loch with him, to repair the eyrie from the storm damage of the winter.

At first, watching the bird in the early daylight, Andy Chalmers was confused. The bird hunted. It dived on a young duck and carried it to the heart of the reed beds. He understood that. He could see that the bird had no grace in its flight but was able to hunt. It was re-

covering from injury, could have been a strike against a pylon's cables or a shotgun wound. After it fed, the bird circled one area at the
heart of the reed beds. It was too immature, without the width thick-
ness in the wingspan, to have a mate nesting below, and at first he
had been confused.

He watched that place.

He waited for some reaction from the other birds: for the ducks to
rise screaming, or swans and geese to clatter for open water, but he
saw only the circling bird, until the afternoon.

Then a single curlew had flown, startled, from the place he
watched. It had taken him minutes to realize that the bird was no
longer over that same place and could not have stampeded the
curlew. In his mind, he made a central point for the arcs the bird
flew, and that point changed, moved gradually away. If he had not
been so tired, Andy Chalmers would have understood sooner. The
central point for the arcs of flight neared the far shoreline of the
marsh, where the trees and scrub merged with the reeds. He did not
know why the curlew had crashed out of the reeds, only that its
flight had been a moment of luck and had alerted him.

There was a pattern here that he was struggling to understand. At
the limit of his vision, he had seen a sparrow break cover from the
scrub.

The bird no longer circled, wheeled, but climbed. It was a distant
speck when Andy Chalmers moved from his cover and went down
into the mass of reeds.

He took the dogs with him, would not be separated from them. It
was only when he reached the focus of the harrier's arcs that he realized it was a hiding place, and as such it was well chosen. Many
years before, enough years for it to be before his birth, the marsh
waters had rotted a tree's roots. The tree had fallen, the branches
had decayed. An empty oil drum had been driven by the winds and
tides against the remaining branches and had wedged. It was a
refuge, a safe place. Where the trunk peeped above the water was
the stripped carcass of a duck, and in the drum was the faint smell
of a man. The bird had shown him the place. He could have passed
within two yards of the tree's trunk and the almost submerged drum
and would not have seen the hiding place.

He had the line. The bird had given him the line to the shore.

Wading through the mud and carrying his dogs, swimming and having them paddle after him, he found not a trace of the man he tracked. He had followed men who had come onto the mountain to raid the eyrie nests, and those men took precautions, faced prison and had cause to be careful. This man was better than any of them. He had the point on the shoreline from which the sparrow had flown. He had the marker.

At the edge of the reeds he lay still in the water, and listened. There was a tangle of bramble a few paces away. He could smell him, but couldn't see him. The dogs were against his body with only their heads above the water. He held his breath and waited. He did not have a profile of the man, could not be inside his mind to know how he would react and how he would move . . . It was more interesting, there was more unpredictability, in tracking a human than a deer. The tiredness had left him. He lay in the water, was fulfilled, and listened.

The dogs would have told him if the man was close.

The dogs smelt him, as Andy Chalmers did, but knew he was no longer there. He came out of the water and the dogs bounded forward, splashing clear.

He found rabbit's bones and the rear leg of a frog.

He knew the man had gone, moved on.

Meryl kissed him. She had her coat on and she held her Stephen's hand. There was another coat over her arm, and four suitcases behind her.

Davies was at the back. Perry couldn't read Davies's face as Meryl kissed him. Rankin was closer: he tousled Stephen's hair, and his machine gun flapped loosely on the webbing when he bent to pick up the child's football.

"You'll be all right?"

"I'll be fine."

"Bill's going to shop for you."

"I'll manage."

The bell rang.

"You won't worry about us."

"I won't."

"I'm just so frightened."

At the third blast of the bell, Rankin peered into the spy hole, then nodded to Davies. The key was turned, the bolts drawn back. Davies watched them. Were they ready? Had they finished? It hadn't been there before, but Perry saw compassion in Rankin's face. And he noticed the sharp movements of Davies's jaw as his teeth bit at his lip— hard bastards, and they were moved. He had not been upstairs while she had packed. He had not found the quiet corner in the house, away from the microphones. She kissed him one last time—her boy wore a new England football shirt that Paget and Rankin had given to him. God alone knew how they'd obtained it, must have had a shop in the town opened up at dawn. Perry felt helpless, as if the eyes, the microphones, and the watchers ruled him. He wanted it over, her gone, before he wept.

"You should go, Meryl."

"I'll see you."

"Sometime soon."

"Keep safe. Be careful. Don't forget, ever, our love, don't—"

"Time you were gone, Meryl."

He could hear the cars outside, the engines starting up.

Davies said, calm voice, "Don't stop, Mrs. Perry. We believe that the area outside is secure, but still don't stop. The pavement time is the worst. Straight out and into the lead car. There's no going back for anything. Keep moving directly to the lead car."

Rankin pulled the door open. Davies hustled them forward, past the two men who waited on the step. They went at a charge. Perry saw his Meryl go, and Stephen with the football, pushed forward by Davies towards the door of the lead car. The two men came behind them with the suitcases and pitched them into the rear car. Rankin snapped the front door shut. He didn't see them go, didn't have the chance to wave. He heard the slam of the doors and the roar of the engines.

"The best thing for now is a fresh pot of tea," he said.

She had taken a position beside the lavatories near the hall. From there she had a view of the gable end of the house and a small part of the green. The light was going. Hours ago, Farida Yasmin had learned the patrol pattern of the unmarked cars, and each time they came by she was behind the toilets and beyond their view. She had hung on there because she had found out nothing that would help him. She stretched her body.

"Hello, my dear, still here, then?"

The woman had come behind her, on the path that led to the beach.

"I was just going."

"I can't remember what you said, why you were here."

The woman would not have remembered because she had not been told.

Farida Yasmin explained pleasantly, "It's a college project on the modern pressures affecting rural life. It seemed an interesting place to come to. I'm getting the feel of it, then I'll be looking to interview people."

"I don't know what you'll learn about us from our toilets."

She had her back to the green and the house. She hadn't seen the cars come. They swept past her. She saw the child and a woman in the backseats of the lead car, and a man who had his head turned away sat in the front. There were cases in the second car, piled high, clearly visible in the rear window. Their headlights speared away into the early dusk.

The woman coughed deep in her throat, drew up the spittle, spat it out through her gaudy lips. She murmured, "They've gone. Damn good riddance."

Farida Yasmin shook. The shock swept through her. She watched the taillights disappear around the corner, at speed. Now she had learned something, but it was nothing that would help him. She began to walk briskly from the toilets, past the front of the hall.

The woman called after her, "Come and see me, when you start your interviews."

She had been cheated.

The bird hovered in the last of the afternoon's watery sunshine, then dived.

Beating its wings, it strutted close to him. He saw the wound. There was a tiny scrap of greaseproof paper, the sort used to wrap the meat his mother brought home from the butcher in Lochinver, and he found soaked, muddied mince, buried in grass, where the bird had walked and pecked. As if it had been tamed, the bird came close to him. The head keeper had a peregrine falcon in a cage behind the house and near to his caravan: it had no fear of him because it had been fed by him since the day he'd found the abandoned fledgling, wounded by ravens. Andy Chalmers had come out of the marsh, stinking of it. The bird trusted him. Other than the head keeper, he knew of no man who would nurse an injured bird and win its trust. The head keeper was one of the very few men that the taciturn and sullen Andy Chalmers had respect for.

The dogs picked up the scent. They meandered either side of the path and crisscrossed over it. Without water to go into, it was hard even for a skilled man not to leave a scent for dogs.

He let them lead through the wood.

He felt a sense of burgeoning regret.

The dogs burst from the wood and tracked at the side of a grazing field. A car's lights illuminated the top of the hedgerows, receding. He went around the perimeter of the field.

He saw the tire marks. He could smell the man and the marsh. The tire marks were at the gate of a field, on the verge of the lane.

He wanted to go home. He had no hatred of a man who had nursed and fed a bird. He wanted to be back with his mountains. He called on the radio for Markham to come and collect him, and gave no explanation.

In the far distance, silhouetted against the darkening sky, was the shape of the church, and the shimmer of the village lights. It was not his place and not his quarrel; he had no business there.

17

"You are certain?"

"It's what I saw."

In the rear car was the heap of suitcases on the backseat, and two men at the front. In the lead car were a child looking out through the window, a woman staring straight ahead, a man with his head turned away, and more men in the front she did not recognize; she had not seen the child before but the woman had been there, weeks earlier, when she had come to photograph the house.

Farida Yasmin had been walking up the road through the village when the two cars had come back past her, the same two men in the front of each but no passengers and no suitcases on the backseat of the second car.

She had walked on in the darkness. There was a cottage with an overgrown garden and a Sold sign over a For Sale board, short of the church, on the other side of the road. The curtains were loosely drawn on the windows facing the road, but at the back of the house they were not pulled across and spilled light onto the garden. The grass at the back, ringed by untended flower beds, was long and leaf-strewn. The shirt the child wore was bright red and there was a crest on the chest of rampant lions and the logo sign of a vehicle-insurance company, the same shirt she had seen him wearing in the car. The child kicked the football round the grass. He played on his own, the hero and the star.

As soon as she'd met him at the field gate, she'd told him what she'd seen, and now she repeated it. In the car, as she'd blistered him with the information, he had seemed no more willing to believe her than he did now.

"The cars came back without him and his wife and the child. It was done fast, to deceive you, in the darkness. They've moved him to make it easier for themselves. Can't you see it? They've made a trap and now they don't have the responsibility of protecting him when it's sprung. They want you at the house on the green—they want to kill you there when they don't have the responsibility for him."

"You are sure?" The doubt creased his voice.

She told him that she was sure. She had seen the boy, the child, with the football on the lawn lit by the back windows of the cottage. The trap was the house on the green, where the guns waited for him. They were beside the car, in black darkness, among the scrub of the common ground beyond the village. It hurt her that she could not convince him.

"Don't you trust me? You should. Without me, on their terms, you would walk into a trap. Trust me. We are a partnership, that's equal parts—don't you see that?"

She told him that he was nothing without her, and he seemed to reel away from her. She would go back, walk through the village a last time—come back and tell him what she had seen. He squatted down, holding the launcher in his hands, as if it were a child's valued toy or a believer's relic. She told him how long she would be. He had already gobbled down the sandwiches she had brought him. He stank of the mud in the marsh and the still water. Farida Yasmin walked back into the village.

There were lights on in the church, throwing multicolors through the high windows, and she could hear the organist practicing.

Over the hedge she saw the child boot the ball into the far darkness beyond the spill of the light, and leap and whoop with pleasure as if he had found freedom.

She walked the length of the green. She saw the cars outside the house and the same drawn curtains as had been there before. She could see, from the streetlight, that the camera set high on the front wall of the house tracked her, then lost interest, its lens veering away.

It was enough. She was certain.

She heard the rustle of a candy wrapper.

"Hello, it's the student, yes? My friend Peggy told me about you—hope I didn't startle you, just walking the dog. I'm Paul. I'm your man when you start your interviews . . ."

She endured his patronizing talk as they went back past the green, the darkened house, and the lens, through the village. It was useful to have him beside her when she went by the lens, when she was caught in the headlights of one of the moving cars. Walking with him gave her the appearance of being a part of the community . . . She told the man, Paul, that she would definitely find him when she came to do her interviews, and he left her at the pub.

The child was no longer in the garden. She saw the shape of a man through the gap in the curtains.

She cut off the road, stumbled across the common ground, wove between the gorse, trees, and bramble thickets, to the car.

"It's as I said it was. I'm certain."

After she had bought the sandwiches for him she had gone to a chemist's in the town, and selected a perfume. Before he had come to the field gate she had anointed her body with it.

"I deserve to be trusted," Farida Yasmin whispered.

He was still hunched down beside the wheel of the car, holding the launcher. He had not moved.

"I want to be with you . . ."

His eyes stayed down, locked to the launcher and the ground at his feet.

"I've done enough to deserve that. I can help, carry what you need. You've taught me. I want to be there when you fire the launcher. I want to see it happen and be a part of it."

She was crouched close to him and her fingers touched the smooth, oiled surface of the launcher's barrel.

"I can do it, help you."

She saw his head move decisively, side to side. He denied her.

Her eyes tightened in confusion. "Haven't you thought about me? Haven't you considered what I want? What about the risks I've taken? Where's my future? Because of you, because of the people who sent you, I've lost everything. I'm hunted. You'll go, be picked

up on the beach—so, who's thought about me? I'll be caught, interrogated, locked up—is that what you want?"

He never looked at her. She caught his hand and held it tight in
her fist. There was no response.

"Are you going to take me back with you? That's best, isn't it, that
I go back with you to the beach and onto the ship? There'd be a life
there, for us, back where you come from, wouldn't there?"

It was her dream. They were together on the great deck of the
tanker. It was night and the stars were above them, and they plowed
through the endless water, and they were alone. And the same perfume that she wore now would be on her neck then. She would be
introduced to high functionaries and her part in the death of an enemy would be explained, and grave men would bob their heads in
respect and thank her for what she had done. She could see the startled faces of her parents, and the astonished, dull faces of the girls at
work, when they learned the truth of what Farida Yasmin had
achieved.

"I'm finished here. So, you don't take me with you tonight, I understand . . . But I go onto the ship with you, don't I?"

In the darkness, he began to clean the firing mechanism of the
launcher.

By torchlight, he had been shown the tire marks.

Geoff Markham had been marched through the wood, had blundered after the light-footed shadow of Andy Chalmers in front, tried
to keep up with him and his dogs, and had then been pushed without ceremony down onto his knees as the torch was shone into the
cavity at the back of the bramble thicket.

He had queried it again, rejecting what he didn't want to hear.

He had been dragged up, pulled towards the water. He capitulated
and said it was all right, yes, he accepted Chalmers's conclusion. If
he had queried again he would have been pulled in his city clothes
into the water and he'd have been propelled towards a tree trunk
and a submerged oil drum.

There was a crunched sound under his feet. The torch beam
pointed out the stripped rabbit bones he stood on.

"I just want reassurance—there is no other explanation?"

"He's gone."

He had been lost. He had driven round a web of lanes. He had finally found Chalmers sitting with his dogs by the gate of a field. He had expressed his first doubts at the grunted report of the tracker, then been hijacked and taken off into the woods. He didn't want to believe what he was told because of the catastrophic implications of Chalmers's assessment.

"Could he merely have moved deeper into the marshland?"

"No."

He said, bitterly, "But we don't know where he's gone."

"Gone in the car."

"Could he be returning?"

"No gear left—hide's empty. He's cleared out."

They walked back to his car. It was the worst situation. He would be on the secure line to Fenton from the crisis center to report that they had lost their man. There'd be the hissed slip of Fenton's breath, and he would repeat that they had lost their man, and then a volley of oaths would bleat in his ear. He was familiar with analysis and intellectual storm sessions and with the computer spewing answers. What he had been shown was a short length of tire marks in the dirt at the side of a lane and, by torchlight, a hollowed place in the depth of a bramble thicket. He took on trust the description of the hiding place. The torch had been switched off. They came through the dense woodland, and the low branches all seemed to whip his face and not Chalmers's, and where there was a soft pit in the ground his feet found it and not Chalmers's. With his scratched face and sodden feet, he followed the smell and could not see the man ahead of him until they reached the car.

The stench of the man and the filth of the dogs filled the small interior. The water dripped off Chalmers and the mud on the dogs was smeared across the seats.

"I want to go home."

"Too right," Markham snapped. "Home you will go, but not much of the journey in my bloody car."

He drove at savage speed down the lanes towards the main road and the town, and the crisis center. They had lost him. It would end at the house on the green, where the bloody goat bleated at the end of its bloody tether. He hit the brakes, swung the car through the lanes' bends, pounded the accelerator. Beside him, Chalmers, stinking and dripping, slept.

"Do you like to talk about it?"

"No, Mrs. Perry, I don't like to."

"I don't want to pry."

"I will say one thing to you only, and then, please, it is a closed book . . . It was over. Molotovs don't win against tanks. We went back to our homes, which was stupid. I was denounced by people who lived in my street. When the soldiers came, I and others tried to flee over the roofs from my parents' apartment. We were identified by the people in our street. When we were on the roofs they pointed the soldiers towards us. They were the same people I had lived with, played with as a child. They were my friends and my parents' friends, and they showed us to the soldiers . . . We saw what happened last night. We heard what Mr. Perry said."

"Thank you, Luisa, thank you from the depths of my heart."

"What I like to talk about is old furniture, and gardening."

"It's a good time to get cuttings in," Meryl said. "I'd like to help you with that."

Blake was long gone, back to the house. Bill Davies had dozed on his bed. The room was in chaos, Blake always left it that way, clothes on the floor, towels on the bed. Davies was reminded, and it hurt, of the room his boys shared. He still hadn't rung home, couldn't face it . . . He climbed off the bed and sluiced some of the tiredness out of his eyes at the basin. He'd call by at the house to collect his car, then search for another dreary little pub to eat in . . . He reflected that the home where Meryl had been taken in was off limits, but he'd have preferred to have gone there, talked to her. She'd kissed him when she'd thanked him, and had cried as he'd held her awkwardly. She'd been so bloody soft and vulnerable. Too long since it had been like that with Lily . . . He changed his shirt. Couldn't go back to the house in a shirt with Meryl's lipstick on the collar.

He went down the stairs. The door to their living room was half open.

He realized she had been waiting for him, listening for his descent. She came with a quick, scurrying step out of her living room and he could see her husband in his chair by the fire, and the poor bastard had some shame in his eyes. She held the sheet of paper in her fingers. He understood.

She handed him the account.

He didn't argue, and didn't say that he had seen her standing in the shadows behind the mob. He took the banknotes from his pocket and paid her for his bed and for Blake's. He went back up the stairs and packed their bags.

She was waiting by the door.

She said, "It's not my fault, I'm not to blame. We need the money. We wouldn't be doing anything like bed-and-breakfast unless we had to. It was Lloyds that took us down, we were Names, you know. What my husband had set aside for retirement went to Lloyds. We can't exist without the money. I've nothing against those people, the Perrys, but we have to live . . . It'll be remembered, long after you've gone, that we put a roof over your head. It won't be forgotten. I'm only trying to limit the damage to our business. A man like you, an educated man, I'm sure you understand."

The door closed behind him.

He carried the bags down the carefully raked gravel drive. He stopped in the road, saw the light peeping from the curtains where she was, then turned and walked towards the village and the green. He was called on the radio and was told the stalker's report: the man had moved, was lost. He started to run.

He pounded down the road towards the house.

There was the slight scent of damp in the air as Meryl unpacked in the small bedroom.

She took from the suitcase only what she would need for that night, and what Stephen needed.

Simon Blackmore came up quietly behind her. "She was tortured. What they did to her was unspeakable. Amnesty International members from all over the world bombarded the dictatorship with letters demanding her freedom, but above all it was her own courage that saved her life, and her determination to come back to me."

"You make me feel small, and my own problems minuscule. Inevitable, I suppose, but already I regret leaving Frank."

"I don't think it appropriate that we start a seminar on man's inhumanity, but it's necessary that you understand us. We all have our own opinions and—thank God—our own consciences to drive us. Enough of that. Now, Meryl, smile, please."

She did, her first in six days. "I'm going to talk to Luisa about antiques and gardening—there's places round here where you can still get a good old table or a chest at a real knockdown price."

"And I'll talk about wine, and downstairs there is a bottle open and waiting."

"So, you've lost him."

Cox was hurrying, and for once ignored his habits: didn't go to his office first to shed his coat, smooth his hair, and straighten his tie. Straight to the central desk in the work area. He had been called from dinner.

"Bloody marvelous. What else have you got?"

He was the man in charge, and he threw the responsibility of failure at his subordinates.

"Thought there were a few things I could rely on, wrong again, thought I could rely on you not to lose him."

Fenton, who had already ladled abuse at his own subordinate, Markham, squirmed. Parker kept her head down. The others at the table, white-faced, avoided Cox's eyes, except for Duane Seitz, who eased his shoes off the table and laid down his Coca-Cola can.

"His advantage is small, and temporary only," Seitz murmured. "He has to come to the house. If he's moved he'll come tonight. You should relax . . . We all get scared when it's out of our hands, you're not unique."

Cox glanced at him savagely. "What's he got?"

Fenton dived for the book on the table, as if it were his savior. "What we think, from Mr. Seitz's questioning of Yusuf Khan, it's probably an RPG-7, rocket antitank grenade launcher. If the indications from that bedside conversation are correct, then he has a weapon with a maximum effective range of three hundred meters, particularly useful at night."

The old warhorse from B Branch snatched the book from Fenton. "It has an internally lit optical sight for night shooting, or might have the passive starlight scope. Against tanks, even a deflection shot, it'll put a five-centimeter hole through around twenty-five centimeters of armor plate. At a hundred meters it cannot miss."

Cathy Parker leaned over the warhorse's shoulder. "It can penetrate at least twenty centimeters of sandbags, fifty centimeters of reinforced concrete, and—not that it applies—well over a hundred centimeters of earth and log bunker . . ."

"Christ . . ." Cox shuddered.

Seitz smiled and swung his feet back onto the table. "But it has a signature, flash and smoke discharge. It's best if he fires, then you locate him and you go get him."

"If there's anyone left alive, afterwards, to get him." Cox left them, in their silence, kicked open his office door, and threw his coat onto the floor.

"It'll be tonight, he'll come tonight."

Frank Perry looked away from Davies. He sat on the floor, his body weight against the bottom of the door. Ask a bloody stupid question and get a bloody unwanted answer.

There was a small, right-angled space between the hall and the kitchen door, protected by interior walls. The question—why had Davies gone upstairs and dragged the double mattress off the spare bed and the single mattress off Stephen's bed and wedged them on their sides against the two interior walls, and made an igloo between the hall and the kitchen door? Why? He sat and cradled a tumbler of whisky, no water. He could have asked Blake and Paget as they heaved in the sandbags they'd filled. The sand and the empty bags had come an hour earlier. There had been a sharp exchange at the front gate because the delivery driver had dumped the sand and said it wasn't on his work docket to stay and help fill the bags. Perry sat with the weight of the vest on his shoulders. Davies was inserting a chair into the igloo space, a hard chair from the dining room, pushing its seat against the kitchen door, and then he draped the ballistic blanket over its back. The sandbags were already in place at the hall end of the igloo. He drank the whisky, which burned in his throat and upper stomach, the third one that Blake had poured him. He thought, pretty soon, he should go and piss.

It was better that she had gone, with Stephen. He could sense the change in the men's mood, like they'd cleared their decks. While Davies built the igloo, Blake was checking the weapons, and he'd cleared all the rounds out of the machine gun magazines, then loaded them again. There was a box on the carpet, beside his feet, with the big red cross on it, and he'd been asked again for his blood group. He'd given it to them a week ago, but they'd said they were just checking—and he'd heard them talking hospitals. With Meryl and Stephen gone, what had changed, he thought, was that they no longer had the responsibility for the protection of a human being. Frank Perry was an item, he was baggage, protected because of its symbolic value. He gulped the whisky. Paget and Rankin were in the hall. They were going off duty, the new shift was in the hut. What he didn't understand was that they seemed neither pleased to be going off duty nor reluctant to leave. By the time they were at the door, Paget and Rankin were already muttering about the different brands of thermal socks.

Davies said, "He's moved. We don't know where he is or where he's coming from. Would you, please, Mr. Perry, go quickly to the lavatory, then settle into the protected space. Because he's moved we think he'll hit tonight."

Perry downed the drink, stood, and slurred his laugh. "Bit overdoing it, yes, bit over the top, yes, for one man with a rifle?"

"We don't think it's a rifle, Mr. Perry, we think it'll be an antitank armor-piercing rocket launcher."

Ask a bloody stupid question . . .

He used the cover of the stones of the churchyard, those that were beyond the throw of the colored lights from the church itself.

Vahid Hossein had the weapon tilted against his shoulder, and the barrel with the two-kilogram projectile loaded, gouged into his flesh. From the churchyard he could watch the lights of cars on the road. It was important to him to find the pattern they made. The slow-moving patrols of security men would be the same here as outside the bases of the Americans in Riyadh or Jeddah. Patrols were always predictable—it was what they did. The slow cars came by, going into the village and out of it every nine minutes, with only a few seconds' difference in each journey.

From the churchyard, he slipped over a wall and into a garden. He crossed that garden, and two more. Often, at the Abyek camp, he had practice-fired the RPG-7, and it was simple and effective. He had fired it in the Faw marshes when the Iraqis had counterattacked against the bridgehead with armored personnel carriers and the T-62 amphibious capability tanks. He knew well what it could do . . . He moved across two more gardens. He would have preferred to be close, so that the target man could see the blade or the barrel. It was better when they saw it, and the fear flitted over their faces. Then he felt the excitement in his groin.

Vahid Hossein was in another garden, crouched and still. A door opened and a dog trotted out into the pool of light. It approached the edge of the light and yapped, but was frightened to move into the darkness. The rain began again. A man stood in the door and shouted for the dog, which knew he was there. Its courage grew because the man was behind it. It was a small dog and it bounced with the ferocity of its barking. If the man came close, he would kill him, a blow to the neck; if the dog came, he would throttle it. He would not be stopped. The rain pattered on him. The man strode towards the dog, towards the place where he crouched, lifted it up, smacked it, and carried it back into the house.

He moved again.

She had given him the exact description of the house on the far side of the road into which the target had been moved.

"A drink, Meryl?"

She shivered. Stephen was upstairs in the room allocated to him, and had said it was a dump. She'd pulled his lorries out of the case and scattered them on the floor for him, on the bare boards.

"That would be nice." She grimaced at the cold air. The window was ajar behind the curtains and the wind rippled them.

"Red or white? They're both from the Rhône valley, Cave de Tain l'Hermitage, it's only a little place but they've been making wine there since the days of the Romans. We're very fond of it. I think the

lovely thing about the study of wine is that one is never an expert, always learning. That's a good maxim for life. Which'll it be?"

"Red, please—to put some life into me."

"Shall do . . . I'm sorry about the window but Luisa likes windows
to be open so that she feels the wind, she can't abide to be closed
in—you understand."

"Of course." She hadn't noticed it before, but he wore a thick
jacket over a crew-necked sweater. She looked at the grate, saw old
ash and clinker.

Simon Blackmore would have seen her glance at the fireplace.
"Sorry, we haven't got round to cleaning it yet, but we don't have
fires. Luisa cannot abide lit fires. They burned her with cigarettes,
but some of her friends were branded with a poker from a brazier."

"I'll get a sweater."

"No, no, don't." He played the gentleman, took off his jacket and
draped it on her shoulders, then poured her wine.

She was quite touched. It was ridiculous but sweet. She'd ring
Frank later and tell him. And if when she telephoned she could not
be overheard, she'd tell him they were daft, but lovely, and they lived
in a freezer. He said apologetically that he ought to be in the kitchen
helping—would she excuse him if he left her alone?

"Let me do that, help Luisa."

"Absolutely not. You're our guest and need a spot of pampering."

There were two bookshelves in the room. She went past the window and crouched to look at the books.

He had the launcher on his shoulder and his finger on the guard.

He was down among a mass of garden shrubs. Beyond the hedge
and the road was the cottage. He had seen the target's shadow
against the moving curtain, then the coat of the man between the
gap in the curtains, then the shadow.

He had the sights set to forty-five meters.

The car came past, dawdling, its lights brightening the hedge in
front of him. He was not concerned with other cars, only with the
cars that carried the guns and cruised slowly. The darkness came
back to the road and he made his last checks.

·   ·   ·

Paget said, "What I always say, you get what you pay for."

Rankin said, "Fair enough—what you pay for—but if you want the proper gear, then, by God, you've got to pay."

They were on their way back to their lodgings in the town after the end of their twelve-hour shift. Behind them, in the barricaded and guarded house, the principal was someone else's headache. For twelve hours they were free of it.

"When we're out in the bloody boat, this weekend, I want to be warm."

"Then it's gonna cost you."

"Daylight robbery as bloody usual."

"As you said, Joe, you get what you pay—"

The flash of bright light exploded from behind the hedge on the far side of the road. It illuminated the dead hedge leaves, an old holly tree, and the trunk of an oak. Across the road, brilliant in color, came a line of shining gold thread, going arrow-straight in front of the car's windscreen.

The flash came, and the thread unraveled in a split moment of silence. The thread line crossed the road, cleared the opposite low wall and a small garden, and went straight into a downstairs window. It was almost in petrifyingly slow motion.

The blast from the flash fire behind the hedge hammered into the car as Joe Paget braked, and with it was the whistle shriek of the gold thread's passing.

The thunder of the detonation pierced Dave Rankin's ears, and he froze. There was a blackness in his mind and he could feel the air stripped from his lungs. This was not Lippitts Hill, nor Hogan's Alley, nor any bloody range they'd ever been on, not any exercise. The wheels had locked when Paget had braked, and his sight was gone. They were slewed across the road and Dave Rankin's ears were dead from the blast sound.

Paget gasped, "It's where she is—"

Rankin bawled, "Get there, get there to it—where she is—"

Paget had stalled the motor. Rankin was swearing at his window, electric, the pace at which it came down. The engine was coughing back to life. Rankin had the Glock off his belt. Paget had the car swerving back onto the center of the road.

"Fucking get there, Joe!"

Paget put the car back into gear and Rankin's head jerked forward and slapped the dash. Paget accelerated. They were coming towards the house. There was just smoke, billowing from the front window of the house, from the black hole where the window had been and curtain shreds, and silence. The reflex for Rankin was to get out of the car, help make the area secure, radio in. He had the door half open when he was thrown back in his seat as Paget hit the pedal.

"Look, for fuck's sake, Dave, *look!*"

Paget's free hand, off the wheel, reached out and caught Rankin's coat front, loosed it, and pointed.

It was a moment before Rankin comprehended, then he saw him.

There was a high wall of old weathered brick that kept him on the road. The headlights caught him. He was running with an awkward, fast stride towards the end of the high wall and the graveyard beyond. The headlights trapped him. He was in army fatigues but the mud on them blocked out the patterns of the camouflage. As he ran he twisted his head to look behind him. The lights would have been in his eyes, blinding him, and he ran on. The car closed on him.

Rankin had his head and his shoulders, his arm, out of the passenger side window, the wrong side window. He tried to aim, but couldn't hold steady. The Glock was a close-quarters weapon. Practice on the range, with the Glock, was at never more than twenty-five meters. The Heckler & Koch that he'd carried all day, that he would have given his right ball for, would have done the job perfectly but was back in the Wendy hut with the relief.

"Brake, Joe, and give me some goddamn light."

The braking bloody near cut him in two. His back thudded against the door frame.

Rankin went out through the window, fastest way, and tumbled on the tarmac. The breath was squeezed out of his body. He dragged himself up, winded and so bloody confused.

Paget spun the wheel.

The headlights hit the man as he straddled the graveyard's boundary wall.

Rankin was down low, kneeling, and saw him. The lights threw huge shadows off the stones. He was at fifteen paces and going fast, but the headlights held him. They didn't practice it at the range, but he knew what to do. Rankin's fists were locked together on the butt of the Glock, and he punched his arms out and made the isosceles. He tried to control his breathing, to hold the aim steady. His finger was on the trigger. Thirty meters, going on thirty-five. He took the big deep breath to steady himself. Forty meters, going towards the shadows thrown off the stones. He aimed at the back of the running man, into the middle of the spine, and squeezed hard on the trigger. The running man was between a cross and the shadowy form of an angel stone. He fired again. The crack belted his ears. He saw the back of the running man as it dropped. Double tap . . .

Rankin shouted, "I got him—I fucking got him, Joe."

The engine was left running.

"Bloody good, Dave."

"Had him, I dropped him."

Paget went over the wall and right, towards the church porch. Rankin covered him, heard the shout, scrambled over, and circled to the left. It was what they had endlessly practiced, both of them, at Lippitts Hill, until it was routine and boring: two guns, never presenting a target, and closing for a kill. One going forward, the other covering, the other going forward, and one covering. They closed on the gap space between the cross and the angel. There was a dark place, a little beyond where the shadows of the two stones merged, and beyond it there was clear lit ground. They stalked the space, sprinting between the stones, freezing and aiming, calling the moves to each other.

"You ready, Dave?"

"Ready, Joe."

Rankin's aim was into the shadows. He was behind the cross. Paget reached up with his torch from behind the cover of the angel. The torch beam wavered through the shadow and fell on the grass. There was no body on the grass, no corpse, and no wounded man. The beam moved over the grass and there was no weapon discarded there, no blood.

"I thought I saw him go down . . ."

"You thought wrong, Dave."

"After fifteen bloody years . . ."

"Sixteen years, actually, Dave—you waited sixteen years and then you fucked up."

Dave Rankin knelt on the grass where there was no body, no

blood, no weapon, and he shook. As a pair they were laid-back, private, superior bastards. They always did well on the range and never had to be sent for a coffee and a smoke to calm themselves before trying again to get the necessary score to pass the reappraisal. They were the best, they were the ones the instructors pointed out to the recruit marksmen. Sixteen years of practice and sixteen years of training—no body, no blood, no weapon. He knelt on the damp grass and the energy seemed to drain out of him. He hung his head—until Paget pulled him roughly to his feet.

"In this life, Dave, you get what you pay for. They didn't pay much."

"I would have sworn I'd hit him."

"There's no blood, Dave . . . They got us."

The noise of the explosion had careered around the village.

It pierced the doors and windows of the houses, the cottages, bungalows, and villas, where the televisions blared the argument of the evening's dramas. It split into kitchens and dissolved desultory meal conversations. It hammered into the talk in the bar and silenced them there. It startled a man with a dog on the road, a woman who was in the back of her garden filling a coal bucket, a man who worked at a lathe on the bench in his garage, and a couple making love in the flat above a shop. The blast sounded in the houses, gardens, and lanes of the village . . . and in the barricaded house.

It murmured its way into the safe area between the mattresses, past the filled sandbags, and Blake swore softly. Davies dropped his hand onto Frank Perry's shoulder, and there was silence. Then the radio started screaming for them . . .

Nobody in the village moved quickly to leave the protection of their homes. There had been the noise, then the silence, then the howling of the sirens. Only after the sirens had come and the quiet had descended again did the villagers gather their coats, wrap themselves in warmth, and come out of their homes to go to look and to gawp.

The rain had come on heavily.

Eventually, they came from their corners of the village. Their shuffled steps muted, huddled under umbrellas, the first of them reached the house, lit by arc lamps, as the ambulance pulled away.

They gathered to watch.

. . .

He came back.

She had heard the explosion and had rejoiced. He could not have done it without her. Now she would persuade him.

Vahid Hossein came as a shadow out of the darkness, to the car, to her. She tried to take him in her arms to hold him and kiss him, but he flinched away. He gripped the launcher to his chest and rocked. Then he slid down, against the wheel arch of the car. There should have been triumph, but his eyes were far away.

"What's the matter? You got him, didn't you? What happened there?"

He never replied to her.

Farida Yasmin stormed away from him.

She blundered across the common ground towards the lights of the village. The rain sheeted down onto her.

She backed off the road as a police car came past her with its siren wailing, splashing the puddled rainwater onto her thighs and waist. She had heard the clamor of the explosion and clenched her fists and believed she was a part of it. She saw the crowd ahead of her, in front of the cottage home she had identified for him.

She joined the back of the crowd. She came behind them and watched as they stared ahead, heard their whispered voices. She was not noticed. The rain fell on her hair and her face. The crowd was held back by policemen but she could still see the blackened walls of the room through the gaping window. The arc lights showed her the firemen picking through the room.

She listened.

"They say it's a gas explosion."

"That's daft, there's no sodding gas."

She was behind them. They were not aware of her.

"Was it the new people?"

"It was the Perry woman, not the new people."

"Was it Meryl Perry?"

"Just her."

"Where's he? Where's Perry?"

"Never came, it was just Meryl who came."

"That's rough. I mean, it wasn't anything to do with her, was it?"

"Frank was in his house with his guards, it was Meryl. The stupid bastards got the wrong place, the wrong person . . ."

She slipped away. She left as she had come, unseen. She walked back, the rain clattering on her. She felt small, weak. Emergency traffic passed her and ignored her as she cowered at the side of the road. She was little and unimportant. She had thought that night, beside the car, as the sound of the explosion had burst in her ears, that she would love him, that she would be rewarded because he could not have done it without her, and he would take her with him—and she would be, at last, a person of consequence. She stumbled across the ground, went between the thicket and gorse clumps, splashed in the rain puddles. She was Gladys Eva Jones. She was an insurance clerk, she was a failure. She was sobbing, as she had sobbed when her mother had carved criticism at her and her father had cursed her, as when the kids at school had ostracized her and the kids at college had turned their backs on her. She saw the outline of the car and the rain spilling from the roof onto his shoulders. He had not moved.

"It was the wrong person. He was never there. It was his woman . . ."

His hand came up and grasped at her wrist. He did not need her. His strength pulled her down. They were not a partnership and there was nothing to share. She was on the ground, in the mud. She would never know love. His hands prized at her clothes, the knee drove between her legs, and she felt the rain beat on the exposed skin of her stomach.

"I want to see her."

It was an hour since the explosion and the first scream on the radio, and for most of that hour no one had told him. They had kept him in the area inside the mattresses and the sandbags, and they'd filled his glass. A man had come in a crisp uniform, rank badges on his shoulder, and had used the soft language that they taught on courses for handling the bereaved, and then gone as soon as was half decent.

"Damn you, I want to see her, listen—"

Blake's chin shook. "Want away, but you can't."

Perry shouted, "I've the right."

Davies said calmly, "You can't see her, Mr. Perry, because there is nothing to see that you would recognize. Most of what you would recognize, Mr. Perry, is on the wallpaper or on the ceiling. It was your decision, Mr. Perry, to stay, and this is the consequence of that decision. Better you face that than keep shouting. Get a grip on yourself."

It was as if Davies had slapped him. He understood. The slap on the face was to control the hysteria. He nodded, and was silent. Paget came in through the front, followed by Rankin, who had his arm round Stephen's shoulder. The child was white-faced, his mouth gaping. The child sleepwalked across the hall slowly, and Rankin loosed his supporting arm and let him collapse against Perry. He held the boy hard against him, and thought about consequences. He saw the stern faces around him, and there was no criticism, there was nothing. If the child had cried or kicked or fought against him it would have been easier, but Stephen was limp in his arms.

He heard Rankin say, "I thought I had him, don't understand, thought I saw him go down."

He heard Paget say, "He's like a dripping tap. He missed, and the daft tart can't accept that he missed with a double tap."

The woman screamed.

They were on the ground in front of her, in the epicenter of her torch beam. She shrieked for her dogs, and ran.

She walked her dogs each evening before going to bed, summer and winter, moonlight or rain.

Policemen from an unmarked car ran towards the screams. It was several minutes before they could get a coherent statement from the panting, shouting woman of what she had seen.

"Black Toby . . . his ghost, his woman . . . Black Toby with her, what he did to be hanged . . . It's where they hanged him, hanged Black Toby . . ."

They went forward with the spot lamps, her trailing behind them, and her dogs skipping ahead in the darkness.

18

He was hunched forward, peering into the misted windscreen. Chalmers was beside him with the dogs under his legs. They didn't speak.

Geoff Markham wrenched the car round the bends in the lanes, back towards the village and the sea.

Once more he had listened to Fenton on the telephone and been too drained of emotion to take offense at the rambling, cursing diatribe thrown at him. He'd just finished at the borrowed typewriter, had just sealed the envelope, when the first news of disaster had broken, and he'd been in the crisis center trying to make sense from the confusion of the reports when the second package of news had come over the radio. He'd collected Chalmers from the canteen. The envelope with the letter in it was jammed in his pocket, like a reproach.

Dear Sirs,

I am in receipt of your letter setting out your proposals for terms of employment. I have changed my mind, and am no longer seeking work away from the Security Service. I apologize for wasting your time and am grateful for the courtesies shown me. Obligations, commitments, duty seem to have overwhelmed me. I'm sorry if you find this difficult to understand.

Sincerely,

He felt sick, small.

"I want to go home . . ."

Markham's eyes never left the road. After two catastrophic news reports and after the battering from Fenton, he needed a butt for his anger and a chance to purge the guilt welling in him. Chalmers was available. Markham snarled, "When the work's finished you go home—not a day or an hour or a minute before . . . We made a mistake. We could have made the same mistake if the target had been in a tower block of a housing estate, in a good suburb, anywhere, but we did it in a village like this at the back end of bloody nowhere. We made a mistake by thinking it was the right thing to move his wife out, get rid of her, to clear the arcs of fire. We lost her. Losing her is damn near the same, to me, as losing him. It was convenient to ship her out, so we took that road. It's crashing down around us, its disaster. Listen hard, if you say that it's not your quarrel, then you're just like them. You are an imitation of those people in that village. They are moral dwarfs. It was not their quarrel, so they turned their backs and walked away, crossed over to the other side of the bloody street. You aren't original; it's what we've heard for the last week. So, find another tune. You're staying till I say you can go. I thought better of you, but I must have been wrong."

"I've no quarrel with him."

Geoff Markham mimicked, "'No quarrel, want to go home'—forget it. Let me tell you, I considered taking you down to the hospital morgue. I could have walked you in there, filthy little creature that you are, with those bloody dogs, and I could have told the attendant to pull the tray out of the refrigerated cupboard, and I could have shown her to you, but I couldn't have shown you her face. You aren't going to the morgue because I cannot show you Meryl Perry's face—it doesn't exist. That's why we aren't going there."

Down the lanes, towards the village . . .

"We all want to cross over the road and look the other way. Don't worry about it, you're not alone. I understand you because, and I'm ashamed, I've said it myself. I went after different work, outside what I do now. 'Crossing the road,' for me, was sneaking out of the office in the lunch hour and going for a job interview. 'Looking the other way' was listening to my fiancée and hunting for a cash increase. I'm ashamed of myself. I wrote a letter tonight, Mr. Chalmers, and the price of the letter is my fiancée. And what I've learned since I came here is that I, and you, cannot walk away from what has to be done."

As they approached the village, the clock on the church tower was striking midnight, its chimes muffled in the rainstorm. To the left were the pig sheds in the field, to the right was the common ground of scrub and gorse, and in front of them was a policeman waving them down. Markham showed his card, and a rain-soaked arm pointed to a pool of arc lights. The dogs ran free and they walked towards it. The wind brought the rain into their faces.

"Why can't you believe you have a quarrel with this man?"

"He's done me no harm."

"There's a woman, damn you, with no head."

"He saved the bird."

"What bloody bird?"

"He's done the bird good."

He thought Chalmers struggled to articulate a deep feeling, but Markham hadn't the patience to understand him.

"You're talking complete crap."

The blow came, without warning, out of the darkness. A short-arm punch, closed fist, caught Markham on the side of the face. He staggered. He was slipping, going down into the mud. A second stabbed punch caught the point of his chin. The pain smarted in his face. He saw men hustle forward, the rain peeling off their bodies. They were grotesque shadows, trapping Chalmers, swarming around him, as his dogs fought at their ankles, their boots, and were kicked away.

"Show him—show him what the bastard did. He doesn't think it's his business, so show him."

They dragged Chalmers forward. Markham heard a squeal of pain, thought Chalmers had bitten one of them, and he saw the swing of a truncheon.

There was a tent of plastic sheeting. Inside it, the light was brilliant and relentless.

He saw her.

"Get him up close, get him to see what the bastard did."

She was on her back. Geoff Markham had to force himself to look.

Her jeans were dragged down, dirtied and wet, to her knees, and her legs had been forced wide apart. Her coat was ripped open. A sweater had been pushed up and a blouse was torn aside. He could see the dark shape of her hair, but little of the whiteness of her stomach above it. The skin was blood-smeared, bloodstained, blood-spattered. Her mouth gaped open and her eyes were big, frozen, in fear. He knew her. There was the old photograph of her in the files of Rainbow Gold: the eyes had been small and the mouth had been closed; she had held her privacy and worn the clothes of her faith. Looking past the policemen and over Andy Chalmers's shoulders, he stared down at the body. He had seen the bodies of men in Ireland and they'd had the gaping mouths and the open eyes, and the fear that remained after death. He had never before seen the body of a raped, violated woman. Before they had built the plastic tent, the rain had made streams of blood on the skin. Except for Cathy Parker, and her report relayed to him that morning, they had all lost sight of Gladys Eva Jones, the loser, and now he saw her. Except for Cathy Parker, and then it had been too late, they had all ignored her because they had rated this young woman from a small provincial city as irrelevant in matters of importance, not worthy of consideration. He saw in his mind the photograph of the face of Vahid Hossein and the cold certainty that it held.

Chalmers said nothing.

Markham stammered, "God, the bastard—a frenzy. He must be a bloody animal to do that."

A man in a white overall suit looked up coldly from beside the body, and said clinically, "That's not a frenzy, she was strangled. The cause of death is manual asphyxiation. That's not her blood—she's not a cut on her. It's his."

"What does that mean?"

"It means that the 'animal' is severely wounded, knife or gunshot. There is evidence of sexual penetration, probably simultaneous with her being strangled. During the sexual act, during the exertion of manual strangulation, he bled on her."

Markham turned away. He said, to no one, to the mass of grim-faced men behind him, "So, there's a blood trail—so, the dogs will have him."

A voice from the darkness said, "There's no blood trail and there's no scent. If you hadn't noticed, it's raining. In pissing rain there's no chance."

Markham gestured for them to loose their hold on Chalmers, and walked away. Chalmers was behind him. He groped back towards the car and the road. For the rest of his life, he would never lose the sight of Gladys Eva Jones. He stumbled and slithered in the darkness. The letter in his pocket would be soaked and the envelope sodden.

"Will you, please, Mr. Chalmers, please, go out and find him?"

"Are you going, or are you staying?"

"Staying."

Frank Perry lay on the floor between the mattresses and behind the sandbags. Stephen slept against him; his head was in the crook of his stepfather's arm.

"So be it."

"Are you criticizing me?"

"I just do my job. Criticizing isn't a part of it. I've some calls to make."

Davies had towered over him.

"What happened to the people who took Meryl in?"

"Mr. and Mrs. Blackmore are unhurt. They won't leave what remains of their house, and they're staying put."

Grimly he turned away and disappeared among the shadows of men whose names Frank Perry hadn't been told. Perry closed his eyes, but knew he would not sleep. He could hear Davies on the telephone. It would be easier if any of them had criticized him.

The brigadier took the call, which woke him from a light sleep on the camp bed in his office. The voice was very faint. The brigadier shouted his questions, but the answers were vague and there was breakup on the line. In his frustration he shouted louder and his voice rippled from the office room, down the deserted corridors, and into empty, darkened rooms . . . He heard the muffled voice of the man whom he had trusted like a son and barked out questions. Had he succeeded? Was he clear? Could he make the rendezvous point on the Channel beach? How many hours would it be before dawn? What was his location? Had he succeeded?

The call was terminated. The pad of paper on which he would have written the answers to his questions was blank. He played back the tape and heard the insisting shout of his questions and the indistinct answers. In the background, competing with the answers he could not understand, was the splash of water. The cold of the night was around him. He thought of a beach in the black night where the sea's waves rippled on the shingle-stone shore, where Vahid Hossein was hurt and waiting. In his mind was the death that would follow his failure. He weighed the options of survival, his own survival. The hush of the night was around him, and moths flew, distracted, at the ceiling light above him. He rang the night-duty officer at the offices of the National Iranian Tanker Corporation across the city, and he spoke the coded message. Twice, in the minutes that followed, the brigadier called the number of the mobile digital telephone and there was no response. He was alone, surrounded by darkness.

Frank Perry heard the approach of the lorry, and then its engine was cut. He heard the voices and the clatter of iron bars being thrown down, as if dropped from the lorry's flatbed. He was thankful, a small mercy, that the child slept and did not criticize him.

The people of the village slept, with guilt and with self-justification, with doubts and with resentment, or stared at their dark ceilings. There were few who had not walked up the road and along the lanes and gone to look at the cottage home when it was floodlit by the generators. Most had seen the wide hole where a window had been and the torn curtains that fringed it, and some, even, the long bag of zipped black plastic carried away to the closed van, and the uncomprehending eyes of a child escorted from the building by the policemen in their vests and carrying their guns. No one believed the bland explanation of a gas explosion. None had cared to examine their part in what they had seen, heard, with their friends and their families. They had gone home when the show was over, and they had darkened the village, made it silent, switched off their house lights, crept to their beds. In a few short hours it would be the start of another day, and there were not many whose lives would be the same. The rain over the village had gone as fast as it had come, leaving the moon to pour bright white light into the homes where they lay.

"What's that? What the hell's happening?"

Frank Perry was careful not to wake Stephen. He eased himself into a half-sitting position but did not shift his arm, against which the child slept. There was the noise of sledgehammers beating against metal at the front of the house and the back.

Davies was cold, without emotion. "You said you were staying."

"That's what I said."

"So, it's because you're staying."

"What is it? What is it that's happening?"

"We call it a *blindicide* screen. It's old Army talk. In Aden, thirty years back, the opposition had a Swedish-made antitank rocket that was used against fixed positions. It detonates the boring charge early."

"Why?"

"You should sleep. It'll keep till the morning."

"You know what? The bastard let me sleep. Joe bloody Paget let me sleep, didn't wake me to tell me. I bloody knew, but there wasn't a body and there wasn't any blood, and the bastard said I'd missed, Joe bloody Paget . . . You're a miserable sod, Joe—you know what you are? Not just a miserable sod, a mean fucker."

Perry, half listening, dozed, with Stephen's warmth against him.

"Letting me sleep when you bloody knew I'd hit him, that's below the bloody belt. How long have you known, you bastard, that I got the shite?"

He could feel Stephen's slight, spare bones. For a moment he had thought he lay against Meryl's warmth. He shuddered. The morning's light seeped into the house through drawn curtains and reached into the safe area between the mattresses and the sandbags. Rankin was cocky, bouncing. Paget was behind him with a slow grin spreading. The assembled company didn't see him. He thought he did not matter to them anymore.

He heard the lorry drive away.

"I mean, telling me I'd missed when I knew I'd hit, that is a professional slur, Joe. If I say so myself, forty meters minimum and no light, a moving target, that is one hell of a shot. What is it, Joe? Come on, I want to hear you bloody well say it . . ."

They were all laughing. Blake and Davies had been up all night, but Paget and Rankin had dossed down on the kitchen floor to catch a few hours' sleep.

Perry asked quietly, "If he was hit, why do we need the *blindicide* screen?"

He had interrupted them. They turned to look down at him and the sleeping child. They were the only friends he had and none of them cared a damn for him, they were strangers.

Davies said, "His name is Vahid Hossein. He fired a single grenade from the launcher. There's a flash at the front and a flame signature at the back. Mr. Paget and Mr. Rankin were going off their duty shift. They engaged him. He ran into the churchyard. Mr. Rankin was presented with a difficult shooting opportunity. He took it, fired twice, but with a handgun at the limit of its effective range. There was no blood and no body. Mr. Paget assumed that Mr. Rankin had missed his target, that's phase one. Later, a woman walking her dogs on the common starts bawling about 'Black Toby.' God knows what she's doing out with dogs in the middle of a deluge. She says she saw a lifeless woman and a black-faced man on the ground. She's going on about some nonsense that happened two hundred years ago. Police officers went to the scene and found a young woman raped and dead, but no man. The young woman was a Muslim convert, and the eyes, ears, fetcher, and carrier for Vahid Hossein. She was covered in blood but it wasn't hers. The man who raped her, while he strangled her, bled on her from his gunshot wound. Mr. Paget and Mr. Rankin use soft-nose bullets in the Glock, and that is phase two. Phase three is incomplete. He is wounded, Mr. Perry, but he is not dead. Although he'd lost considerable quantities of blood, he was strong enough to leave the murder scene. He is out there, in pain, and still in possession of the RPG-7 launcher. The rain in the night has washed away the chances of tracker dogs finding him. He did not take the convert's car. We do not believe he has tried to leave. An hour ago, an inflatable was launched from an Iranian tanker in the

Channel and came to a rendezvous on a beach. He was not there to be lifted out. We had it under surveillance but took no action. Thus we believe he's still here. The military are beginning a search for him. Now, we classify Vahid Hossein as more dangerous than at any time. You, Mr. Perry, are the cause of his pain, his suffering. If he has the strength, in our assessment, he will make a last attack on your home. That, Mr. Perry, is the reason for putting up the screen around the house that will prematurely detonate—we hope—an armor-piercing grenade."

"And is that why you were laughing?"

The wind swept the cloud away, leaving the sun balanced precariously on the sea's horizon.

Geoff Markham thought the young man tolerated his presence on the bench overlooking Southmarsh.

They had dossed down in the car. He had woken at the first smear of light, but Chalmers had slept on, curled in the backseat with his dogs, a baby's peace on his face. Only when he'd woken had the sourness replaced the peace. Once it had been light enough to see the village, the expanse of the green and the high iron poles in front of the house with the close wire mesh netting hanging from them, he had eased out of the car.

Chalmers hadn't spoken, hadn't given any explanation, but had called for his dogs and emptied out the last of the biscuits from his pocket for them. He hadn't said where he was going or what he intended, but he had walked away with the dogs scampering at his feet.

Geoff Markham, not knowing what else he could do, had heaved himself out of the seat, locked the car, had stretched, coughed, scratched, then went after him.

His shoes sloshed with water, his socks were wringing wet, and his shirt and coat had not dried out in the night. The letter was damp in his pocket. The wind was sharp off the sea, raw on his face. A coastal cargo ship nestled on the sea's horizon line. The birds were up over the beach and over the marsh. He was cold, damp, and his stomach growled for food. Where did the arrogance come from, the belief that his small efforts had changed the movement of events?

He wanted to be in bed, warmed, close to Vicky, and ordinary, without responsibility, free from the consequences of his actions. If he posted the letter he would have none of the things he thought he wanted. He slogged on. It would be the supreme moment of conceit if he posted the letter, it would be the statement of his belief that he changed events.

He found Chalmers sitting, very still, on the bench, and the dogs were beside him. Chalmers, never looking at the sea, wouldn't have seen the coastal cargo ship; he was watching the Southmarsh. What disturbed Markham most about him was that the young man seemed merely to tolerate him and feel no need for his company.

The bench was where Geoff Markham had met Dominic Evans, the shopkeeper. It was set high enough for him to overlook the sea, the beach, the seawall, and the marshland where the reed tips whipped in the wind. The sun, throwing low light shafts, made it pretty. His mother would have liked it there, and his father would have taken a photograph.

Eight of them materialized, in single file, along the path behind the bench where Markham and Chalmers sat in silence.

Buried under the weight of their equipment, they marched past the bench and briskly down towards the trees that shielded the shoreline of the marsh from his view. It would have been settled after the death of Meryl Perry. The secretary of state would have bowed to irresistible pressures and taken the control out of poor old Fenton's hands. The military would have stepped eagerly into the void—he knew the men, or at least the unit, from Ireland. He knew the kit they carried and the weapons. He had seen the troopers from the Regiment slip away at dusk from Bessbrook Mill and the fortress at Crossmaglen, seen them run towards the threshing blades of the helicopters on the pads in the barracks at Dungannon and Newtown Hamilton. They were the quiet men who seldom spoke, who waited and nursed their mugs of tea and rolled their smokes and moved when the darkness came or the helicopters started up the rotors.

Markham watched the column snake down the path towards the Southmarsh and the black water where the wildfowl bobbed in the low sun's light. Two carried the Parker Hale sniper rifles. One had the snub sixty-six-millimeter antiarmor launcher; another cradled a general-purpose machine gun and was swathed with belt ammunition across his torso; one had the radio, the stun grenades, and the gas grenades. Three went easily with their Armalite rifles held loosely. They didn't look at him, nor at Chalmers and his dogs. Geoff thought it was the moment that his relevance, and Cox's and Fenton's, ended. Their faces and hands were blacked up. Sprigs of foliage were woven into their clothes. It was as if, he thought, in bitterness, the job was taken from boys and given to men. He looked obliquely at Chalmers beside him and the very calm of his face abetted the bitterness. Control had gone to the guns of the killing team. Everything he had done was set at nothing, snatched from him by the men with guns who went down into the marshland and the reed beds. The last one had slipped from his sight.

"That's it, we're wasting our bloody time," he said savagely.

Chalmers remained impassive, silent.

"Time we were gone. Time, if you know how to use one, for a bloody bath."

Chalmers sat on the bench and his eyes searched the clear gold blue of the skies over the marshes.

"Sending you was ridiculous, a humiliation for the Service. They should have been put in twenty-four hours ago. They're the professionals, they're the bloody killers. They'll find him." He stood up.

Chalmers squinted at a point high above the reed beds.

"They won't find him." His head never moved, his gaze never shifted.

"Enlighten me. On what is that stunning insight based?"

"They won't find him because he isn't here." Chalmers spoke from the side of his mouth. His head was stock still, and he peered into the lightening sky.

"He isn't here?"

"Not here."

"Then, excuse me, please, tell me, what the fuck are we doing?"

"He saved the life of the bird, and I have time for that, and now he's hurt . . . I have respect for the beasts where I work, I have a duty to them when they're hurt. He fed the bird and treated the bird's injury. The bird is searching for him and cannot find him. If the bird cannot find him, then he's not here."

Markham sagged back down onto the bench. He looked out over the reed banks and the water. The wind came into his face and his eyes smarted.

He peered into the clearing sky. Far below where he looked were the birds of the marsh and the Regiment's troopers. He searched for it, but it was a long time before he saw the speck of dark against the blue. He held it, and perhaps it turned, and he lost it. It was very high, where the winds would be fierce. Chalmers's eyes were never off it. Geoff Markham blinked and his eyes watered as they strained, again, to locate the speck. Beside him, Chalmers sat rock still and relaxed, leaning back as if to be more comfortable. His dogs scrapped at his feet. When Markham found the bird again, he could have yelled in triumph. He was trained in the analysis of covert computerized data, he was offered work at what they'd call the summit of fiscal interpretation, and he could have shouted in excitement because his wet, sore eyes identified a speck moving at a thousand feet up, about a thousand yards away. He saw the bird, and it had moved, gone north, and it still searched. He could have hugged Chalmers because the keenness of this stinking youth's eyesight had given him hope, at last.

"I am sorry—what I said was out of order. I apologize. Did you think of telling them, the military, that he wasn't here?"

"No."

He wanted only to be alone.

A woman police officer, a cheerful, pleasant girl with a blonde ponytail of hair and a crisp clean uniform, knelt awkwardly because of her belt, which carried handcuffs, gas canisters, and a stick, on the hall carpet to help Stephen with a coloring book and crayons.

To be alone and to think of her.

Blake, dressed but with his shoes kicked off, slept on the settee in the living room. While his eyes were closed and his breathing regular, his hand rested on the butt of his gun in the holster of his chest harness, his radio burping staccato messages from his jacket pocket.

To remember her.

Davies, in shirtsleeves because he had two bars of the electric fire on, was at the familiar slot of the dining room table with the newspaper spread out, reading the market and the financial comment. He coordinated the radio link to the crisis center and the locations of the mobile patrols.

And to mourn.

He was not allowed, by Davies, to go upstairs to their bedroom. "Not protected there, Mr. Perry, I'm sure you understand."

He was not allowed, by Paget, to go out through the kitchen door into his sunlit garden. "Rather you didn't, Mr. Perry, wouldn't be sensible."

They denied him the space that he yearned for.

Perry sat on the floor between the mattresses and behind the sandbags.

Chalmers moved.

It was a full half hour since Geoff Markham had given up on the search for the speck. The sky was clearer, brightening blue with pale cirrus corrugated lines of cloud, and it hurt more to look for the bird. He was thinking of the future of his career, whether he would be positioned back with Rainbow Gold, whether he would be assigned to a university town where there were faculties of nuclear physics and microbiology growing botulisms at which Iranian students were enrolled, or whether he would be dumped into the new team working on illegal immigration, or the old Irish unit or narcotics . . . when Chalmers moved.

Chalmers was already twisted round, his eye line no longer on the skies above the marsh. The Regiment men would be down in the reed banks and the water now, and there was nothing to show their presence. Chalmers stood, his back turned to them, and moved.

There was no discussion, no conversation, no explanation.

Chalmers whistled softly for the dogs to come to heel, then started to track back up the path towards the village.

He walked with his head craning upwards, as if the sight of the bird, the speck, was too precious to be lost, and Markham was left to trail behind.

The path brought them back to the village between the hall and the pub. Chalmers strode surely, briskly, never looked down to see where his feet trod, and puddles splashed onto his trouser legs.

Cars scuttled past them, and a van with a builder's ladder lashed to the roof, but that was the only motion of life in the village. It was a bright, sunny morning with cheerful light and a bracing wind, but no one walked and took pleasure in it. He thought the fear and the shame were all around, in the houses, the road, and on the lanes . . . as if a plague had come and the inevitability of disaster was upon them.

A fierce rapping, knuckle and glass, and a protest shout startled him. He saw a woman at a window, her face contorted in fury. The woman pointed at her cut front lawn. One of the dogs had crapped on it, the second lifted a stumpy rear leg against the Venus statue that was a birdbath. Chalmers didn't call off his dogs, didn't look at her or seem to hear her, just walked on, and all the time he studied the skies. Markham stared pointedly at the far side of the road.

They went by the house on the green, the sun making silver patterns on the new wire of the screen.

Chalmers never glanced at the house, as if it held no interest for him.

They went through the village.

A few times, Markham looked for the bird and could not find it. He thought of it, high in the upper winds, soaring and circling and searching, and he thought of the power of the bird's eyesight—and he thought of the man, Vahid Hossein, in pain and in hiding. Andy Chalmers had talked of respect and of duty to a beast that was hurt. He didn't think they would understand at Thames House, and it was pretty damned hard for him to comprehend why respect was due to a wounded killer and what duty was owed him. Chalmers walked remorselessly through the village, and out of it.

Beyond the village was a river mouth, then more wave-whipped beaches; at their farthest point were the distant bright colors of a holiday community nestling in the sunlight.

A path ran alongside the river on top of an old flood-defense wall. In the fields between the village and the path, cattle grazed on grassy islands among the pools of the winter floods. Chalmers was ahead of him, high above the river and the fields, and all the time he gazed upwards.

Hungry, thirsty, the foul taste in his mouth, his shoes sodden, his feet cold, his back stiff, Geoff Markham followed blindly, thinking of food, coffee, a shower, dry socks, a clean shirt, and dry shoes, and . . . he careered into Chalmers's back, jolted against it. Chalmers didn't seem to notice him. Beyond the fields, going away from the village and the banks of the river and the raised pathway, was Northmarsh. The sunlight gently rippled the water.

The sun caught the flight of the bird, now lower in the sky, but still high above the swaying old reed heads of the Northmarsh.

The bird had come down from the upper winds and now it quartered over the marshlands. It was as he had seen it over the Southmarsh. The bird searched.

Chalmers walked to where the path cut back towards the village, then stepped over a fence of sagging, rusted wire and settled himself down on the small space of rabbit-chewed grass beside the water and the reed beds. His dogs began to fight over a length of rotten wood. There was peace, quiet, and serenity, until Markham heard the bird's call.

"Do you want help? Do you want the guns here?"

"No."

He watched the bird search, and listened for its shrill, insistent cry.

It was the most important call that Joel Burns had made in the nine years he had worked for the Federal Bureau of Investigation, by far the most important since he had started doing shifts as a night duty officer at the J. Edgar Hoover Building. He was shivering with excitement as he dialed, heard the call ringing out, and waited for Marv Williams, a regional director, to wake on the other side of the Beltway. That he had been entrusted by Duane Seitz, a man who was a living folk hero to make the call pumped his flushed pleasure.

The call was answered by a sleep-ridden voice.

Burns babbled. "Mr. Williams? It's Joel Burns, night duty officer. I am sorry to disturb you . . . Yes, I know the time. You'll want to hear this, Mr. Williams. Duane Seitz has been on, I've just had him on the secure line out of the London embassy. You are familiar with all details of Mr. Seitz's mission—of course you are . . . The British have the jerk winged and holed up. Mr. Seitz says it's close to over . . . I

need your say-so, Mr. Williams, for getting the wheels moving—
y'know, cameras, microphones, lights, and *action*. It seems we can
guarantee that the mullahs are about to have a very bad day. They
are going to squirm like never before . . . *But*, Mr. Seitz says that it
won't fit the British end game when we go public . . . Mr. Seitz says
we should go quiet till there's a prisoner or a corpse, then hit the
mullahs and hard, the full publicity and the evidence they can't wriggle away from. Why I'm ringing—can I start to move the wheels, Mr.
Williams? . . . That's all I need, thanks. Oh, the jerk got the target's
wife last night—they are so fucking incompetent it's unbelievable . . .
Sorry again to have disturbed you."

How many sausages for Stephen? How many for the nanny policewoman? Did Davies like his eggs turned over? Should Blake be
woken? Rankin had found one of Meryl's aprons and wore it tied to
his lower stomach so that his waist holster cleared it.

And Perry hadn't been asked how many sausages he wanted, nor
about the raid on the refrigerator. There would be a plate for him in
the kitchen with sausages, bacon, and eggs, whether he wanted it or
not. He wasn't consulted because he was only the bloody principal.
He felt a sickness in his stomach. He ached for Meryl. Paget came
past him carrying two loaded plates, heading for the dining room,
the French windows, and the outside hut, where the new team were
on duty.

He had to be with her and alone, to kneel and cry for her forgiveness.

The policewoman shepherded Stephen into the kitchen. Davies
followed with his newspaper, and Blake in his stockinged feet.

He was an afterthought. The life of the house went on, they were
all sitting at his kitchen table.

Paget called out, "And you, Mr. Perry—got to keep body and soul
together."

They did it for Stephen, forced their cheer down his throat.

"Just going to the toilet—start without me."

The window in the lavatory had an antithief lock, and the key was
in the small wall cupboard. He bolted the door behind him. They
were his only friends and the mark of their regard for him was that

they tried to clear the mind of her boy from what he had seen, heard, the night before. They tried hard, had to, because what he had seen would have been so hideous, brain-scarring. He heard the banter and the laughter round the table as he unlocked the window. He crawled out through it, took the one fast step across the narrow concrete path, climbed Jerry and Mary Wroughton's fence, and dropped into their garden. He had to be alone.

19

He'd avoided, on the way out from London, all her attempts at conversation, kept his eyes closed and his head turned away. Seitz climbed out of her car and hoisted his bag from the rear seat. Gruffly, he wished her well. She told him it was only a drop-down zone, asked him to check that he'd his ticket, and said that she couldn't stop. Cathy Parker didn't offer her cheek to him, or her hand. He watched her drive away and she didn't wave or look back. By the time he was inside the turmoil of the terminal, she was far from his thoughts.

He was early for the flight back to Riyadh and he would have a decent time to search among the air-side shops for chocolates for Mary Ellen and something, maybe a scarf, to post to his wife. He always took chocolates back to Mary Ellen, and Esther had a drawer filled with the tokens he'd sent her.

He queued at the check-in.

"Morning, Duane."

He turned. Alfonso Dominguez took the chore of administration work at the Bureau's offices in the London embassy.

"Hi, Fonsie, didn't think you'd make it."

"Apologies for not being able to drive you down here, but the good news, I've gotten you an upgrade. It's the least you deserve. Have you been in contact the last hour?"

"No, wasn't able to—thanks for swinging the upgrade."

The embassy man shouldered forward to lift the bag onto the scales and was smarming the girl at the ticket desk. He liked to think he had a reputation as a fixer, and eased the formalities. His arm was round Seitz's shoulder as they walked together across the concourse, and his voice had the hushed whisper of confidentiality.

"I hear you done really well, Duane, that's why I bust my gut to get you the upgrade. You're not up to speed on the news? I just got it. State Department's lining up, trumpets and drums, the briefings. Everything'll come out of Washington. It's gonna be our show. There's decks all being cleared. I guess you'll have a personal call from the director tonight, that's what Marv was saying, could even be a call from the attorney general. It's our show, and we're going to milk it for all we can."

"Do the Brits know?" Seitz grinned.

"They'll be told, when they need to be."

"I did well—better, actually, than I thought."

"You're too modest, Duane."

He enjoyed the admiration. "Good of you to say that, Fonsie. I said at the start it would take a week, and this is the seventh day, and it's pretty much all wrapped up."

"Soon as the State Department gets the word he's in chains or a body bag it'll be the big blast, coast to coast, round the world, live TV . . ."

Seitz said gently, "I've been working for this for so long. What I've finally achieved, Fonsie, what nobody else has achieved to the same degree, is the fracturing of the code of deniability. Tehran's deniability is crucial in their operations, and it's broken. It's been the screen they've hidden behind, and we're taking the screen down."

"And going public."

"And hold on to your seat, Fonsie, hold on tight, because the repercussions can be ferocious. What I'm saying, we have the mullahs by the balls."

"Too right, Duane."

"Whether the Tomahawks fly, whether it's resolutions and sanctions at the Security Council backed by teeth, it's going to be a hell of a rough ride—but we've the evidence of state-sponsored terrorism,

we've got the smoking gun. But you know what? The massive repercussions of the breaking of deniability have turned on events in
some shitty backwater—Fonsie, you wouldn't believe that place. It's
been played out among folk with clay on their feet, Nowheresville."

"I think I have your meaning, Duane. Shame about the casualties . . ."

"You might have heard me say once, Fonsie, that you have to keep
the focus on the big picture and tell yourself the casualties are irrelevant. I'd have said, once, that if you don't have the casualties, then
you don't win . . . Let me sidetrack. I kicked the Brits in the right direction—what surprised me was that they bought the crap I sold
them, ate it out of my hand . . . Right now, Fonsie, I have a problem.
The cost of the big picture was that I brought the war to Nowheresville. I am responsible for the casualties . . . It sits heavy, believe me, on my shoulders. But that's the job, isn't it, that's the
goddamn job."

Fonsie said cheerfully, "You did your bit, did it well, Duane. You're
top of the pile."

"If you say so—do we have time for a drink?"

The slick in the water lapping against him was an ocher mix from
the mud he disturbed and the blood he dripped.

Vahid Hossein had gone to the limit of his strength to reach his
hiding place. A filthy handkerchief from his pocket had been used as
a field dressing to staunch the wound when he had left her.

After the woman had screamed and her dogs had snarled, when
the beam of her torch had found him, then bounced away as she had
fled, he had pushed himself up from her body. He had not realized
he had bled on her until the torch showed him the blood. He had
gone away into the night and pressed the handkerchief into the
wound but it had pumped blood onto his vest, his shirt, his sweater,
and his camouflage tunic. He had known that he must absorb it, not
permit it to fall on the ground he crossed, because there would be a
trail for dogs to follow. In the darkness, he had gone through the pig
fields, skirted between their half-moon huts, smelt the disgusting
odor of the creatures. Guiding him was the call of the seabirds and
the soft motion of water ahead. It was as he reached the water, went

down into it, that the numbness of the wound gave way to the pain in his chest, and with the pain came the exhaustion.

There had once been a track leading through the heart of the marsh, an old pathway long since flooded. Under the pathway, in dense reeds, a culvert drain had been built of brick. Lying on his side, Vahid Hossein kept the wound above the level of the water. The pain came in rivers now. If the marshes had been at the Faw peninsula or on the Jasmin Canal, if he had been with colleagues, with friends, the pain would have been lessened by morphine injections. There were no colleagues, he was far from the Faw and the Jasmin, there was no morphine. The pain sucked the strength from his body.

If he lost consciousness, he would sink lower in the drain's water and drown. He reached into his pocket for the muddied, soaked photograph, held it in his hand, and gazed at the small, distorted face of his target.

The sun shone on the water at the entrance of the drain, dappling among the reed stems. If he drifted to sleep, if he sank into unconsciousness, he would drown; if he drowned he would never look into the face. But sleep—unconsciousness—would kill the pain. The bullet had been from a handgun. One low-velocity bullet, fired at the extreme of range, was still, misshapen and splintered, somewhere inside the cavity of his chest. The entry wound was low under his armpit and he had not found an exit wound. The bullet had struck the bones of his rib cage and been diverted deeper into the chest space.

He coughed. He could not help himself. It came from far down in his lungs. He writhed in the confines of the drain. He needed space, air, and couldn't find it. He held his sleeve against his mouth to muffle the sound of his cough, and he crawled towards the segment of bright light at the mouth of the drain. He saw the blood on his sleeve and it eddied from the coarse, soaked material into the flow of the water.

Vahid Hossein did not know how he would survive through the sunlit hours. He prayed for the darkness and prayed to his God for strength. With darkness, with strength, he would go for the last time to the house. The blood and the mucus ran from his hand and over the photograph he clutched, and into the water . . . They would be waiting to hear of him, and learn of what he had achieved. He thought of Barzin, and her body in darkness, the awkwardness with which she held him, and he wondered if she would weep. He thought of the brigadier with the bear-hug arms, and the laughter that was between them, the trust, and he wondered if the tears would come to the cheeks of his friend. He thought of Hasan-i-Sabah and the young men who had gone down on the narrow, steep rock path from the fortress at Alamut and who would never return . . . He thought of them and they all, each of them, succored his strength.

The image of the young woman, living or dead, was never on his mind. She was past. The sun was on his face. Protected from sight by the waving reed banks, he eased his head, and the shoulder above the wound, out into the light. He was so tired. He wanted so desperately to sleep. It was not an option. He recognized the delirium that snatched at his concentration, but could not resist the call for him to show strength and courage. They were all around him, the people he knew in his heart and in his mind. He heard their words, and they cried to him from close by. He reached above the drain, his fingers groping in soft mud against the reed stems for the launcher. The voices, near to him and shrill, told him he must hold the launcher through the sunlight hours, and never sleep, hold it until night came . . .

It was blurred, small.

The bird cried out above him and flew its search over him. The pain was back, the dream was over. He saw the bird searching for him and heard its cry in the silence. It was the same silence he had felt before, when he had believed a man watched for him. He struggled to get back into the recess of the mouth of the drain, but he did not have the strength, and his fear was the same as hers had been when she was under him and choked and scratched at his face. The bird hunted him.

Chalmers saw the bird dive.

The man, Markham, slept beside him, lying on his back with the sun bathing him, sheltered from the wind, and the dogs were close to him. Andy Chalmers had heard the bird call and it had not been answered. He saw it tuck its wings against its body and plummet, a stone in free fall, bright light shimmering on its wings.

He watched it, for the briefest moment, pull out from its dive and spread its wings to cushion the impact of the fall. He heard its cry. For a few seconds it hovered over the reeds, then dropped. As a marker, he took an old, withered tree that rose above the flood marsh, dead branches with a crow perched on it. The bird came up, sky danced over the reeds, then dropped again. A faraway tree draped in ivy, which was alone among the willow saplings on the distant extreme of the marsh, was his second point. His mind made the line between the perched crow and the ivy tree. The bird stayed down, and he knew its search was over.

Chalmers leaned across the sleeping man, ruffled the hair of his dogs' necks, murmured his order to them, and slipped into the water. He moved away from the shoreline, where Markham slept and the dogs watched, without sound. He had the line to guide him. He half swam, half walked, and although the water was icy against his body, he was not aware of it. He kept the line in his mind. He felt no anger, no passion, no hatred. The shore was behind him, hidden from him by the reed banks. He went quietly, slowly, along the line his mind had made.

Cathy Parker said to Fenton and Cox, "What I think, Seitz has operated on a different agenda to ours. It was all in the body language. He's not a man who'd lie, and he pretended he was asleep all the way to the airport, and then he was gone like a scalded cat. He didn't want to lie to me, about our agenda and his. What you do about it is your problem."

Twice he had flapped his arm at the bird, the second time more feebly than the first. He could not drive the bird away from him. If Vahid Hossein could have reached it, the bird he loved, he would have caught it, held it while it clawed his hand and gouged at his wrist, and he would have throttled the life out of it, but he could not. When his hand came close, the bird fluttered farther away, eyeing him, and flew and circled him, but when it came down it was always beyond his reach. To survive, he would have killed the creature he loved, and all the time the silence grew around him. Again, digging for strength, the pain surging, he lunged. He was on his knees and groping at air. The bird mocked him, danced in front of him.

As he sagged back, his face screwed in pain, he saw, in the far distance, the man walking towards him. On the raised pathway, coming closer, alone and unprotected, was his target. The photograph had fallen from his hand when he had reached for the bird, floating on the muddy water near to him. He gripped it, looked once more at the crumpled photograph and at the man. The pain in his body told him it was not the delirium that comes to the wounded before sleep and then death. The man walked towards him. Vahid Hossein thanked his God and grasped the launcher in his hands as firmly as he could.

"Is that you, Fenton? Penny Flowers here. Did you know our esteemed American allies were already counting their chickens? They're planning to go public as soon as there's a corpse or a prisoner. They reckon, a little bird tells me, that it's going to be their day, which is in direct contradiction of what I understand to be our policy on this. Thought you should know . . ."

He walked in the beauty of the landscape and did not believe he deserved to.

Meryl was dead, the woman he had slept with, loved with, bickered with, lived with was lying on a tray in the mortuary's racks. Because of him . . .

When they had walked on that path together, after going to the beach, she was always on his right side so that she could better see the waterbirds in the marshland. His right arm dangled at his side and his hand was open, as if she were about to take it and hold it, as she did when they were alone and together.

The sun warmed his cheeks, but his body was cold, insensate. He had not taken a coat out through the toilet window, but had escaped in the pullover that had been warm enough for the house. As he'd walked on the beach the self-pity had dropped away from him, and now, on the path going towards the marshland, he remembered only what he had done to friends . . .

For Frank Perry, friends had been the rock of life. And she was gone because of what he had done to friends, burned them to death. He could remember each meeting with them, and how he had bought them. He had purchased his friends, and they were burned to death because of him. And Meryl had paid the final price.

In a quiet, private voice, he asked for her forgiveness, and the agony of his crime distracted him from the beauty all around him.

Poor Meryl—innocent, ignorant Meryl—Meryl who knew little of the world beyond her door, for whom Islam was a mystery. Into her home he had carried history and faith, terror, warheads, and a killer, and he tried to ask for her forgiveness.

She had been innocent and ignorant, and happy with it.

It was a country and a culture, a people, an aspiration of power of which she had known nothing and wanted to know nothing, and he had dragged it into her life, and that nothing had killed her. His friends, too, were in his mind, their faces, their kindnesses, their laughter, and their burned bodies, and she was dead and she had not known them. She was gone from him . . . too late to ask for her bloody forgiveness. Life went on.

He said it out loud to make it real. "Life goes on . . ."

The dogs pounced at him from hidden ground below the pathway, came through the old sagging fence beside the water where it turned towards the church tower.

"Life bloody goes on."

The dogs tripped him from his dream state. He lashed at the nearer one with his shoe and it danced clear of him. He peered over the fence and saw the sleeping minder, Markham. He could have walked on. The man lay and slept in the sunshine and breathed easily. Markham had told him the consequence of his actions. Enough of asking for forgiveness and enough of thinking on friends, because life bloody well went on, like it or not. He stepped over the fence, slipped down past the leafless willows, and crossed the short-cropped grass. The dogs snarled and cuddled down beside the sleeping man, Markham. He crouched, shook the man's shoulder. Eyes opened, the face contorted in astonishment.

"What the hell—what the fucking hell are you doing here?"

Markham looked around him fast—the empty grass, the still water, the unmoving reed beds—and he reached up and dragged Perry down.

"I could ask you the same question. Nothing better to occupy yourself? What are you doing?"

"Shit . . . because he's here . . ." Markham stared out into the impenetrable mass of slow-swaying reeds, then glanced down at the dogs. "Because the tracker's gone in there after him . . . Get down."

The sarcasm was wiped from his lips. Perry lay on his stomach beside Markham.

"Here? So where are the guns?"

"There are no fucking guns, there's just an unarmed civilian tracker in there searching for him," Markham spat. "What the hell are you doing out of the house?"

He said weakly, "I wanted to be alone. I went out through the toilet—"

"You're serious?"

"I wanted to think."

"That is about as irresponsible as is humanly possible."

"I'm just a parcel, nobody cares."

"You're a bloody symbol. Men protect you because of your status as a symbol. Christ, you weren't idiot enough to think it was personal, were you? We're not here because we bloody *like* you. It's our work, it's what we do. What were you thinking of?"

"I thought you were as much my friends as the men who burned to death. Where is he?"

"Somewhere out there, being hunted."

He lay on his stomach. Nothing moved ahead of him to disturb the peace. He closed his eyes and pressed his head down onto the short-cropped grass. The sun was on his neck, and he felt only the chill of regret. In his mind, he saw the burned bodies.

Cox said to the secretary of state, "If our American friends, our dear and closest allies, are allowed to run with this, then we sail on uncharted waters and among unknown reefs. We will be sucked into their vortex. Do we want that? Are we prepared to be tugged along by the nose, at their beck and call and in the interests of their propaganda coup? It's a huge step . . . so often the quiet passing of a covert signal achieves more than the beating of cymbals. But, sir, it is your decision . . ."

Pandemonium broke loose.

In the domestic routine, plates clean, food finished, washing-up done, the principal had been forgotten.

Where in God's name was he?

The kid had been the center of attention and the requirement to distract him, and the military were doing their thing, and that had softened the alertness. It was only when the nanny policewoman had gone to the downstairs toilet and shouted back that it was locked from the inside that he had been remembered.

They scattered: Blake upstairs to check the bedrooms, Paget going out to search the garden, Rankin hustling through the ground floor, Davies scanning the green and the road—and not a sniff of him. As they pounded around her, the nanny policewoman told the kid it wasn't anything to worry about.

Paget broke down the toilet door. The window was open, the sunlight streaming in. They were gathered behind him to look.

"The bastard's done a runner."

The cacophony of voices filled the hallway.

"After all we've bloody done for him . . . Bloody put ourselves on the line for him . . . Sort of thanks you get from a selfish bloody bastard . . . What the fuck is he thinking of?"

Forgotten in the melee, the child shouted, "Don't, don't—you're his friends."

They stood for a moment, heads hung, shamed.

Fenton said, into the telephone, "So good to speak to you. Of course, I feel I know you although we've never met. Let's put that right. Lunch today, I think. I apologize if you've something in your diary, but I promise you it would be worth your while to scratch it out. There's a nice little place off St. James's, on the right, third street up from Pall Mall, Italian—one o'clock? Excellent. I've heard so much about you . . . what's it concern? Try remembering a man known as Frank Perry . . . One o'clock? I look forward to it hugely."

• • •

The chance was given him by his God. The bird was above him, sometimes coming down into the reeds to perch and watch him, but always beyond his reach. One final chance was given him by his God, to take him to the Garden of Paradise. He thought of the great men who had gone before him, slipped from the mountain at Alamut, made long journeys, stalked their target, and he would meet them as an equal in the Garden of Paradise, and sweet-faced girls would wash the wounds on his body under trees of fruit blossom and take the pain from him. He was weak and could move only slowly. He had seen where the target had come down off the high pathway, and he had not seen him climb back. He knew where he would find him and prayed that he had the strength to take him.

He smelt the burning of the bodies as the flesh melted on the bones. He heard the terror of the screams. He saw the women weeping. He had been in their homes and they had cooked celebratory meals for him and their husbands.

Frank Perry jerked up his head from the ground.

"What's happened?"

"Nothing's happened," the minder, Markham, whispered sourly.

"What about the tracker?"

"Don't know, haven't sight nor sound of him."

"And for him, the hunter, is it just a job—or does he care?"

"You wouldn't understand."

"I understand what I did."

"You were convenient—they used you every inch of the way."

"Does he care, the man out there, the man who killed Meryl?"

"He's professional, doing a job for his country, as we're doing a job for ours. As a person, he doesn't care."

"Dying for his country?"

"Let me tell you something, Mr. Perry, that might help you to comprehend . . . The Islamic activists in Egypt blow up tourist buses, but it's not personal. They get caught, they get tried in courtroom cages, and are sentenced to hang on the gallows. You and I would beg for mercy, but they don't. When the judge passes the death sentence they jump up and down in excitement, and they are smiling and laughing and praising their God. He won't give a shit, but you cannot comprehend that."

"Would he know about the bus? Would he know what I did?"

"He'd know."

"Could you live with that, the sight of the bodies and the smell?"

"I don't have to. It's not my problem."

"But I do, and it's my torment."

He pushed himself up, onto his knees, onto his feet, and stood at his full height. The minder, Markham, was tugging at his trousers and trying to drag him down, but he braced himself and stood straight. He saw the birds gliding in the dark water pools, and the gentle motion of the wind in the reed heads, and the calm, unbroken reflections. He saw the harrier swoop low over the reeds. There was an awesome beauty in the sunlight, and peace. He identified the corruption that had led him to the crime of responsibility for the burned bodies and the smell. He had been "somebody"; he had been the man who was valued, who was met at the airport with the chauffeured car, who was taken into the room in the house behind the Pall Mall clubs, who talked to a quiet audience and explained the detail of the satellite photography.

He had rejoiced in the attention of being "somebody," as if a corporate badge hung from a neck chain on his chest. He had thought himself important, but he had only been used. He shouted, "I am here. I am worthless. It is what I deserve."

The minder, Markham, struggled to pull him down.

"I know what I am. I am nobody."

The harrier danced on the reed heads at the edge of his vision and the sunlight caught on the barrel of the launcher.

"Do it, because I deserve it!"

In the depth of the reeds there was the dazzle of fire. With the fire was the gray belch of smoke and the telltale gold-thread signature climbing away from it. The sound thundered towards him. The birds rose screaming, threshing, shrieking from the pools between the reed banks. The trail of fire rose high above his head, away into the blue denseness of the skies, then seemed to hover as the harrier had, and then it fell. A white line of smoke marked its passing. There was a dull explosion away on fields to the north. The birds quietened and circled.

"And who would have looked after the boy, Mr. Perry?"

"I didn't think . . ."

"Then start thinking—get down."

He dropped to his knees.

Ahead of him, the reeds erupted—as if spitting out what before had been hidden. The young man stood. He was small and thin. The water ran from his shoulders and from his face.

He reached behind him and lifted up the launcher tube, and without hesitation he threw the tube far from him, over a bank of reeds, and it splashed down in clear water. Then he bent before reappearing. Frank Perry could see the dangled legs across his chest and the lolling head behind his shoulder, and he came slowly as if a great weight burdened him.

Frank Perry watched.

The young man carried the body of Vahid Hossein through the reed banks and out of them.

The minder, Markham, went into the water when they were close and made to help the young man, but the weight of the carcass was not to be shared.

The young man stepped from the mud and onto the cropped grass. The water and mud cascaded off him, and off the corpse. He climbed the bank, grunting at the effort of it, and straddled the fence of rusted barbed wire. He whistled for his dogs. He went up onto the high pathway with the weight of the body on his shoulders.

Frank Perry noticed the harrier soar above, and wondered whether the bird was watching them.

They walked in file back towards the village, led by the young man with his burden.

The villagers had heard the explosion. Some pretended they had not. Some broke from the link of their conversation, listened, then talked again. Some heard it and crept away to a corner of privacy. It was not possible to escape the sound of the explosion . . . Davies heard it, and Blake, Paget, and Rankin, and the nanny policewoman clutched the child to her in the moments after the windows had rattled at the house. The soldiers working through the Southmarsh towards the snipers' rifles heard it.

Gussie brought the news to the pub. He had run at full pace from the pig fields overlooking Northmarsh.

"They've got him. They're bringing him in. He's dead."

. . .

At the edge of the village, Geoff Markham hurried to keep up with Chalmers, who carried the body easily, moving with a fast, loping walk. Perry was behind, and it was as if it were nothing to do with him. He saw the crowd gathered on the green across the road from the house, standing loosely, watching and waiting. When Markham caught up with him he walked beside Chalmers, and the head of the carcass lolled lifelessly against his arm.

"Why did you do it?"

There was no answer, no turn of the head, no attempt at explanation. Markham thought he understood the gesture of respect for the beast.

"How did you kill him?"

Chalmers's lips were set tight . . . Markham looked into the dead eyes of the corpse and saw the pallor on the face. There was a clean-cut bullet hole in the tunic and a great bloody stain discoloring the material round it. At the neck there was the mark of a bruise, a deeper color, just below the ear. He saw them together, very close, two filthy, soaked, wild creatures. There would have been no fear on the hunted man's eyes in those last moments, and there would have been a gentleness on the hunter's face as he had readied the heel of his hand. The same gentleness on the moor and the mountain when he came close to the wounded beast and its pain.

"Did he say anything?"

No answer.

"Did he fight?"

No answer.

"Did you feel anything?"

Geoff Markham thought that Andy Chalmers wouldn't be feeling sadness or remorse. It was what was owed to a wounded beast. It was not about a quarrel, it was about ending the misery of pain . . . He had no more questions, there was nothing more that he could think to ask . . . And maybe it was right that he should have no answers to the last moments of the life of Vahid Hossein. He thought of his commitment to the ideology he believed in, and of his untamed defiance—and he thought of the death of Meryl Perry and of Gladys Eva Jones . . . He thought of those who had milked the access knowledge of Gavin Hughes, and those who had put the launcher in the killer's hand . . . He thought of those who had tied the rope to the ankle of Frank Perry, tethered him, and armed the guns, and waited for the predator to close on him . . . He had no answers. It seemed unimportant, at that moment, to Geoff Markham that he would never know what had happened in those last few seconds as the launcher was fired high into the sky and away from the target. He would never know whether the Iranian had fired it, or Chalmers, or whether it had been fired as they struggled. He would never know how the final moments of the confrontation between the two dirty, dripping men in the marsh had been played out.

The crowd edged back as Andy Chalmers walked across the green with his burden.

Davies was at the open door, and Blake, and Paget with Rankin, watching.

The young man came to the front gate of the house and dropped his shoulder so that the body fell easily from it. It crumpled, twisted, onto the grass.

The crowd stared down at the death mask and the bloodied uniform as if at a creature from the darkness. The water oozed from the uniform and the last of the blood. Markham reflected that, somewhere, a woman would weep for Vahid Hossein.

The crowd stayed back, as if they were still in fear of this intrusion into their lives, who had made them make choices, as if he still might sting, might bite, as if he still possessed the power to hurt them.

The first of the soldiers to come said it. "Come on, you bastards, it's not a fucking peep show. Show him some dignity . . ."

Geoff Markham said quietly, "If we went now, Andy, I think we could make the afternoon train to get you home."

He walked towards his car, unlocked it, opened the door for Chalmers and his dogs. Before he climbed in, he walked with purpose to the shop where the postbox was. He wanted to be the solitary, private man, the man who sat alone in the corner of a bar or a train carriage. He wanted to be a part of the strange, neutered, unshared life of a counterintelligence officer. He wanted to walk into people's lives and be able to walk out again. He wanted to be lonely, like the woman with the red hair who was a legend . . . He took the sodden letter from his pocket and dropped it into the post-box.

As he drove away, with Chalmers sitting expressionless beside him and the smell of the marsh water filling his car, Markham saw the crowd reluctantly dispersing, and he saw Paget spreading a bedroom blanket over the carcass of the beast.

He had welcomed his guest at the restaurant's door, smiled, and held out his hand in greeting. Harry Fenton had seen the rank suspicion on the intelligence officer's face. He had led him to the corner table. Fenton had grinned before they sat, and his back to the restaurant's clients, he had quickly unbuttoned his shirt, lifted his vest, had exposed his chest, as if to convince the guest that no recording device was strapped to his body.

"I thought it was good that we should meet, because misunderstandings can so damage our mutual relations."

He had laid his mobile telephone on the tablecloth, taken the menu cards, and he'd told the intelligence officer that he would order for him. He had thought the intelligence officer would have cleared the short-notice invitation with his head of section, with his ambassador, and ultimately with his Tehran control. The man had been wary but not nervous, and Fenton had thought him an experienced professional.

"There are four names that I wish to throw at you, my friend, and you should listen most carefully to what I say, because the implications of our conversation are a matter of some importance."

They ate, Fenton heavily and the intelligence officer with little enthusiasm. The mobile telephone had lain silent beside Fenton's place.

"It's a question of deals. We are into the business of negotiation. Let us begin with the names. There is the name of Brigadier Kashef Saderi. For the mission mounted into this country, we have ample evidence of his involvement. Yusuf Khan, formerly Winston Summers, currently under armed guard in hospital. Farida Yasmin Jones, now dead, strangled . . . There is Vahid Hossein."

Each time he had given a name, Harry Fenton had smiled and looked up into the intelligence officer's eyes. The man didn't blink or turn away. Himself, confronted with names, he would have wanted to puke up his food. Of all those he knew at Thames House and worked with, he'd thought only little Miss Prim Parker would have held her composure as well as the intelligence officer had. Of course she would; it was Cathy who had come back from the airport with the idea of shafting the bastards, the esteemed allies. Smiling into his guest's face, he let the names sink, then resumed eating. He cleared his plate. He had ordered gelati for them both, and requested espresso coffee to follow.

"Around Vahid Hossein a net is currently tightening."

The tables around them had cleared. Bills were paid. The restaurant staff found coats, umbrellas, and shopping bags for their clients. Fenton admired the calm of the intelligence officer. The coffee was brought.

The mobile telephone bleeped.

Fenton sipped at his coffee.

He let the telephone ring.

He returned the cup slowly to the saucer.

He lifted the telephone and listened. A smile played on his face. He thanked his caller. The intelligence officer watched him for a sign. He drank again from his coffee cup, wiped his mouth with his napkin, then leaned forward.

"Vahid Hossein is dead—my condolences. He was brought out of the marshes like a stinking, slime-ridden rat, dead. It's the way these things end, I suppose, without decency. We are faced, because of the weight of evidence, with a most serious situation involving relations between our two countries—yes?"

Harry Fenton raised his hand, flicked his fingers imperiously for the bill to be brought him.

"Allow me to answer my own question. No—it can be that it never happened, but 'never happened' comes at a price."

Astonishment spread, for the first time, on the intelligence officer's face, and he bit his lip.

"It never happened, and therefore it never happens again. I repeat, it never happened. And your agents never again threaten the life of Frank Perry. It's an attractive solution to both of us."

The intelligence officer reached out and grasped Harry Fenton's hand. The deal was done with their locked fists.

He paid the bill and carefully pocketed the receipt. It was the last
of Harry Fenton's lunches. A few minutes later, after the close whispering of details, they were out on the pavement and he waved down
a taxi for his guest. He started to walk back towards Thames House.
The body would go from a closed van into the cargo hold of the aircraft. The threat against the life of Frank Perry would not be re-
newed. The Americans, arrogant shits, were shafted and their
staffers would have no brief to spell out in front of the cameras.
Peace was preserved, deniability ruled, and the bridges remained in
place. The bottles would be broken out of Barnaby Cox's cabinet to
celebrate a good, most satisfactory show.

He walked at a breezy pace, and he laughed out loud.

It had never happened.

Back at Thames House, he told Cox what he had achieved, and the
raid on the cabinet began.

Fenton was downing his second drink, might have been the third,
when an assistant director wandered into the office.

"I've just heard—well done, Barney. Up on the top floor we're all
very pleased, but then we always had confidence that you'd get it
right. My congratulations, Barney."

The body had been taken.

Davies had gone.

Paget and Rankin had left before him, loaded their kit into the car
and driven away.

Geoff Markham had stayed as little time as possible.

The workmen had dismantled the poles and the screens hanging
between them; the crane would be there in the morning to lift out
the hut, and the technical people to disconnect the electronics. The
workmen had carried out the sandbags and had helped to manhan-
dle the mattresses back to the beds upstairs.

Only Blake, the last of his friends, remained, but would leave at
dawn.

The dusk fell. He had opened every heavy curtain in the house,
and the lights blazed out over the green. He had torn out all of the
net curtains, peeled the sticky tape from the mirrors, and placed
their pictures back on the walls. He had pushed his easy chair, in the
living room, away from the fire and into the window. He sat in his

chair and the brightness of the lights lit the path, the front gate, and the fence. He saw them come—Jerry and Mary first, then Barry and Emma.

They came out of the darkness beyond the throw of the lights and they laid the flowers against the gate and the fence. The gang from the pub followed them with more flowers. A few minutes afterwards it was Mrs. Fairbrother, Peggy, and Paul. The call had come from London. A drink-slurred voice, against a background of laughter and bottles clinking with glasses and music, had told him that the danger was past and would not return, that he was free to live his life.

The boy, her child, sat at his feet and watched with him as the cluster of flowers grew—the vicar brought fresh-picked daffodils. The voice had said that what had never happened was over.

Early in the morning, after Blake had gone, he would ring for a van, and after he had fixed for it to take away their possessions, he would make the arrangements for the funeral, and after the funeral he would drive away from the village with her child. He would drive to a place where he and her child could remember her and give her love, a place where they were safe together from guns and friends.

He sat in the chair, his fingers gripping the boy's shoulders, and watched the stream of shadowy figures come in silence from the darkness, pause by the gate, before hurrying back to the safety of their homes. Together they listened to the distant sound of waves breaking relentlessly against the shore and stared out, beyond the floral penance, into the emptiness of the black night.